OUT OF THE SHADOWS

JUSTINA IRELAND

WITHDRAWN

PRESS

LOS ANGELES·NEW YORK

© & TM 2021 Lucasfilm Ltd.

All rights reserved. Published by Disney • Lucasfilm Press, an imprint
of Buena Vista Books, Inc. No part of this book may be reproduced or
transmitted in any form or by any means, electronic or mechanical, including photocopying, recording, or by any information storage and retrieval
system, without written permission from the publisher. For information
address Disney • Lucasfilm Press, 1200 Grand Central Avenue, Glendale,
California 91201.

Printed in the United States of America

First Edition, July 2021

10 9 8 7 6 5 4 3 2 1

FAC-020093-21162

ISBN 978-1-368-06065-3

Library of Congress Control Number on file

Design by Soyoung Kim, Scott Piehl, and Leigh Zieske

Visit the official *Star Wars* website at: www.starwars.com

STAR WARS
THE HIGH REPUBLIC

The galaxy celebrates. With the dark days of the hyperspace disaster behind them, Chancellor Lina Soh pushes ahead with the latest of her GREAT WORKS. The Republic Fair will be her finest hour, a celebration of peace, unity, and hope on the frontier world of Valo.

But an insatiable horror appears on the horizon. One by one, planets fall as the carnivorous DRENGIR consume all life in their path. As Jedi Master AVAR KRISS leads the battle against this terror, Nihil forces gather in secret for the next stage of MARCHION RO'S diabolical plan.

Only the noble JEDI KNIGHTS stand in Ro's way, but even the protectors of light and life are not prepared for the terrible darkness that lies ahead. . . .

STAR WARS TIMELINE

THE HIGH REPUBLIC

FALL OF THE JEDI

REIGN OF THE EMPIRE

THE
PHANTOM
MENACE

ATTACK OF
THE CLONES

THE
CLONE WARS

REVENGE OF
THE SITH

THE
BAD BATCH

SOLO:
A STAR
WARS STORY

AGE OF REBELLION

THE NEW REPUBLIC

RISE OF THE FIRST ORDER

REBELS

ROGUE ONE:
A STAR WARS
STORY

A NEW HOPE

THE EMPIRE
STRIKES BACK

RETURN OF
THE JEDI

THE
MANDALORIAN

RESISTANCE

THE FORCE
AWAKENS

THE LAST JEDI

THE RISE OF
SKYWALKER

PROLOGUE

Sylvestri Yarrow tried not to scream in frustration as she looked at the numbers before her. Why hadn't anyone warned her how expensive it was to own a ship? Between the rising cost of fuel and the Nihil threat forcing them to alter their routes, she and her crew were barely scraping by. Once the shipment of gnostra-berry wine—the most lucrative cargo they'd had in *months*—was delivered, they'd still be in massive debt because of the cost of their last fuel pickup in Port Haileap. Not to mention the bill they still owed on Batuu. At this rate she was going to be in debt to half the galaxy.

Syl leaned back in her seat in the cockpit of the *Switchback*, her pride and current frustration, and watched the peaceful blue of hyperspace stream by. The cockpit was dark enough that she could clearly see her own reflection in the viewport, and the dark-skinned face that looked back at her was long past worried; it was positively distraught, and if her copilot, Neeto, saw her, he would know things were bad. Syl took a deep breath, closed her eyes, and forced herself to think.

There had to be an answer. If they had still been part of the Byne Guild, which was dissolved because of its abuse of indentured crews, there would have been some protection from creditors, but without the guaranteed jobs and profit sharing of the Guild, Syl was at the mercy of her own business sense. Which was why she was floundering, searching for an answer to her money problems. She'd spent her entire life as a hauler, but somehow that didn't seem like enough anymore. The galaxy had changed, and not for the better. And as always, it was the folks who were barely scraping by who felt the biggest pinch.

What to do? Lengthen routes? Haul passengers? Double fees, which were already higher than they had been a year earlier? What was the magical equation that would make shipping profitable, especially in a time when the Nihil—space pirates without any sense of honor or self-preservation—plagued the shipping lanes? How did she get herself out of debt and keep her home?

If her creditors came calling, they would take the *Switchback*, and then Syl would be left with absolutely nothing, and so would Neeto and M-227. Just considering it made her stomach ache. She had to find a way to keep things afloat like her mother always had. But she didn't know the answer, and trying to puzzle it out was giving her a headache, too.

"Emtoo," she said, opening her eyes and turning toward the droid sitting in the copilot's seat. "I think we might be in trouble."

The security droid turned his head with a shrieking sound, and Syl winced. "And we need to quit buying you that cheap oil." She grabbed the nearby oil can and went to work on the droid's joints. At over two hundred years old, M-227 was the oldest droid Syl had ever met, and was also pretty worthless at security. Like the *Switchback*, he had been part of Syl's inheritance after her mother was killed by Nihil raiders, and he was one of the few things Syl could call her own. She should have traded him away after the past few weeks of mounting debt, but she couldn't bring herself to sell the droid. He was like family. He reminded her there had once been better times.

Just a few months earlier, in fact. It was a time that Syl had started thinking of as *Before*. Before the Nihil had destroyed a good portion of Valo's capital city and killed hundreds of thousands of people. Before the Republic had realized they were a real threat. Syl's mother, Chancey Yarrow, had known the Nihil were dangerous from the beginning, their violence plaguing the edge of the galaxy more than anywhere else. She'd joined with a number of other shippers to demand that the frontier planets align to try to protect the shipping lanes from the Nihil, especially after the dissolution of the Byne Guild. But it hadn't done much good.

It hadn't stopped Chancey from losing her life to the raiders, either.

Syl dashed sudden tears from her eyes.

"Please. Do not worry," M-227 said in his stilted voice. His vocoder hadn't been updated in years, and in the past few months the problem had progressed more rapidly. Just one more task Syl had been putting off until she had some extra funds.

"Too late," Syl whispered, mostly to herself. She rested her head in her hands and took a deep breath, running her fingers through her dark, frizzy curls until they stood even farther out from her head. Syl loved the *Switchback*. She loved flying through the darkness of space and jumping into the cool blue of hyperspace. She enjoyed meeting new people and going places that seemed impossibly strange and exciting. And most of all, she loved that no one questioned her about any of it. She had far more independence than so many other eighteen-year-olds in the galaxy.

But at this rate she wasn't going to be able to feed herself or Neeto, let alone repair the finicky hyperdrive or improve the engines the way she wanted to.

The *Switchback* came out of hyperspace with a bump, and every single proximity alarm began to blare all at once.

"I leave for one minute and things go sideways," Neeto Janajana said, strolling down the corridor from the crew mess. The Sullustan did not run, just stretched out his legs a bit more. His liquid black eyes never reflected the slightest hint of worry, and it was rare to see his facial ridge tensed with concern. Syl sometimes wondered if he knew the meaning of "hurry up" or if that was something he didn't believe in, like minding his own business. "What did you hit?"

"Nothing! We were just in hyperspace. And before you ask, I didn't do anything, we got kicked out. This seems to be a bit early," Syl said, looking at the readouts. She put her datapad to the side, facedown. No need for Neeto to know they were not only broke but hemorrhaging credits. He might seem unflappable, but the threat of indenture could get a rise out of anyone, and he'd been down that road once before.

Not everything about the Byne Guild had been great, now that Syl took a moment to think about it. Neeto had been one of the numerous victims of its predatory indenture contracts prior to coming to work for Chancey Yarrow, and neither Syl nor her mother had discovered that until after the Guild was dissolved.

M-227 stood with a screeching of metal, and Neeto sat down in the copilot's seat, taking the droid's place. He frowned, the ridges around his large black eyes narrowing a bit and his large ears twitching. "Well, it wasn't debris, otherwise you and I would be having this conversation with a lot less oxygen."

Syl nodded. "Running diagnostics right now to see what happened."

"Good idea." Neeto said. "You think the rumors back at Port Haileap were true?"

While picking up their cargo, a dockside gossip had told Syl and Neeto about ships going missing from their hyperspace routes, mentioning that a few of the more superstitious haulers thought it was the Nihil. "You saw what they did to the Republic Fair on Valo," Migda, the crusty old spacer, had said, mandibles clicking. "What if they have Force users?"

"The Jedi would never allow it," Neeto had said, and Syl agreed. There was no chance that the most powerful Force users in the galaxy would let the Nihil exploit the Force for violence. According to the holos the Jedi were at that moment fighting the Nihil at the behest of the Republic, a combined operation that promised to shortly put an end to the threat.

Syl still didn't think the ragtag group of pirates could do something so sophisticated. "Maybe we ran afoul of a solar flare," she said.

Neeto grunted, neither agreeing nor disagreeing. "This feels off."

Syl swallowed dryly. Because he was right. When they'd lost her mother there had been a bit of strangeness before the attack: weird readouts, alarms, and then the sudden appearance of ships bearing down on them. But surely it couldn't be the Nihil again? She had planned a route that avoided any sector that had ever had any reported sightings of the marauders. It should be safe.

Syl pushed her worries aside and began to run system tests on the hyperdrive as the ship drifted. It was standard procedure. It wasn't common for a ship to get knocked out of hyperspace, but with the *Switchback*'s sketchy hyperdrive it did happen occasionally, especially if they'd rushed the calculations and the triangulation wasn't tight. They needed a new hyperdrive and probably a new navicomputer, one of the more modern, more accurate models.

And just like that, Syl was worrying about credits all over again.

"This is wrong," Neeto said, dragging Syl from her despair spiral. "Did you see this? It looks like we somehow got pulled out into the Berenge sector. Nothing out here but a dead star and a whole bunch of nothing."

Syl blinked as a number of ships appeared on her readout. "How—nonononono. Not again."

Neeto looked out the viewscreen. "Is that . . . ?" he asked, voice low.

She and Neeto exchanged looks, and a chill ran down her spine. "Nihil," she said.

Neeto nodded. "Sure enough. Guess Migda's rumor mill had a kernel of truth."

Dread blossomed in Syl's middle. "You don't think they're the reason we got kicked out of hyperspace, do you?"

Neeto shrugged. "No clue. But I am not about to sit around and wait to ask them."

Syl nodded, all her worry focused on the ships bearing down on them. "Let's get out of here."

"Already on it," Neeto said, flipping switches.

The *Switchback* powered up and moved around, away from the approaching ships and back toward the spot where they'd been ejected from hyperspace.

"I can't find a single beacon," Neeto said. In rarely used parts of space like the Berenge sector, beacons were the best way to chart a path. Beacons were like miniature lighthouses in deep space, strategically placed transmitters that emitted a faster-than-light signal a navicomputer could use in hyperspace when a safe route wasn't known. They were a vital resource for outdated navicomputers like the one on the *Switchback*.

But jumping while only knowing the location of a single beacon was dangerous. Ideally, a pilot would be able to calculate a jump off of at least three beacons. The more hits, the better a ship could understand its precise location, and how to get somewhere else, hence the need for triangulation.

"Can we jump without a destination?" Syl asked, trying to coax even a short jump from the navicomputer. It was a rhetorical question. She knew the answer; she just didn't much like it.

"It's not a good idea, but it's preferable to whatever our

friends on the approach have planned. And yes, I know. But it's a risk we have to take."

Syl grimaced. "I was afraid you were going to say that."

"All right, found a beacon. Hold on," Neeto said, rerouting their jump based on that single signal.

That was, of course, when the engine blew.

The sound of the ship shutting down, of every component losing power, left a cold lump of dread in Syl's middle. "Oh, no. Not now."

Neeto grimaced. "I'm guessing that the coaxium regulator couldn't wait to be replaced, after all," he said, not a hint of fear or stress entering his voice. The only sign that he was not having a great day was the extra line that had appeared between his large, liquid eyes.

"We're spine fish in a barrel," Neeto said, watching the approaching ships. "We have to evacuate."

"No," Syl said. Her fear hadn't lessened at all, but she straightened just a bit.

"Yes. The Nihil want the cargo and maybe the ship, which we do not have time to fix. If we run we can maybe save our lives. I doubt they'd notice an escape pod. Emtoo? Tell Syl our odds of survival if we evacuate now. Before they get to us."

M-227 turned creakily. "Evacuation is best."

"No," Syl said, hunching over in her seat. She wrapped her arms around herself, suddenly chilled at the idea of leaving the *Switchback*. She'd spent her entire life aboard the ship, hauling cargo with her mother. Every memory of her mother she had, good and bad, was there on that beloved heap. "This is all I have, Neeto. And you know running is not my style. If the Nihil want my ship, then they can take it from me. Beti and I can handle them." Syl reached down and pulled the modified blaster rifle from its holster under the control panel. It had been a joke when her mother had first given her the rifle, naming it after her childhood doll. But the name had stuck, and Syl and Beti were a lethal combo. She'd never missed a shot with the snub-barreled blaster rifle, and it had only been because of the gas the Nihil used that she hadn't killed the marauders who'd boarded their ship the day her mother was killed.

Neeto sighed. "Syl."

"A captain doesn't quit their ship, no matter how bleak things get." Syl blinked away hot tears and turned back to Neeto. "This is all I have left and it's worth fighting for."

Neeto stood and pointed through the cockpit's window at the ships approaching. "How many people do you think have died just like your mother? We have to tell someone what is happening out here. Do you think the Republic or the Jedi know that the Nihil are even in this sector? They've already killed so many, but this means nowhere is safe. We have to let someone from the Republic know. Otherwise, how will we keep other haulers from routing through here?"

Syl blinked, and M-227 began to move toward the escape pod like a very old man, each movement punctuated by a squeal of rusty hinges. It was really something when not even her security droid wanted to fight. Syl knew they were right, but in this moment she couldn't help herself. She didn't want to do the smart thing. She wanted her heart to stop breaking.

"The *Switchback* is my home," Syl said.

"It's become my home, too," Neeto said, his voice clogged with a rare show of emotion. "And I promise you we will get it back. But first we have to survive."

Syl nodded and reluctantly stood, sliding Beti into the backpack holster she wore. And then she ran to the escape pod with Neeto and M-227, fleeing for her life, giving up one of the last things she had left of her mother.

They made it to the escape pod just as the sounds of the Nihil breaching the air lock reverberated through the ship. As they launched out into the darkness of space, Syl's thoughts were only for the *Switchback*.

She would do everything in her power to get her ship back.

Either that, or she would extract its price in Nihil blood.

ONE

Vernestra Rwoh closed her eyes and breathed deeply. The Mirialan's green face smoothed, the frown of concern she usually wore melting away, leaving the markings at the corners of her eyes—six tiny diamonds arranged in two vertical rows—uncrinkled for once. The tiny trickle of a babbling brook grew into a steady stream, which in turn grew into a rushing river, pouring into the wide sea that was the Force. Every Jedi perceived the Force slightly differently, and for Vernestra it had always been a waterway that connected all life in the galaxy.

As she sank into the power and possibility of the Force, Vernestra felt more at peace than she had all day. The meditation garden on Starlight Beacon was hands down Vernestra's favorite place. Peace, tranquility, the cloying scent of gherullian vines . . .

. . . and sweet, blessed silence.

Vernestra breathed slowly as she meditated, her entire being linked deeply with the Force. She was still not great at emptiness; she often too quickly landed back in her physical self as her daily worries gnawed at her, but she was getting better. Not that she'd had a lot of time to practice. As often as she'd been sent out on missions in the past year, this kind of personal time was a gift. The steady detachment made her feel more at peace and more centered, which was exactly what she needed.

Having a Padawan was *hard*.

Passing her trials at fifteen had seemed like a remarkable feat, but it was nothing compared with trying to teach someone else how to be a Jedi. At sixteen Vernestra had taken her first Padawan learner, and a year later, she still struggled under the responsibility of teaching another Jedi. Especially someone as unconsciously connected to everyone around him as Imri Cantaros. A veritable empath, Imri was able to sense the slightest shift in the moods of those around him.

Including his master.

When Vernestra had taken Imri as her Padawan, it had been because she felt like she'd let him down when they'd been stranded on Wevo. Imri had been mourning his previous master, and Vernestra had missed the telltale signs of grief, of all the anger and doubt that could blossom in such a fertile emotion. She'd thought she could help him be more self-assured, show him that he could be a Jedi if he worked hard and followed the Force. Teaching was a cornerstone of the Order, the sharing of knowledge nearly as important as protecting life. Vernestra thought that taking a Padawan would be easy, a natural extension of her Jedi abilities.

But that was then, and in the past year she and Imri had grown a lot closer and had learned a lot about the intricacies of the master/Padawan relationship. She'd learned that the path to knighthood was different for everyone, and that she had to focus less on what worked for her and more on what would work for Imri. Which was hard. Vernestra wanted Imri to learn the same way she had, because that felt like the best course of action. But it wasn't for him.

So Vernestra was trying to help Imri forge his own path to knighthood. Sometimes that meant knowing that he had to find his own way, that she had to be less involved in his daily studies. She'd tried having him shadow other Jedi Masters on Starlight, since there were a handful who did not currently have an apprentice. Plus, she figured that it was good for him to see that even though the Jedi were united in their cause they were all very, very different.

She was beginning to think part of the problem was how well she and Imri got along. She was only a couple of years older than Imri and often saw him more as a colleague than a student. She always felt a bit silly telling him to do this or that. Not that he argued, but her own master, Stellan Gios, had taken a much firmer hand with her training and she'd always been a little intimidated by him. Maybe she should try seeing Imri more as her responsibility and less as a friend who needed a little extra help.

That didn't mean Vernestra wasn't trying, wasn't teaching Imri how to be a Jedi. It just meant that she spent more time than she should wondering whether or not she was doing a good job. Force knew how hard she was trying, but she still had a niggling feeling that she should be doing something else.

Something *more*.

"Vern! There you are."

Vernestra opened her eyes to see Imri standing before her, his pale cheeks ruddy. Only one person on all of Starlight called her Vern, so seeing her Padawan in the meditation garden was no surprise. The boy, who was quite a bit taller than her and stocky to boot, grinned as though he'd just discovered a new secret to the Force.

"I take it your lightsaber conversation with Master Avar went well?" Imri had talked about the Jedi Master's distinctive hilt and lightsaber technique for months, so much so that Vernestra had finally given in and asked the marshal of Starlight whether she would be willing to spar with the boy. Surprisingly, she had readily agreed. Master Avar was beyond generous with her time, especially where Padawans were concerned, and Vernestra secretly hoped that one day she could be as competent as the Jedi Master was with Padawans. Because she felt anything but.

It seemed ironic that the first time she ever questioned her competency as a Jedi was when training a Padawan. Wasn't she supposed to be the one with the answers?

Imri bounced on the balls of his feet, seeming much more like a youngling than a Padawan. "Look!"

Imri thrust out his lightsaber for Vernestra to inspect. The hilt bore a new secondary set of tubing, which would light up when Imri powered up his saber.

"I was telling Master Avar how much I liked her lightsaber, and she helped me create a bit of my own design for the hilt. She said the extra weight will make it better in the backswing, and it really does feel a lot better in my hand. And I promise I will not lose this one." He grinned. Imri was a bit sensitive about his lightsaber. His previous saber had been lost nearly a year before, and until just recently he'd been using a loaner from the armory on Starlight Beacon. It had only been a couple of months since he'd been able to make a pilgrimage to find a new kyber crystal, a trip made dangerous by the looming threat of the Nihil. And after the tragedy on Valo, so many lives lost in a single terrible day, it was even more important for the Jedi to keep their choice weapons nearby. The attack had put every Jedi on high alert. There were not many who still believed the Nihil were a small, localized threat, and the past couple of weeks had seen even the most pacifist Jedi more readily draw their lightsabers at the first sign of danger.

Everywhere except for the meditation garden.

"Imri," Vernestra began, uncrossing her legs and climbing to her feet. "Meditation garden."

"Oh, right! Sorry," he said sheepishly. Even if Imri did turn into a bit of a nexu cub when he was excited, he was quick to correct his mistakes, which was one positive.

Because he made a lot of mistakes.

"Also, there's a comm droid waiting for you outside," Imri said, tucking his lightsaber back into his holster. "I guess they're also not allowed in the meditation garden."

Vernestra smiled and ruffled Imri's hair, even though the boy was half a head taller than her. "That would be correct. Did it say who was calling?" Live holos to Starlight, as opposed to recorded ones that were sent daily, were uncommon and usually saved for important alerts. Vernestra didn't know anyone but Master Avar who used live holos regularly.

Imri shook his head. He followed closely behind Vernestra as she exited the garden, the peace and tranquility of the space giving way to misters raining down water vapor and then finally a long gleaming white hallway that spit them out onto one of Starlight Beacon's main concourses. The cacophony of the space station was jarring after her time spent in the meditation garden, and Vernestra sighed.

Perhaps she should have gone back to Port Haileap when

Master Avar had offered her the chance. Jedi Master Jorinda Boffrey, a Delphidian with stripy, leathery skin and a gentle manner, had stopped on Starlight Beacon and told Vernestra that there would be space for her in the small temple there, but had also encouraged her to listen to the Force and go where it willed. Vernestra was not sure it was the Force that had kept her on Starlight Beacon for so long, but her presence had allowed her to assist in a number of lifesaving missions. Plus, if she had left Starlight then, she and Imri would have missed learning so much. There wasn't much happening on Port Haileap, and Vernestra had delayed her return to fully experience life on Starlight Beacon, which was less outpost and more thriving city. Perhaps she'd dallied too long and the Order was sending her back to Haileap.

"Oh, here it comes," Imri said as a two-wheeled droid bobbled toward them, looking surprisingly unsteady as it rolled along. A silver pole connected to the droid's wheelbase extended up into a flat screen blinking Vernestra's name.

"I'm Vernestra Rwoh," she called as the droid lurched past, and the thing nearly fell over as it tried to turn around. The comm droid bumped into a passing astromech, which let out a set of furious beeps as it backed up and went around, before it finally stopped in front of Vernestra and Imri.

"Vernestra Rwoh," she said again, and the screen bearing her name blinked once and then revealed a number pad.

"Please enter your passcode," the droid said.

"Umm, I don't have a passcode." They stood in the middle

of the corridor, so foot traffic had to go around them on either side, and Vernestra tried to move closer to one of the walls to get out of the way of droids and people as they went about their business. Imri blinked once and then again, his normally ruddy cheeks going pale.

"Does it seem like there are a lot more people here today?" he asked.

Vernestra nodded. "There must be a large transport passing through from the frontier."

"Is it okay if I catch up with you at dinner?" Imri asked. The boy looked ill, and his eyes darted to the left and the right as he took in the bodies flooding the concourse.

"Overwhelmed?" Vernestra asked. Ever since the disaster on Valo, Imri had seemed even more sensitive to the moods of those around him, and large groups of non-Force users seemed to affect him the worst.

"Very," he said.

"Why don't you go back to the meditation garden? I'll come get you after I figure out this passcode thing," Vernestra said. "And remember to keep your lightsaber holstered!"

Imri nodded and hurried back the way they had come, and Vernestra turned her attention back to the blinking screen before her.

"Please enter your passcode," the comm droid said again.

"Oh, that one is broken," came a voice from the middle of the concourse.

Vernestra turned to see a human she knew too well grinning at her.

"Reath!" Vernestra said. "Are you already back from the ruins on Genetia?"

The Padawan nodded. Reath Silas was a studious human with pale skin, brown hair, eyes that shone with intelligence, and an utterly adorable aversion to adventure. Vernestra had known Reath ever since they were younglings, which was why it was always so strange to see him with a Padawan braid. He was a visual reminder that she was far ahead of her peers, even if she was feeling a bit unmoored at the moment.

Reath scratched the back of his head and laughed a little. "Yeah, it turns out that the ruins were actually much smaller than we'd thought, and with the tragedy on Valo, Master Cohmac thought it would be better to return instead of waiting for the eventual recall order. I think we might be more useful here, working against the Nihil."

"Yes. Valo was . . ." Vernestra's voice trailed off as she thought back to the carnage of the disaster on the recently added Republic planet. The Republic Fair was supposed to be a grand event that would unite the galaxy and show the strength and diversity of the Republic while also welcoming Valo to the fold, but instead it had turned into a mass casualty event when the Nihil attacked. So much pain, so much loss. None of the Jedi who had been there seemed to be able to talk about the enormity of that moment, even if the Republic feeds were full of nothing but chatter about the disaster and conspiracy theories about where things had gone wrong. "It was a lot."

"Oh, I didn't know you were there," Reath said. "I'm sorry."

"Everything happens for a reason, even if the why isn't clear right now. That's the way the Force works. I mean, that's what I keep telling myself. And I know that doesn't erase the tragedy of the attack, but I have to focus on that for the moment." Otherwise she would maybe find a way to spend all her time basking in the calm tranquility of the cosmic Force and never return to the messy day-to-day business of the living Force.

The living Force was the energy that connected all living things to one another, but the cosmic Force was the galaxy itself and was wide and vast. It was easy to get lost in the massiveness of it all if one desired. Some Jedi frowned on those who neglected their physical selves for too long to pursue the calling of the cosmic Force.

Still, sometimes Vernestra could feel the cosmic Force calling to her like far-off waves, and she wondered what she would find if she just followed that sound to the edges of the known galaxy. It wasn't an impulse she indulged too often.

"Please enter your passcode," the communications droid intoned.

"I don't have a passcode! I swear, I am going to use my saber," Vernestra growled.

"Is it okay if I . . . ?" Reath pointed to the communications droid.

Vernestra stood a little to the side. "Be my guest."

Reath slammed his palm into the side of the droid, causing several people on the concourse to turn and look, and the screen flashed before displaying an empty room.

"Hey, thanks!" Vernestra said.

"No problem! Well, I'd better get back to helping Master Cohmac unload the ship. See you around!" Reath melted into the crowd on the concourse, and Vernestra turned her attention back to the comm droid. Whoever had called her must have already gone about their business. She peered at the screen, trying to parse out just where and what the background could be. She'd half expected to see Avon Starros staring back at her. It wouldn't be the first time her former charge had spliced a comm unit for a friendly chat.

"Hello?" Vernestra called through the screen. It didn't seem like anyone was actually on the other end.

"Vernestra!" Master Stellan Gios leaned into the frame, and Vernestra's face split into a grin. "I'm sorry, I think I underestimated how long it took to connect to Starlight."

"Master Stellan! Did you stop trimming your beard?"

"I did! Well, I mostly just haven't had the chance, I've been so busy." He rubbed his face and smiled ruefully as he contemplated the hair dusting his cheeks and chin. Master Stellan reminded Vernestra of Reath, and that wasn't because all humans looked the same, but rather because they had the same pale skin and brown hair. But where Reath slouched to avoid notice, Master Stellan strode into a room and fairly demanded someone give him a leadership position. He had a way of taking charge that had always awed Vernestra and made her proud to be his Padawan.

"Unkempt looks good on you, Master Stellan," Vernestra said with a smile. "You look just like the human hero from one of the adventure holos, *Frontier's Peril*."

The older Jedi laughed. "Between you and me, I mostly grew it so I would look more dignified. The Jedi Council is very serious business." Then his expression sobered. "How are you doing in the aftermath of Valo? I think the attack on the Republic Fair has impacted us all, but that was the last time we saw one another, and I was sorry we didn't get to catch up after the counterassault."

After the Nihil had murdered thousands on Valo, the Jedi had assailed the Nihil stronghold on Grizal, scattering the Nihil and severely limiting their abilities to wreak havoc. Now a combination of Jedi and Republic forces was waging battle after battle across the galaxy, with the intent of eliminating the Nihil threat once and for all.

Vernestra crossed her arms. She'd rather not dwell on the battle, but she couldn't exactly give a Jedi Master the brush-off. "I'm as well as can be expected. And I am glad to speak to you again. I was worried. After Valo . . ." Vernestra's voice trailed off. Everyone had seen the image of Master Stellan standing amid the wreckage, people wailing in pain while a single tear slid down his cheek. He had become the hero of Valo in a moment when everyone else was considered a villain—including the Chancellor, who was still in recovery— and it was strange that the Jedi who had ushered Vernestra through her Jedi training was now a galactic celebrity.

Stellan nodded. "Valo changed everything, which is actually why I'm contacting you. I wanted to let you know that I'm recalling you and your Padawan to Coruscant."

Vernestra blinked. Her pulse picked up a bit, and she took a few calming breaths. Everyone knew that being assigned to the main temple was important, and she felt the weight of responsibility settle over her. This was good, right? "Is there a reason why?"

"Yes, actually." Stellan grinned again. "Your heroism and courage have distinguished you more than you know, and a Republic senator asked for you by name to handle an issue we're having in the Berenge sector."

"Berenge?" Vernestra said, running through what she knew about that part of the frontier. She adjusted the tie holding back her purple-black hair, using the time to buy herself a moment to think. "But there's nothing out there."

"Which is exactly the problem. Anyway, I'll give you the details when you get here."

Vernestra nodded. "I'm guessing you've already run this past Master Avar?"

"She is going to be my next call. Don't worry, Vernestra, this is a good thing for you. To be a Jedi Knight who has already distinguished herself, and at such a young age? The Order is better for having you. May the Force be with you."

"And you," Vernestra said, ending the call, gnawing on her lip as she did so. Master Stellan's news should have filled her with joy. Serving as a Knight in the main temple on Coruscant had once been her dream, and here it was coming true when she was only seventeen.

But instead, Vernestra was filled with despair. She had so much left to learn on Starlight Beacon, and the station had become her home. She also didn't want to leave Master Avar. The older Jedi was planning a big mission, and Vernestra wanted to be a part of that. She wanted to help eliminate the Nihil from the frontier, to help keep the settlers trying to build their lives safe from any more attacks.

Vernestra took a deep breath and went back to the meditation garden to fetch Imri. First they would eat dinner, and then she would seek Master Avar's counsel. If anyone could provide guidance in a moment like this, it was her.

TWO

Reath Silas didn't exactly feel happy to be back on Starlight Beacon, but there was definitely a sense of relief. For the past year, ever since his fight with the Drengir on the Amaxine space station, he'd been steadily getting used to adventuring. Master Cohmac might be a historian and folklorist, but he also had a penchant for seeking out artifacts that were in very, very dangerous places.

So far Reath had been shot at innumerable times (never hit), kidnapped twice (only once successfully), and had fought more Nihil and Drengir than he could count. He had even taken a few lives, a burden that weighed on him if he let himself wallow in the moment. But despite all of it he still thought he had made the correct choice in asking Master Cohmac to be his master after the loss of his previous master, Jora Malli, who was killed fighting the Nihil in the aftermath of the *Legacy Run* disaster.

But there were times, like when he was unloading the ship after their latest mission, that he sort of regretted it.

"Master Cohmac, did you really need, um, all sixty-four volumes of Leric Schmireland's *Almanac of the Unknown*?" Reath asked, looking at the crate before him. As much as he loved the information contained in the datatapes, they were heavy.

"The datatape edition has a few locations and some information that the databank version does not," Master Cohmac said, levitating the crate onto the cart waiting nearby. "Schmireland is one of the greats of the Age of Exploration, and we would be remiss not to have a copy of his work here in Starlight Beacon's library."

Reath said nothing and went back to levitating crates onto the nearby cart. The droid piloting the cart beeped in annoyance, and Master Cohmac sighed. "It takes as long as it takes, friend," he said in response to the droid's complaint that it had somewhere else to be.

Reath held his hands out and used the Force to stack the final two crates. It was a ridiculous number of artifacts and tapes, but Master Cohmac was adamant that it was important they preserve as much as they could from Genetia, since the planet was spiraling toward civil war. The Order usually didn't get involved in such matters, but Master Cohmac had found the petition from the planet's academic community compelling, and he'd managed to save almost two entire libraries and a museum's worth of artifacts. One day when things were stable once more, the Order would return the artifacts and tapes to the ruling government. But until then, they would be stored on Starlight Beacon.

"That seems to be the last of it," Master Cohmac said, swiping his hand across his sweaty brow. Like Reath, Master Cohmac still wore his mission attire, the brown tunic only a little darker than the warm tan of his skin. His dark beard was slightly unkempt—their last few days on Genetia had been spent hiding from revolutionaries who thought the Jedi were emissaries of a demon king—but overall the Jedi looked content. It was an expression Reath had not seen on his master since before the tragedy on Valo and the resulting attack on the Nihil Tempest Runner Pan Eyta. The trip to Genetia had been exactly what the older Jedi needed after so much full-scale battle, and Reath felt a measure of relief at seeing Cohmac look less . . . concerned.

"Should we go get something to eat?" Reath asked.

"After we see Master Avar. I want to see if she's heard any news on my request to get a copy of Master Evelyn Qwisp's *Meditations* from the archives on Coruscant."

Reath didn't sigh out loud, but his stomach did let loose a loud growl, and Master Cohmac laughed. "You go ahead and go eat. I'll find you after I speak with Avar."

Reath didn't wait for his master to change his mind. He set off with long strides to the community dining area. One of the things he was looking forward to was real food, not the pastes and packets that travel sometimes required.

The scent of roasting vegetables and savory breads greeted Reath as he entered the dining area, and he nearly wept with joy. The dining facility on Starlight Beacon was a grand affair, just like the rest of the station. Long rows of gleaming white tables lined the wide-open space, maintenance droids cleaning them as Republic officials and other travelers ate and left. At the far end of the room was the serving line, and the kitchen droids overlooked nearly a hundred different dishes, all held in shining silver chafing vessels. The dining area was always open because of the varying internal clocks of the many different species that passed through Starlight Beacon. But for once it seemed less busy than usual, and Reath was able to grab a tray and walk right up to whatever food items he wished without waiting.

He was going to eat his weight in roasted harmony squash and freshly baked seed bread with thick blue butter and even thicker yellow chime fruit preserve.

After piling a tray high with food Reath walked over to the long rows of tables and was just about to sit at an empty one when a familiar green figure waved at him. Reath grinned at Vernestra's happy look and changed course so he could sit with her and the boy who accompanied her.

"Reath! Have you met my Padawan, Imri Cantaros?" Vernestra said as Reath sat down next to her.

Reath blinked. He'd heard Vernestra had a Padawan, but the reality of a Jedi he'd known since he was a youngling already having a Padawan learner left him feeling a little unmoored and maybe a tiny bit inadequate. Reath knew he wasn't ready to take his trials and become a Knight, but Vernestra's effortless competence made him feel like he should be working harder. He pushed aside the unwanted doubts and turned his attention back to the conversation. "I haven't. Uh, Reath Silas," he said, waving at the boy across the table. From his size Reath had thought the boy was maybe the same age as him, eighteen, but sitting across from him Imri looked a bit younger. There was something in his wide eyes and slightly worried frown that reminded Reath of himself when he'd been younger.

Imri waved at Reath and went back to his own plate of food, the frown lines never leaving his pale brow. Reath raised an eyebrow at Vernestra, but she waved it away, as though whatever was bothering the other boy was nothing of consequence.

"So, now that I'm not fighting with a comm droid, tell me about Genetia. Was it as pretty as they say?" Vernestra asked. "Imri, aren't you from there?"

Imri nodded and then shrugged. "Yes and no. My father was from Genetia, and my mother was from Hynestia, and we lived on both planets before my parents took me to the temple on Hynestia when they discovered I was Force-sensitive. I only remember it a little bit." He frowned and kept looking at his plate of food, as though he was reluctant to be involved in the conversation. Reath didn't know Imri well enough to know whether this was unusual for the boy, and he wasn't especially good at reading the emotions around him, so he tried to offer Imri a friendly smile.

The other boy never looked up.

"Oh, then, Reath, you have to tell us what Genetia is like now. For Imri's sake." Seeming not to find Imri's behavior odd in the least, Vernestra smiled, the tattoos on the outsides of her eyes crinkling, and Reath was suddenly taken back to their days together as younglings. Back then, Vernestra had been a quiet, studious girl who always spent far too much time trying to perfect her lessons. Perhaps not too much time. She was a Knight while Reath was still a Padawan, one whose master had not even mentioned preparing for the trials.

Imri's head shot up, and his frown deepened a bit. "It's okay. I feel that way sometimes, as well," the boy said, patting Reath's hand solicitously. The tiny bit of annoyed jealousy that had been threatening to well up in Reath melted away, and he blinked.

"What did you just do?" Reath asked, ignoring Vernestra's question about Genetia.

"I—I didn't do anything," Imri said, his pale cheeks going ruddy.

"Yes, you did. I felt it, as well," Vernestra said, her polite smile fading away. "It felt like"—she did a motion with her hand—"like smoothing. But what were you smoothing?"

"I just—Reath seemed a bit upset, and I wanted him to feel better."

"You soothed my annoyance," Reath said, intrigued by Imri's use of the Force. "Not so much manipulated it but just, kind of dulled the sensation."

Vernestra stood. "That can't be good. Imri, you can't use the Force to manipulate others."

Reath opened his mouth to defend Imri—he'd met Loden Greatstorm before he'd been lost, and knew that the technique was rare but when used correctly could be greatly beneficial—but he was cut off by a burst of emotion from the other Padawan.

"I didn't mean to!" he said, and Vernestra raised her hands in surrender.

"Tranquility, Imri. Take a deep breath. I know it might have been instinctual, but we're going to have to work on this to make sure you can control it. But first, let's go talk to Master Maru. He may know what it was that you did and may know of some exercises for it. Or there might be something in the library we can research." Vernestra gave Reath an apologetic smile. "Sorry, I really did want to hear about your trip. Things have been hard since the tragedy on Valo, and this is one of the things we're sort of working on."

"Oh, no worries. It was good talking to you again,

Vernestra. Hopefully I'll see you around." He realized it wasn't just polite chatter. He really did want to see her again. His face heated a bit with a happy flush.

Imri gave him a sideways look, and not a friendly one, and Reath wondered if the boy could read his emotions that easily. He coughed to cover his discomfort, and as he watched Imri and Vernestra go, he felt a strong sense of relief.

He knew such things were frowned on by the Order, but he couldn't help having a crush on Vernestra. She was smart and friendly and took the Order just as seriously as any Jedi Master. It was hard not to like the Mirialan. But that didn't mean he liked her romantically, did it? Marriage and children weren't things Jedi sought to have, and there was no way Vernestra would ever take her vows anything other than seriously.

For some reason Reath's thoughts bounced back to Nan, the Nihil girl he'd met what felt like nearly a lifetime before. He suddenly wondered if he would ever see her again, and just what she was doing. Was she even still alive, or had she been killed in one of the numerous battles the Nihil had fought with the Jedi and the Republic peacekeepers?

Reath didn't know, and he didn't know why he was even thinking about Nan, or why he suddenly wondered what it would be like to kiss someone. Remembering that Nan had been sweet to him just so he would feed her information, he pushed all the weird, uncomfortable feelings aside and threw himself into his food, knowing that sooner or later Master Cohmac would come looking for him, and then it would be time for yet another task.

There was no sense in working on an empty stomach.

THREE

Nan stood off to the side of the temple in the *Gaze Electric* and watched as the Eye met with his Tempest Runners. Like most of the ship, the room was dimly lit and smelled faintly of rust and decay. Once, this room had been a place of worship, even though Nan didn't recognize any of the symbols etched into the walls. Once, the Eye never would have dreamed of having Tempest Runners come to his ship, but in the past few months the Republic and their Jedi had done a number on the Nihil's many hidden bases, leaving them scrambling to muster up a response.

"You're not supposed to be here," whispered a boy a few

years younger than her, his pale blond hair covering most of his face.

"And you are?" Nan said, smoothing her dark hair back and pretending to be unbothered by the challenge. Krix was right. She wasn't technically supposed to be in the room, but if that annoying mynock was going to hang out and eavesdrop, then she was going to do the same. "Leave me be before I slide a blade between your ribs."

The boy laughed in his throat before moving away, and Nan considered how she could end his life just to remove the stench of him from the room.

In the past year Nan had lived a hundred lifetimes. She'd fought Jedi and raided shipyards. She'd collected more intelligence for the Eye than any of his other trusted spies. Her young appearance and effortless ability to lie had made her invaluable. She could make just about anyone believe whatever she wanted, and she had used that ability all in the name of the Eye, Marchion Ro.

She had earned her place at his side, unlike Krix, who was nothing but a slimy, bucktoothed human who spent more time causing trouble than bringing glory to the Storm. Nan really did want to murder the pale boy, but she worried that Ro might actually like him for some reason, so instead she glared at him from across the room and hoped that he'd end up on the wrong side of a blaster bolt.

"Why am I hearing reports of a Nihil loss at Dalna?"

Marchion Ro asked. He slumped in a massive chair that looked down on those occupied by his Tempest Runners, seeming for all the stars bored by the conversation. It gave Nan a thrill every time she saw him like this: helmet off, black hair free to hang over his bare, leathery skin and his star-marked shoulders. His pitiless eyes were all black, and Nan stood close enough that she could see the slight ruffle on the edge of his ears. No one knew just who Ro's people were. Every time someone asked him his species they ended up dead. He was as deadly as he was beautiful, and Nan counted herself lucky to be allowed to occupy the same space as him.

"It's just another ploy by the Republic to undermine our victories," said the newest Tempest Runner, Kara Xoo, a brutal Quarren who thought torture was a spectator sport. Nan liked Kara's way of doing things, which was mostly smash and a little grab. The one time Nan had gone along with the Quarren's Tempest on a run, it had been great fun, if not particularly lucrative. She was only a Tempest Runner because Pan Eyta had gone missing in the aftermath of the attack on Valo. Most everyone thought him dead. He was not missed.

"If that's the case, why is your fleet down twenty ships?" Lourna Dee said. Like Ro, she reclined in her chair, utterly at ease. Lourna was a sickly green Twi'lek who wore armor and was much deadlier than she appeared, and it was a mistake for any opponent to underestimate her ruthlessness. She didn't bluster or brag like Kara or the previous Tempest

Runner, Pan Eyta; she smiled prettily and then killed anyone who annoyed her. Members of her Tempest were just as coldly efficient as she was, and just as reserved. She was the only Tempest Runner who made Nan uncomfortable. Not because she was dangerous, but because her speech patterns sometimes slipped into a moneyed Hosnian Prime accent. No matter how much Nan had tried to discover Lourna's secrets, she'd always come up dry.

"Twenty ships?" the Eye said, straightening. "Who was in charge of that run?"

"I was," said an Ithorian, his translator crackling as he spoke. "I lost half of my Strike and all of my Storm. The Republic was waiting for us. We didn't have any kind of chance, not even with the Path drives." The Ithorian still wore his mask, which Nan took to be an insult to Lord Ro. The *Gaze Electric* was the safest ship in all the galaxy. The Jedi had managed to ransack the base on Grizal and a number of other safe houses the Nihil used. But the *Gaze Electric* was so far untouched, and some of the younger Nihil had begun speaking of Marchion Ro as though he were more than a mere man.

Nan didn't think the Eye had any unusual abilities, but he was a survivor just like her and knew to plan accordingly, with several plans going at any single point in time. She liked that about him.

Marchion Ro picked up a small object next to his chair and threw it at the Ithorian. Nan had only a glimpse of it before it attached to the Ithorian's face. The other pirate pulled at the thing, which Nan now could see was one of the sticky charges the Nihil sometimes used to get through particularly stubborn airlocks.

There was no time for the Ithorian to say anything before the entire top half of his body exploded, the detonation also taking out his friends who stood too close to him. The rest of the Nihil didn't even flinch.

It wasn't a party without at least a little murder.

"Speaking of ships, Lourna, where is my weapon you promised me?" Ro said, turning on the Tempest Runner just as Kara gestured for a couple of her followers to drag away the bodies. Her Tempest was now down at least another Strike's worth of Nihil, but Marchion Ro had moved on. "And my promised Jedi? With the last one gone, the butcher grows anxious for test subjects. I'd hate to see him start finding volunteers in other places."

Lourna shrugged, unbothered by the threat. "Science takes time, Ro. We're still mapping the overlapping routes that pass through the area. And as for the Jedi, I'm on it. Politics, as you also know, are impossibly slow. But the Graf family and I have enjoyed a long and fruitful partnership. You will have your replacements."

"The Jedi are less important than the weapon. The Republic has more than enough of our Path drives to begin researching in earnest. It is only a matter of time before the Republic understands the Paths," Ro said. He didn't seem to be any less bored than he was before, but the drum of his obsidian talons on the arm of his chair gave truth to the lie of his posture. "You promised me a way to disrupt that."

"And the Gravity's Heart will do just that. But without understanding all of the routes in the sector, we can't disrupt anything but those manifests we already hold. You did get the tithing of coaxium, did you not?"

"Yes, but that was not what I tasked you with," Ro said.

Lourna Dee smiled at him. "If you were to give me the assistance of your savant I could finish the project more quickly."

Ro's scowl melted into an expression of surprise. "Is that so?"

"Yes. She knows and has forgotten even the most tenuous Paths, untold byways through hyperspace. She can help us route and track the energy spikes in the area. She was the one who suggested the Berenge sector in the first place."

Ro sat up, suddenly interested. "She did? Have you been poking through my currents, Lourna?"

"Not at all. It was the Path I asked you for in the aftermath of Valo. Or have you forgotten?"

Lourna's words were nearly a direct challenge to Ro, and everyone in the room heard it. A collective breath was held, and everyone adjusted slightly as they waited to see whether Ro would take her words as a threat or not. The Nihil were always ready for a fight, but with their dwindling numbers Nan worried that a full-out brawl was unwise.

If there was a fight, Nan knew exactly where she was aiming. As though Krix heard her thoughts, his eyes met hers across the dim room, and Nan showed the boy her teeth.

But Ro merely smiled, flashing his own jagged teeth at Lourna before settling back into his chair. "And why should I give you my savant? Where is the benefit?"

Lourna sat up and gave Ro a sly look. "Where do you think I got the coaxium? The weapon is already a success, but is imprecise. Better mapping, along with better intelligence, would mean more profitable hauls. And the weapon could be most powerful in an offensive the next time the Republic comes calling. After all, it would be disastrous if we were taken unaware again like Pan was on Cyclor."

Marchion Ro's nails dug into the arm of his chair, shredding the metal. The reminder of their defeat on Grizal was a risky subject for Lourna to bring up. So many Nihil had been lost, and their scattered forces had been on the run ever since.

"Eye, I can see that I have displeased you," Lourna said to Marchion Ro with an incline of her head, her challenge melting away into obeisance. "I only meant to indicate that your impending travels will render the Paths useless to you in the interim. With the help of your savant, we could better prepare the weapon so that it will be ready after your travels."

Ro stared at Lourna Dee, and there was a long moment when Nan's heart pounded. She did a mental calculation of the knives she wore and the location of Lourna's faithful in the hall. Just in case. She liked to be ready when the killing started.

But the Eye did not stand in challenge. Instead he laughed heartily. "Yes, yes, of course. Perhaps I should have you bring your mysterious scientist to the *Gaze Electric* instead of giving you my savant."

Anyone who had not studied Lourna Dee would have missed her surprised blink, but Nan saw it. Just as she saw the way Lourna stretched and sighed, her languorous movements drawing the eyes of any number of people in the hall as she settled back into her chair. "Eye, you know how academics are. If I bring you my scientist she will be unsettled for weeks, and then the final adjustments to the weapon will never be made. But, as always, I am at your disposal. As faithful as I have always been."

Marchion Ro smiled, and this time it was genuine. Nan relaxed. Her lord was amused, which meant that he found something Lourna said funny. Nan wished she knew what it was. "I see. It's all starting to make perfect sense. You can borrow the savant. I have no use for her on my undertaking. But she isn't going alone. Nan!"

Nan startled and ran over to kneel near Marchion Ro. "Lord Ro, I am at your command."

"You will accompany my savant to Lourna's *Gravity's Heart*. Safeguard my prize with your life."

Nan's heart pounded in her ears, and she fought to hide

her disappointment as she stood. She'd seen the savant once, a frail human woman who looked like she'd died thrice over. Everyone knew the woman had been alive as long as there had been Nihil. She was ancient. What if the old woman perished from a heart attack while Nan was supposed to be caring for her? There was no mistaking what Ro meant by Nan putting her life behind guarding the old woman.

If the crone died, so would she. This wasn't a task; it was a death sentence. What had she done to earn the Eye's ire? Where had she failed?

Not a flicker of her distress made its way to Nan's face. Instead, she bent over at the waist in one last show of respect.

"I am honored to have this duty, Lord Ro."

"Indeed," Marchion Ro said, his gaze not on her but on Lourna. "Go to the labs and find the doctor. Tell him to prepare the savant for travel. He will accompany you."

Nan gave a short nod. "For the Storm!"

Nan turned on her heel and left. But not before she saw Krix grinning at her evilly from across the way.

She decided that maybe she would kill the boy after all. Not today, but soon.

FOUR

Syl walked into the first dockside tavern she could find on Coruscant and heaved a sigh of relief at the familiar smells of cheap food and even cheaper liquor. This was more like it.

For the past two days Syl had been running through a gauntlet. She had reached out to just about every Republic official she could find, from shipping officers to transportation clerks. No one cared about the hyperspace anomaly out in the Berenge sector, or the fact that Syl had a pretty good idea the Nihil were behind it. Either Syl got a pat response—the Republic is seeing to the issue of the Nihil as quickly as possible; thank you for your concern—or she got shuffled to yet another Republic official to file a report.

She had yet to give any kind of testimony to anyone important within the Republic, just a lot of reception clerks who were clearly trying to get her to leave. All she wanted was for someone to flag the routes that went through the Berenge sector as dangerous so that people who traveled them knew they were taking a chance. It was frustrating and aggravating, and she was beginning to lose hope. What if she'd abandoned the *Switchback* for no reason? What if no one ever stopped the Nihil on the frontier? The handful of skirmishes thus far weren't enough. If they had been, Syl would still have her ship.

Syl shook her head. The Republic and the Jedi needed to do better. Most of the clashes had been in the Outer Rim, with the farthest outposts still scrambling to defend themselves from relentless attacks. She wasn't on Coruscant just because she'd lost her ship. This was also about doing the right thing for those who didn't get a voice on Coruscant, so far away from the fear and bloodshed of the Nihil attacks. If enough people spoke up, the Republic had to listen, to see that the Nihil were more than just space pirates stealing from hapless haulers. She was going to keep yelling until someone paid attention.

Besides, without her ship, it wasn't like she had anything else to do.

Syl took a deep breath and made her way into the tavern. She missed the reassuring weight of Beti, left back in the lockbox in her room in the cheapest hotel she could find. Normally she would carry the modified rifle strapped across her back in the holster she'd had made for it, but Coruscant was civilized, which meant that people there tended to look down on folks carrying blasters out in the open. And Syl was trying to blend in just a bit. It was annoying, but not much of an issue. She was a resourceful girl.

Syl found an empty table in the back with a communication module set into the wall. It was a common feature in dockside taverns. Haulers and shippers often liked the relative privacy of a public comm unit to call home. Ships could be claustrophobic, gossipy places, and sometimes the last thing a person wanted was their crewmates knowing all their business.

For Syl, she was only half certain that the Ithorian who ran the sketchy hotel where she was staying wasn't also an information broker, and the last thing she needed was her business being aired throughout the galaxy. Not that she had many secrets. But better safe than sorry.

A server droid ambled over, and Syl ordered the special and a mug of the local swill. She wasn't going to get drunk, but a drink would be nice. Especially since the food might be completely inedible. She needed at least one thing to go right for her.

Once the server droid left, Syl powered up the comm unit, plinking in a couple of credits. She didn't have much left to her name, but she'd promised Neeto she would send him a holo. They hadn't had enough credits among the three of them to book passage from Port Haileap to Coruscant for everyone, so M-227 and Neeto had remained behind to work in the docking yard, where they had found positions as laborers. Neeto had promised to send along enough money to get Syl back to Haileap, but she wasn't going to ask the old Sullustan for a single credit. She already felt guilty enough leaving them behind, but coming to Coruscant and getting the Republic involved had seemed like the best way to change things on the edge of the galaxy. Now she wasn't so sure. It was only her deep hatred for the Nihil that had even brought her to Coruscant. It was, for the first time in her life, the lesser of two evils.

That didn't mean she didn't still loathe the planet. It was overcrowded and filled to the brim with buildings that stabbed at the sky. Syl couldn't wait to get back to the wide-open spaces of the frontier. But she refused to leave until she had something to show for her trip, even if that was just a weeklong case of indigestion.

A slim woman wearing a plain tunic and trousers walked by, and Syl's heart leapt before it settled back down to a normal pattern. This was the other thing she hated about Coruscant: the chance that she might see her ex-girlfriend again. She found herself looking for Jordanna far too often, as though the girl would be happy to see her. For a moment Syl was back on Tiikae, laughing with the girl and teasing her about her silly San Tekka manners, sneaking kisses with her when no one was around to catch them—not Syl's mother and definitely not Jor's stern aunt. It had been the best few months of Syl's life, and the last time she'd been happy.

Less than two weeks after Syl had left Tiikae, Syl's mother, Chancey Yarrow, was dead and Tiikae was ravaged as part of the Drengir attacks, leaving few survivors. Was Jordanna still there? Or had she gone home in defeat?

Syl mentally chastised herself. Expecting to see Jordanna in a dingy dockside pub on Coruscant was silly. She'd never come to such a place. Her family owned a tower somewhere in the city, San Tekka wealth being the kind that leaned into big gestures. If she was out it would be at some swanky place that only catered to the ultrarich.

Still, Syl couldn't stop herself from hoping for just a glance of the girl she'd come close to loving.

Hope is for fools and holos, Syl thought, reminding herself of one of Chancey Yarrow's favorite sayings. Too bad Syl couldn't tell her heart that.

The comm unit began to flash, startling Syl from her ill-timed reveries, and she smoothed her wild, kinky curls and put on her best smile. He wasn't picking up, so her call would go into a message queue for him to listen to later. "Hey, I hope you and Emtoo are enjoying Port Haileap! Everything is progressing kind of slowly here on Coruscant." She didn't tell Neeto that she had yet to even talk to anyone who took her seriously. "It's just a lot more complicated than I thought it would be, filing a report and all. You know how busy it is here." She was rambling. Neeto would know something was wrong. "I'll send you another update when I have news. Love you guys!"

"Are you Sylvestri Yarrow?" someone with a robotic voice asked as soon as Syl had clicked off the comm unit, her credits spent too quickly.

Syl looked up. And up. All she saw at first was snow-white fur and a mane of beautiful cream-colored hair. Above that, a mask of some sort over what Syl assumed to be a mouth, and a pair of black eyes that shone with intelligence. Syl had never seen a Gigoran before, but there was no mistaking their size: equally as tall as a Wookiee but broader through the shoulders. And pale where the Wookiees were mostly shades of brown. The strange voice came from the vocalizer the Gigoran wore, and Syl forced herself to relax.

"I'm Sylvestri Yarrow," she answered, hoping that the Gigoran was not an enforcer for one of her many creditors. Who else even knew she was on Coruscant? Just Neeto, but he wouldn't give her up without a fight. A spike of worry stabbed her before she was able to push it aside. Neeto was a survivor; he'd taught her much of what she knew. And whatever this was about, Syl had no doubt she could get out of it.

She glanced at the Gigoran again and swallowed dryly. Maybe not. Syl was clever and decent in a fight, but the Gigoran was at least twice as tall as she was, and there was no way she would end up anything other than mush in a fair fight. Or an unfair fight.

Stars, she should've brought Beti with her. To a red sun with whatever anyone thought.

To Syl's relief the Gigoran stepped to the side to reveal a slender human standing at the edge of her table. Syl didn't recognize him, which meant the man was unlikely to be a creditor. The people she owed money were of the sort to track it down themselves.

They were also nowhere near as pretty. The stranger wore a deep-green tunic that probably cost more than Syl had made in the past year. His dark hair was shorn closely on the sides, with the top left long and artfully sculpted into a high wave, and his skin was a lighter brown than Syl's, with a reddish tint to it. His eyes were the sort of blue that was rarely natural and usually the result of beauty treatments, and seemed incongruous next to such a dark complexion. Everything about the man screamed wealth, and he was as out of place in the tavern as a Jawa in a crowded city.

"Do you mind if I join you?" he asked, his voice as soft as snowbird down. Syl realized she was staring, and she shook herself. Who was this man, and what in the known galaxy could he possibly want? Syl was curious, which was how she usually got herself into trouble. But in this case, she had nothing to lose.

"Do I know you?" Syl knew she didn't, but it was a not-so-subtle way to provoke an introduction.

"No, I'm afraid not. But a friend of mine told you me might be here." He folded himself into the seat across from

Syl and gave her a friendly smile that did not reach his unnervingly blue eyes. Perhaps he wasn't human as she had originally thought but some other species she'd never met in her travels. Everything about him seemed constructed, as though he had built himself out of the expectations of others. Syl had met a scoundrel once, a dance hall owner on Neral's moon, who had looked much the same way and given off a similar vibe. She'd been charming until she arrived to collect a debt, and then she had happily performed any brutality necessary to secure her credits.

Syl blinked, and it suddenly settled into place. The memory of Lesha and her penchant for violence gave her a good idea of who this man might be. She didn't need this, not right now. "A friend of yours? Ah, you mean the hotel proprietor. Look, I already told her I didn't need any company. Besides, you, ah, aren't what I usually go for. Not that you aren't very pretty," Syl said hurriedly as the man's expression slid into horror. "It's just that you're a little too, uh, fancy. I like my partners to have a bit more of an edge, if you know what I mean. Again, no offense, but I'm good. I'm also broke, so I wouldn't be able to pay you properly even if I did take advantage of your offer." Syl was rambling. It happened sometimes, and her mother always used to chide her for it. *Don't go letting your mouth get ahead of your brain, Starshine,* she'd always said.

Too late.

"I am not a pleasure escort," he said, each word as chilly

as a Hynestian sunset. "But I do have a matter of utmost importance to discuss."

"Oh, sorry," Syl said. The server droid chose that moment to plunk down Syl's mug of beer, and she drank deeply of the bitter brew. Stars, could this get any more awkward?

"Basha," the man said to the Gigoran still standing over the table. "Would you like to wait outside?" It was not truly an invitation to leave, but a gentle command.

"Yes, thank you. Call if you need me." The Gigoran left as quietly as they had arrived, remarkably light on their feet despite their size. The man gave Syl an apologetic smile.

"Basha is my bodyguard, and normally I would have her join us, but I'm afraid the booth you chose would not accommodate someone so large, and it seems in poor taste to have a lurker."

"I didn't exactly expect company when I sat down," Syl said, crossing her arms. He'd spoken to her like he was chiding a small child, and every single bit of kindness she'd felt toward him when she thought he was just trying to nab a gig disappeared. This was why she didn't like fancy people like him. They spoke to everyone as though they were the hired help.

"Of course you didn't," the man said, chuckling softly to himself. "But really, you should have after your little performance this afternoon at the Ministry of Commerce. Threatening to string that Twi'lek up by her lekku if she sent you to one more department was quite the spectacle."

Syl flushed. It had been a stressful day, and that had not been her finest moment, but how in the seven valleys of Laveria did this man know about it?

Syl's already thin patience evaporated. All she wanted to do was drink her beer, eat her food, and be left alone. She leaned forward. "Look, I don't know who you are—"

"But I know you. Syl Yarrow," he said, his expression unchanging. "Your mother, Chancey, was a bit of a rabble-rouser, organizing the Lastelle Collective before it went defunct, not to mention her petitioning to deregulate and open up a number of private hyperspace lanes." His voice was flat. "She was killed a few months ago in an unfortunate attack on your ship, the *Switchback*. And you have been the captain ever since, working with a skeleton crew and doing your best to remain afloat. Not very well, but things are rough right now for haulers. Well, legitimate ones."

Syl leaned back in her seat, arms still crossed. "Nice bio. That still doesn't tell me who you are."

He leaned back in his chair, too. "I am Xylan Graf. And yes, before you ask, of *those* Grafs."

Syl uncrossed her arms and glanced around for possible exits. She couldn't run out the front door; the Gigoran would be waiting for her. She could say that she had to use the lavatory and hope that there was a back exit. She gnawed on her lower lip as she considered her options. This was bad. Everyone knew of the Grafs, one of the most powerful families in the galaxy. Not only had they heavily financed Starlight

Beacon, but they controlled a large part of the shipping in the Inner Rim and had a huge stake in the Outer Rim. They had made their money a generation before as hyperspace prospectors, mapping out new lanes and byways. At least half of the more readily traveled hyperspace lanes had been discovered and marked by the Grafs, and rumor was that they even had private hyperspace lanes that could be used for a very hefty fee.

Chancey Yarrow had spent her entire life fighting against people like the Grafs—people who had too much money and too much power and were happy enough to grind the rest of the galaxy into dust beneath their expensive bootheels. It seemed disastrous that one would want to speak to Syl now.

All this flashed through Syl's mind in less than a heartbeat, and she cocked an eyebrow at Xylan. "What do you want?" She was curious, blast it. It was her fatal flaw.

He held his hands out in supplication. "Lady Yarrow, please. I realize the weight my family name carries, but I assure you my presence here is to your benefit." He pulled out a small silver cube and set it on the table. With a start Syl realized it was a datacron, a very small one, probably worth more credits than the *Switchback*.

The server droid returned with her food, and when Xylan saw the plate of undefinable stew, he wrinkled his nose in a way that Syl found hilarious. She got the feeling that not much unsettled the man, but it seemed as though her food had done exactly that.

"Perhaps we should go somewhere a bit more . . . refined and eat."

"I've already got my food," Syl said, relishing the shift in power. She spooned a bit into her mouth and was pleased to find that the sauce was heavily seasoned, numbing her tongue just a bit with some piquant spice she didn't know. Still, much better than she'd hoped.

Syl gestured to the datacron. "Show-and-tell time, Graf. You made a point to interrupt my supper. So, what've you got?" When all else failed, bluster was always an excellent standby. The truth was that Syl wanted nothing more than for the man to leave; there was something inherently untrustworthy about him, but she wasn't silly enough to think he'd depart before he had his say, so better to pretend that the whole interaction wasn't making her uncomfortable.

Xylan Graf grimaced but did as instructed. With a slender, well-manicured finger, he pressed a button set into the design of the cube. There was no sign that he'd done anything until a beam of light flashed up from the datacron and a Togruta man began talking. "We have inexplicably been kicked out of hyperspace in what my navidroid is saying is the Berenge sector. There is nothing here, and we didn't read any anomalies in the lane before we were ejected. We are currently looking at—what was that?" The man in the holo leaned from one side to the other, as though his ship had suddenly lurched and he was trying to maintain his footing. "It's just as you said, Lord Graf. I am sending along the readings you requested. All of our instruments have begun to give us readings that make zero sense, and we're experiencing very real turbulence, as though we are flying through an asteroid field. What the—"

The holo cut out and went back to the beginning, playing on a loop.

"This was the last dispatch from my hauler, the *Belt Runner*. This ship was carrying approximately a million credits' worth of coaxium," Xylan said, closing the datacron and secreting it away somewhere within the folds of his tunic.

"So, what's that got to do with me?" Syl said. "Do you think I'd be here if I had that kind of money?" The stew was almost gone, and her belly still felt impossibly empty. Maybe she could swing another bowl if she skipped breaking her fast in the morning.

"I'm sure that I do not have to tell you we have people willing to look out for our families' interests throughout the Republic."

Syl sighed, the pieces sliding into place. "Including the shipping and transportation offices."

Xylan inclined his head in acknowledgment. "The story you have been telling is a familiar one, and I am hoping you can tell me a bit more about your experience."

"Why do you care? I mean, a million credits in coaxium and a ship aside, I'm sure you don't normally concern yourself with hauling problems out on the frontier." Syl gazed at him before gesturing at his very shiny tunic. "As for the money, you look like you can spare it."

"The *Belt Runner* was not working the frontier. It was traveling a hyperspace lane between Hosnian Prime and Kessel."

Syl blinked. "Wait, so how did it end up in the Berenge sector? That's all the way on the other side of the galaxy." The man was lying and took her for some kind of rube if he expected her to buy that story. It was a long haul between Kessel and Berenge, and no self-respecting hauler could get themselves that lost without trying at it. Next he'd be telling her he had a starflower-scented bantha for sale. But Syl wanted to know the pretty boy's end game, so she played along.

"Indeed, it is. And this is the fourth ship the Grafs have lost in the past month."

"Truly?" He didn't sound like he was lying about that last part.

"Yes. It has become quite the issue for my family."

Syl took a moment to let that sink in. She had thought what the Nihil were doing was just a localized problem, making life difficult for those on the edges of the galaxy. Life was already hard on the fringe of civilized space, so it wasn't a surprise to run up against pirates every now and again.

But a Graf sitting in a dingy dockside tavern spinning her wild tales meant there was something very different going on, something that would unsettle life for haulers even in the relatively safe Inner Rim.

Xylan Graf could be the best scam artist Syl had ever met. Maybe. But there was a story here, and the more Xylan Graf spoke, the more Syl wanted to know what it was.

"I'm sorry, I don't know how something like that works. I only know that one moment we were in hyperspace, and the next we were hauling through realspace. I'm no scientist to give you the nuts and bolts of it." That was true enough, even if she knew more than she would let on. She could beat this fancy fellow at his own game. She would find out what he knew and then plan her next move accordingly.

Xylan leaned forward, resting his elbows on the table. "You may not be a scientist, but I am. Which is why I am hoping you can walk me through what happened to you so that I can understand. You see, Lady Yarrow, you are the first person to survive after experiencing the anomaly."

The server droid wobbled over, and Syl grinned before pointing to her empty bowl and cup. "Tell you what, you buy me a proper dinner and I will tell you everything you want to know about my last haul, including the calculations we used." If nothing else, Syl would give this lying fashion holo a bit of conversation in exchange for a good meal. She had nothing but time, since the Republic offices were closed for the day.

The truth was that she wanted to know what the man knew, wanted to know what kind of scam was worth traveling to one of the meanest parts of town to search out a grubby hauler with a dead mom and a stolen ship.

Xylan Graf dropped a few credits on the table like they were trash—the amount had to be several times the value of Syl's bill—and began to stride toward the exit. If Syl had doubted the truth of the man's identity, that behavior would have put the matter to bed. Syl scooped up a couple of the extra credits and put them in the pocket of her trousers before nodding to the droid, who quickly grabbed the rest.

And then Syl, who was usually much smarter but was starting to realize that when she was curious she got more than a little bit reckless, followed the well-dressed man and his bodyguard out into the night.

FIVE

Vernestra and Imri made their way from the shared dining area toward the restricted section where the Jedi of Starlight Beacon lived and worked. When she had first arrived, Vernestra had been awed by the view from the Jedi's main tower. The lift emptied out onto a windowed balcony that pointed not toward the rest of Starlight but the vastness of space. The stars of the galaxy pressed in all around in a way that could make some feel small and insignificant but made Vernestra feel part of something much larger. The Force was all, and the endless view was an awe-inspiring reminder of that fact.

But in the past few weeks, Vernestra had stopped noticing the view, instead always focused on getting to her bed or speaking with one of the other Jedi about this issue or that. But knowing that she would soon be leaving Starlight Beacon, Vernestra paused in front of the bank of windows and let the cosmic Force wash over her, feeling it in the ebb and flow of the stars and in the rushing life of the station, a dozen streams coming together into the crash of waves.

"I'm going to miss it, too," Imri said, coming up to stand beside Vernestra.

"I thought you wanted to return to Port Haileap?"

Imri shrugged. "I did. I do! I miss the noodle cart next to the dockmaster's office and Avon's reckless experiments and the scent of marblewood trees. I even miss Jay-Six's weird behavior," Imri said with a laugh. "I've still never met a droid like her. But I don't know if I would be the Jedi I am now if I hadn't ever left. It would still just be me and Master Douglas, talking to travelers and occasionally chasing off pirates."

Vernestra felt Imri's unspoken compliment and warmed slightly. "Yeah. Life would be very different if we'd never left Port Haileap," she said, but Imri's reassurance did not push aside her worry.

"You're afraid of what will happen if I go someplace crowded, like Coruscant," Imri said.

"You are entirely too good at reading emotions," Vernestra said with a wan smile. "But, yes. Imri, ever since Valo I've felt unsteady. The suffering we saw there, the loss of life . . ."

Vernestra's voice trailed off, and she took a deep breath, recentering herself. "I never thought something so terrible could happen. But I've been able to meditate to help with those feelings. But I sense that for you, you've been directing it to other places. And I'm worried about you." A few moments spent in one of Starlight's meditation gardens helped Vernestra feel more herself, but Imri came out of the sessions antsy and anxious, as though the quiet moments only made things worse for him. Vernestra had been hoping it was a short-term issue, but the sensation she felt while he meditated was too close to what she had felt in the dining facility just moments before.

Imri walked over to the bank of windows and stared out into the distance for a few heartbeats. "Something changed on Valo, Vern. I feel . . . I feel everything. Too much."

Vernestra walked to stand by Imri's side. "Is that why you tried to, I don't know, stop Reath from feeling jealous?"

"No, I didn't stop him. I just sort of tried to help him feel a little better. It's like a smile through the Force." Imri turned to look at Vernestra. "Look, maybe it's easier if I show you?"

Vernestra nodded, and Imri put a heavy hand on her shoulder. Her worry and concern began to melt, as though the feelings were an ice cube and Imri a summer sun. Reath had called it soothing, but it was less than that. It was like Imri was sharing a happy moment with her.

And she did not like it one bit. There was something about it that felt wrong, but she was hard-pressed to explain why. She always worried that Imri would find himself on a dangerous path with his Force abilities, and this raised new concerns.

"Hey," she said, pulling away, and Imri's expression quickly went from surprise to hurt.

"I'm sorry," Imri said with a heavy sigh. "All those people on Valo were hurting so much, and I wanted to make it better for them. So I practiced fixing it just in case it happened again."

"Who were you practicing with?" Vernestra asked, concerned.

"Just by myself and with some of the other Padawans. I discovered that I could create bonds with my friends and help them feel better, so I've been practicing doing it with them."

Vernestra nodded. "Wanting to help is a good thing, but this is too much, Imri. A Jedi should be able to sense and understand those around them, but changing their emotions is something else."

"Is it a dark side ability?" Imri asked, face stricken.

Vernestra shook her head. "No, it's not that, not in the least. The old stories say that the Sith used emotions as a weapon, which is one of the reasons the Order cautions against things like attachment. You're trying to make people feel better, trying to ease their pain. It's less a bad thing and more that you're overstepping. People should be allowed their emotions, to deal with them as they see fit. You're taking that choice away from them."

"Ah," Imri said. "I see." He looked absolutely miserable and more than a little deflated, and Vernestra felt like she was suddenly in water that was deeper than she'd expected. She didn't know what to do with Imri's growing empathic abilities. Her skills had always been in dueling and diplomacy. She could read intent, but not like Imri could. She was certain his abilities had already surpassed hers in that regard.

So how was she supposed to train him in such a strange and unique skill set? Vernestra was struck by a memory from her own time spent as a Padawan. For a while she'd suffered from a strange talent where she would lose herself in hyperspace, her consciousness traveling while in that liminal space. The first time it had happened it terrified her: she'd never exhibited the ability when she'd been a youngling. But Master Stellan had seen it as an impressive and wholly unique skill, and had urged her to practice it whenever they traveled through hyperspace.

Until one day the ability stopped, and she could no longer do it. Shortly thereafter she'd taken her trials and been promoted to Knight, and she'd never had the problem again. She didn't think of her hyperspace gift often, but something about Imri's friendly emotional nudge brought the memory back.

Vernestra took a deep breath. "You have a great talent, Imri. I'm certain you are very gifted empathically, beyond what most Jedi achieve, and this skill is something that will be useful to the Order. But I want to talk to the Council.

They may be able to provide guidance that I cannot, and since we're headed to the main temple, I think this is a great time to see what I can do to make sure you get exactly what you need."

The worry melted from Imri's face, and he grinned at Vernestra. "Thanks, Vern. You always know just what to do."

Vernestra sighed. She didn't know how other Jedi interacted with their Padawans, but there were only a couple of years between her and Imri, and this was one of those moments when she felt more like an older and wiser friend than a true mentor. "I just wish we weren't going right at this moment. There is so much at stake with the Nihil prowling on the frontier. I really wonder if we should try to delay our travel a short while in order to help out here."

Imri nodded. "Maybe you should talk to Master Avar. She would know what to do."

Vernestra pursed her lips. Imri had a touch of hero worship—maybe even a bit of a crush—on Master Avar, and it had become readily apparent in the past few weeks, since the disaster on Valo. No one had been more adamant about defending the galaxy against the Nihil than the marshal of Starlight Beacon, probably because she knew the toll the marauders had taken on the frontier. Ignoring them and hoping they went away hadn't just been silly; it had inevitably led to more suffering and pain. How many lives had they taken so far? Millions? Hundreds of millions?

Master Avar and a number of other Jedi had been campaigning for swift and decisive action against the Nihil before they could spread their misery any farther, but the Jedi Council and the Republic had been slow to act before the tragedy on Valo. And now the Republic pursued the Nihil in earnest, but the battles against the Nihil had been slow and far-flung, a net cast too wide and not precisely enough to snag the marauders. Vernestra had seen what the Nihil could do, how little they cared for the lives of others and how destructive they could be. She had agreed with Master Avar more than many of the other Jedi, who saw any kind of aggression as antithetical to the goal of the Order. Wasn't it the calling of the Jedi to provide relief to those who were suffering? Shouldn't they help those who could not help themselves? How could they protect life if they stood by idly while it was wantonly being taken?

It was a conversation Vernestra had learned not everyone saw eye to eye on, so it made sense to seek the counsel of a Jedi whose beliefs were similar to her own. Surely, if Master Avar thought Vernestra should stay a little while before traveling to Coruscant, then that was what she should do. Imri would be fine for a few more weeks. And Master Stellan would understand.

It wasn't truly as though Vernestra had a choice. A Jedi should go where the Force needed them, and most often the Force worked through the wisdom of the Jedi Council. But it never hurt to try to negotiate a better path. It was something Vernestra had learned not from Stellan Gios but from Imri's first master, Douglas Sunvale, who had never found an argument he couldn't win.

But Vernestra did not say any of that aloud to Imri; instead she gave her Padawan a crooked grin and teased, "You just want to talk to Master Avar because you're hoping you'll get to see her lightsaber again."

Imri flushed. "It is a great lightsaber," he said, and Vernestra laughed, feeling a bit better now that the tense moment had passed.

"Well, then, let's go see what the Master is up to."

Master Avar was, as per usual, in the marshal's grand office. Vernestra pressed the door chime, and the door opened for her. Positioned near the control center, which bore a dizzying array of holo screens and droids and was overseen by Master Maru, the marshal's office was purely functional and held nothing more complicated than a few chairs, a plush carpet, a desk, and a comm unit. The entire back wall of the office overlooked Starlight Beacon's active docking operations, the flow of traffic somewhat diminished so late in the day but still busy. Vernestra had expected to find Master Avar reading one of the dozens of reports that came across her desk or meditating, but instead she found the blond, pale-skinned human Jedi engaged in a very tense conversation with someone who sounded like none other than Master Stellan Gios.

"Maybe we should come back later," Imri murmured.

"No, stay," Master Avar said, closing the door behind them with a wave of her hand. "This conversation concerns you." It didn't take an empath to sense the frustration and annoyance radiating off of Master Avar.

"Is that Vernestra? Good, perhaps talking to her directly will clear up some of this." Master Stellan's voice was curt and bore none of the warmth he'd had earlier for Vernestra.

"Stellan, I'm not finished—" Avar began.

"I expect to see my former Padawan as soon as possible for this tasking. May the Force be with you, Avar." Master Stellan, never one to back down from a battle, disappeared from the comm unit, ending the call.

Master Avar sighed and pushed her hair out of her face before she turned to Vernestra and Imri. She looked paler than usual, with the exception of the two spots of color high on her cheeks, and the diadem on her forehead glittered dully in the office lights. "Master Stellan tells me that he talked to you earlier about returning to Coruscant," she said, as though Vernestra and her Padawan hadn't witnessed the tense scene. "I was just expressing to him that I think the timing is abysmal."

"Master Avar," Vernestra began, but Avar held up her hand.

"You cannot stay, even if I need every Jedi able to hold a lightsaber for this upcoming mission." Sadness flitted across Master Avar's face before her usually determined expression returned. "What I will ask is that you return as soon as this favor, whatever it is, is completed. The Nihil may be on the run, but they are far from finished, and the Jedi are going to have to take the fight to them in earnest or countless others will suffer the consequences. We need swifter action, not more politicking."

Vernestra smiled because it was easy to agree with the Jedi's sentiment. "I will, Master Avar."

Her face relaxed, and she gave both Imri and Vernestra a warm smile. "I've enjoyed having the both of you here. Your service has been invaluable."

It was a dismissal, and Vernestra nodded and turned to leave, Imri on her heels. She paused. "Imri, can you give me a moment with Master Avar?"

Imri blinked and then nodded. "Sure." He left the office, the door closing behind him quietly.

"Vernestra. What is it?" Master Avar asked, standing and walking around her desk.

"I have a conundrum."

"Is it Imri?" Avar asked, looking past Vernestra toward the closed door. "The boy's empathic abilities are growing expeditiously. You should be proud that your tutelage has led to him advancing so much in his usage of the Force."

Vernestra shook her head. "No, it's something else altogether. It's about my lightsaber."

Master Avar nodded and crossed her arms. "Ah, your whip. You've gotten quite proficient in dueling with it this past year. You should take comfort in that."

"I'm concerned, Master Avar. I haven't had leave to document my changes with the Temple, and I want to show Master Stellan. But—"

"But he is a stickler for protocol and you are afraid that he will object to the modifications you've made."

"Yes," Vernestra said, sighing loudly. "He always taught me that my lightsaber was a tool, one to be used defensively and in the protection of life, but I don't know that this light-whip meets the same standards."

"Your whip has been very effective at both ending conflict and protecting you and your fellow Jedi. I do not see any issue with it. But that being said, if you would like to keep the information from the main temple for a bit longer, until you've worked out your own feelings about the modification, I see no problem with that. But remember that secrets too long held can become destructive."

Vernestra nodded, and some of the worry she'd held on to melted a bit. "Thank you, Master Avar."

"You already had the answer, Vernestra," Avar said with a warm smile. "You just needed to find it within you. Now, go find that Padawan of yours before he starts to worry that he is the problem."

Vernestra took her leave and found Imri pacing back and forth.

"Tranquility, Padawan. My discussion wasn't about you. I had to get some clarification on another matter." She smiled to ease any sting from the words.

Imri let out a deep breath. "I wasn't just worried about you! I don't think I've ever seen Master Avar angry before," he said.

"Me either," Vernestra agreed.

"What do you think got her so riled? Us leaving or Master Stellan telling you before he told her? Or something completely different?"

Vernestra didn't answer. The scene, however mild it was, had left her unsettled. Both Stellan and Avar were usually so controlled. It was unusual to see them at odds over something. And Avar's observation—that Master Stellan was very enamored with the rules—and a measure of time spent away from Coruscant had taught Vernestra that the rules of the Order were better considered guidelines. Yes, some were there to benefit the Jedi, but so many seemed to hinder the Jedi's effectiveness in protecting life if adhered to too strictly.

But Imri was right. Surely this wasn't over them leaving Starlight? Theoretically neither was still supposed to be on the station. Their official posting was Port Haileap. They'd only remained on Starlight so long because there had been a number of missions and many Jedi assigned to the station had been delayed in their arrival by first the hyperspace lane shutdowns and then the rising Nihil attacks. But for now they would not remain on Starlight Beacon. Vernestra had her orders, and she would follow them.

If Master Stellan needed them for a mission on Coruscant, then that was where they would go. Vernestra was a Knight, not a Jedi Master. Whatever had caused the friction between Master Stellan and Master Avar had nothing to do with her.

At least, that was what she tried to tell herself.

"The issue between Master Stellan and Master Avar is no business of ours. Get a good night's rest, Imri," Vernestra said. "Tomorrow we head to Coruscant."

SIX

Reath was completely unable to sleep. He laid in the too-comfortable bed in his quarters for a handful of hours, willing himself to rest, even going so far as to meditate his way into the cool blue reassurance of the Force. But every time he began to drift off, he was pulled out of it by racing thoughts.

It had been too long since he'd spent a night in the bosom of safety. He was used to falling into a fitful sleep, exhausted and wondering what the next day would bring, not stuffed full of good food and snuggled into soft covers.

Maybe adventuring had broken him.

The corridor lights were dim as Reath left his room. It was technically the sleep cycle, even though there were still Jedi up and about tending to their business. Not all the species were diurnal, so there was activity on Starlight Beacon at any given hour, even if it tended to settle into something more sedate after most found their rest.

He made his way through the corridors, his feet leading him even though he had no real destination in mind. When he stopped in front of the bank of windows near the lifts, he stilled and turned toward the vastness of space.

"Can't sleep?"

Reath turned to find Vernestra standing nearby. Sweat dotted her brow, and she held a glass of water. Reath saw the door to the practice room sliding closed a short distance down the hallway.

"No."

"It happens. Every time we leave and come back, it takes about a day for my body to readjust to the gravity here on the station." She drank deeply of the water while looking out the windows into the darkness of space beyond. "Dueling helps me when I can't sleep."

Reath nodded, and Vernestra gestured back toward where she'd come from. "Since you're up, come duel with me. The practice droids are getting tired of me walloping them, and I'd love a partner."

Reath nodded. "Sounds like fun," he said, and Vernestra laughed in response.

"You sound like a man headed to death," she said as they walked back to the practice room.

"Uh, it's just that I usually practice with Master Cohmac, and he is really, really enamored of forms."

"Well, then, dueling with me should be fun, because I like to use a little bit of everything. You can critique my form. That should be a nice change for you." Vernestra winked as she said it, and Reath found himself flushing. When they were Padawans, Vernestra's form had been a thing of beauty, sinuous and efficient, and more than one Master had come by the practice room to see it for themselves.

Reath had always seen dueling as part of the requirement to be a Jedi, and so he had taken it on with the same dogged determination with which he approached every task he was not particularly suited to.

After tossing Reath a practice tunic, Vernestra grabbed a practice saber off the rack in the corner, and Reath did the same, testing them out until he found one that felt nearly the same as his own lightsaber. When he powered it up, it glowed a sedate blue, and the one Vernestra had chosen glowed a peaceful green. These lightsabers, while carrying a slight charge, did not have the killing ability of real lightsabers. That didn't mean that getting hit by one didn't hurt. It just meant that neither Reath nor Vernestra had to worry about accidentally cutting off the other's hand. The tunic was also made of a material that was sensitive to heat, and a direct hit would show on the snowy material as an angry scorch.

"Ready?" Vernestra asked, and Reath nodded, his heart pounding.

Vernestra was not like Master Cohmac, who was patient and steady in his attacks. She ran forward and delivered a flurry of blows, all of which Reath parried, much to his surprise. Vernestra smiled, seemingly unbothered, and the sense Reath got from her was of a stream charting its rightful course to the sea, all intent and purpose.

"Breathe, Reath! You're going to end up exhausted if you hold your breath the whole time!" Reath let out his breath in a whoosh, taking another deep breath as Vernestra swung her saber in a wide attack and exhaling it as he blocked the blow.

They went on like that for a long while, Reath forcing himself to remember where to put his feet, to keep his shoulders square, to watch Vernestra's shoulders to understand what her next move might be. Minutes passed, and Reath found himself wiping the sweat off his brow, hard-pressed to keep up a competent defense against Vernestra's enthusiastic attacks.

She was even better than he remembered.

Finally, Reath felt himself slowing, and Vernestra slowed her attacks, as well. When she launched herself into a backflip in the air over his head and caught him from behind, the saber sizzling across his back, he groaned and raised his hands in surrender.

"I yield," he gasped, and Vernestra's laughter was equally winded.

"Cohmac must be an amazing teacher. Your form is impeccable," Vernestra said, powering down her saber and flopping onto the padded floor, arms akimbo.

"Maybe," Reath said, sitting down hard. "But I still lost."

"Only because you wanted to." Vernestra rolled over onto her side, propping her head up on her hand. "You could have won any number of times. But you were so focused on defense that you never took up the attack. I get it, the Order wants us to defend life," she said, her eyes sliding out of focus as her thoughts drifted. "But I think sometimes we can best defend life by going on the offensive."

"Are we still talking about dueling?" Reath asked. Vernestra sat up and sighed.

"No, not really. It's just that, when I was a Padawan I thought all of the older Jedi had everything figured out and the Force would give me that same kind of insight when I became a Knight. But here I am more than a year later, and I still feel just as confused and conflicted as I did when I was a youngling." Vernestra fell back onto the mat. "And not only that, I'm worried no one takes me seriously because I'm so young, except for my Padawan, and I'm not sure I'm giving him the right tools to be a good Knight." She turned her head and smiled at Reath. "So, you know, normal late-night musings."

"Yeah," Reath said, lying back, as well. "The entire time Master Cohmac and I were on Genetia, Master Cohmac kept saying that he had to get this volume or that, that the Force had led him to be in this place or that. But I don't know if he truly believed it. The destruction on Valo was hard on everyone, but ever since, I feel like Master Cohmac has been volunteering us for more and more dangerous missions. I've sensed guilt in him, but I don't know what it's from, and he isn't one to share such personal thoughts."

"I probably shouldn't have, either, but I consider us friends," Vernestra said. "But I have felt this sense of apprehension from so many Jedi lately, especially the more we go up against the Nihil. Is it the right thing to seek them out and destroy them before they claim more lives? So far they've tampered with the hyperspace lanes, seeded the Drengir throughout the galaxy, and attacked the Republic Fair. I can't see how they'll be any less dangerous if we leave them be."

"But that feels like it goes against the Order and the balance in the Force," Reath said. Nothing Vernestra was saying was alarming. He'd had the same thoughts on more than one occasion, and in the end it always came back to his faith that the Force was guiding him on the path best suited for him.

"Exactly. And so I end where I began, questioning if I am doing as the Force wills or as I want. But since I haven't thought about returning to Coruscant, I suppose leaving Starlight Beacon is wholly the workings of the Force," Vernestra said with a laugh. "I'm sorry you can't sleep, Reath, but I am glad you were up to spar with me."

"Me too," Reath said as Vernestra climbed to her feet and put away her dueling materials before taking her leave. "And next time I won't spend so much time on the defensive."

Vernestra laughed. "I look forward to it."

Reath didn't move as she left, choosing to remain flat on the practice mats as he let his mind wander.

Vernestra's misgivings were no different from his own, and like her he had thought that he would somehow feel different once he was promoted to a Knight. Not that he believed that would happen any time soon. If his trials required researching something obscure like the history of Genetian wedding rituals, he'd have no problem, but for most Jedi their trials required dealing with something they weren't skilled in. And while Reath didn't think he was a lost cause, he definitely felt like he had a lot of learning left to do before he took on any more responsibility.

The whole question of the responsibility of the Order in relation to the Jedi just proved how unprepared he was to be a Jedi Knight. Reath had heard Master Cohmac have the same conversation with other Jedi, the argument about how much the Order owed the Republic. Some Jedi were concerned that their focus was at risk of turning from research and education and the workings of the Force to war and politics. Master Cohmac certainly had expressed worry over how comfortable the Chancellor and her aides had become inserting themselves into Jedi Council meetings even after the Great Disaster had been resolved. And Master Cohmac might be a bit of a worrier, but he greatly disliked feeling beholden to the whims of the Republic, even if he also thought the Nihil were a dangerous threat.

Reath didn't know how he felt on the matter. He could see both sides, and it wasn't like anyone was looking to Padawans to make the decision. Thank the Force.

Reath picked himself up from the practice mats, his muscles warning him that he would feel the effects of this training session long into the next day, and after putting away his practice saber and tunic, he returned to his room and promptly fell into a blissful sleep.

SEVEN

Vernestra woke feeling better than she had in a long time. Dueling with Reath had been surprisingly enjoyable, and she thought that he would one day be just as good as his master—that is, if he developed a little more faith in his abilities. Reath had always been the studious sort, given to long ruminations on philosophy and theory, able to quote some of the most obscure Jedi to have ever lived, but Vernestra thought that with a little prodding he could be the kind of Jedi who did great works.

He just had to take a chance on himself.

Vernestra washed and changed into clean attire before packing her things quickly. She had very little. Like most Jedi her belongings consisted of her white temple robes, a spare set of boots, and a spare set of mission attire, just in case Stellan's favor required it. Once her bag was packed, her belt with its many pouches strapped on, and her lightsaber holstered, she went to find Imri.

Vernestra easily found her Padawan, who carried a pastry from the dining facility for her, as well as a cup of tea. "I figured you would try to skip out on breakfast," he said with a sheepish grin. His own knapsack was thrown over his shoulder, and he wore the same daily attire as Vernestra.

She took the tea and pastry gratefully. "Much thanks. Are you ready?"

Imri nodded, even though his expression was one of sadness. "I'm going to miss Starlight Beacon."

"You'll be back. I promise," Vernestra said, sinking her teeth into the flaky, fruit-dotted pastry. "Let's get ourselves a ship."

They headed down to the quartermaster's office near the first level of the docking bays. As they got off the lift—the traffic to this part of Starlight thin so early in the day—they had to stop for a trio of Ithorians in restraints, their flat faces scrawled with a number of Nihil tattoos, being escorted by Republic coalition troops through the hangar onto a nearby cruiser, most likely headed back to Coruscant to stand trial.

"Nihil," Imri murmured, and Vernestra nodded, drinking her tea as anger surged through her at the sight of the pirates.

She realized with a jolt that she really, really wanted to teach the Nihil a lesson. Vengeance was not the way of the Jedi, but Vernestra could not stop seeing the destruction on Valo. She woke some nights to the wailing of the people hurt in the attack, the cries of pain and terror echoing in her mind even though it had been weeks. Master Josiah, a Jedi counselor who helped ensure Jedi remained balanced after terrible events, had told her once that remembering was part of how one dealt with the pain and trauma of a disaster, but Vernestra would have liked to remember a little bit less. Her anger over the Nihil could become a liability if she gave into it completely instead of acknowledging it, letting it go, and remembering her oath as a Jedi.

"Vernestra?" Imri said, giving her a concerned look as they stood outside of the lift.

"I'm fine, Imri, thank you," she said, feeling the Padawan's query. She took a deep breath and vowed to take some time to meditate as soon as they had a break when they hit hyperspace.

"When was the last time you were at the main temple?" Vernestra asked, changing the subject. Imri frowned and pursed his lips as he thought.

"I don't know, maybe when Master Douglas took me on as a Padawan?" Imri's bright, happy expression dimmed for a moment, and Vernestra was sorry she had asked, but just as quickly his smile was back. "Do you think we could see the opera house while we're on Coruscant? I never got to see that last time I was there."

"Yes, most definitely," Vernestra said, smiling in relief. She knew she was probably worrying a bit too much about Imri; he was a great Padawan and was learning something new every day, but she couldn't shake a creeping feeling that something bad was going to happen to the boy and she would be helpless to stop it. She wasn't sure where it came from; perhaps the destruction at the Republic Fair on Valo, seeing so many dead, had affected her even more than she had acknowledged.

"We can go after we've determined the extent of your empathic abilities," Vernestra said. She still felt some resistance in him to being examined, most likely because Imri became worried when he thought he was about to let Vernestra down, but they were far past his objections. Like communicating with beasts and meditative battle tactics, empathic abilities tended to need additional training, although some Jedi were naturally better at it than others. Some Masters practiced their entire lives to hone their skills in one area, but Imri seemed to have a natural gift that was growing far beyond the usual. Vernestra always liked to have a second opinion. Not because she didn't trust her own instincts, but because it never hurt to be certain.

The crowd of people grew as they got farther away from the lifts and closer to the docking bays. Even at an early hour people of all species went about their business. Here was a Mon Calamari arguing with a human man about the cost of some repairs, and there was a family of Twi'leks hurrying to catch their flight. A little farther away a dark-skinned human in a hoverchair laughed with a trio of green-skinned Neimoidians in coppery-hued robes. In the past year Starlight Beacon had become the crossroads of this part of the galaxy, offering asylum and hope to people of all species.

It made Vernestra sad to leave, for different reasons than before. She was going to miss the station. It had become home in a relatively short time. The chaotic rhythms and constant flow of life thrilled her and reminded her of the responsibility of the Jedi in a way that overcrowded places like Coruscant and vacant outposts like Port Haileap had not. Here on Starlight, the battle between light and dark felt more immediate, more important. She was proud to be part of that.

"Vern?" Imri asked hesitantly, and Vernestra shook her head. She'd fallen into reverie, and she gave the confused boy a smile. "Sorry, got lost in my thoughts. Let's go find the quartermaster."

The quartermaster's office stood at the end of a long hall marked with signage in several languages that warned only Jedi were allowed. A droid scanned all those that entered the hallway, a new addition since the attack on Valo. Everyone on the frontier was rightfully on edge because of the Nihil attacks, which had gone from a handful total to several daily. A number of the ships that found their way to Starlight

Beacon reported some skirmish or another, and sometimes the reports were much grimmer, of sighted wreckage and distress calls that no one answered.

Master Avar sent regular patrols to check out the reports, but by the time they arrived there was nothing to be done. The Republic was attacking known Nihil sites, but it seemed like the more they attacked the Nihil, the more they found—like lifting a rock and finding skittering arthropods underneath. Something more had to be done. Which was one of the reasons Vernestra was happy to be called to Coruscant, even if she was trepidatious about leaving Starlight. Perhaps there was something the main temple could do to ease the suffering of the frontier.

Vernestra and Imri walked past the droid and several closed doors that led to uniform issue and the armory. Their goal was a desk at the end of the hall, which opened up on its own docking bay. Behind the desk was a nervous-looking human Padawan who was tapping on a screen. Next to her was an empty cylindrical jar as tall as Imri and nearly as wide.

The human was small for her age and had burnished brown skin and straight black hair in a short angular cut, her Padawan braid hanging only to her shoulders. She was young, perhaps new to Starlight Beacon judging by both her wide-eyed fear as she tapped into the terminal and the fact that Vernestra did not recognize her. She gave Vernestra a panicked look, but when she spied Imri her shoulders relaxed a bit.

"Hey, Preeti," Imri said with a wide grin.

The girl smiled back, showing every single one of her teeth. A bit of pink crept into her cheeks, and Vernestra had to hide a knowing grin. Imri had an admirer.

"Hi, Imri. Oh, uh, is this your master?"

"Yep! Preeti, please meet Master Vern Rwoh."

"Um, it's Vernestra Rwoh," Vernestra said with an apologetic smile. She had let Imri continue to call her Vern, a nickname from the dearly departed Master Douglas Sunvale, but she refused to let it become commonplace.

Preeti blinked, her brown eyes going wide. "You passed your trials at fifteen."

"Umm, yes. And now I am seventeen." It wasn't supposed to sound dismissive, but it was, and Vernestra smiled to soften the blow. "Do you have a ship we can use? We're going to Coruscant. It's just the two of us, so a skiff should work nicely."

The Padawan bobbed her head and looked down at her terminal. The thing beeped and glowed red, and the girl swallowed. "I'm sorry, Master Vern—I mean, Vernestra. You are not allowed to be issued a ship."

"What?" Vernestra said, unable to keep the surprise from her voice. "I've been reassigned to Coruscant. Surely that's in there?"

"Yes, um, it is. But the order banning you from having a ship comes from Master Nubarron."

"Is the Master here so that I can have a few words with them?" Vernestra asked sweetly.

Preeti looked upward, and there hovering near the ceiling was Master Nubarron, their amorphous body tinged purple and pink.

YOU MAY NOT HAVE ANOTHER SHIP TO DESTROY, VERNESTRA RWOH.

Vernestra winced at the volume of the voice in her mind as it vibrated through her body. No one knew just what species Master Nubarron was. Some had theorized that they came from a planet in Wild Space, that they were perhaps an unknown race of Filar-Nitzan, with their purple coloring; others speculated that whatever species they came from was especially good at avoiding discovery, opting to blend in as part of the weather. Stories about Master Nubarron had run rampant once they were assigned to Starlight Beacon, even though they were legendary before they were Starlight's quartermaster. Vernestra's favorite was that of their discovery as a sideshow in a not very reputable circus, and that when a Wayseeker Jedi found them, the youngling Nubarron had been relieved to finally meet someone they could communicate with, then demanded to be liberated.

The purple cloud might be cantankerous, but that was one of the reasons Vernestra adored them so. Master Nubarron was not the least little bit afraid to be themself, no matter how unpleasant that could be.

"Master Nubarron—" Vernestra began, but was very quickly cut off.

NO. I LISTENED TO YOUR STORY AND PLEADINGS LAST TIME YOU WERE HERE. AND YOU PROMISED TO RETURN MY JUNK HAULER IN REASONABLE CONDITION. AND THUSLY, IT WAS UTTERLY DESTROYED.

Vernestra smiled sweetly. "But it was damaged in the attack on Valo. Surely, Master Nubarron, you cannot expect me to be responsible for every single thing that occurs in the galaxy?"

AND WHAT OF THE VECTOR BEFORE THAT?

"That one was shot down by the Nihil," Imri offered helpfully. Preeti winced, which was exactly how Vernestra felt. Later, she was going to have to remind Imri that sometimes less was more.

Master Nubarron merely shaded from purple to scarlet, small lightning bolts illuminating their puffy curves. The bolts were not sent singing across the room, so Vernestra and Imri were still quite safe.

NO SHIP FOR YOU. YOU ARE A TERRIBLE PILOT, VERNESTRA RWOH, AND I WILL NOT LET YOU RUIN WHAT IS LEFT OF MY FLEET, Master Nubarron sent, the message ringing with finality in Vernestra's mind.

"Master Nubarron, what is the matter?" a masculine voice echoed down the hall behind Vernestra. "You are likely to give all of Starlight a headache, carrying on so."

MASTER COHMAC.

Vernestra turned to see the older Jedi striding toward them, Reath not far behind. Each carried a knapsack similar to the ones Vernestra and Imri held. Master Cohmac looked more like a senator of the Republic than a Jedi. The human male's robes were carefully tailored to set off his slim frame, and his dark beard was knife's-edge precise against his dusky skin. Vernestra had seen more than one person make an effort to cross the Jedi Master's path, but he seemed more resolute in his vows than many others. Vernestra had heard rumors that he had been in love once, but like most idle chatter, she took it to be the result of too much time and too little to do. And probably a bit of jealousy. Master Cohmac was very handsome.

"Master Nubarron, are you out of ships?"

I AM NOT.

"Then why not give Vernestra and her Padawan a ship?" Cohmac said, raising a single perfect eyebrow, and Vernestra could swear she heard Preeti sigh just a bit.

VERNESTRA RWOH IS NOT GOING TO BE ISSUED A SHIP. NOT AS LONG AS I AM QUARTERMASTER. IF SHE NEEDS A RIDE SHE CAN CHARTER ONE OF THE CRUISERS FOR HIRE.

"Those ships are rarely spaceworthy," Vernestra exclaimed, unable to remain calm. "I've already been stranded on a moon once. It is not an event I care to repeat."

"Why don't you ride with us?" Reath asked, brows pulled together. "You're going to Coruscant, and so are we."

"That's a great idea," Imri said, smiling in relief. He had started to seem a bit worried as Master Nubarron became angry. Vernestra wondered if he'd heard the rumor that Master Nubarron didn't carry a lightsaber because they could create their own lightning. Vernestra knew it wasn't true; she had seen the amorphous Master using a green lightsaber in the practice rooms, but she wasn't about to reveal Master Nubarron's secret. They also taught a number of logistics classes for the Padawans, and supply chain principles were much harder than anyone ever believed. Master Nubarron needed every advantage they could get.

"Excellent," Master Cohmac said, inclining his head at Vernestra. "Then it looks like we shall need something slightly bigger than a skiff to make our way to the Temple."

Master Nubarron shaded back to lavender and sank into their jar while Preeti issued Master Cohmac the ship.

"I heard that Master Nubarron once sent lightning at their entire youngling class when a teacher asked if their species ate food," Imri whispered as they followed Cohmac and Reath to the docking bay.

"I heard that it was their Padawan class," Reath said over his shoulder. He adjusted his stride to walk next to Imri. "It's why no one has tried to research Master Nubarron's origins."

Vernestra stepped around the Padawans, leaving them to their gossip, and fell into step next to Master Cohmac. He looked down at her humorlessly. "You must be quite the pilot indeed to have riled Master Nubarron so. How many ships have you destroyed?"

"Two," Vernestra said.

"Well, that's not so bad in the lifetime of a Jedi—"

"That's just since I came to Starlight."

Master Cohmac hid his surprise behind a cough. "Who was your master?"

"Stellan Gios."

"Well, that explains it," Master Cohmac said with a nod. "Excellent Jedi, wasn't always the best pilot."

"Oh, really?" she asked, hoping that Master Cohmac would elaborate, but the older Jedi only shook his head and led the way to their ship.

Vernestra made a note to ask Stellan when she saw him just how many ships he'd crashed. And to have Imri along in case her former master decided to try to lie about it.

EIGHT

Syl paced. She couldn't help it. The room that Xylan Graf had generously paid for, after declaring that her previous lodgings were "a good way to contract a hemorrhagic fever," was beyond sumptuous. Her worn boots sank into plush carpet in shades of blue and green, and one entire wall was taken up by a tank full of a rainbow of exotic fish from throughout the galaxy. There was a sleep area that adjusted depending on the species of the room's guest, and she had spent the night tossing and turning on the most luxuriously decadent bed she had ever laid upon. Every quarter of an hour that she wasn't pretending to sleep, a server droid came through and asked Syl if she wished for anything. It seemed rather put out as she told it no time after time. She had thus far only said yes twice: the first time to figure out where the facilities were (behind a hidden door that concealed a lavatory and shower stall, in addition to a number of other things Syl could not name and probably weren't meant for humans) and the second to order breakfast, which had been so lavish that she had been compelled to sample everything, which led to her feeling like vomiting after. Rich-people food was nothing like shipper rations.

It was still pretty good, though.

Syl knew when she was out of her element. And usually she could suss out the rules of a place and adapt. It was how she had come to understand several languages, including Shyriiwook. She figured out what she had to do to get by, did it, and moved on to the next task. One thing at a time, as her mother had always said.

But the room was so bizarre and unfamiliar that she couldn't seem to relax. What if she left fingerprints all over the glass?

At some point the night before, her curiosity had morphed into pure avarice, hunger for a taste of the good life far outpacing her common sense. She knew this would come back to bite her; the question was only how and when.

Xylan Graf had listened to her story and seemed to be the first person who cared not only that the Nihil apparently had a way to force ships out of hyperspace but also that there was something peculiar happening in the Berenge sector. He would not, however, tell Syl just why he was interested in the daily activities of the Nihil. Or what his scientific thought was on the mystery of the hyperspace anomaly. Or why he had made up that ridiculous story about a coaxium hauler disappearing and reappearing halfway across the galaxy.

"Trust me, I will happily tell you everything once I verify your story. But for now, just try to enjoy the surroundings," he'd said when he showed her to her room after dinner. He'd taken her to a restaurant where their table had been a room of its own, completely sealed away from the other patrons, jammed with dining pillows made of an airy foam that cradled her body luxuriously while a mister sent down a variety of floral scents paired with the dishes as they were served. The parade of tiny delicacies left Syl wondering when the main dish would arrive, but she realized when the bill came that the tiny dishes were all there was. It was a good thing that was her second dinner.

Syl sighed and did another circuit of the room, the pacing helping her think. She was being foolish, trusting a complete stranger, even if he was flush with credits. Wasn't that how people ended up sold to the Zygerrians? Plus, there was something about Xylan Graf that was unsettling, despite how kind he seemed. Syl kept wondering what his grift was. After all, rich people got that way for a reason, and honesty usually wasn't it.

But the room's comm unit had let her send a message to Neeto without even charging her for the holo, and she was free to come and go as she wished, so Syl figured that whatever Xylan was about, it was not slavery.

Which made her wonder what exactly he was up to. And just like that she was deeply curious all over again. Plus, she had to admit the breakfast had been really, really good.

On her eleventh circuit across the carpet, Syl caught a glimpse of herself in the mirror that occupied the wall across from the sleeping area. When she had awoken that morning, it had been a window, not a mirror. A knob turned the glass clear, revealing a dizzying view of Coruscant's daytime traffic streaming by. Syl had watched the sky cars zipping past for exactly ten seconds before she had closed the glass once more. It was nauseating to consider how many beings flooded the planet. No wonder the Republic officials had completely ignored her pleas for help. How could they care about a handful of frontier lives when they had all this around them?

The Nihil must seem like a vague and distant threat to a people with their own busy lives.

Now, a wide-eyed Syl stared back from the glass. Her kinky-curly hair was snarled and flattened to one side of her head from her restless night. Her dark eyes seemed too large in her dark brown face, making her look like a frightened child. Was this why none of the Republic officials had taken her seriously the day before? She was an absolute mess.

Syl took a deep breath and let it out in a growl as she half-heartedly tried to fluff her hair into some semblance of order. She wasn't built for this! Give her a broken compressor, pirates, and a risky flight plan and she was fine. But dealing with government officials and fleecing the ultrarich apparently sent her to absolute pieces.

"Your heartbeat is elevated," the server droid said, coming through on its quarter-hourly cycle. "I will dim the lights and play soothing music."

"No, I'm fine," Syl said. But the lights had already dimmed, and the discordant sounds of a Saleucami harp filtered through the room.

"Since you are from the frontier, I have selected music popular to the Outer Rim. If you would like something else, please specify."

"I didn't want any music at all," Syl said, crossing her arms. Could a droid be too helpful? Because this one was.

A chime echoed throughout the room, and Syl looked around in surprise. The server droid was less startled.

"There is a visitor," it said as it walked by. It was a gangly model, with an extra set of arms and a polished silver body. The middle spun around as it headed toward the door, one of the arms spraying some kind of floral scent into the air. "You are nervous. This scent has been designed to calm anxious humans."

"Uh, thanks?" Syl said. She sort of missed the flop in the bad part of the city. There, no one had much cared how she felt, and the biggest annoyance had been the giant insects gnawing on the insides of the walls. Syl hadn't seen any in her short time there; the sound of the chewing had changed to scattering feet when she'd entered the room in the run-down hotel to grab Beti and her small knapsack the night before, but at least pests were a thing she knew how to deal with.

The droid approached the door, which slid open soundlessly. "This room's occupant did not yet order the midday meal," the droid began. That was all it got out before two blaster shots felled the mechanical servant, a charred hole where its processing unit had once been.

Syl got a glimpse of a Mon Calamari male in a ragged hotel uniform before she threw herself behind a nearby chair. Two more blaster shots sizzled the air, leaving char marks on the carpet where she'd been standing just a moment before.

"Oy, now, be a dear and make this easy," the man called. His Basic was heavily accented, like that of many on the frontier, and it made her think he wasn't from Coruscant. Did the Mon Calamari leave Mon Cala? Not that she much cared where he was from. He was obviously trying to kill her.

It was strange the thoughts that ran through one's head when trying not to get blasted.

Syl considered her options as she crouched behind the chair. It was her good luck the room was dimly lit and the man didn't seem to know the layout or the fact that one whole wall was nothing but a mirror. He stalked into the room carefully, his blaster at the ready. Syl could track his progress in the reflective surface across from her. He was a dark shape against more recognizable shadows. Every couple of breaths the droid sparked, brightening the dim space and throwing everything into stark relief. Syl needed a plan and quickly, before the man discovered he could see her just as she could see him.

The lavatory was toward the back and the door could be locked, but she would be trapped. She could try to fight back, but she didn't have her blaster; Beti was in a closet near the lavatory, and by the time she grabbed it she would be dusted. Still, Syl considered fighting back her best option. Only, what was she going to use as a weapon? A decorative sculpture?

That actually wasn't a bad idea.

Syl very slowly reached for a nearby knickknack—a small, heavy vase that looked to be made from some kind of very fancy pink rock. She pulled her arm back and hefted the vase. Not as heavy as she wanted it to be, but better than just a fist.

"Emergency. Emergency," the droid bleated, its voice processor severely damaged and the sound jarring. The sudden noise was enough to make the man turn around, and Syl did not waste the moment. She planted her foot in the seat of the chair she'd hidden behind and launched herself over its high back, landing behind the man with the blaster. As he turned toward her, she swung with all her might at his head, but he dodged at the last moment. Syl adjusted her swing slightly, and the vase hit the blaster he held. He yowled as his long fingers bent in all the wrong directions.

Syl did not give him time to recover. She aimed a kick at his midsection and he went flying backward, falling into the prone form of the droid. Syl grabbed the blaster—a heavy, outdated model—but before she could level it at the man, he had rolled out of the still open doorway, scrabbling to his feet and running away toward who knew where.

Syl let the hand holding the blaster fall to her side. A security droid, all black with arms disproportionately long compared with its body, burst into the room.

"There has been a distress call. Please state your emergency," the droid said, a number of yellow lights on its torso flashing.

"Someone just tried to kill me! If you run you might be able to catch him," Syl said in annoyance. Now that she was no longer in any immediate danger she was mostly just really, really angry. How dare someone try to *kill* her?

The droid hurried off in the same direction the Mon Calamari man had fled, but Syl had a feeling the assassin was long gone. As busy as Coruscant was, it would be a futile search.

Syl threw the blaster onto an end table and put her hands on her hips as she surveyed the damage to the room. The carpet was smoldering, and the droid was leaking various fluids all over the place. There were a couple of cracks in the fish tank, the see-through material melted and warped. Syl wondered who she should call about that. If the side of the fish tank went, she was going to have one giant mess on her hands.

"By the stars, what happened here?" came a voice from the doorway. Syl pulled her attention away from the damaged fish tank to find Xylan Graf standing there, the Gigoran Basha a looming white wall behind him. Xylan was dressed in red and white: deep red cape with an edge lined in beige, pale shirt and pants, each decorated with a pattern that swirled in shades from deep red to scarlet as Syl watched. Where in the galaxy had he found such an outfit?

Before Syl could explain the past couple of minutes, a cracking sound came from behind her. Instinctively she jumped onto a low-slung fainting couch. As she did, the wall of the tank gave way and a wave of water spilled across the room, lifting the murdered droid and surging toward the door. To Xylan's credit he didn't cry out or panic, merely raised a single perfectly edged dark eyebrow as water and dozens of flopping fish rushed toward him and over his shoes, soaking him up to his knees.

"This is unfortunate," Basha said, her vocalizer making it less an exclamation of woe and more a statement of fact. She ducked her head to look at Syl directly, the doorframe not built to accommodate her height. "Is this the result of some kind of attack?"

"Yes! Someone tried to kill me," Syl said, crossing her arms and remaining where she stood on the sofa. Xylan might have other shoes, but she was wearing her only pair of boots and she had no intention of getting them soaked. She'd had enough shenanigans for one day.

"We're going to have to move you somewhere safer," Xylan said, looking at his boots with an expression somewhere between woe and annoyance. "If an assassination attempt was made, it must be that someone thinks you have some critical piece of information."

Basha nodded, her white hair shifting as she did so. "We should also alert the hotel. They are going to need a new fish tank."

Syl didn't know whether to laugh or cry. But one thing was certain: she was definitely going to start carrying Beti with her everywhere she went.

Coruscant might glitter more than the frontier, but the flashy planet was every bit as deadly as the far reaches of the galaxy.

NINE

Nan looked out the viewport of her ship, the *Whisperkill,* at the central hub of the Gravity's Heart and tried to understand why she'd been exiled to such a sludge hole. If most of the Nihil ships were a hodgepodge of parts and modifications, then the Gravity's Heart was the queen of them all. Flying in, Nan had taken her time perusing the wheel-shaped station, which sat in the midst of an orange-and-yellow radiation cloud in the Berenge sector. It looked as though someone had spliced together more than a dozen ships, connecting them to form the outside of the wheel, while hollow shipping containers made up the spokes. A handful of Nihil ships, all on the smaller side, moved around the outside of the station, providing protection for the people who welded this and that, combustion torches flashing as they worked on the *Heart*.

It was not the superweapon that Lourna Dee had promised Marchion Ro. It was a salvage yard. And Nan truly did not want to be there.

Nan sent a docking request and waited for the instructions to come back. She saw no evidence of a hangar, so she let her ship drift while she went back to check on her cargo.

The Oracle slept in her pod, the rotund doctor Kisma Uttersond puttering with the knobs and dials that controlled the hoses running into the clear tank, his robotic leg clanking as he moved around the space. The old woman wore nothing but a simple shift, and the one time the doctor had opened the tank to bathe her Nan had run to the cockpit to take care of a made-up task. There was something about the human woman, her loose wrinkled skin, nearly bald head, and staring vacant eyes, that repulsed Nan in a very physical way. Even just looking at her in the tank, asleep, made the Nihil a bit nauseous.

But Nan's life was linked to that of Ro's Oracle, so she still had to check on the old woman, whether she liked it or not.

The life-support systems of the pod rattled as they recycled the fluids through the ancient crone, and Nan turned away as the Oracle murmured to herself in her sleep. "Is she going to be able to help Lourna's scientist? She looks dead."

"Ah, that is just the effect of the rejuvenation chamber, to be sure, to be sure," the squat Chadra-Fan said, his mismatched eyes looking almost past her, as though the concerns of one Nihil brat were beneath his brilliant mind. The doctor had said few words to Nan during their days of travel, opting to remain in the cargo hold with the Oracle, except for the time he'd demanded they stop on Tiikae so he could pick up a few supplies from some haulers there.

"How long until she'll be, uh, awake again?" Nan asked, watching as a glowing green liquid flowed through a clear tube that disappeared somewhere in the vicinity of the woman's heart. Nan wasn't afraid of death—she would die as she'd lived, on her own terms—but this artificial life the Oracle enjoyed was a horror. Nan didn't much ponder the difference between good and evil—it was all a matter of perspective, after all—but the Oracle's fate was definitely terrifying.

"She is awake right now," Uttersond said, a note of disgust in his voice. As though Nan were the one with greasy matted fur and dirty goggles. "Would you like a word with her?"

"Uh, no," Nan said. "You still have the box?" Before she had left, Marchion Ro had pressed a small puzzle box into Nan's hand. It was some trinket the Oracle enjoyed, and Nan had given it to the doctor.

"She grows more fragile and more distant by the day, and I have found that the old motivations don't always work," he'd said, eyes as dark and unreadable as they always were. Nan had seen the way Ro used electric shock on the old woman to gain her compliance, and she was easily able to fill in the unsaid things. "Use this. It will prove valuable if you need to force her cooperation."

The doctor nodded and gave Nan a dismissive wave, so she went back to the cockpit with a shudder. This mission had to be a test from Marchion Ro. She had been the most loyal, the bravest spy in his arsenal. Surely he was trying to see if she could take on bigger responsibilities by giving her care over his most priceless weapon? Everyone within Ro's very limited inner circle suspected that the Paths came from the Oracle, and it was the Paths that, when used correctly, gave the Nihil an edge over the Republic and the Jedi. It was the Paths that would let them tear down the galaxy and forge their own way.

Nan wasn't an expert on hyperspace; her education had been spotty at best, and she had no head for navigational sciences. But she knew that the Paths allowed the Nihil to jump into hyperspace through places that seemed impossible, places where the gravity would interfere with the calculations from even the most advanced navicomputer or droid. The Paths were what made the Nihil unpredictable and highly successful, and those calculations came from the Oracle.

And here Nan was, caring for it all. She realized this wasn't a test or a punishment. It was an *opportunity*. She would use this moment to grow her influence, to climb even higher within the Nihil. Perhaps she would one day have her own Tempest. Not marauders and thieves like Kara Xoo's or assassins like Lourna Dee's, but a squad of spies and information brokers, those who realized the value in a secret known and an official bribed.

She sat back down in the pilot's chair and smiled as she imagined it. The docking instructions from the Gravity's Heart began to filter in, and as she changed the ship's trajectory, the intercom crackled to life.

"You, girl," came the creaky voice of the doctor. "There is a problem."

Nan's heart began to pound, and she schooled her face into a scowl. "If the Oracle is dead, you will soon follow." And so would Nan if Marchion Ro found out. Perhaps there was some newly discovered frontier planet she could run to?

"No, no, the Oracle is still quite fine. But the puzzle box is missing. We have been robbed."

TEN

The Jedi settled quickly into their ship, the *Fraunesaa*, an old cube-shaped hauler that had been confiscated from a Hutt slaver who had been intercepted when he was forced to stop on Starlight Beacon. The ship had obviously seen better days. A new array of laser cannons had been arranged around the hull, late additions to all the Starlight Beacon ships in light of the increased Nihil threat, but that was the only modification Vernestra could see. Once the ship was powered up and the navigation was set, they were off with a minimum of fanfare. Cohmac took the pilot's seat, and Reath took the copilot's seat after a nod of tacit agreement from Vernestra.

"I think Master Cohmac might be a bit concerned about your flying abilities," Imri murmured. The passenger compartment was directly behind the cockpit in this model, making for awkwardly close quarters. Reath turned around to interject, but Vernestra shrugged in response.

"I don't care who flies as long as we get to Coruscant." She was unable to stifle a yawn, and Imri frowned at her as Reath turned back to the controls. Not flying really wasn't a concern for her. Catching a ride with the other Jedi was still a far sight better than hitching a ride on a public transport. Faster, as well, since the flight would be direct.

"Master Cohmac, Reath, do you mind me inquiring why you're headed to Coruscant?" Vernestra asked, partly to change the subject from her terrible flying but mostly because she was curious.

"The atrocities we witnessed on Genetia have attracted the attention of the Senate, so we've been summoned to testify before a committee consisting of a few well-known senators and the Jedi High Council," Cohmac said with a sigh. "I am not a fan of bureaucracy, but I do hope this will convince the Republic to intervene in the civil war. Good people are suffering, and so far they've ignored their pleas for help."

"Why couldn't you just holo in?" Vernestra asked. It seemed silly to ask two Jedi to leave their work behind to testify in person.

"Apparently the Senate likes to have people in the same

room," Master Cohmac said, his lips quirking in a pained smile. "And this is a Republic meeting, not a High Council one, so what the Republic wants, they get."

"Is that something the High Council would normally do? Ask the Republic to get involved?" Imri asked, frowning. Master Cohmac shook his head.

"Not usually. But since the Great Disaster, the High Council has gotten more and more involved in the affairs of the Republic. The Republic is out of their depth at the moment, and the Order helps all those who ask for our assistance. And of course, there are those who truly feel this work takes us away from the more important work of the Order, from our meditations and philosophies. This is a time of change for all of us. The Nihil prowl the hyperspace lanes, the Republic has grown larger and more powerful than ever before, and as more and more planets are brought into contact with each other, things are bound to change."

"You don't sound like you agree with the High Council working with the Republic," Vernestra said, feeling that the conversation was an echo of the one she'd had with Reath in the practice room.

"That's not it at all. The Jedi have a duty to protect life and maintain balance, so working with the Republic government is a given. But the Jedi follow the Force. We are the light, and we cannot blindly follow any other edict but that one. We go where we can best chase away the darkness in the galaxy, and we must not serve any other cause but that." Master Cohmac shook his head. "Historically, fighting the Republic's battles hasn't always gone well for the Order."

"Master Cohmac, are you talking about the long ago massacre on Dalna?" Reath asked, but Master Cohmac sighed.

"Yes, but I forget myself. Let us leave the political talk for the High Council and do as the Force wills us." And that was the end of the conversation as Master Cohmac turned his attention to the navicomputer, leaving Vernestra feeling as though the older Jedi truly felt as conflicted about the current path of the Order as she did.

"Are we jumping into hyperspace so close to Starlight Beacon?" Imri asked. Usually ships traveled well away from the satellite's mass before calculating a jump.

"Yes, but only because I'm planning on taking a short initial jump to avoid some of the lanes that have been flagged by the Republic," said Master Cohmac.

"Why were they flagged?" Vernestra wondered aloud, alarm tripping through her. "Surely there haven't been any recent Emergences?" More than a year earlier, the *Legacy Run*, a ship carrying thousands of passengers, had been destroyed in hyperspace, splitting into numerous pieces that emerged in different parts of the Republic. For many months after, everyone thought the incident was the result of a problem in the hyperspace lanes, until it was discovered the Nihil had been behind the whole thing.

Reath twisted around in his seat. "There have been

rumors that some of the lanes have become unstable. On our way back to Starlight we heard stories of ships being forced out of hyperspace into realspace and then disappearing."

"You think the Nihil have something to do with it," Vernestra said. Hyperspace had been stable and predictable before the Nihil came along, so it made sense to wonder if they were behind every anomaly.

Master Cohmac shook his head. "It's hard to say. There is much our experts still do not know about hyperspace, despite thousands of years of prospecting and analysis. But I am also a cautious sort, so it's definitely a much safer idea to stick to the better-traveled lanes at this point."

Vernestra nodded in agreement, and Master Cohmac went back to preparing for the jump to hyperspace. But she could not quite let go of the strange feeling that somehow the Nihil had a part in the newest instability in hyperspace. Just what could cause ships to fall out of the lanes and back into realspace?

Vernestra was not an expert on hyperspace by any stretch of the imagination, but like most younglings and Padawans, she had sat through extensive classes in how hyperspace worked, both literally and philosophically. There was some thought among Jedi scholars that hyperspace was a part of the cosmic Force, the lanes rivers of energy that sprang from some unknown font. Others saw hyperspace as another dimension, a shadow of the world occupied by the living Force, and said that was why planets and other real objects impacted hyperspace as they did. Vernestra did not know who was right; philosophy was rarely about proving a theory as far as she had seen and more often about embracing the possibilities, and there was no final answer on just what hyperspace *was*. Everyone knew how to use it, but only the scholars still debated its nature.

But to have objects fall out of hyperspace was strange and unnatural, and it had been her experience that if there was something terrible afoot in the galaxy it was probably safe to blame the Nihil.

The whine of the hyperdrive powering up on the small ship drew Vernestra away from her thoughts, and she was surprised to find Imri watching her with concern. Vernestra frowned. "Is something wrong?"

He shook his head. "Just a feeling. But I don't know what it is. Don't mind me," he said, leaning back against his chair and closing his eyes, his breathing becoming deep and even as he began to meditate. Or nap. Vernestra wasn't sure which one.

The ship bumped and jumped, and then the blue of hyperspace streamed past the cockpit windows. Vernestra yawned once, and then twice, and the next thing she knew—

She was in the desert on a planet she'd never seen before. She walked forward in a dreamlike state, everything around her a little hazy and unreal.

Oh, no, she thought, alarm surging through her. *It's happening again.*

Vernestra had enough awareness of the moment to know she was having one of her hyperspace visions, which she hadn't had since becoming a Knight, but she was thoroughly unable to pull herself from the reverie. She found herself carried along, so she eventually relaxed and let the vision show her what it would.

The red sand of the desert gave way to scrub brush and a small culvert with a sickly trickle of blue moss growing thick at the lowest point. Vernestra walked along the top of the ridge toward a small town that consisted of a handful of weathered buildings. At the end of the town's lone road was a Jedi temple, the Order's insignia painted on the front the only thing in the landscape Vernestra recognized.

Blasters fired and people roared. A ragtag group fired haphazardly into the buildings, unchallenged.

"For the Strike! For the Tempest! For the Storm!" they yelled. A blue-skinned Jedi came out of the temple, his lightsaber powered up and ready to do battle.

Someone was calling her.

Vernestra walked as a ghost, stepping away from the battle raging in the street and slipping into the shadows of a lodging house. A family of Ugnaughts huddled in a back room, their eyes going to something on the table.

"I told you it was a bad idea to steal from the Nihil!" the woman yelled at the man. "You have killed us all."

"The old Jedi will handle it," the man said, even as he flinched at every sound of blaster fire. Sitting in a tray on the table was a box. It looked like a holocron, but there were glyphs Vernestra did not recognize on the outside. Squiggles and slashes in shades of black and silver.

Take it. Find me. I have something for you, said a voice Vernestra did not recognize and was definitely not her own.

In the dream, Vernestra reached out for the box, for the secrets it held, for the chance to answer a call—

"Vern! Hey, are you awake?"

Vernestra startled upright, blinking as the last remnants of the dream—vision?—fell away. Imri stood over her, and he took a step back as Vernestra straightened.

"I—I must have fallen asleep," Vernestra said, rubbing her eyes, heart pounding with the lie. "Are we still in hyperspace?"

"No, we just exited, and now we're heading to the next jump point. Are you okay?" Imri asked, a dozen questions in the look he gave Vernestra.

"I'm great, just fine." She hated the way she was pulled from her body, the lack of control as she was moved from one part of the scene to the next. But Vernestra still wanted to take some time to analyze what she had seen, meditate on it and pick it apart as she did every problem. Before, when she was still a Padawan, having one of her attacks left her feeling scared and shaken, like she was somehow misusing the Force.

Now Vernestra was just wondering why they were happening again.

Visions were not uncommon to those connected deeply

to the Force, but prophecy was no gift; rather, many Force users saw it as a curse to be endured. Vernestra was not prone to prophecy. Those Force users were usually discovered very early on, and none of her previous mental wanderings had ever come true, so the vision must be something else entirely. Was someone trying to reach out to her? Was she seeing things that were happening in that moment? But how, and why now?

Imri, ever the sensitive one, frowned as the questions raged through Vernestra. He gave her a concerned look and opened his mouth to speak. But whatever he was about to say was cut off as the comm unit began to beep.

"What's happening?" Vernestra asked, standing and walking away from both Imri's concern and the lingering strangeness of the vision.

"It looks like the temple on Tiikae has sent out a request for aid. They're reporting a number of Nihil fighters looting and menacing the local populace."

"How far away is that?" Imri asked, coming up behind Vernestra. She could feel the questions he wanted to ask her, but she would put him off for now. This was no time for pondering her wayward abilities.

"Not far," Reath said, worry twisting his pale brow. "We should assist."

"Agreed," Cohmac said. "Reath, update our course. Vern and Imri, I can drop you in from above to save time? From the message it seems as though the fighting just began."

"Of course, Master Cohmac. We'll do what we can. Come on," Vernestra said to Imri. "The sooner we can stop these Nihil, the better the chances there won't be too many casualties."

"I'll come along, as well," Reath said as he finished inputting the new location. He unbuckled from his seat. "The ship only needs a single pilot to land."

"Once we're over the heart of the fighting, I'll open the loading ramp," Master Cohmac said. "Looks like I'm going to take this fancy array for a spin."

Vernestra nodded, and the three Jedi ran to the loading ramp. She pushed the strangeness of her vision aside to be dealt with later and turned all her attention to the battle that lay before her.

It was time to remind the Nihil that the Jedi would not tolerate their violence.

Vernestra handed both Imri and Reath communicators to slip over their ears before placing one over hers. After a quick comms check to make sure she could hear not just Imri and Reath but also Master Cohmac, she palmed her lightsaber and took a deep breath, centering herself in the Force. Vernestra wasn't much worried about Reath—she knew he was capable enough—but she turned back to Imri.

"You think you've got this?" she asked. Imri was a proficient fighter, but Vernestra tended to worry about him anyway. She worried that every battle left more of a mark on

Imri than it should. He was no coward, but he lacked the fire of Jedi like the Trandoshan Master Sskeer.

Imri pulled his lightsaber from his holster and tossed the hilt from hand to hand, spinning it around to limber up his wrist. "Let's handle these Nihil."

Reath nodded and shifted his stance but said nothing.

The door to the loading dock opened slowly, and they all peered down at the landscape below. Master Cohmac kept the ship about ten meters off the ground. They were above a city in the middle of a desert. Roofs curved into brightly painted domes, and below them was a market square with a fountain and a number of combatants. Blaster fire rained down from windows and flew from doorways, and in the midst of the chaos, a lone Jedi in ivory temple robes repelled the incoming blaster fire, his bright green lightsaber a blur as it moved. He looked to be fighting completely by himself.

The scent of heat and sunbaked sand made Vernestra blink stupidly for a long moment. She knew this place, although she had seen it from a different point of view last time.

The town was the one she had just seen in her vision.

"Vern?" Imri said uncertainly, his voice loud in her ear, both through the communicator and because he was standing next to her. She shook away the memory and her sense of unease at having one of her visions actually be true and gave him a quick nod.

"Let's go. As soon as your feet hit the ground, protect the Master."

And then Vernestra was leaping through the air, letting gravity pull her toward the surface of the planet, too fast. This was the part where jumping from such a great height could be tricky. Giving in to fear, letting one's focus wander and losing that vital connection to the Force, could mean disaster, and then instead of using the Force to control her fall at the last possible moment and landing nimbly on her feet, she would plow into the ground, and that would be the end of Vernestra Rwoh.

There was, of course, little chance of that.

Vernestra pointed at the ground rushing up toward her and used the Force to push until she landed, bending her knees to absorb the impact. Reath landed next to her on her left and Imri on her right. Less than a meter away was the Master, a bright blue Chagrian with a missing horn, the edge singed halfway down. He sagged as Vernestra and the Padawans fell in around him, repelling the blaster bolts. As a group they moved the elder Jedi into the safety of an alcove between two buildings, where he collapsed against the wall.

"Master, I am Vernestra Rwoh. Are you injured?" Vernestra said, one eye on the Jedi Master and the other on the threat behind them. The blaster fire had stopped, but Vernestra could not see where it had come from. As far as she could tell, the streets were completely empty. It was different from her vision, yet almost exactly the same, and the disconnect between what she'd seen and the current land-scape gave her a strange feeling.

"Jedi, I am Master Oprand Qwen, the marshal here. The sludge pots got one of my horns," he said, wincing as he reached up to his head. "But otherwise I am unharmed." Chagrians bore a set of ivory horns on the tops of their heads and softer lethorns that hung below their jawlines. It was lucky that he'd only lost a horn, judging by the volume of blaster fire pointed at him.

"What's going on here? The alert said there were Nihil," Reath said, gesturing toward the windows. A spate of blaster fire erupted once more, coming close enough to make Reath jump a bit deeper into the alcove but missing the Jedi.

"There are. Five that I counted. But that blasted gas makes it difficult to be certain. That building across the way there is the town's one lodging house. The Nihil have taken it over and have declared it theirs. And they have a handful of hostages. They're demanding something that was stolen from one of their number when they stopped here, in exchange for releasing the family inside, but I am certain they are just buying time, waiting for reinforcements to arrive."

Vernestra's mouth went dry. She recalled the small cube the Ugnaughts had in her vision. Was that what the Nihil were after? "Can't the town officials send in help?" Vernestra asked. "Where are your coalition protection troops? This is a signatory planet."

The Master sighed. "Perhaps, but the Republic presence

consists of a force that only makes visits sporadically, and not even that now that the Republic is fully occupied with the Nihil and is bringing resources to bear in other places. Even the San Tekkas, who own most of the area and have a deputy on planet to see to most issues, have been hard-pressed to get supplies to their vassals. And our temple here has a bit of a dual purpose. We were originally established as a waystation for Jedi bringing younglings from the frontier—before Starlight Beacon was built, of course. But we also settle disputes within the town proper. Tiikae is a small planet and sparsely populated. Settlers have only been here for the last seventy-five years or so, and that is thanks to the San Tekkas. There is not much here but what you see with your eyes."

"So, no backup then," Vernestra said, gnawing on her lip as she considered the situation.

The Jedi Master shook his head. "I am afraid not."

"Are you here all by yourself, Master?" Imri asked. He was right to wonder. It was strange to see a Jedi alone in such a protection role.

"I wasn't, but we have had a run of misfortune. One of our Jedi was killed just last week in a Nihil attack, and I lost another at Valo. The last was called to assist with dispersal of a Nihil cell in a nearby quadrant, leaving me by myself. This normally isn't a problem, as the San Tekkas' appointed deputy is a competent woman who is exceptionally good at protecting the people here. But she has been out all morning trying to round up the scattered bantha herds. We thought they'd run because of a dust cur, and it wasn't until after she'd set out that the Nihil attacked. She'll be back, but I'm afraid it won't be before things take a tragic turn." The Jedi frowned. "I thought I could take them myself, but I was wrong. Thank the Force you arrived when you did."

"Thank the Force indeed." Reath nodded.

Vernestra looked across the dusty square at the lodging house. Time was their enemy, because without a doubt the Nihil would start killing their hostages sooner rather than later. If they hadn't already started killing the people inside. In Vernestra's experience the Nihil were not known for their restraint. They had to keep the pirates busy so they didn't take out their violent tendencies on innocent bystanders.

"Where is the Nihil ship?" Vernestra asked. It seemed strange to see the Nihil planetside without a way to make a quick escape. The Nihil weren't soldiers; they were thieves. They usually overran a place, took what they wanted, and then ran before they could be confronted by anything more threatening than farmers and haulers.

"I'm not sure," Master Oprand said.

"It's to the north of town, Vern," Master Cohmac said in her ear. "I'm flying over it right now, and there's no mistaking that Path drive. It doesn't look like they left anyone behind, so you're probably dealing with one of the smaller teams."

Vernestra swallowed a sigh. So now the esteemed Master Cohmac was calling her the hated nickname? Good grief.

She put the minor annoyance aside and focused on the

mission. "Okay, here's what I think we should do, Master Oprand," Vernestra said. "Reath and I are going to get inside the lodging house. Once we're inside, the Nihil should be distracted, and then you and Imri will follow us from behind. Can you do that?"

The Master nodded and pushed himself to his feet. "Yes, my injuries are not so severe as to take me from the battlefield."

"Remember to move quickly, and do not let your guard down around the Nihil," she said to the Padawans.

"They have no honor," Imri said with a solemn nod of agreement.

"So I have heard," Master Oprand said. "But, Jedi, how are you and the Padawan going to get into the lodging house in the first place?"

"Oh," Vernestra said with a grin, "I have a few tricks up my sleeve. Reath?" Vernestra powered up her lightsaber, the purple blade bright in the dimness of the alley.

"Right behind you," he said, his own lightsaber a sedate green.

Vernestra took a deep breath and ran from the alley, right toward the lodging house. The Nihil were ready, and the blaster fire erupted after only a couple of steps. Vernestra repelled the blaster bolts that came near with her lightsaber at first, her connection to the Force guiding her movements, but as they got closer the accuracy of the shots improved and Vernestra had to move faster.

She was going to be exhausted by the time she hit the front door.

"Reath, give me a bit of room and then fall in right behind me," she said, leaning to the left to dodge a blaster bolt as she twisted the bezel at the top of her lightsaber. The blade seemed to melt, sparks flying up where the tip of the lightwhip touched the ground. And then Vernestra spun the whip over her head fast enough that it was little more than a blur of purple. Instead of trying to anticipate where each bolt would land using the Force, Vernestra was able to provide herself and Reath a constant shield of protection.

They sprinted the rest of the way toward the building.

"Reath, door," Vernestra said, and the Padawan held his hand out toward the front of the lodging house, ripping away the door and its frame and sending the whole thing careening down the street to the right.

As they crossed the threshold, Vernestra turned her bezel once more to shift the lightwhip back into a lightsaber. As useful as the whip could be, it was terrible in close quarters, and there was no telling what they would find inside the lodging house.

The door opened onto a dimly lit foyer, a human body slumped over a table. The Nihil hadn't waited to kill their hostages after all.

A maskless human man rushed through the doorway from another room, blaster raised, and Reath held his hand out, using the Force to pick up the man and throw him across the room before he even had a chance to get a shot off. The Nihil grunted and slumped against the wall, and Reath checked his pulse before standing.

"Not dead, just unconscious."

"Leave him to Imri and Master Oprand. It seems like the rest are through that doorway," Vernestra said, feeling a sense of menace when she considered the arch through which the first Nihil had come. The rest had to be behind that door.

"Agreed," Reath said, adjusting his grip on his lightsaber. More than most Jedi, Reath hated conflict; he much preferred the safety of libraries, and he had been the one to help Vernestra learn to use the library on Starlight Beacon for her research into Imri's empath abilities. But even though he was more at home in a library than a battle, Vernestra was glad to have him with her. She knew he was a competent fighter, especially after their sparring match, even if he disliked it.

Vernestra took the lead as she walked through the doorway. She kept her steps slow and deliberate as she scanned for threats with not just her physical senses but also the Force. The room beyond was dim, but her lightsaber cast a deep purple glow that revealed more closed doors, two of them.

Find the cube.

The voice came out of nowhere, distracting Vernestra for an instant.

"Left!" Reath shouted, just as the doorway opened up and a hail of blaster bolts flew at them. There was no time to repel them with the lightsaber, so Vernestra dove behind a nearby chair while Reath stepped backward out of the room.

"We've got you outnumbered, Jedi," called someone with a high voice.

Vernestra didn't say anything. If the Nihil were talking, it was a distraction. Instead she stood and held her hand out, pushing with all the power of the Force that she could muster. The Nihil went flying backward into the room and Vernestra followed, letting the memory of the destruction of Valo give her energy and propel her forward.

Vernestra entered the room, expecting blaster fire. Instead she found a door hanging open and a family of Ugnaughts bound and gagged in a corner. The blaster burns in the middle of their chests made her heart seize, but the signs of torture lit a fire in her. The Nihil had tortured and killed the family.

The same family from her vision, Vernestra realized with a jolt. But this was not the time to reflect on what that meant. The Nihil were getting away.

Vernestra ran through the open doorway, prepared to be greeted by blaster fire, but all she saw was a speeder bike tearing off across the dusty landscape. Reath followed, running into the alley and standing next to Vernestra.

"We have to go after them," he said.

Vernestra powered down her lightsaber and sighed. "Master Cohmac, can you see the Nihil fleeing?" The departing speeder kicked up a thick dust cloud as it streaked across the landscape.

There was nothing but static, and Vernestra turned back to Reath. "I think he might be out of range. We need to go after them."

Another speeder bike came careening around the corner, a slender rider with a full helmet covering their face driving the vehicle. "Get on," shouted a feminine voice.

Vernestra hesitated for less than a heartbeat before jumping on the back. "Keep trying to call Master Cohmac," she yelled at Reath as the speeder bike took off after the retreating Nihil.

She would stop the Nihil before they had a chance to hurt anyone else.

ELEVEN

Syl followed Basha and Xylan Graf through an echoing corridor located in the grandest building she had ever seen. After deciding that Syl could not be left to her own devices—as if the assassin who had blasted the droid and the fish tank had been her idea—Xylan had ordered her to pack up her things and follow him.

"I greatly dislike being wrong, and I seem to have miscalculated your potential for assassination," Xylan had said, which both pleased and annoyed Syl. "Either way, it's bad form to have a guest murdered, so you're going to stay in my house where I can be assured of your safety."

"It is also much nicer than the hotel. You will like it,"

Basha had said as they all walked to the waiting sky car. Syl had thought that the Gigoran was Xylan's bodyguard, but it seemed she also functioned as a sort of companion or secretary. Syl wondered how the two had met.

Normally Syl would have balked at being whisked off to some man's house, but after her near death that morning, she was willing to be a little bit flexible. Besides, she was wondering where a man like Xylan Graf, who had not once complained about the destruction of his outfit, lived.

She wasn't disappointed.

Xylan Graf lived in the penthouse of a glittering jewel of a building. The main floor featured a number of protection droids, another Gigoran as well as a Wookiee, and feral-looking human guards, their uniforms not dampening the glint of malice in their eyes. The people in the lobby looked less like hired security and more like gladiators, but when they saw Basha they nodded to her and saluted.

"I am head of security," she said in response to Syl's raised eyebrow.

"Does everyone in this building know you?" Syl asked. She was talking to Basha and Xylan both, since there had been a number of head nods and chest-thumping salutes as Xylan passed, as well.

"I should hope so," he said, his now red-and-pink boots squelching as they walked across a floor that looked to be made of priceless Baffian marble. "I own the building."

Syl looked around once more, taking in the structure

with fresh eyes. The foyer was nearly twice the size of the *Switchback* stem to stern, and dozens of art pieces filled the space. At least, that was what Syl figured they were. How else to describe the twisting plants and blobby multihued rocks that decorated the lobby?

"There are two thousand floors," Syl said when they reached the lift, her gaze flicking over the numbers. "How does a person live on two thousand different floors?"

"I don't, I only live on the top ten. And technically there are two thousand one hundred and twenty-five floors in this building, but a few hundred of them are below level. For the sky cars." His lips twisted in amusement. "Not all of them mine, of course. I rent out the floors I don't occupy. This is just my private entrance," he said, gesturing to the grand foyer behind them.

Syl's wonder died, and confusion took its place. She couldn't quite reconcile this level of wealth. Instead of making her feel better for taking advantage of Xylan Graf, it just made her feel silly. She thought she was perpetrating a grand scheme, but someone with this much wealth wouldn't even blink at a few hundred credits. "I don't get it. How do you own an entire building? One that comes with a private army? You're, what, twenty? Twenty-one?"

"Twenty-two, actually, and yes, your point is valid. My grandmere gave me this building as a present for my eighteenth birthday when I accepted my place in the family, with the understanding that it was my job to make it not just self-sustaining but profitable." A pensive expression wiped away the mirth on Xylan's face, and he pursed his full lips in thought. "It took me two years, but I did it. And when I did, the building was mine in truth. The Matriarch is harsh, but fair. She would like you."

"Because I managed to destroy a hotel suite in less than a day?"

Xylan laughed. The man had a strange sense of humor. "No, because you're a survivor. Grandmere often tells stories about the early days, of how the Grafs went from the dirty business of hyperspace prospecting to shipping. She admires grit and determination, and you have both in abundance, Sylvestri Yarrow."

Syl didn't say anything, and the lift mercifully chose that moment to arrive with a soothing bong that echoed throughout the lobby. Xylan and Syl stepped in, but Basha remained behind. Syl felt a bit of loss at watching the Gigoran leave. She rather liked her dry sense of humor, though whether it was because the vocalizer stole the emotion from Basha's voice or because she was truly funny, Syl didn't know.

She decided that she didn't like Xylan Graf complimenting her. She didn't much like him at all. His attitude felt condescending. So what, he'd taken a piece of prime real estate and made it profitable? Pfft, he'd started off winning. She'd been born losing, a whole life led trying to survive on the fringes of the galaxy. Growing up on a ship, scraping by from cargo to cargo, sometimes fighting for her life against pirates and other scum, she'd never had it easy. And things had only gotten harder after her mother died. For the past few months she had scraped and planned and haggled and done everything she could to make a go as a hauler, and in the end it hadn't mattered. She'd lost it all in a random attack.

Nothing about life in the galaxy was fair, but somehow standing next to Xylan Graf and inhaling his too-expensive cologne just made the fact all the more obvious. And that made Syl mad. Anger was a far better emotion than despair, so she held it close with everything she had.

It would also make it easier to squeeze a few more credits from the man without her conscience getting in the way.

The lift doors opened, the ride to the top floors so smooth that Syl hadn't even realized they'd been moving. Xylan squelched out of the lift—his wet boots seemed to be disintegrating the longer he wore them; who in their right mind would pay for such flimsy footwear?—and waved expansively at his foyer and the sitting room beyond.

"I'm going to change," Xylan said with a wry smile, oblivious to Syl's annoyance and discomfort. "Make yourself at home. Well, that is, try not to set anything on fire." He winked at the joke and then flowed down a hallway with his long-legged stride.

Syl turned her attention to the room spread out before her. Like the room at the hotel, it was decadent in a way that was obvious in the careful crafting and uniqueness of each item. Here was an end table carved out of some peculiar black-and-white striped wood; here was an entire carpet made of gherlian fur, a king's ransom tossed haphazardly across the floor. If Syl had been any kind of scoundrel, she would have pocketed some of the assorted knickknacks scattered around the room and hightailed it to a resale shop. She could have easily bought an entire fleet with the value of the decorations in that single room.

Instead, she plopped onto a strangely shaped chair and sighed as she sank into the warm material, resigned to feeling forever unbalanced and angry around the beautiful enigma that was Xylan Graf. She might not like him, but maybe by helping him she could convince him to sponsor her with a ship or something. She didn't have to like him to like his money.

He was her best chance at making sure her trip to Coruscant hadn't been a colossal waste of time.

"You know that isn't a chair, right?" Xylan said as he strode back into the room. His cream-and-red outfit had been changed out for a simple shirt and trousers, the kind a mechanic might wear. It looked like the sort of thing one would find dockside, normal and unremarkable. Syl decided she liked his understated look better than any of his high-fashion ensembles, and then she wondered if he had changed just to make her feel more comfortable. That put her once more on edge. She didn't like being manipulated, especially by pretty men.

"If it isn't a chair, what is it?" Syl asked, scrambling to her feet.

"That's Plinka, my Grand Theljian snow dog. Don't worry, she doesn't mind."

The creature stood and shook herself out as Syl watched, horrified. "I sat on your dog."

The beast was huge, with six stocky legs and a wide, smiling mouth. Two sets of eyes blinked at Syl, and a huge blue tongue licked her before she could fend off the attack.

"Ugh," Syl said, scratching the dog behind its tiny ears—the only small thing on the beast—as it growled appreciatively. Some of Syl's annoyance melted away. It was hard to hate someone who had such a great pet. "I suppose I deserve that slobber, since I sat on you."

Xylan laughed. "She does it all the time, crouches and waits until someone decides to see if she's as comfortable as she looks. She is a scoundrel." The beast padded over to Xylan, her head nearly even with his. As he petted the dog, Syl tried to imagine having such an enormous creature riding around on the *Switchback*. She couldn't.

And thinking of the *Switchback* gave her a keen sense of homesickness, so she clamped down on the thought and focused instead on how annoyingly pretty Xylan Graf was. She would make sure he gave her a new ship.

"Okay, you asked me to wait to discuss the attack until we got here," Syl said, gesturing to Xylan's splendiferous living quarters. "Now I want to know why someone went to the trouble to try and kill me, a simple hauler."

Xylan's expression darkened, and Plinka, as though sensing his mood, moved off to lie in what looked to be a giant dog bed. "You're right," Xylan said with a sigh. "I'm afraid I only gave you part of the truth during our dinner last night. To get the whole of the matter I have to show you something. Please follow me."

Syl nodded but said nothing. At least now she knew her instincts had been correct.

Xylan turned and walked through the foyer to a room that looked to be some kind of gathering area and then onward to yet another lift, this one without numbers. Inside he pushed a series of buttons, none of which seemed to indicate where they were going. "What language is that?" Syl asked, gesturing to the strange scribbles above each floor.

"That is Graffian. It's my family's secret language."

Syl blinked. "Your family has a secret language?"

Xylan grimaced. "I think perhaps when I explain things to you fully you'll understand just what is happening here, and why someone sent an assassin to kill you. Ah, here we are."

The lift doors opened to reveal a completely different room, a laboratory full of gadgets and devices that looked expensive and complicated. Xylan walked past them all to a board that glowed with a number of points. It was a map of the galaxy. It took up an entire wall, and various points blinked red or green or blue, with systems glowing in gold.

"Whoa," Syl said. She'd seen a similar star map only once in her life, at a museum her mother had taken her to the one time she'd gone to Hosnian Prime.

"Yes, it's impressive. I think to explain to you just what I'm about, I have to tell you a little bit about my family history. The Grafs were not always rich. A few hundred years ago we were once haulers like you, and then my family had the great idea to split off into hyperspace prospecting, discovering new lanes and byways through space. Dangerous work, which also meant it was profitable."

Syl nodded. She'd heard of prospectors. Once, it had taken months to crisscross the galaxy. Travel was faster now because of the hyperspace lanes, those shortcuts between places that somehow bent time and space.

"I don't want to get into the debate as to the nature of hyperspace," Xylan said with a rueful grin. "Some will tell you hyperspace lanes are navigable wormholes, and others will claim they are routes carved out by some ancient race that no longer exists. Either way, when the Republic was expanding, there was a sort of rush to map and claim the existing, yet unknown, routes. It was a little bit of math, navigation, and a whole lot of good luck. My family, of course, mapped out several routes, some of which were private until your mother and people like her campaigned to have the Republic make them accessible to all."

Syl bristled and opened her mouth to respond, but Xylan

raised his hand. "I'm simply stating facts. To understand what's happening now you have to understand the history and theory behind hyperspace."

"I'm not stupid," Syl said, crossing her arms. "I'm a pilot. I get how hyperspace works. My questions are how I was kicked out of hyperspace while minding my own business and why someone would try to kill me over sharing that fact."

Xylan scrubbed his hand over his face and pointed back to the map. "That's the problem. I don't know how you were kicked out of hyperspace. The theories for such a thing are purely hypothetical, and there are few instances that could account for such a phenomenon, such as supernova fallout or collision with an object or its mass shadow."

"We didn't hit anything," Syl said.

"And there haven't been any supernovas reported in the Berenge sector, I've looked."

Syl gestured at the map. "What do all of these lights mean?"

"That's the second piece of the puzzle, the other thing the Nihil are doing that defies explanation. These are places where they popped out of hyperspace and then dipped back in. I've been tracking Nihil sightings and trying to figure out how it is that they're basically appearing where there's no real navigational beacons to build reliable jump coordinates. There's a theory that hyperspace could be entered from any-where, including a planet's atmosphere, but the calculations for such a thing would be far beyond any navigational unit, or even an astromech. Not to mention the adjustments that would need to be made to account for the gravity! They're using what are basically unmapped roads to pop in and out of realspace and avoid both the Jedi and the ships the Republic has sent after them."

"How?" Syl asked, suddenly feeling like maybe she didn't understand hyperspace as well as she'd thought.

Xylan shrugged. "I don't know."

"I thought you worked in theoretical hyperspace physics," Syl said, walking as she studied the map of the galaxy, the blinking lights suddenly less pretty and more ominous now that she knew what they represented.

"I do. But this is even beyond me. And not to boast, but I am considered to be near the top of my field," Xylan said. It sounded like a brag. Xylan Graf was, unsurprisingly, not very good at being humble.

"So what do you think is happening?"

"I think the Nihil are using temporary paths through hyperspace, lanes that are only useful for a small period in time due to the orbits of nearby heavenly bodies. Like this right here." Xylan pointed to a dot near Valo, a small out-of-the-way planet that had entered everyone's minds after the disaster there. "There was a report of a Nihil ship jumping to hyperspace here, but the occlusion of these moons' orbits should have prevented that. And two days later the triannual eclipse would've made that jump location a death sentence."

"Aren't these just some of the stored calculations that navicomputers have?" Syl asked with a shrug.

"No navicomputer has every single possible route. The Nihil are able to map these routes without using any of the beacons, even in sectors where they have never been spotted before or places where the beacons are disabled. Because they already have the information."

Syl had felt unbalanced ever since she'd come to Coruscant, but this revelation put all that to shame. The Nihil weren't brilliant or strategic; they were cruel opportunists who had somehow stumbled upon a way to use hyperspace that surpassed everyone else. This seemed like weird, magical kind of stuff, like those stories people sometimes told about the Jedi and their great feats, stories that sounded half like typical cantina tales and half like hopeful musings. If the Jedi were so great, why hadn't they prevented the attack on Valo? Or the crash of the *Legacy Run*? If they were so great, why hadn't they shown up to save Syl's mother?

Syl took a deep breath. It was silly how her grief for her mother could reappear without warning. This was not the time for it.

"So, okay, how do we stop them? How do we get the Republic to intervene?" Syl asked, stopping at the edge of the map and turning on her heel to face Xylan. "Surely you've shared this information with them?"

He nodded. "But it isn't enough. The Republic is currently

trying to stamp out the Nihil threat by attacking their known locations, and with the Jedi helping, the attack is going well. But unless we can figure out this other piece of the puzzle, along with just how much of the nature of hyperspace they're exploiting, we will always be chasing our proverbial tails."

Syl shook her head. "Why do you think I can help you? I've already told you everything I know about the day the *Switchback* was stolen."

Xylan gave Syl a direct look, and she realized that the man she'd seen before had been an act, even if a poor one. His kindness evaporated and his eyes turned hard as he stared directly at Syl.

"Because," Xylan said, crossing his arms as he studied Syl, "there is a theory your mother is the one behind all of it. And I think that is why someone wants you dead."

TWELVE

Vernestra regretted jumping on the back of the speeder bike seconds after she and the other woman took off after the fleeing Nihil. Not because she didn't want to catch the murderers, but because she didn't have a helmet and the driver was reckless enough to make Vernestra wonder just what she'd gotten herself into.

Force protect her, it would be a shame to die from something as silly as a speeder bike accident.

The wind whipping past made Vernestra's eyes water, and she squinted as they gained on the speeder bike in front of them.

"Shoot back," the woman driving said.

"With what?" Vernestra asked, yelling to be heard over the wind.

"You don't have a blaster?"

"No, I have a lightsaber!" This was probably not the time to tell the woman that Vernestra did not particularly care for blasters. Why would one need such a crude weapon when one had a lightsaber?

The woman grumbled something and reached down to the holster on her leg, then handed the blaster to Vernestra. "Here."

Vernestra holstered her lightsaber and took the blaster, the movement of the speeder bike making shooting difficult. Still she managed to get off a couple of return shots, enough so that the speeder bike in front of them veered and changed direction.

"Got you now!" the woman driving said as the Nihil took a low path through a gully.

"Aren't you going to follow them?" Vernestra yelled as the speeder bike turned to hug the outline of a ridge that veered slightly to the right.

"I am!" the driver said. "Get ready to jump."

"Jump?" Vernestra asked, looking around. The Nihil were down in the dry gully below, just a little bit ahead.

"You can jump or you can drive," the woman said, and when Vernestra didn't answer her, she shrugged and stood up on the seat, climbing deftly onto the front of the speeder bike and gesturing for Vernestra to take her place. Vernestra awkwardly moved forward as the bike began to slow down, handing the blaster to the woman before taking the controls.

"Get me ahead of them!" the woman yelled. Vernestra wondered just who this foolhardy person was. Surely she didn't actually think she was going to jump? It would be a risky move for a Jedi, utterly reckless for anyone else.

Vernestra pushed the speeder bike, the thing bucking a bit then clanking angrily as she gave it as much throttle as the machine would allow. The engines kicked off a curious whine, smoke beginning to billow slightly as the speeder overheated, but the bike pulled ahead just enough for the woman to launch herself through the air and into the valley below.

Somehow, the woman actually landed on top of the fleeing speeder's driver, sending the vehicle into a spin before it slid to a stop.

Vernestra tried to ease the speeder bike back down, but the engines were fully engulfed in flame, so she vaulted off the back of it, using the Force to land feet first on the ground when she would've face-planted. It was a near thing though, definitely not her finest moment, and she coughed as she waved away a plume of smoke. Vernestra gained her bearings and looked down below as the woman kicked backward, knocking the Nihil passenger off of the speeder before using her blaster on the driver. She vaulted off of the machine, stalking the lone remaining Nihil as she scrabbled backward across the ground. The stolen speeder bike drifted, riderless, and Vernestra ran down the sheer side of the cliff to help the woman subdue the Nihil.

"That was quite impressive," Vernestra said, still coughing a bit from the smoke of the burning speeder bike above. "I didn't actually think you'd make the jump."

The mystery woman removed her helmet to reveal she was human, with long, dark curly hair drifting down to the middle of her back. Her sandy-hued skin had a smattering of freckles, and her dark eyes cut through Vernestra.

"You owe me a speeder," she said, voice flat and unaffected.

Vernestra looked up along the ridge, where the bike was most definitely on fire. "Yeah, that's probably fair. Should we get this one back to town?"

"No reason, she's dead," the woman said, pointing to the deep claw marks in the middle of the Nihil woman's chest.

"You killed her?" Vernestra asked in disbelief.

"No, Remy did. She was out hunting but must have come to check out the action. She likes hunting here in the gullies. It's how I know this place so well." A hunting cat with rosettes of green and blue, nearly the size of a small human but nowhere near as large as Chancellor Soh's targons, prowled around the dead Nihil, electricity crackling between the elegantly curving horns on her head. The human woman made a clicking noise, and the massive cat slunk over to her. She scratched the ears of the beast. "The pirate threatened her, and the vollka defended herself, like she's supposed to."

This woman was strange and seemed curiously indifferent

to the dead people at her feet. She was detached from every-thing happening around her, as though she had better things to do than stop murderers. Was life truly so brutal on the frontier?

"I'm Vernestra Rwoh, by the way." Maybe if Vernestra changed the subject, the other woman would warm up a tad.

"Jordanna Sparkburn," the slender woman said. "I'm the San Tekka deputy here on Tiikae. Where's your braid? And sash? Or is the Order not doing that anymore?"

Vernestra blinked. Was it her imagination or did this woman seem to dislike the Order? "I'm, um, a Knight," Vernestra said, feeling awkward being on the receiving end of Jordanna's unflinching gaze. She felt like she'd waded into a pond only to find it was much deeper than she'd expected.

"A Knight—what are you, like, twelve? Mirialans might not age like humans, but you look seriously young."

Vernestra pursed her lips in annoyance. "I'm seventeen. I passed my trials early."

"Congratulations," Jordanna said flatly. Remy, the vollka, yawned widely as if to punctuate Jordanna's lack of enthu-siasm. She sat next to Jordanna and leaned down to butt her head against the woman's hip. Jordanna scratched the cat's ears some more as she looked into the distance at . . . nothing, as far as Vernestra could tell. The combination of the strange behavior of the deputy and the appearance of the vollka had thrown Vernestra off balance so that she struggled to remember there were two very real dead people on the ground nearby.

"Do you often get Nihil attacks here?" Vernestra asked, changing the subject again. Perhaps there was an explanation for the woman's iciness.

"In the past year this planet has become a war zone," Jordanna said, gesturing to the bodies on the ground with a half-hearted wave. Her expression showed none of the horror that Vernestra would expect in such a situation. The deputy just looked tired. "My family, the San Tekkas, settled this planet nearly a century ago, and most of the other families have been here since the beginning. Tiikae used to lie at the juncture of two decently sized hyperspace lanes, but a comet came through a couple decades ago and the debris left behind made one of the hyperlanes too dangerous to traverse. And since then it's just been . . . awful. First the Nihil came, so we hired mercenaries who drank too much and then wreaked their own havoc on the town instead of doing their jobs. Once we got rid of them, we thought things would get better, but they haven't. We've lost a few of the temple Jedi and then had Zygerrians come through trying to kidnap settlers, and Hutts right after that. And all that doesn't even count the Drengir." Jordanna turned to look Vernestra in the eye. "So, yeah. We've had an interesting year. And we're supposed to handle all of this with very few resources since they are all being diverted to other, more lucrative San Tekka holdings."

The vollka suddenly straightened, looking at one of the bodies and hissing. Energy danced across her horns and Jordanna tensed. Vernestra drew her lightsaber instinctively, shifting her stance slightly in anticipation of a new threat. Jordanna held up her hand and walked over to the corpses.

"Relax, Jedi, they're still dead. Remy found something else." Jordanna rifled through the Nihil woman's pockets and pulled out a small cube-shaped item.

"What is that, a holocron?" Vernestra asked, holstering her lightsaber and walking over to where Jordanna stood examining the box.

"Seems like. But these markings are strange," Jordanna said, puzzling over the cube before handing it to Vernestra. "You recognize these?"

Vernestra took the box. A chill ran across her skin despite the heat radiating from the crimson sun overhead.

It was, not so surprisingly, the box from her vision.

It was smaller than most holocrons, intricately decorated and well-made. It was sturdy, as though it could survive a fall or maybe even a pitched battle, and it obviously had. The box was decorated in a rainbow array of colors. The glyphs on the outside looked like a cross between Aurebesh and a child's frivolous scribbles; if they were words or letters, they were nothing Vernestra had ever seen.

"No, I don't recognize the writing. I don't think it's a holocron. This doesn't look Jedi at all," Vernestra said, fighting to keep herself calm. "Do you mind if I hold on to it? We're on our way to Coruscant, and maybe one of the archivists at the Temple can decipher the outside. It seems important, since the Nihil were willing to kill for it."

Jordanna shrugged. "Maybe. They're Nihil. From what I've seen, they aren't so choosy about when they kill." She searched the rest of the Nihil's pockets, moving on to the man when she'd finished with the woman. "Nothing else here except a few credits."

A landspeeder crossed the landscape toward them, dirt billowing up behind it, and Vernestra powered up her lightsaber once more as the vehicle approached. Jordanna merely stood with her arms crossed, an annoyed expression twisting her lips. The vollka flopped to her side and began grooming herself.

Jordanna pointed toward the approaching vehicle. "That's a Jedi. One of yours?"

"Yes, that's one of the Padawans." As the speeder drew even with them, Vernestra could easily make out Reath's silhouette against the reddish sand, his face twisted with concentration as he sped toward them. He pulled up short a few meters away and stood.

"Hey, looks like you got them," he said.

"Master Oprand said there were five," Vernestra said.

Reath nodded. "They ran back to their ship and got away. Master Cohmac tried to stop them, but they jumped into hyperspace right in front of him."

"Figures," Jordanna said as Vernestra jumped into the

speeder. The older woman pointed at the nearby speeder bike. "I'll ride this one."

"What about the bodies?" Vernestra asked, feeling strange about leaving the dead behind, exposed and uncared for.

"Leave them for the carrion serpents." Without another word, Jordanna and her hunting cat ran toward the speeder bike.

"Is everything okay?" Reath asked, his face pinched with worry.

"Well enough, I suppose. Let's get back to town," Vernestra said. "She's the San Tekka deputy here. I think she knows what she's doing."

Reath turned the landspeeder back toward town, Jordanna riding alongside on the speeder bike, her vollka veering off to take a different path than the one they followed. Reath drove like he was being chased, the landspeeder racing over the sand, and Vernestra had to meditate to calm her pounding heart. In her mind the image of the family, blaster burns in their chests, bodies showing signs of torture, and the way they had looked in her vision, alive and scared, came back to her. Why had the Nihil wanted the cube so very badly? Did it hold some kind of secret?

Was that why she had been pulled toward it in the vision? And if so, why was her vision true for the first time ever?

The landspeeder pulled into town, and Vernestra did not wait until it had fully come to a stop before she vaulted out of the vehicle. Imri and Master Cohmac stood with Master Oprand, the three of them conversing in hushed tones. They turned around when they saw Vernestra.

"Is everyone okay?" Vernestra asked, and Master Cohmac shook his head.

"Unfortunately none of the hostages made it," the older Jedi said, his expression somber.

"But there would have been more casualties if you had not answered our distress call," Master Oprand said.

"Yeah, it seems like there's a first for everything," Jordanna muttered, loud enough that everyone could hear.

"Master Cohmac," Master Oprand said, ignoring Jordanna's aside, "you said that the marauders jumped before you could capture the ones who fled?"

"Yes. To hyperspace. The Nihil have a way of making hyperspace jumps from just about anywhere," Master Cohmac said.

"A conundrum I am sure the Republic is working hard to solve," Master Oprand said. He smiled politely and gestured toward the woman staring at their group with crossed arms. "Oh, I forget my manners. Master Cohmac, please let me introduce the San Tekka deputy, Jordanna Sparkburn. She is responsible for the welfare of the homesteaders here on Tiikae. Jordanna, these are the Padawans Reath Silas and Imri Cantaros. It appears you have already met the Jedi Vernestra."

Reath gave a half-hearted wave. "I want to check out something I saw in the rooming house, if that's okay," he said. Master Cohmac nodded, and Reath took his leave.

Imri gave Jordanna a shy smile. Jordanna gave a curt nod, arms still crossed. She opened her mouth but was interrupted by Remy's approach, and her grim expression melted into one of joy when the vollka bumped into her as though seeking her own introduction. "Ah, and this is Remy. She's a vollka and has much better manners than I do."

Imri's pale face split into a wide grin, and he stepped toward Remy. "Stars, a real vollka?" he asked, eyes wide with awe.

"Yes," Jordanna said. The cat straightened and took in Imri through slitted eyes.

"I've read about them, but I didn't realize that they left Mirran Six. Oh, look at you," Imri said, reaching out to scratch the cat between her spiraled horns.

"She's been in my family for over a century, found long ago as a kit by one of my more adventurous ancestors. And she bites," Jordanna said just as the vollka snapped at Imri's extended hand. The Padawan snatched his hand back before the cat could catch his fingers, but the near miss did not dim his grin in the faintest.

"You are so pretty," he whispered to the vollka, who decided she had better things to do and walked off to inspect a nearby rain collection barrel.

Master Cohmac cleared his throat, drawing everyone's attention. "So, Master Oprand, it seems as though your settlement should be safe for the moment. But what are you going to do should the Nihil return?"

Master Oprand shook his blue head and scratched one of his lethorns. "I am not sure. I wish I knew why they plagued us in the first place. We are a small settlement away from the most popular hyperspace lanes, with very little in the way of value. There is no reason they should find us a worthwhile target time and time again."

"We should reach out to Coruscant for advice, Master Oprand," Jordanna said. "This is the third Nihil attack, not to mention everything else that has plagued the settlement, and the violence is only getting worse. We either need additional Jedi to help us defend the people here, or we need to relocate the settlers somewhere safe until the Nihil are handled. The disorder they cause has made far too many others too bold. We can't hold the settlement with just the two of us."

"I'm afraid you are right, Jordanna," Master Oprand said, his voice heavy with sadness. He turned back to Master Cohmac. "I have been sending requests to the Temple on Coruscant to ask for assistance, but my promised reinforcements keep being routed to other locations. Do you think there are Jedi able to assist on Starlight Beacon?"

"Perhaps. I would not know. I'm afraid my time spent

on the station has been brief, as I, too, have found myself engaged in a number of continuous missions," said Master Cohmac.

"How many settlers do you have here?" Vernestra asked. There was space aplenty for refugees on Starlight Beacon if the Jedi Master had a way to transport everyone, and there was no way Master Avar would turn anyone away. It could be the most reasonable short-term solution.

Master Oprand sighed and tucked his hands into the large bell-like sleeves of his robe. "Before this massacre? Two hundred and sixty-three people, not including us."

Vernestra turned to where a group of humans were taking the bodies out of the rooming house. Everyone looked grim, but no one cried or sobbed, typical emotions after such a catastrophe. These settlers were used to hardship and loss. Perhaps that explained Jordanna's brusqueness to some degree.

"If you have a way to ferry everyone to Starlight Beacon, that would be an option," Vernestra said. "Master Avar Kriss, the marshal of Starlight, has space to accommodate and has made a point of welcoming those displaced by Nihil attacks."

"Yes, Vernestra is right," Cohmac said. "I can send a direct message to Starlight ahead of your arrival, or even request a pickup from them. Starlight Beacon is only a few hours' travel from here, all on hyperspace lanes that are patrolled by the Republic's volunteer corps."

"And we can take a few people to Coruscant if they'd rather," Vernestra said. "We have room."

"We can and will," Cohmac agreed.

Just then there was a commotion near the entrance to the lodging house. The Nihil Reath had subdued earlier broke free of his captors, snagging one of their blasters as he did so. He aimed at the Jedi and fired once and then again, missing both times.

"Die, Jedi scum!"

Jordanna jerked her chin toward the man, and Remy took two steps and then seemingly disappeared.

Vernestra didn't have time to wonder where the vollka had gone; she pulled out her lightsaber and ignited the purple blade. But she needn't have bothered. Remy reappeared in front of the Nihil, horns crackling and teeth bared, and with a single leap ripped out the Nihil's throat with her sharp teeth. Blood sprayed in an arc and the Nihil fell to the ground, dead.

"It's true," Imri breathed, his eyes going wide.

Vernestra powered down her saber and put it back in its holster, her heart still pounding from the sudden violence of the cat's attack. "What's true?"

"Vollka's have the ability to fade into their surroundings and become invisible," Imri said.

"Vollkas are just very fast when they are hunting. The invisibility is a rumor," Jordanna said, but she sounded as though she was regurgitating a line more than anything else. "The vollka have been hunted nearly to extinction by scientists trying to test and replicate that idea, but it just isn't true."

"Do you think maybe that's why the Nihil keep attacking here?" Vernestra asked. "Remy seems like she might be valuable."

Jordanna narrowed her dark eyes at Vernestra in an expression reminiscent of the vollka and shook her head. "I think the Nihil keep attacking us because we are an easy, soft target that cannot put up much of a fight. There might be a couple hundred settlers here now, but there were once thousands. And these buildings? They're what's left. We haven't had a chance to rebuild. We are all survivors of a dangerous year, and this settlement might not look like much, but this is home for a lot of people. Never forget that the Nihil attack here for the same reason they attacked Valo: because they can."

Vernestra couldn't help wincing. Jordanna didn't know she had been on Valo during the attack. She didn't know the survivor's guilt that Vernestra carried around like an overstuffed knapsack. Was there something more she could have done? A quick glance at Imri confirmed that he didn't sense any of her sudden grief, and she took a deep breath and released it. As long as she could control her emotions well enough to keep her Padawan from sensing them, she was still coping as well as could be expected.

Perhaps she would find some space to meditate when they were on their way once more. It was the only way Vernestra knew to calm the maelstrom of emotions that had plagued her since the Republic Fair attack.

"Yes, yes, indeed. Thank you, Jordanna," Master Oprand interrupted, a look of disgust mingled with despair crossing his face as he took in the dead Nihil bleeding all over the dirt and the hunting cat fastidiously grooming the blood from her whiskers, "However, I think it's a brilliant idea for me to take those who are willing to Starlight Beacon."

Jordanna nodded. "We'll take every ship we can find, and I'll let the homesteaders who want to remain know that they do so at their own risk. I'll take one of the smaller skippers to Coruscant and reach out to the San Tekka conglomerate office there and see if I can't negotiate new postings for those willing to stay on as San Tekka vassals."

"You are more than welcome to ride with us, if that would be easier," Master Cohmac said. "We are currently on our way to Coruscant. It would be no hardship to include you."

The deputy nodded. "Much obliged. That way there's one more vessel to transport folks to Starlight Beacon. I'll get my things."

She moved away from the group toward a small building at the end of the dusty road, her vollka padding along behind her, their footsteps kicking up small puffs of dust. The squat building bore glyphs marking it as a San Tekka conglomerate office. Vernestra had not been on many planets like Tiikae, but she had seen the advertisements of corporations like the San Tekka conglomerate looking for settlers to come to out-of-the-way planets, their labor in establishing local infrastructure handsomely rewarded, especially when the planet became an important outpost.

It probably wasn't enough credits to continue to endure so many attacks.

"Imri, go find Reath and tell him we'll be leaving shortly," Vernestra said, and the Padawan ran off.

Cohmac nodded at Vernestra in thanks and then turned back to Master Oprand. "Is Jordanna going to be a problem?" Master Cohmac asked. "She seems capable, but I sense much . . . discord in her."

"Jordanna has spent far too many years on the frontier," Master Oprand said, squaring his shoulders. "She was an assistant until very recently. The previous deputy was lost in the Drengir attack a few months ago, and when I arrived she had been fighting for months on end, her and that cat doing what they could to protect the local citizens. She is headstrong and has an uncanny knack with animals, but she has a penchant for violence that I find . . . disturbing." Master Oprand sighed heavily. "But I am also afraid that I have been on the frontier for a long time, and I have met a number of settlers just like her. This is why our light is so important to the galaxy. The more we can ease the suffering of those like her, the better to protect life."

Master Cohmac gave a curt nod. "Too much time on the

frontier can make anyone lose perspective, and we're happy to have another along for the ride."

Reath and Imri returned, Reath's face pinched with despair and Imri sending him quick side glances of worry. Vernestra frowned as she caught the hint of confusion and upset from Reath. If she could feel his distress, then something very bad must have happened. Poor Imri must be overwhelmed, and she moved nearer to him to rest a hand on his shoulder and lend her Padawan a bit of strength before she turned her attention elsewhere. "Reath. What's wrong?"

Both of the Jedi Masters turned toward the Padawan, and Reath flushed at the sudden attention. "I was poking through the rooming house, trying to figure out what could have drawn the Nihil to such a place. And, well, I found something I think you all should see."

Master Cohmac gestured for Reath to lead the way, and as Vernestra entered the rooming house once more, she realized that she'd had only the briefest impression of the space her first trip through. Then she'd been focused on finding the Nihil and stopping them from hurting the settlers they held hostage. Now she took the time to truly observe the space: the burn marks from the Nihil's blasters, the curious stains on the floor where lives had been lost. It was all so pointless. Why had the Nihil killed all those people? What did they hope to gain?

And why weren't the Jedi stopping them more quickly?

Imri gave Vernestra a sharp look, and she took a deep

breath before grabbing hold of her rampant emotions. It had been a very eventful day, but she still needed to set an example for Imri, and falling to pieces was not it.

Reath crossed the dusty floor and went to a panel in the wall, one that had been closed the last time Vernestra was there, making it appear to be part of the wall. "I heard a strange beeping when I entered earlier, and I just now found this panel. Look."

The Jedi crowded around the narrow doorway, peering into the small space beyond. It was little more than a closet, but it was filled with a high-powered comm unit, the kind used to send offworld messages. It blinked with a recently received holo. Reath pressed the play button so they could all view the message together.

"We know you took it," said a pretty, pale human girl. She was the kind of girl you noticed but immediately forgot, unremarkable in her features. Round cheeks, pale skin, dark hair with blue streaks that was a common style among the Nihil, even though nothing else seemed to mark the girl as such. No facial tattoos or piercings and definitely no mask. "And in a very short time you will be dead. So stop resisting and give us what we want. Or call down the fury of the Storm."

"Is she Nihil?" Imri asked, confused.

"Yes, her name is Nan," Reath said. "Whatever the Nihil were doing here, it wasn't a soft target they were after. It was something someone took. It seems like maybe this family was working for the Nihil? This isn't the only message I found. And if Nan is involved, it's bad. She's not like most Nihil. She's clever and cunning." A pained expression crossed Reath's face before he caught himself and schooled his features once more to blankness. "Master Cohmac and I met her while stranded on the Amaxine station. If she is somehow involved in what happened here, it can mean nothing good. She is relentless."

Master Cohmac nodded somberly. "I believe transporting those who are willing to leave Tiikae is a very good idea."

The weighted cube in Vernestra's belt pouch felt suddenly heavier than before. "I think I might know what it was they wanted," she said, pulling out the holocron-like object that Jordanna had taken off of the dead Nihil, who had most likely taken it from the family of Ugnaughts she had seen in her vision. The family who was now dead. "Jordanna and I found this on one of the Nihil. I supposed this could be what they were after?"

Master Cohmac stroked his beard as he narrowed his eyes. "Perhaps. And if so then we might finally be a step ahead of those pirates. Did you open it and survey the contents?"

Vernestra shook her head. "I don't understand the glyphs, but maybe one of you do?"

Master Oprand took the small cube from Vernestra and turned it over in his blue hands. "I do not recognize these glyphs," he said before handing it to Master Cohmac.

Cohmac shook his head. "Neither do I. But it looks to be very, very old. I would say that it reminds me of an ancient puzzle box, but not knowing the language upon the sides it would just be an educated guess. Reath?" The Padawan shook his head, and Master Cohmac handed the cube back to Vernestra. "You should take this to the languages expert when we get to the Temple. Perhaps she will be able to translate it for you."

"And perhaps then we will get an answer for why so many lives were lost today," Master Oprand said. "But this discovery also makes it very clear that to stay here will only lead to more misery. You are correct in that deduction, Master Cohmac. I must go and advise the remaining settlers to depart with me while you take that cursed thing back to the Temple."

"Yes, we must be on to Coruscant. We are, after all, expected," Master Cohmac said.

As they filed out of the building, the mysterious cube weighed heavily in Vernestra's hand.

What could be worth so many lives?

She was almost afraid to find out.

THIRTEEN

"**I'm sorry,** could you repeat that?" Syl said. Her hands were fists at her sides, and she wondered how long it would take Basha and the rest of the security team to respond if she took a swing at Xylan Graf.

"You heard me. Come now, Sylvestri Yarrow, you are no actress and we are both very smart people," Xylan said, leaning his tall frame against a nearby counter. A smirk played around his lips, tinder for the flame of Syl's temper.

Just one punch. Oh, how satisfying would that be? It was a good thing Basha had taken Beti back at the hotel; otherwise Syl might end up in jail for murder. "I'm not pretending like I want to hit you. Trust me, I really do. And I'm not playing stupid, either. My mother is dead. Not that she was some kind of hyperspace mastermind, anyway."

"Nonsense. Your mother was the most brilliant student I ever taught, far smarter than Xylan here. Surely you know that?" came a voice from the doorway.

Syl turned. Standing in the entryway to Xylan's lab was a gray Gungan, his long ears laid flat against his head. Long whiskers hung off of his bill, and a pair of spectacles made his eyes appear huge. He wore matching pants and shirt, both bearing a curious pattern of cross-hatched blue and green stripes. Syl had only seen one other Gungan in her life, and that one had spoken Basic with an odd patois that made him seem silly and a bit stupid, an affectation he used so he could more easily separate his marks from their money in the dock-side gambling dens.

Xylan approached the Gungan with a wide grin. "Professor Wolk! What a delightful surprise. I thought you were back on Naboo."

"Nonsense, I sent you notice of my return two weeks ago. You are still a terrible liar, Graf." The professor ducked his head to enter the room. Even though most of the security team were other species, the dimensions of the space accommodated humans first and foremost, which Syl figured was something of a status symbol for Xylan, a slight toward anyone not like him. The few rich people Syl had met in her life always liked the power of being comfortable while others were not, and the smirking, grinning, smiling Xylan Graf seemed no different.

"Also you did not answer my question," the Gungan said, his bulbous eyes fixed on Syl.

She looked from Professor Wolk back to Xylan. "I don't understand why you both seem to think my mother, who by the way is dead, was some kind of hyperspace genius." She'd been too hasty in thinking she could squeeze something out of Xylan Graf. After all, he came from a family capable of not just great works but also great horrors. People in the Outer Rim and on the frontier still whispered about the role the Grafs had played in the Hyperspace Rush more than a hundred years before. Being desperate wasn't an excuse to throw caution to the wind, and the whole time she'd been plotting how best to cajole him into sponsoring a ship for her he'd been manipulating her for his own ends.

"Perhaps you and Professor Wolk should be properly introduced before we get into, ah, less savory topics of discussion," Xylan said with a winning smile.

"Look, I can't help you," Syl blurted out. It was time to play the hard-luck card. "I don't have a ship, and my current crew consists of an old Sullustan and a twice-rusted security droid. So good luck trying to blackmail me into helping you. All I have to my name are three credits, a spare set of coveralls, and a roll of breathfresheners. I have no idea what you're talking about, and you're starting to scare me, and I just—I just—" Syl sniffed and tried to make a few tears fall, her eyes burning from the effort. Stars, she was bad at this.

Professor Wolk made a curious croaking sound that Syl realized was laughter. "Oh, very dramatic. Your mother was the same way at your age." Professor Wolk walked over to a nearby stool and sat on it, folding his long limbs into a pose that was a bit too relaxed for Syl's liking.

Xylan sighed loudly. "Syl, this is Professor Thaddeus Wolk, the preeminent expert on theoretical hyperspace physics."

Syl blinked. "The smartest hyperspace scientist in the galaxy is a Gungan?"

"Rude," Wolk said, but there was no heat in it. "And yes. I realize the irony, as my kind are not fond of leaving Naboo— for good reason, I might add, in light of recent events—but I have published a number of studies on the possibility of superluminal transit through a particulated atmospheric medium and the proposed tangled-superstring projection that has hyperspace and the Force sharing a cord in a five-brane worldvolume."

Syl blinked. It was a lot of words, and she understood maybe six of them. "The Force? That's Jedi stuff. You two are making less sense the more you talk."

"Perhaps," Professor Wolk said. "But I'm afraid dear Xylan is obfuscating the important matter here, which is why the logic is so fuzzy: I knew your mother. She was my student when I taught at the Academy of Carida."

"What?" Syl said, feeling suddenly dizzy. Xylan caught her elbow, guiding Syl to a nearby stool. She sank onto it gratefully, and Xylan gave her a kind smile before releasing her arm. Even if his chivalry was one more part of his act, she was glad he hadn't let her fall to the floor. Her mother, Chancey Yarrow, activist and champion of the oppressed, had attended military college? The thought was ludicrous.

"Yes, I suppose this might be quite the shock to the system if you did not know your mother was a theoretical hyperspace tactician," Professor Wolk said, tapping the end of his bill.

Syl blinked, feeling like someone had just sucker punched her, and Xylan grimaced. "Professor, perhaps you should start at the beginning. This is going nowhere."

Professor Wolk climbed to his feet and inclined his head toward Xylan in a nod of acknowledgment. He steepled his long fingers for a moment before he straightened.

"Apologies, I was just gathering my thoughts. I suppose I should start at the beginning, since it would explain how I met your mother.

"As you no doubt know, the Academy of Carida was once a preeminent school of study for not just war but the very difficult business of discouraging conflict. In our time the college has fallen out of favor with most, because peace in most of the Republic tends to make us indulgent and happy. There are still a few planets where war is the norm and the instruction of the war college is coveted, but not nearly enough to round out the student body. The college, in dismay at its declining enrollment, instituted a program of recruitment amongst the Outer Rim and less populous planets in order to remain relevant."

Syl took a deep breath and gathered her wits. "Meaning they let dirt scrabblers on the frontier go to their fancy school for free so that people wouldn't forget they existed." Syl knew how the interior saw the frontier planets. And who could blame them? There was nothing so fine or so fancy as what she'd seen on Coruscant.

Professor Wolk bobbed his head and paced as he continued, his words taking on the rhythm and tone of a practiced lecturer. "Yes, if we are to speak plainly. Certain senators were even then pushing for a standing navy, something to keep the established lanes safe, while planets newly joined to the Republic did not want to send their citizens to fight. Anyway, I am getting ahead of myself. The course of instruction still focused primarily on tactics, but programs in several arts and sciences were brought in to round out the instruction and make it more palatable to students who never thought their lives would be touched by war.

"I was brought in to lead and guide the hyperspace theory and philosophy department, with a focus on how hyperspace could best be exploited in times of combat. But students also spent a large amount of time theorizing the true nature of hyperspace and its possibilities beyond traditional travel. That is how I met your mother. Might I have a glass of water?"

"Of course," Xylan said, and a droid trundled forward to offer the professor refreshment.

"I don't suppose I could get a glass of something a bit stronger?" Syl murmured.

Xylan's eyebrows jumped, and he left the room only to return with a decanter of something blue.

"Toniray. From Alderaan," he said as he poured Syl a glass. She nodded and drank half of it. It could have been bantha piss and she wouldn't have cared, as long as it fixed a bit of the pounding that had started up in her head. Xylan said nothing, just raised a perfectly arched eyebrow and refilled her glass before pouring one for himself.

"Yes, yes, very nice," Professor Wolk said, licking the water from his whiskers with his prehensile tongue before handing his glass back to the droid. "As I was saying, your mother approached me after one of my lectures. She had a bright, inquisitive mind, and she was not shy about challenging the assumptions of her colleagues and the professors on the team. I wrote a letter of introduction for your mother to the Ministry of Transportation, but she decided that she would rather continue her studies. You see, she had a theory about artificial gravity wells, and how they could be used to force ships out of hyperspace at opportune moments. It was the perfect meld of the battle tactics she'd learned and the hyperspace theory she loved.

"But Chancey Yarrow was reckless. Hyperspace tactics during times of conflict had always revolved around modifying beacons or encrypting them, a passive tactic meant to confuse navicomputers, never something violent. Why, the energy necessary for such a machine, to be able to replicate the gravity of a planet, would be massive. And the calculations required to know when a ship would be at a specific point in hyperspace for the device to work . . ." Professor Wolk's voice trailed off before he chuckled once more, shaking his head at the silliness of such a thought. "They believed your mother had gone mad. She was so enamored of her idea that when the college ejected her just shy of receiving her doctorate, she didn't even argue, just packed up her work and left. Now it seems like the Nihil might have a very similar weapon. And I do not believe in coincidences."

Syl tried to keep her expression neutral, but she knew she was failing miserably. This story was so utterly unbelievable, she had to consider that maybe it was true. No one was this good at lying. Not even the holo adventures had tales so far-fetched.

"So, you think I'm the daughter of some evil hyperspace mastermind who happens to be working with the Nihil," Syl said, the pieces falling into place. "Is that why someone tried to kill me?"

Professor Wolk stopped, his long ears rising a bit in surprise. "Someone tried to murder you, you say?"

Syl nodded. "Earlier today."

"Ah. Then we are not the only ones who noted your arrival here. Perhaps the Nihil have decided you are a liability, as it is possible that they have sympathizers even here on Coruscant. If it brings you comfort I have had several attempts on my life, as well. It is my belief that the Nihil are not the only ones behind Chancey Yarrow's experimental weapon, and I am currently building such a case to present to the Republic. Which is why your assistance is so vital."

Syl slurped at her blue wine once more. It was starting to taste better with each sip. Which wasn't really saying much. She'd much rather a tall, sudsy grain beer and a hot bowl of stew. She wasn't cut out for the fancy life.

She sighed before turning back to the Gungan. "I didn't even know my mother went to college." All of this was like hearing a story about a stranger. Here was this woman who had studied complex hyperspace calculations and theory for years, a woman Syl had never known. Her mother was more likely to shoot at a problem than do complicated equations. Chancey Yarrow had been brash and sometimes embarrassing, loving and stern, but a hyperspace physicist?

Syl didn't know that woman. And hearing these stories from a stranger was like losing her mother all over again. Chancey Yarrow had led a full life before having her daughter, but Syl hadn't known just how much her mother had done.

"Well, that is going to make my work a bit more difficult, then," Professor Wolk said, bobbing his head.

"None of this has anything to do with me," Syl said. She took another drink of the blue wine, but it didn't make her feel any steadier. The opposite, in fact, and that just annoyed her. "I can't help."

Professor Wolk crossed the distance to rest a heavy hand on Syl's shoulder. "Are you certain you don't know anything? The last project your mother was working on, before she was ejected from Carida, was an actual gravity-well projector. She'd been denied a research grant for the work no fewer than three times, before pretending to change her research directions and securing a grant meant to lead to an increase in the energy economy of hyperspace jump drives. But she had lied on her application, and when it was discovered that she was in reality trying to build a gravity-well projector anyway, she was dismissed from the university. And now there is a disturbance in the Berenge sector that defies all rational explanation."

"So you think my mom gave her plans to the Nihil and they built a gravity-well projector in the middle of dead space? How would they even do that? There's nothing in the Berenge sector. It's why everyone cuts through it. No worries about going off course. And no resources to speak of, so how would anyone even build something there?"

"We don't think your mother gave her plans to the Nihil. It's doubtful they have anyone who would understand the complex calculations required to predict the proper positioning and timing to use such a weapon," Xylan said, his words carrying a note of exasperation. "We think she *built* it."

"No," Syl said, struggling to her feet. She had to get away

from these men and their wild accusations. Her mother was dead. She'd been there when the Nihil attacked, woken up with the headache from the gas. She'd seen the blood in the maintenance hallway. There was no way her mother was alive. And if she was, she wouldn't work with the Nihil.

But what if she would? a tiny voice in the back of Syl's mind whispered. *You didn't even know she'd almost been a doctor.*

"Ms. Yarrow," the Gungan said, lowering his head so he could look Syl in the eyes, "your mother is alive, and she is working with the Nihil. And one way or another, I am going to stop her."

FOURTEEN

Reath jolted awake as the ship touched down. Master Cohmac had sent him off to take a rest break once they made their final jump—their new companion, Jordanna Sparkburn, more than capable of playing copilot if needed—and his sleep had been full of half-remembered shadows and waking nightmares. It was no wonder his head ached and he felt out of sorts.

Every time he'd tried to close his eyes during the flight, he'd been transported to the overgrown corridors of the arboretum on the Amaxine space station where he'd first met the Nihil. And where he'd first met Nan. His heart clenched as he thought of the girl, the pretty blue streaks in her dark hair, the way she'd asked question after question about the Jedi, the way she'd looked so in awe.

All of it a lie. He had been just another mark for her to work, another informational source to be bled of every last bit of data. He hadn't thought he'd had any lingering feelings about the memory, but seeing her face appear in the holo had taken him right back to the shame and embarrassment he'd felt then.

Vernestra would tell him to meditate the distress away. Master Cohmac would take him to the practice room and try to duel the distress from his heart while gently chiding his form. But Reath didn't want to ignore the feeling or somehow sweat it away. He was not the same Padawan he'd been last time he'd run up against Nan. And he never would be again. She had taught him a very valuable lesson about caution and how some could twist kindness into a blade. If he saw her again he would thank her for the lesson.

And then he would take her into custody so the Republic could deal with her and her crimes, whatever they might be. He had no doubt she had something to do with the deaths on Tiikae, and those people deserved justice.

But Reath wasn't bitter or upset. He was, in some place deep inside, glad Nan was still alive. Because that meant she could, if she chose, somehow redeem herself, Force willing. And that gave Reath hope that all the Nihil could one day become better people and respect life in the galaxy.

Would it happen? Probably not. But he could hope.

Reath climbed to his feet and gathered up his belongings. A quick glance out of a viewport revealed the heavy traffic of Coruscant. He was back where he'd once thought he belonged, but that was before hyperspace accidents, a Drengir infestation, and weeks spent saving artifacts from an impending civil war. Now Reath felt like he belonged out among the stars, doing what he could to protect the galaxy from people like Nan. He was anxious to get back to Starlight Beacon and the mission there. It was a strange realization.

"Are you going to stand there like that all day?"

Reath turned around. Behind him stood Jordanna with her small knapsack, the vollka pressed up against her leg. Jordanna had not said a word to anyone the entirety of the trip, and Reath realized the woman was only speaking now because he was blocking the ship's boarding ramp.

"Sorry," Reath said, disembarking. At the bottom of the ramp, Imri fairly bounced on his toes, his face split in a wide grin.

"It's just as amazing as I remember it," Imri said, pointing to the Temple in the near distance. The sun was rising over the city, and the five spires of the Temple gleamed gold and white in the brightness. Reath immediately forgot his fatigue, and his heart swelled. This was the closest thing to a true home he had ever known, and just seeing the Temple once more made him glad. He enjoyed Starlight Beacon, where he felt like he was making a difference in the galaxy for the better, but the main temple buoyed his spirits and strengthened his resolve in the Force.

"Whoa. Did they add another spire?" Jordanna said, shielding her eyes as she took in the Temple.

Vernestra was walking down the boarding ramp, but stopped in shock at Jordanna's words. Reath knew his expression mirrored hers, and Imri just looked upset. "The Temple has always had five spires," Vernestra said, her words a bit clipped. Reath wondered what had transpired between the two in the desert. He had never seen Vernestra be anything but kind to anyone, even the Nihil who were sometimes taken prisoner.

Master Cohmac blinked. "She's teasing you."

Vernestra turned back to Jordanna, who grinned and winked at her. "I was. Remy and I are off to report to the conglomerate office. Thanks for your help on Tiikae, and thanks for the ride."

"May the Force be with you," Cohmac said as Jordanna and Remy left, and Vernestra gave Reath a sidelong glance.

"Strange sense of humor," she said, but Reath shrugged.

"I thought it was funny."

"Yeah, who knew San Tekka deputies could be so hilarious," Vernestra said, voice flat. She was definitely out of sorts. There was a story there, and Reath decided next time he had a moment alone with Vernestra he would ask.

Reath, Master Cohmac, Vernestra, and Imri made their

way to the Temple's main entrance. The building loomed over them as they approached, and the city sounds all around them seemed deafening after so much time spent on the frontier. Even Starlight, with its constant flow of travelers and bureaucrats and Jedi, did not feel as chaotic as Coruscant. Airspeeders flew past, and droids pushed their way through the crowds, hawking wares and offering services. As much as he had missed the Temple and its coolly reassuring energy, he had not missed the chaotic energy created by so many people living in and around it.

Reath turned to Imri and was about to ask him a question when he noticed Imri's expression had gone from happy excitement to near panic. Reath flashed back to the scene in the dining facility on Starlight, the way the boy instinctively created Force bonds with those around him, and he wondered what it would be like for someone as sensitive to the emotions of others as Imri was to suddenly be plunged into the seething mass of life on Coruscant. It had to be a bit like being pushed into a raging river, especially after so much time spent on the sparsely populated frontier, and judging by Imri's wide eyes, the boy was drowning.

Before Reath could do anything, Vernestra was there at the boy's side.

"Imri," Vernestra said. At Master Cohmac's raised eyebrow, she waved him and Reath on, but Reath stood his ground, as did Master Cohmac.

"Reach out to the boy. Show him how to block out what

is happening around him and focus on just his own emotions," Master Cohmac said. Vernestra nodded, eyes wide with her own muted alarm.

She closed her eyes and put her hands on either side of Imri's head. "It's okay. Just let it wash over you. Breathe."

Reath watched as Imri matched his breathing to his master's, the high color in his cheeks fading to something more akin to his usual complexion. Vernestra's tension also melted away, and a smile crossed her lips as she opened her eyes and let go of the boy.

"Better?" Vernestra asked, and Imri gave her a shaky smile.

"Yeah. It was just so much. It was like everyone's emotions came flooding at me all at once and there was nothing I could do about it." Imri bit his lip in worry. "I've never experienced anything like that before."

Vernestra placed a comforting hand on Imri's shoulder.

"Imri, is this the first time you've been overwhelmed like this?" Master Cohmac asked as they resumed walking. They joined the flow of people entering the Temple: Jedi and Republic officials, citizens and a few vendors who tried to sell trinkets as visitors approached.

"No, but it's never been this bad. It's weird. Ever since we left Starlight I've felt odd. Like I should be looking for someone. I even heard a woman whispering to me. So when we got off the ship I found myself reaching. I don't know why I did that."

Vernestra stopped short, and a nearby vendor took that as an opportunity to approach. "Jedi! Look! I have authentic kyber crystals from the Holy City of Jedha!" the Weequay said, thrusting a handful of crystals at her.

Vernestra gently pushed him away and Reath was struck with an idea.

"Imri, have you read the philosophies of Samara the Blue? She was a Jedi who was posted in a temple on Genetia. The Genetians have very violent emotional swings, one moment happy, the next angry, and they instinctively project these emotions at one another through the Force. She came up with a series of meditations to help her while posted at the temple there. Master Cohmac and I sent a copy back here to the main library. You may find her techniques helpful."

Master Cohmac nodded. "Good thinking, Reath. The answers to our current troubles are so often found in the writings of those from the past. I do believe that is an excellent idea. Reath, why don't you and Imri go to the library while Vernestra and I see to our business here. Unless, of course, you object?" Master Cohmac said, directing the last bit to Vernestra.

"No, I think that's a great idea," Vernestra said, but there was a strange expression on her face, like she wanted to say something else. Reath worried that he had overstepped in suggesting Imri try something different. But then she shook her head as though to clear away an errant thought, her hair coming loose from its fastener with the effort. "Reath, thank you."

Reath nodded, and as he and Imri walked to the library, which was located inside the main ziggurat of the Temple, he had the comforting thought that he was exactly where he was supposed to be, just as the Force willed it.

So why then did his mind keep going back to the holo of Nan on Tiikae and the certainty he felt that they would cross paths once again?

FIFTEEN

Vernestra watched Imri walk away with Reath and felt conflicted. She was happy that Reath seemed to think he had some teachings that would help Imri deal with his sensitivity to the emotions of others. It was a good idea, and she hoped it did help. But at the same time, she'd wanted a moment to discuss what Imri had said about hearing a woman's voice.

Had he somehow heard the same voice that had plagued Vernestra since her hyperspace vision? It was a voice that seemed to come from the Force itself, because that was the only explanation for it. How else could someone have spoken to Vernestra through her vision and also while on Tiikae? Who could exist so completely in so many places at once?

Vernestra didn't know, and she'd wanted the chance to question Imri about it. Because if someone else had heard the woman, then maybe her visions hadn't returned after all. Maybe it was something else entirely. Which was even worse. If there was one thing Vernestra disliked, it was feeling uncertain about herself.

She and Master Cohmac entered the Temple silently, the guards waving them through, and inside the shadows were blessedly cool. Grand statues of brave and honorable Jedi decorated the hallway, and a huge tapestry depicting the battle between the Jedi and the Sith hung over the entrance, causing both Jedi to stop and stare like wonderstruck younglings. In the tapestry the Jedi, depicted as soothing blue swirls, battled the Sith, characterized as red lightning bolts. In the center of the tapestry was a human female Jedi standing atop a Zygerrian Sith lying on the ground, his hand outstretched as if seeking the mercy and forgiveness the Jedi were best known for.

"This is amazing," Vernestra said, coming to stand next to Master Cohmac.

"This wasn't here last time I visited," he said. "And yes, it is quite impressive."

"Welcome back to the Temple, Jedi," said a Devaronian Jedi with a light dusting of powder-white fur and a smattering of freckles. Her steps as she approached were so light she seemed to float. "I see you have noticed our newest addition to the entry, a gift from the Republic for the Jedi's assistance during the disaster last year."

"Yes," Vernestra said. "It's beautiful."

"It is. It truly evokes the duality of the Force, does it not?" the Temple guide replied.

"Who made it?" Master Cohmac asked.

The Devaronian pointed back toward the artwork. "This tapestry was made over two hundred years ago by the famous Jedi artist Sherche La Plenn, an Ubdurian who served as the first marshal in the temple on Sag Kemper. This fine piece was thought lost to history, but we are fortunate to have it with us once more."

"Interesting. Thank you for that bit of information," Master Cohmac said without a hint of sarcasm.

"Of course. Enjoy your visit, and may the Force be with you," she said before moving away to greet other Jedi entering the Temple.

Vernestra and Cohmac made their way through the hallways, strolling past Master Jedi debating some issue loudly, and dodging a class of younglings running through the hallway, laughing and playing some game only they knew the rules to. They stopped before the bank of lifts, and Cohmac pointed to the last one.

"That one will take you to the level used by the Council,"

he said. "I'm afraid my appointment lies in another part of the building."

"Well then, thank you again for the ride to Coruscant," Vernestra said with a grin. "And maybe next time you can let me fly a little."

Master Cohmac chuckled low in his throat. "Not a chance. Give Stellan my best, and ask him about the first time he flew a Vector by himself."

Master Cohmac left, and Vernestra entered the lift, the only one with a Temple Guard, who stood masked near the panel of buttons.

"Who are you going to see?" he asked, his voice a deep rumble.

"Stellan Gios."

He punched a few buttons. As the car began to rise, Vernestra bounced on her toes, excited to once again see her mentor. The last time they'd met had been in the midst of the fighting on Valo, and there had been precious little time for niceties then. She had so much to talk to him about.

Vernestra exited the lift into a hallway crowded with Jedi, Republic officials, and droids going about their daily tasks. It was daunting, and she stood in the middle of the hallway for a moment just trying to figure out which way to walk.

"You are lost," came a familiar voice, and Vernestra turned around to see Master Yaddle walking toward her with a group of very serious-looking younglings in tow. The green-skinned Jedi was no taller than the little ones with her, barely reaching Vernestra's waist. The sight of the younglings made Vernestra's heart melt. Had she ever been that small?

"Master Yaddle! How are you? I thought you were still on sabbatical on Kronk!"

"I have returned, for a moment at least." The Jedi's long brown hair was braided as usual, and she wore the same gold-and-white temple robes as Vernestra. "I missed my time with the younglings. I have heard great rumblings of your deeds, Vernestra Rwoh."

"Thank you, Master Yaddle. I hope I am living your teachings."

The older Jedi chuckled as though Vernestra had said something funny, although she didn't know what. Master Yaddle rested a hand on Vernestra's arm, her green-gold eyes boring into Vernestra's. "Do not reject your instincts, Jedi. Understood?"

A shiver of premonition ran down Vernestra's arm. "Yes, Master."

Just as quickly, Master Yaddle straightened. "Looking for Stellan?"

"Yes. Could you tell me which office is his?"

"On the left, last one. Be well, Vernestra Rwoh."

Master Yaddle left, returning to her lecture about the responsibilities of the Jedi in a changing galaxy, and

Vernestra walked in the opposite direction to the door the older Jedi had indicated.

The door slid open even before Vernestra reached it, and a tall, dark-skinned human male with kind eyes exited, Vernestra's former master a familiar figure at his side. "Please keep me apprised of what you uncover. Your Republic liaison will be . . . difficult. Keep the larger mission in mind," Vernestra's former master said, his voice low.

"Master Stellan!" Vernestra said, perhaps a bit too loudly. But there was something about Stellan's meeting that felt a bit clandestine, and she didn't want to seem like she was eavesdropping. Most cultures she'd come across found that to be rude.

Master Stellan frowned in Vernestra's direction before his face broke into a genuine grin as he recognized her. "Well, I see you've finally made your way across the galaxy." He waved Vernestra over. "Emerick, do you know Vernestra Rwoh, my favorite former Padawan?"

The man smiled warmly at Vernestra as a calm feeling came over her. It was as though she'd known the man her entire life, and she had the strangest urge to tell him her life story before she realized that he was causing the feeling.

"Emerick Caphtor. Pleasure to meet you," the dark-skinned man said. "Stellan has spoken at length of your accomplishments, and I hope we get to work together one day so that I can see you duel. I have heard your style is quite unique."

"Ah, not so different from Master Yoda's. But nowhere near as proficient," she said, laughing. Master Yoda's dueling style was one she admired and wanted to one day emulate, but it would take much more practice before she got there. "But I am always looking for a new challenger, so I hope we get the chance to meet in the practice ring one day." Vernestra felt a little flustered; praise always did that to her. But knowing that Master Stellan spoke highly of her made her feel centered and calm.

With another nod at Stellan, Emerick Caphtor took his leave, and Vernestra found herself intensely curious about the man. Why was he meeting with Master Stellan, anyway?

"Well, I'd expected you a bit earlier," Stellan said, indicating that Vernestra should enter his office. It was like most rooms in the Temple, spartan and utilitarian, with a number of circular seating pads and a datapad placed on a nearby table. The room was just as she remembered it from the last time she had been on Coruscant, when the office had belonged to Rana Kant, Stellan's former master. Coming to visit Stellan now, in the same space, gave Vernestra a peculiar feeling of traveling in a repeating pattern, not moving forward but occupying the same spaces over and over again.

This time, however, Stellan sat on one of the meditation pads and indicated that Vernestra should take the one directly across from him. Vernestra settled onto the disk before answering Stellan's implied question.

"We were waylaid by a call for help from Tiikae. They

had an issue with some Nihil and we were nearby, so we gave them our assistance."

Stellan nodded. "I'm glad you were in the area. You were traveling with Master Cohmac, then? The Council is expecting him, as well."

"Ah, yes," Vernestra said, her face heating. "There was a, um, lack of ships."

Stellan laughed, a belly-deep sound. "Are you sure it isn't because someone keeps wrecking them?"

Vernestra groaned. "It's a terrible reputation. And only a little bit true."

"Avar may have called me again after you left to complain about losing a competent Jedi as she prepares to launch her own offensive. And she might have mentioned that my former Padawan was as bad a pilot as I once was." He smiled ruefully. "Don't worry, Vernestra, you'll get better. One of the challenges of becoming a Knight so soon is sometimes certain things take longer to master than others. Have patience with yourself."

"Are you speaking from experience? I've heard that you have your own legend involving a Vector, according to Master Cohmac."

Stellan let out a single bark of laughter. "That Jedi remembers far too much," he said, eyes going misty with some long-ago memory. "But, either way, that is quite the tale and definitely one for when we have more time."

Vernestra nodded. "I am glad you spoke to Master Avar.

And I hope the Council is heeding her warnings about the Nihil. If they are not stopped sooner than later I'm afraid they will find a way to tear the galaxy apart."

Master Stellan nodded. "I agree. But here on Coruscant the issue of the Nihil is a very fraught one. Half of the Senate think the Nihil should be destroyed by the Order, and the rest think the Nihil are the frontier's problem and the matter should be left to the local planets affected. A number of planets have sent troops to help, but with Chancellor Soh still recovering, it has been difficult to mobilize some of the reluctant senators, even if they agree that the Nihil must be stopped."

Vernestra wanted to prevent the Nihil from taking any more lives and had no trouble helping out. But it couldn't only be the Jedi fighting against the scourge. It sounded as though the Republic was more interested in debating the matter than stopping the danger stalking their hyperspace lanes.

Vernestra realized that she really didn't like politics. How exhausting to fight about the how when everyone already agreed a matter needed to be handled.

"Either way, you should be aware that there are still ongoing discussions. So far the Council has agreed something must be done to remove the threat, but I'm afraid we're still a bit split on what that should look like, even though we all agree our piecemeal response needs to be more cohesive. Which is why I called you," Stellan said.

Vernestra forgot about the troubling idea of the Jedi fighting a war on behalf of the Republic and perked up. "You have a secret mission for me?"

Stellan shook his head. "Settle down, it's just a diplomatic assignment. Senator Ghirra Starros asked you to accompany a very influential member of the Graf family to the Berenge sector. According to the Grafs, the Nihil might have some experimental tech that they're testing, and your task is to go out there and verify that it's not some sort of hyperspace anomaly."

"Why would they need a Jedi for that? That sounds like work for a scientist." Vernestra tried not to be disappointed, but she was. She'd traveled all the way to Coruscant for—as people on Haileap called it—a boondoggle: an assignment that was nothing but a waste of time.

Stellan frowned. "Have you not been testing your abilities in hyperspace like we discussed? I thought you would be a good fit for this detail because of your affinity for hyperspace."

Vernestra squirmed a bit in her chair. "I told you, that was just a fluke." She didn't want to tell Stellan about her recent vision, because he would make more of it than it was, especially if she told him that this time it had come true, that she had seen something real and definable, not only impressions of places she'd never been. Master Stellan had always thought highly of her, but sometimes his expectations were difficult to meet, and even though Vernestra was no longer his Padawan learner, she still didn't want to disappoint him.

Stellan sat up a bit straighter and gave Vernestra a searching look. "I have never known another Jedi to be able to navigate using only the Force in hyperspace. And I know you deny that was what was happening, but I am not convinced. Your strange visions could be a precursor to such a rare ability. You know, there is talk that in ancient times the Jedi were the first to jump to hyperspace and they did it using only the Force."

Vernestra couldn't help laughing. "Stellan! That's a youngling's tale! Next you'll tell me that the Sith were able to become immortal by drinking the blood of babies." Vernestra stood, shaking her head. "I may have passed my trials early, but I'm not special. I'll go along on this trip. Maybe Imri will enjoy traveling to a nearly empty sector of the galaxy. It's not like we'd be of more use fighting the Nihil with Master Avar back on Starlight." Her tone was bitter, and she regretted the words as soon as they were out.

"Hey!" Stellan said, climbing to his feet. "This is a serious assignment, Vernestra. You should treat it as such. Also, head over to the senator's office right after this. She's expecting you, and I'm counting on you to demonstrate the quality of the Order's youngest Knights."

Vernestra took a deep breath, centering herself. She was annoyed. She couldn't help it. Here she was, thinking she was getting a real mission, something important, and she was being sent to do the same kind of Padawan busywork

Stellan had given her once upon a time. And here he was bringing up her weird hyperspace experiences just like in the old days. The feeling of being stuck rose up once more, but Vernestra swallowed it with the rest of her frustration.

"I will, Master Stellan. I'll report back to you when I return."

"That's more like it," Stellan said with a kind smile. "And maybe try practicing those exercises when you're in hyperspace. Consider it a favor to me. Now, was there something else you wanted to discuss with me? I keep getting the feeling there's something you're not telling me."

Vernestra froze as she remembered her conversation with Master Avar. It wasn't just her hyperspace vision that she was keeping from Master Stellan. She'd wanted to show him her lightsaber whip on Valo, but there had been no time as they headed into battle. She'd planned on showing him her modifications the next time they met, but Avar's warning loomed in her memory, and she found that telling her former master about the changes made to her lightsaber seemed like a much bigger thing than it once had.

Vernestra suddenly remembered the strange cube in her belt pouch. "Oh! I almost forgot." She pulled out the cube and held it up so Stellan could see. Better to show him this than her lightwhip or to bring up her strange vision. "Do you know what this is?"

He took it from her, turning the box in his hands. "Where did you find it?"

"On one of the Nihil who was attacking Tiikae. I think they might have been sent there to retrieve it. There was also a holo from a Nihil that Padawan Reath Silas dealt with, threatening violence if the cube wasn't returned."

Stellan glanced at Vernestra before turning his attention back to the box. Vernestra couldn't quite read the expression on his face, and she was a bit sorry she had even shown the box to Stellan. Did he feel this was beneath his notice? Was this something she shouldn't have shared with him? It seemed important since the Nihil had wanted it, but she could be wrong, and she hated to waste Master Stellan's time. It was very possible he saw such matters as trivial, now that he was on the High Council.

Vernestra had a strange sense of knowing and not knowing the man standing before her. The Stellan she had known as a Padawan had been thoughtful and approachable. This Stellan wore his mantle of office like it was a burden. As he studied the puzzle box, she took in the dark circles under Stellan's eyes and the fact that his tunic hung on him looser than usual, an indicator of lost weight. "Master Stellan, are you well?"

Stellan startled from his perusal of the puzzle box and gave her a wan smile. "I have been better, that is for certain. But don't worry, I am well." He handed the cube back to Vernestra. "That looks like an old-fashioned puzzle cube. They used to be popular, perhaps a hundred or so years ago?

The puzzle was usually solved by entering a phrase, and inside was either a melody or a holo that would play as a reward."

Vernestra nodded. "That is what Master Cohmac thought it might be."

Stellan probed at the puzzle where it lay in Vernestra's hand, but even though he touched the outside in a number of different ways, the cube did not respond. "Every time these puzzle cubes were solved, they would reconfigure themselves. Most of the puzzles had a number of answers, but I don't understand these sigils. Wait." Stellan took the box from Vernestra's hand and turned it over before placing it back in her palm. He pointed to a glyph that looked like an arrow with multiple tips. "I think this is an old prospector symbol. I saw images like it when I visited the temple on Hon-Tallos."

"Prospectors?" Vernestra asked. She placed the puzzle box back into her belt pouch.

"Hyperspace prospectors. Hmmm, you should go by the Senate offices and ask to speak to Professor Wolk. The old Gungan was brought in as a consultant to analyze the Nihil actions on Valo. He might know how to decipher this. If my memory serves, he was boasting about interviewing a few of those old-timers before they passed on."

Vernestra nodded. "I suppose it's on my way. Thank you, Master Stellan."

"May the Force be with you, Vernestra," he said, stifling a yawn. "And give those old exercises a try. Don't be afraid of what you might be capable of. We have learned in the past year that there is much we still don't know about hyperspace."

Vernestra left Master Stellan's office without another word, but she knew she wouldn't be trying anymore hyperspace Force nonsense—not now, not ever. The events on Tiikae had been unavoidable, but whatever the voice wanted would have to wait. She didn't have any time for side quests. And there was no way she was going to practice those silly hyperspace navigation exercises Stellan loved. That was something she had indulged as a Padawan, but no more. She was already unsettled enough from the most recent vision. What if his exercises just provoked more to appear?

Some things were best left in the past.

SIXTEEN

Syl woke feeling angry. When she was a kid the same thing used to happen, especially if her mother sent her to bed before she was ready.

"You're more tenacious with a grudge than a Solubrian jungler with a bone," Chancey Yarrow used to tease, finding Syl's temper charming. Now the memory came back to Syl and she rolled over in bed angrily, pulling the covers over her head to block out the light streaming in through the frosted glass of the window.

Xylan Graf's window.

Syl flopped onto her back and let loose the angry tears she'd managed to hide the night before. After Professor Wolk had shown Syl a few flickering holos he'd brought—all of Chancey Yarrow giving some lecture while wearing clothing cut in the square lines of military garb and nothing like the flowing dresses Syl remembered—he'd finally accepted that Syl knew nothing of her mother's past. Nor was she a hyperspace genius pretending stupidity.

She was just a girl with a dead mother who might have been a secret evil genius.

That premise would've been hard to swallow in any of the holo adventures Syl loved, but in her own life it was downright unbelievable. Chancey Yarrow had not been a hyperspace genius, positing theories that made her colleagues jealous in their complexity. The Gungan had to have been lying. Syl had heard of droids who could doctor holos. At least, maybe. It was possible she was making that up.

Syl rolled over onto her stomach and pulled the pillow onto her head. She wanted to believe the Gungan had been a hired actor, that this was all some elaborate scheme cooked up by Xylan Graf to . . . what? What did she have that a Graf would want? The Grafs were rich enough to fund a project as massive as Starlight Beacon. Sylvestri Yarrow was an insignificant pilot with a pile of debt and a crappy ship, a ship that had been stolen and was in the hands of the Nihil. There was no reason for Xylan to have been lying to her. He'd been quiet throughout the entire affair, not even commenting when she'd drank all his wine without so much as a thank-you.

Syl knew it was true, every single word the Gungan professor had said. The problem was that she didn't know how to fit that knowledge, that huge piece of her mother that she'd never known, into the memory of the woman she'd mourned for months.

But the more she turned it over in her mind, the more she played with the possibilities, the more the strangeness of the Berenge sector made sense. Of course someone had built a gravity-well projector to kick ships out of hyperspace. What else could it have been? And one of those people had most likely been her mother, because why else hadn't the Nihil attacked and killed her and the rest of the crew as they escaped? The Nihil weren't known for being strategic or kind, so why had it been so easy to escape? Obviously because they had let her.

Syl laughed to herself. She was going insane. Was she actually considering that her mother could be alive, working with the Nihil in a deserted sector of the galaxy?

No, she wasn't. She could never believe her mother capable of such a thing. What else could she do in light of all the evidence Wolk had shown her? Either Syl's mother was dead or Chancey Yarrow was being held hostage, forced to work for the Nihil. Those were the only logical explanations, even taking into account Wolk's theories. He didn't know Chancey like Syl did; he hadn't lived years and years with her, scraping by, learning how to be a hauler, and fighting for his life.

And hoping that Chancey Yarrow was still alive was too much for Syl. Her mother was dead, and entertaining any other kind of outcome was silly. Syl had to focus on surviving and on her next steps. After all, Neeto and M-227 were counting on her.

The door chimed before sliding open, and a droid trundled in. "I have brought the morning meal," it said, carrying a tray laden with a number of delicacies and a very noticeable packet of painkillers. "Master Xylan would like you to dress and join him at your earliest convenience. The wardrobe contains clothing created based on your measurements and should accommodate your form nicely. And please make haste. You have an early-morning appointment."

The droid set the tray on a nearby table before departing, and Syl climbed from the bed reluctantly. There was nothing about the day that she was going to enjoy, but at least Xylan had been considerate enough to figure that she would have a headache. She had imbibed—no, guzzled furiously would be a better descriptor—far too much of the blue wine for the morning to be her friend.

Syl took the pain meds, which fizzled on her tongue, before digging into the breakfast of fruits and cheeses. There was a meat-filled pastry, which she avoided, as she always felt intensely guilty after eating any kind of meat, but luckily the flaky roll she broke open had no animal flesh hidden inside. She thought that she should tell Xylan she wasn't fond of meat, but then immediately thought that was presumptuous of her. How long was she going to take advantage of his hospitality?

Syl sighed. It was time to leave Coruscant. There was just nothing more she could do there. She would make a call to Neeto and let him know she was returning to Port Haileap shortly, and that it might take her a while to find a ride. She was a competent pilot and a halfway-decent fighter. Surely she could hire on to some hauler going to the frontier?

Syl finished breaking her fast and went to the wardrobe to see what the droid had referred to. Inside was a small army of dresses, all extra flouncy and complicated looking, with straps and fasteners and entirely too much sparkle. Syl slowly slid the door closed once more. Where exactly were they going?

Xylan had said something the night before about aiding him in . . . what? The memory was fuzzy—definitely too many revelations for one evening—and she realized that even though the droid had spoken like Syl knew exactly what was on the day's agenda, she had no clue what Xylan had planned. She would have to find him and ask. But not in any of those outfits. She'd had enough of changing for Coruscant. She was going to start doing things her way.

Syl ate one more roll, jumped into the shower, and got dressed in her one change of clothing. Then she grabbed a cheese pastry, wrapped it in a napkin, and stuffed it in her pocket before going to find Xylan. You never knew when you'd need a snack.

The room where Syl had slept was at the end of a long hallway that led out to a sitting area. A strange floral scent tickled Syl's nose as she walked, making her homesick for the scent of joint oil and burned elasta bun that would've greeted her on a trip through the *Switchback*. Her work boots sank into the plush carpet, and the reminder that she was completely out of her depth made Syl square her shoulders as she strode into the room. Just because she was uncomfortable didn't mean she had to show it.

Xylan stood talking to Basha in low tones in the middle of the room, his arms crossed and his expression concerned as the Gigoran related something in quiet words through her vocalizer. When his eyes lit on Syl, his worried expression melted into one of happiness, and the look took Syl aback. No one had been so happy to see her in a very long while, and the resulting emotion was far more unsettling than Xylan's casual wealth.

But Syl didn't have long to worry about the feeling, because Xylan's happy expression quickly melted into a frown of dismay.

"Sylvestri, what are you wearing?" Xylan asked, and Syl blinked for a moment at the question.

"I—I'm wearing my clothes," Syl said, looking down at her utilitarian blue mechanic's coveralls. She'd also strapped on her backpack holster for her blaster, even though Basha had taken the weapon when they left the hotel the day before and Syl hadn't seen it since.

"You're going to wear coveralls to visit the Galactic Senate?" Xylan asked incredulously. "To meet a sitting senator?"

Syl shrugged. She'd forgotten that was where they were going, but that definitely explained the parade of dresses in the wardrobe. It didn't much matter what the day's plan was. She was comfortable. "These are the only clean clothes I have."

"I had appropriate outfits made for you last night. They were in your closet," Xylan said, speaking slowly as if she were a child.

"I prefer my own clothes, thanks," Syl said with a tight smile. "Besides, I think you're fancy enough for both of us." He wore a sleeveless sheath tunic in a swirled pattern of blue and green that hugged his torso before flaring out around his hips. Matching trousers, also fitted, ended at his knees. The better to show off the knee-high silver boots he wore.

He was, to put it kindly, a spectacle.

"Those were very nice dresses," he began, but Syl raised her hand to cut him off.

"Xylan, you have been more than generous, but I think I'm at the point where I doubt I can in any way pay back your hospitality. You were kind to me because you thought I could help you in the search for my mother, or that I knew something, but I don't. I'm afraid I'm not nearly as useful as you thought I would be. And I have to be honest, I was hoping I could turn your kindness to my advantage by talking you out of a ship, but I don't think that's going to happen now. So, I think it's probably for the best if I grab Beti and try to find myself a trip back to Port Haileap," Syl said, taking a deep breath.

"Absolutely not," Xylan said. "Did you not see how you completely flattened Professor Wolk yesterday? Your presence has been absolutely worth it."

Syl blinked. "I remember thoroughly disappointing the professor."

Xylan's eyes lit with excitement. "Yes, you completely blinkered his theory that you were a Nihil operative sent here to lure the Republic into a trap."

Syl frowned. "I don't follow."

Xylan grinned. "Professor Wolk is no ally of mine. He is a blockade. My family has been campaigning within the Senate to have the Berenge sector set aside for some hyperspace experiments since we have been tracking the anomaly there. The original lease was held by the San Tekkas, but since they've had a rash of bad luck with their investments, they relinquished the rights years ago. It is exactly what my family needs: a vast, unoccupied area of space. The Republic was agreeable at first, but the lease has been put on hold pending Wolk's silliness about a potential Nihil weapon. And foremost among those listening to Wolk is Senator Starros. She blocked our application, based on Wolk's theory that there must be some sort of hyperspace weapon operating in that part of space."

"You don't think there's a weapon?" Syl asked, thinking of the holo and the ridiculous story he'd told her that first night in the tavern. "What about your missing ships?"

"Ah, that." Xylan looked rueful for a moment before shrugging. "A bit of theatre, I'm afraid. I wanted to test you before I introduced you to Wolk, on the off chance that you were a Nihil operative sent to Coruscant to gather intel."

Syl's anger was swift and quick. "The Nihil killed my mother. I would never align myself with them in any way."

Xylan waved dismissively. "Of course not. And there obviously isn't a weapon. That is just one of Wolk's wild flights of fancy. My holo simply showed a regular Nihil attack. But if you were a Nihil operative, then your reaction to the video would not have been so utterly disgusted. An actress, you are not."

Syl grimaced. "I'm glad I could be useful."

"Oh, immensely. And having you say basically the same thing to Wolk was very convincing. So I now need you to bring that same energy to Senator Starros. If she agrees to go along with us, then I will ensure that you are repaid. Handsomely."

A bitter taste filled Syl's mouth. This was the kind of politicking that kept simple folks away from Coruscant, and here was Syl smack-dab in the middle of it all. She hadn't ever really trusted Xylan Graf, but she was standing in his living quarters after eating food he'd provided, all because it made her life a little easier.

"So, Professor Wolk lied?" Syl asked quietly, changing the subject while she gathered her rushing thoughts. How could she make this situation work for her?

"Oh no, he believes everything he said, the old fool. Do you understand the level of resources required to build the kind of machine he's saying the Nihil have built? An artificial gravity well? Or rather, a gravity-well projector? It's ludicrous. But since Wolk has the ear of Senator Starros I had to prove to him that his theory was complete bantha fodder. And you were the perfect way to do that."

Syl felt like puking, her breakfast suddenly uneasy in her stomach. But she crossed her arms and stared at Xylan Graf, hoping her expression revealed none of her outrage. "So, I help you convince the senator that Wolk is a few bolts short of a droid. What's in it for me?"

Xylan smiled, this one genuine judging from the flash of a rarely seen dimple under his dusting of facial hair. "As the daughter of Chancey Yarrow you are in the peculiar position of being able to refute Wolk's claims. You saw your mother die, and you can help me convince Senator Starros that the old Gungan is chasing shadows. If you can help me get the sector lease, I will clear your debts and make sure you leave Coruscant in your own ship with a line of Graf credit for the next year."

Syl's heart did a painful double thump. "You're serious."

"Indeed," Xylan said. He'd stopped with the false kindness that had colored his face the past couple of days. His eyes glittered, and he stared at Syl as though she were one more thing to be bought and sold, just another good on the open market.

And in a way, she was. But at least he was being honest with her now.

Too bad he wanted her to lie.

"If Wolk is wrong, why did my ship get ejected from hyperspace?" Syl asked. "I can tell this senator of yours that my mother is definitely dead, but that doesn't really change the fact that when everything happened the Nihil were right there to play welcoming party."

"A simple error of your faulty hyperspace engine. Did you not tell me that your ship was basically on its last thruster? It seems fairly logical that your ship malfunctioned and the Nihil just happened to be there to take advantage of your woe."

Syl scowled. That seemed far-fetched and highly unlikely. And lying to a senator about the possibility of a Nihil threat was the opposite of why she'd come to Coruscant. But Xylan was offering her a life-changing amount of money. The ship alone would be worth more money than she'd seen in her life, and the line of credit besides? Syl gnawed on her lip as she weighed Xylan's offer against her conscience.

Turned out even her better nature had a price.

"Fine. But I want Beti back, and I want you to send ten thousand credits to my friends in Port Haileap by the end of the day as a show of good faith." It was a king's ransom, and Graf didn't even blink.

"Done. And in exchange, you will accompany us on a trip to the Berenge sector as our pilot."

Syl frowned. "Why do we need to go to the Berenge sector?"

Xylan sighed heavily. "It's likely to be part of Senator Starros's list of conditions. She'll want verification that Wolk's theories are untrue, so that will require a complete evaluation of the sector. I plan on offering to send a crew to visually inspect the sector rather than relying on droids, since she's already rejected that data once before. We'll need to most likely accommodate Wolk coming with us, along with whoever Starros designates as her representative."

"Good. I want to speak with Wolk again," Syl said. Her decision to lie to a senator she'd never met already rubbed at her, and maybe another conversation with Professor Wolk would alleviate some of the apprehension she felt.

"That shouldn't be a problem. He's a silly old Gungan who has nothing but time on his hands," Xylan said, waving dismissively. But Syl knew Xylan Graf well enough to know that the man was lying about something, that there was something he wasn't telling her. He'd agreed to give up those credits too easily, regardless of how rich he was. He wouldn't see something like Syl lying as worth such a high price.

But if he was willing to pay so much for the pleasure of Syl's dubious company, she wasn't sure she cared all that much. If his family wanted control over the Berenge sector, so be it. She'd tried going about things the honest way; maybe it was time to try other methods. As long as she could care for her crew, that was the most important part. Anything beyond that was just details.

"Do we have a deal?" Xylan asked.

Syl flushed with excitement. Her own ship. And the Graf name backing any venture she decided to take on for a year. It was the answer she'd been looking for not all that long before, and here it was falling right into her lap.

So why did she feel like she was getting played?

"Deal," Syl said, pushing the niggling uneasiness away. She might not like Xylan Graf or his family's reputation, and she might not like the idea of lying, but his credits spent just like anyone else's, and he seemed more generous with them than anyone else she'd met. She and Xylan shook on the agreement, like they did on the frontier, and he adjusted his clothing.

"And to be clear, we could have settled this last night after Wolk took his leave, but it felt cruel to try to negotiate with you after you'd drank so much Toniray."

"If it makes you feel any better, I'm never drinking any of that blue wine again."

Xylan chuckled, picking up a silver cape from a nearby chair and tossing it across his shoulders with a flourish. "Well then, let us be off. We've already kept Senator Starros waiting. Basha, would you please fetch Sylvestri's blaster?"

Xylan strode toward the lift, and Syl followed. She should

have been happy. She should have felt excited that she was getting exactly what she wanted from Xylan Graf.

Instead all she could think was that nothing so easy ever turned out well.

SEVENTEEN

Nan stood in the control room of the Gravity's Heart and fumed. The Strikes she'd sent to Tiikae had one job. Just one. And they had botched it terribly.

"It was a family of Ugnaughts," Nan said, smoothing her dark hair behind her ears. "How hard could it have been?"

"There were Jedi," cried out the Weequay who had led the mission. He was small of stature and had a way of clicking his teeth as he spoke that set Nan's already frayed nerves on edge.

"Jedi can die just like anyone else," Nan snarled. "How is it you survived when the rest of your Strike is now carrion on Tiikae? Where is your sense of courage?" She was taking her fear out on the lone survivor of the Strike, and for good reason. At some point she and the Oracle would return to the *Gaze Electric*, once they'd finished their work on the Gravity's Heart, and when she did, what would she tell Marchion Ro about his missing box? That she'd lost it? That she'd been distracted and a family of Ugnaughts had snuck onto the *Whisperkill* and robbed her? And now they were all dead and she had nothing to show for it. She looked weak and stupid, and she was neither.

Nan drew her blaster and shot the Weequay in the chest. He fell over, and as she holstered her weapon, she turned on her heel and strode into the laboratory where the Oracle was being kept.

There the scientist, Chancey Yarrow, stood with a small tablet, speaking to the Oracle in a low voice. As far as Nan could tell, the elderly woman was still unconscious, but the scientist, a dark-skinned human woman with long hair twisted into a multitude of tiny braids, laughed before patting the tank, as though the two were in the middle of a conversation. The woman was like no Nihil Nan had ever met. She wore billowy, free-flowing dresses that seemed better suited to a farming community than to raiding, and she was barefoot, her feet tattooed in a swirling pattern that meant nothing to Nan. The woman seemed younger than she was, and her conversations with the mostly dead Oracle made Nan more than a little nervous. She was one of those people Nan had trouble reading, and the younger girl decided she disliked the scientist on principle alone.

When the older woman turned and saw Nan, her mirth faded away. The dislike was mutual.

"Did I just hear a blaster?" Chancey Yarrow asked.

"Yes. The Strike returned, without the item I sent them after," Nan said.

"So, you shot one of my people without asking me and without my permission?" the woman asked, her eyes still on her tablet.

Nan shrugged and knew immediately that she'd made a mistake. One moment she was opening her mouth to tell the scientist that she was a Nihil and she did as she pleased, and the next she was flat on her back, the woman's bare foot pressing into her windpipe.

"You do not kill my people. You might be Marchion Ro's pet, but this is my domain, and next time you raise your hand or a blaster against any of my people, your life will be forfeit. Am I understood?"

Nan nodded and gurgled out what assent she could. The scientist moved away immediately, and Nan sat up, coughing wetly, her throat already beginning to ache. She was going to have a marvelous bruise, but it was worth it. She now knew more about the scientist than she had a moment before, and sometimes the price paid for information was steep.

She wouldn't make the same mistake again though.

"Get up and find something to make yourself useful," Chancey said, going to one of the navicomputers lining the walls and making some kind of note. As far as Nan could tell, the entire room was laden with the machines, and there were even a couple of navidroids toddling about. Why did they need so many navicomputers? It wasn't like they were flying the hunk of junk anywhere.

"My job is to watch the Oracle," Nan said, her voice raspier than she liked. She swallowed dryly.

"The Oracle. That's what you call her? How funny," the scientist said, even though she didn't laugh.

"Why is that funny?" Nan said, moving to sit in the chair she'd brought to the room earlier for her guard shifts. She and the doctor had agreed to alternate shifts caring for the old woman, which mostly meant that Nan sat and watched as the crone slept in her strange pod.

"She's no oracle. She's the legendary Mari San Tekka. I'd thought Lourna was teasing me when she said that Ro had a hyperspace savant as his prisoner, but now, after seeing her? I have no doubt that's who she is. No one else could do what she does. Not even a room full of Siniteens."

"Mari San Tekka?" Nan asked, looking at the wizened old woman. "Like, as in Joral San Tekka?"

"Same, although what relation she is to him, I'm not certain. Here, there's a holo about the girl. It's at least a hundred years old. It's from right after she went missing."

There was a holo unit in the corner, and the scientist pressed a button on the side and it flickered to life.

"The San Tekka family beseeches all those who can hear and see this broadcast to assist them in finding their lost child. They ask that their youngest daughter, Mari, be returned without incident," the announcer droid said in a low, halting voice. An image of a laughing young girl flashed on the screen, and Nan found it difficult to consider that the crone and the girl in the holo were one and the same. "Her loss is a misery to all those who knew the child."

The holo began to repeat, and Chancey switched the set off. "Mari San Tekka's disappearance was one of the greatest mysteries of a hundred years ago. This was after the Hyperspace Rush, when hyperspace in the outer regions was not nearly as well mapped as it is now. The San Tekkas had always been a bit hardscrabble, but they suddenly ran into a bit of luck, mapping new routes through places like the Relgim Run and the Bitmus Cloud, high-value routes. The Graf family, their competitors, hired an information broker to find out their secret, and it was her," Chancey Yarrow said, pointing at the pod. "That woman has an ability to see all of the possible routes through hyperspace, time and location phased. Do you know how impossibly rare that is? Her brain is the equivalent of nearly ten thousand navicomputers, all working together. At least."

"You're telling me no one in the galaxy can do what she

can do?" Nan said, giving the Oracle's pod a sidelong glance.

"Not in hundreds of years. There are some ancient texts that reference it being a trick of the Jedi and their long-gone enemies the Sith, but who knows what is true and what is fable." Chancey shook her head, a slight smile on her face. "Most thought her family faked her disappearance to protect her, since there were a few attempts on her life shortly after rumors of her ability began to get out. But this? The San Tekkas would spare no expense to destroy the Nihil if they knew that all this time their Mari had been here, being held prisoner."

The woman tapped her lips, pursing them as she thought. "You know, I think I am going to have to rethink you and that doctor's role here on my *Heart*. There is really no telling just why Marchion Ro sent you."

Nan knew that the Gravity's Heart was Lourna's, not this scientist's, but that didn't mean the woman couldn't make Nan's life miserable. The woman went to a call button, and a set of large human men, both heavily muscled and wearing the garb of Lourna Dee's Tempest, walked into the room.

"I need to have Mari's keeper given new, more secure quarters. And find the Chadra-Fan and ensure that he is similarly restricted. We must assume that they are all a direct threat to my work here."

The men nodded, and one walked over to grab Nan by her upper arm and drag her from the room. Just that quickly she'd gone from a respected member of the Nihil to a prisoner.

Chancey Yarrow went back to her work, and as she was dragged out, the wheels in Nan's head began to spin. She was loyal to Ro, but that didn't seem to be an asset here. Besides, she had every reason to fear him now. She had seen him kill others for lesser offenses than a lost valuable, and blaming the doctor would get her nowhere. There was no way she could go back, not without the cube and not without the old woman, but maybe she could find another explanation for why the device was missing. It was just a stupid puzzle box, after all. And maybe, if the old woman died, there could be a good reason for that, as well.

Maybe this half-built weapon wasn't quite as stable as it looked.

Nan began to formulate a plan, one that would cover her mistakes and help her hedge her bets. Maybe even make her look like Ro's most valuable asset.

She was a survivor, after all.

She could definitely find a way to come out of this mess in one piece.

EIGHTEEN

Syl was pleasantly surprised to find that Senator Ghirra Starros of Hosnian Prime was completely and absolutely normal. During the airspeeder ride to the senator's office, a peculiar blend of excitement and fear had come over Syl, so that she began to worry she was going to embarrass herself when she actually met the senator. Perhaps it was Xylan's pointed comments about her attire, with Beti strapped across her back and under her coveralls, the way he kept giving her sidelong glances as though she were a wild bantha let loose in the civilized streets of Coruscant. Syl wasn't even sure Xylan truly wanted her to accompany him, despite his insistence that she was the puzzle piece he had been missing. Regardless, she would do what she had to in order to keep up her side of the bargain.

But when Xylan and Syl were escorted into Senator Starros's office—Basha opting to remain outside and guard the door because she didn't entirely trust the building's security, especially since they'd so easily overlooked Syl's blaster tucked under her coveralls—Syl found someone who looked much more like her than like Xylan. Senator Starros was a small woman who wore a plain, heavy robe in deepest green with a body-hugging underdress in a paler shade of green. Her only jewelry was a heavy bronze necklace with a medallion that sat just above her breasts. Her skin was deep brown like Syl's, but where Syl's wild curls were given free rein, Senator Starros's hair was knit into ropey locks that had been piled on top of her head. She wore no cosmetics that Syl could ascertain, not even a hint of lip tint, and the realization that the senator's beauty was completely unenhanced knocked Syl a bit off balance.

The woman was gorgeous, and if Syl's heart hadn't been so recently broken, she might have found herself with a bit of a crush.

Her emotional equilibrium was quickly put to rights when Senator Starros placed her hand on her heart and bowed a little. "Xylan Graf. I see you are still wasting my time with these visits. But at least you brought me someone worth speaking to today. Sylvestri Yarrow. I knew your mother, and you are her absolute image."

Syl returned the frontier greeting, hand over heart and half bow, before frowning. "Are you another hyperspace professor?" There had been enough revelations about Chancey Yarrow's past that whenever her mother was mentioned Syl felt herself tightening like a fist.

Senator Starros laughed, the sound surprisingly deep for such a small woman. "Oh no, your mother's work to open all the hyperspace lanes was directly in opposition to work I was doing with the San Tekka family," Senator Starros said with a rueful smile. "But even though your mother and I disagreed on the proper remuneration for hyperspace travel, I always respected her deeply."

"As did my mother and grandmother," Xylan said with a kind smile. "And Senator Starros, even though you are a San Tekka ally, please don't forget that your debt at the moment is to the Grafs. Without us, Starlight Beacon and your Dalnan treaty would be nothing but the hopes of a woman quickly falling out of favor."

"Xylan, I was negotiating deals on the Senate floor when you were still learning to walk. My agreeing to meet with you on this ridiculous matter of the Berenge sector is a kindness, and do not forget it. The lease should be set aside for academic purposes, not so your family has a bit of empty space to test your weapons, especially since we have no idea what they would do to the hyperspace lanes that route through there. Can you imagine the difficulty in rerouting all of the traffic that flows through that part of the galaxy? This seems like quite a lot of effort for one little sliver of space. But I suppose you are here yet again to convince me otherwise."

Senator Starros indicated that they should sit, and Syl collapsed into a nearby chair gratefully. This was nothing like what she'd thought it would be. Senator Starros clearly disliked Xylan Graf; her lip twisted every time she looked in his direction, and his own sneer of distaste made it clear that he returned the sentiment.

This was going to be much, much harder than Syl had expected. How was she supposed to lie to this woman? Especially since it seemed like the senator already had her mind quite clearly made up. And Syl couldn't blame her. Why go through so much trouble for this nothing sector of space? Surely there were other places where Xylan's family could conduct their experiments?

Once Xylan had settled onto his chair, Senator Starros took the chair that was obviously meant for her because it sat a bit higher than the rest in the sitting area. Syl wondered if that was a Hosnian custom or just Senator Starros and her pettiness.

"Ghirra, I again thank you for seeing us," Xylan said. "I know you are very busy pushing through bills that help your kin make money off of the most recent disaster. Congrats on the Valo Restoration contract going to one of your family's holding companies." His sarcasm was pointed and cruel, but he spoke like a man complimenting the décor. Syl sat a little straighter in her chair. She didn't want to miss a single barb.

Ghirra laughed, the sound melodious. "The Republic has come together beautifully in the light of the tragedy on Valo, and I am fortunate to have a number of highly skilled kin who won that contract through their own merit. But you didn't come here to discuss politics or my most recent bills in the Senate." A server droid bustled through the room with small cups of tea, and Syl was pleased to find the brew fruity and cool rather than astringent and hot. She sipped the tea while Xylan and Senator Starros spoke.

"You're correct," Xylan said with a chuckle, even though there was no humor in the words. "I am here once more to ask that you and your faction approve the lease to the Berenge sector, and I am now in a position to submit to your demands. Sylvestri is here as a sort of goodwill ambassador, to show that I am indeed taking Wolk seriously. If Chancey Yarrow's daughter does not think the woman is capable of building a weapon out in the middle of space, or that she's even alive, for that matter, then perhaps Wolk is seriously mistaken."

Senator Starros smiled, unfazed by Xylan's words. "I am busy. And yet you and your clan ask me increasingly for favors that do nothing but further your own agenda. The Senate just passed the bill that gave a five-year privacy clause to any new hyperspace lanes mapped by private companies, a bill your family were especially interested in seeing become law. That should keep the old tooka cat you call a grandmother off of my back for at least a fortnight, and you tell her I said as much when you relate my most recent rejection of your request."

Xylan waved away the senator's statement. "Pshaw. That bill was a waste of your time. It would have been better spent sending me a reply to my many calls. The Grafs have not undertaken prospecting in decades. The people who will benefit from such a law are dust chasers like the San Tekkas, which is why you really passed it." Xylan put his cup down on a nearby table and leaned forward. "I want your agreement that if I finance a crew to go out to the Berenge sector and record the readings while also surveying the area, and find no weapon, you will cease this silly exercise of blocking my request for the Berenge sector lease."

"And how do you aim to prove this weapon doesn't exist? Fly the entire sector, meter by meter?" Senator Starros scoffed.

Xylan tapped his chin as he considered the question. "A weapon like Wolk believes exists would have a distinct energy signature. My crew and I will survey the area, and if it turns out that the readings indicate a weapon of some sort, we will return to Coruscant immediately and share the information."

"You've done that already with your scout droids," the senator said, her expression bored. "I saw your earlier reports. There's no indication of any unusual activity." Ghirra picked up the delicate cup and sipped its contents thoughtfully. "But Wolk seemed to think that having the weapon powered down would lead to similar results."

"Perhaps, which is why I was so happy to make the acquaintance of our dear Sylvestri here. She confirmed she doesn't believe that her mother lives, let alone that she could be working with the Nihil. So much so that she has pledged her assistance in this matter. What I am asking, Senator, is an opportunity to prove to you once and for all that there is nothing in the Berenge sector. No Nihil, no deep-space anomaly, nothing. Sylvestri has agreed to go in order to clear her dearly departed mother's name, and I would love to invite Professor Wolk, as well. All I need from you, Senator, is an official letter of sanction."

Syl shifted in her seat at Xylan's lie. Only it wasn't a lie so much as a withholding of information. It was still enough to make Syl reevaluate her deal with Xylan, but the more Syl considered whether or not she should say something, the more she just sat there with her mouth shut. All she could think was that one day, when she was a successful hauler, she would look back on this moment and know keeping her mouth shut was the right thing for her to do.

What if Wolk is right, though? a little voice whispered in the back of Syl's mind. She ignored it.

Senator Starros climbed to her feet and walked over to the desk that dominated the back of the room, her expression thoughtful. Syl didn't understand why Xylan needed an official letter of sanction from the senator. Was that to keep her to her word?

"Will the letter of sanction get you your lease?" she whispered to Xylan.

"It will force me to adhere to whatever the official findings are, so yes, if Xylan happens to be correct," Senator Starros said. "Your proposal is interesting, Xylan. I can offer Wolk's assistance in studying the space, taking readings and whatnot. He's already asked me for dispensation to do something similar to what you are describing."

"So, then," Xylan said with a victorious smile, "we are in agreement. I will undertake this mission with Wolk and Sylvestri here, and you will endorse my family's request upon my return."

Syl looked from Xylan to Senator Starros. Things had gone exactly the way Xylan had said they would. She didn't quite believe it could be this easy.

"Not quite," Senator Starros said. "I need an unimpeachable observer. How do I know you won't bribe Wolk? Or what if he never makes it back?"

Xylan sighed heavily, not even taking offense at the senator's insinuation that he might try to have the old Gungan killed. "Ghirra, if you wanted to go along with me, you just had to ask."

"Don't flatter yourself. I was thinking something more along the lines of Jedi." Senator Starros pressed a button, and a door next to her desk slid open.

Syl climbed to her feet, watching openmouthed as a

Mirialan girl and a stout human boy entered the room. They both wore the tunics and tabards of the Jedi Order, and a feeling somewhere between awe and anger flowed through Syl.

What were the Jedi doing on Coruscant instead of out on the frontier fighting the Nihil? Everyone knew that the Jedi had powers far beyond anyone else, with their mysterious Force, not to mention plasma swords that could cut through just about anything and also repel blaster bolts. It seemed ridiculous that they should be here, waiting to help Xylan Graf claim rights to the Berenge sector rather than fighting back the Nihil.

Where had they been when the blasted pirates were stealing her ship? Where had they been when the Nihil murdered her mother?

Rich people really weren't like everyone else.

Syl blinked hard to keep back the angry tears that threatened to spring forth. She couldn't do this, not even for thousands of credits. She couldn't work so closely with people who reminded her of everything she'd lost. She couldn't.

Especially when they would easily see through her lies. Syl might be able to keep her mouth shut and convince the senator that Xylan Graf wasn't just a very pricey hustler, but there was no way she would be able to fool Jedi.

Not only that, but this was *exactly* why she had come to Coruscant! She finally had her audience, a senator and Jedi, who could do something about the strangeness she'd experienced in the Berenge sector. Was she really willing to sit there and say nothing, to secure her own future?

Not just mine, she thought. *I can't forget Neeto and M-227.*

Deep breaths. Syl took a breath, held it, and let it out. She wanted to run from the room, but instead she held her ground. She twisted her hands in her coveralls and counted her breaths the way her mother had taught her long before. She could do this. For Neeto and M-227 and her future, she could lie to Jedi.

A Jedi can only use their mind tricks on you if you're unwary. By focusing on your thoughts, by fortifying your mind against them, you can keep them out of your head. As long as you are strong and truthful with yourself, there is no reason to fear them. The memory came back, the way her mother had smiled at the Jedi standing outside of the temple on Tiikae, the way she'd always smiled at and spoken highly of the Jedi. Syl pushed that and all her emotions down, so deep down that she would never think of Tiikae again. Because it was entirely too close to the memory of the day Jordanna had dumped her.

She was done thinking about the past; it was time to turn toward the future.

Now was not the time for Syl to let her emotions run amok, so she breathed deeply and imagined the way the *Switchback* felt as it lifted off, the familiar jolt and swoop that had always filled her heart with joy. Soon she would have another ship that would feel even better. She imagined that new ship, and the modifications she would make with Graf credit available to her for a whole year. Anything to avoid the conflicted feelings that threatened to overwhelm her.

"So, you had Jedi waiting in the wings. You'd already planned on granting my request, and still you let me sit here and try to convince you of the logic of my proposal," Xylan said, a muscle flexing in his jaw. Syl could understand why Xylan was upset. Senator Starros had treated him to a large dose of his own medicine.

The senator completely ignored his vexation. "Xylan Graf, please meet Vern Rwoh and her Padawan, Imri Cantaros. They will provide security on your trip in case you run into trouble," Senator Starros said, her smile returning. It didn't warm Syl as it had before; now she knew it for the lie it was. Both Starros and Graf were vipers, and Syl just had to stay out of their way.

She actually felt a little sorry for the Jedi, because they both looked so young and guileless. They had no idea of the mess they'd happily walked into.

"Um, it's Vernestra," the Mirialan corrected, but no one bothered to acknowledge her words. The senator and Xylan's gazes were locked on each other, and then Xylan's jaw clenched as he looked at the Jedi and back at Senator Starros, his face flushing. Syl realized he was angry. But she couldn't understand why. The Jedi were negotiators and academics. Didn't he want someone to help him parse out whatever readings he got? Because it definitely wouldn't be Syl.

Or maybe that was the problem. He wouldn't be able to bribe Jedi the way he'd so easily convinced Syl to lie for him. Just what was out in the Berenge sector that the Graf family wanted? Syl couldn't believe that securing a place to conduct experiments was really their end game.

"We are most definitely not going to run into trouble, so why the Jedi? They're children!" Xylan said. "This is ridiculous even for you, Starros. You want to send me off with a spacey Gungan and children? I don't care if they are Jedi."

The Mirialan's expression flickered a bit at Xylan's insult. Syl could imagine just how she felt.

"I am a full Jedi Knight," she said, looking Xylan right in the eye. "Lord Graf—"

"Xylan," he corrected curtly.

"Xylan, trust me when I say that my Padawan and I are experienced in not only fighting the Nihil but providing security."

"Vern and Imri are the ones who managed to keep both my Avon and that Dalnan boy, Honesty Weft, safe when the Nihil destroyed the *Steady Wing* last year," Senator Starros said.

"We were also on Valo when the Nihil attacked," the Jedi, Vern, said, crossing her arms.

"Oh, you Jedi did a bang-up job on that one didn't you?" Syl said, suddenly annoyed at the haughty tone in the girl's voice. She was trying to keep her mouth shut and stay out of the argument, but something about the green girl was starting to irk her, especially since seeing the Jedi had stirred up fresh grief in a way Syl hadn't been expecting. Her loss was like that sometimes, whether it was the memory of Jordanna or her mother. She would be going along, living her life like always, and the next thing she knew she was angry and upset, the trigger something as benign as smelling the cookies her mother had loved or seeing a slim figure that reminded her of Jordanna.

But Syl's instant dislike of the Jedi girl was something different. Maybe it was the way she said every word in a low voice, like nothing ever ruffled her, the polar opposite of Syl. The girl appeared calm and self-possessed, everything that Syl, who had felt especially unmoored ever since arriving on Coruscant, was not. Or maybe it was that the Jedi, who had stood against cruelty in the galaxy more than anyone else, were a stark reminder that Syl had sold out her conscience for a king's ransom in credits, and that was not such a great feeling. Turning her misgivings over her choice toward the Jedi seemed like as good a plan as any. "I think you'll have to excuse me if I trust Beti more than a couple of monks in funny robes," Syl said, letting her frustration out on the Mirialan.

"Beti?" the green girl asked. She seemed completely unfazed by Syl's tone, her earlier pique already dissipating. It bothered Syl that the girl was actually pretty cute, with her facial tattoos on the outside of each eye. Syl couldn't tell what the design was at this distance, but it had the effect of making her eyes seem larger than they were.

Gah, she was not about to fall for a *Jedi*, was she? Maybe it was the blasted uniform. *Get it together, Yarrow.*

"Her blaster rifle," Xylan said, interrupting Syl's thoughts.

"Xylan, please don't misunderstand my offer. It comes at the behest of your grandmother. She was the one who suggested that perhaps the Jedi would be the best way to settle this matter."

Xylan's demeanor changed immediately. He took a deep breath before running a hand through his dark hair, even though not a strand was out of place. He seemed to have come to some kind of decision, and Syl desperately wanted to know what he was thinking. Too bad she wasn't a mind-sifting Jedi.

"Senator Starros," Xylan said after a couple of heartbeats, "I thank you for your offer, but I cannot believe my grandmother would ask for such a condition without alerting me to the changing situation. These are children."

Senator Starros leaned back in her chair and sighed heavily. "Are you calling me a liar?"

"Absolutely not. But I will not take babes into the mouth of the beast, so to speak. Do you honestly expect me to believe this is the concession Grandmere agreed to? You know that the Grafs do not negotiate." There was no heat to his voice, just a statement of fact. His family was so powerful that what they wanted, they got. "I asked for an adult solution. You offer me children."

"We're Jedi," the pale boy muttered under his breath, and the Mirialan girl made a shushing motion.

Syl suddenly felt like the last place she wanted to be was in that room with those people, fighting over minutiae and pretending her conscience wasn't gnawing at her. So she stood, turned, and walked toward the door to make her exit.

"Syl?" Xylan called. Syl stopped, surprised he'd even deigned to notice her departure.

"I still want to talk to Professor Wolk while we're here," Syl said. "And it looks like you and the senator have some things to discuss." Syl didn't know how politics worked, but Chancey Yarrow had often talked about how nothing was ever as it seemed on Coruscant. And it turned out Syl did not have the temperament to watch such a display of petty maneuvering in the pursuit of profit, even if the returns were hers. It had been intriguing at first, but now it was just upsetting.

"Professor Wolk?" the green Jedi said, her bored expression melting away. "We need to speak with him, as well. I have a puzzle box that he might be able to decipher for me." The Jedi pulled a small box out of her belt pouch, and the look of it reminded Syl of the datacube Xylan had shown her when they first met.

"Why don't you all go down and speak with the professor while Xylan and I finish hashing out the details of this agreement," Senator Starros said, her smile tight. "I'll have an aide accompany you."

"Grand idea," Xylan said, teeth flashing as he smiled wide. Syl suddenly had the feeling that whatever happened once they left would not have even the barest hint of civility. As she stepped outside the senator's office, Syl took a deep breath. She already felt better.

Well, she would if it weren't for the blasted Jedi following her like lost children.

NINETEEN

Vernestra did not know what she had
done to the dark-skinned girl who stood outside
Senator Starros's office with them, but dislike flowed from
her in heavy waves, enough so that every time Imri glanced
in her direction he grimaced as though he were in physical
pain. The girl really, really did not like Jedi.

Vernestra wasn't surprised. She just wanted to know why.

Not everyone loved the Jedi. Of course they didn't. There
were those who found the Order too restrictive, other Force
users who didn't think balance was as important or freely
used the Force in a way the Jedi forbade. And then there
were the cultures that found themselves at odds with the Jedi

regularly—the Hutts and the Zygerrians, plus smugglers and rogues of all types. And of course the Nihil, the most recent addition to that list.

But most people, especially those within the bosom of the Republic, saw the Jedi not as a necessary evil but as heroes of good order and peace. Because, of course, that was what they were.

Sylvestri Yarrow did not seem like a smuggler or a rogue, and she was very obviously a human. The girl wasn't Nihil; she didn't look at the Jedi with the sneer of disgust most Nihil did. Rather, she seemed saddened by the appearance of Vernestra and Imri, like they reminded her of something she missed.

"What?" the girl said all of a sudden, turning to look at Vernestra. As they exited the senator's office, she unfastened her coveralls, tying the sleeves around her waist so the trousers stayed on her slim hips. Underneath she wore a fitted shirt that would've been at home on a ship but looked out of place in the hallway of the Senate building. With the coveralls down it was easy to see the backpack holster she wore, a modified blaster rifle—the aforementioned Beti—nestled in the space between her shoulder blades.

"I was just wondering if I somehow offended you," Vernestra said. "You seem prickly." She did not think to lie. In her experience that only led to more trouble. Best to tell the truth or say nothing at all.

"Not personal," the girl said. "You just remind me of something I went through."

What was the girl's name again? Vernestra searched her memory.

"Is that all?" Imri asked, and the girl scowled. Sylvestri Yarrow! That was her name.

"Did you know Senator Starros was going to use you like that?" Sylvestri Yarrow said to Vernestra all of a sudden, a brutal yet effective way to change the subject.

Vernestra frowned. "Like what?"

"As a way to get under Xylan's skin." The human girl looked from Imri to Vernestra and back. "Come on, you know she used you to provoke the pretty guy, right?"

"We were brought here to help by special request," Vernestra said. She looked to Imri, but he was also confused by Sylvestri's words.

"Oh, come on, Vern. It was Vern, wasn't it?"

"I actually prefer Vernestra—"

"Vern, she had you hide behind a secret door—a door we couldn't see until it opened, by the way—and had you pop out when he asked about one of the final details of his trip. Don't you think that was strange? You both should have been involved in our conversation from the beginning." Sylvestri laughed hollowly. "Stars, I hate Coruscant. Too many politics and not enough honesty."

Vernestra shook her head. "Master Stellan said—"

"Your master guy set you up. Or he was set up. She used you to show Xylan that his concerns were trivial. She must have some angle she's working, as well, what with that comment about his grandmother. . . ." Sylvestri's voice trailed off as she considered something. "She's definitely up to something, or they both are. The vibes were all off."

"Yes, I would concur. Imri said much the same thing to me," Vernestra offered, but the girl wasn't really paying attention to her, still puzzling through whatever it was that had sent her down a path of rumination.

"Why would a senator try to use Jedi like some kind of trick? Just consider what it looked like from my side: 'Here's a couple of kids for your *very important* mission. Good luck.'" The girl shook her head. "She was really trying to provoke Xylan. I know an insult when I see one, no matter how pretty the words are that it comes wrapped in. The question is, why? Is academic research really so important?"

A pale-skinned human woman with red hair knit into a similar style as Senator Starros's appeared in the hallway in front of them. "Hello," she said, her smile not quite reaching her eyes. "I am Kyrie. I'm supposed to take you to see Professor Wolk. He's in another building, so we'll have to take a speeder. If you'll follow me?"

Sylvestri Yarrow clamped her mouth shut and—after shooting Vernestra and Imri one last look, eyebrows raised in an expression that said, *Can you believe this?*—turned on her heel to walk after Kyrie. As their group silently followed the senator's aide, Vernestra began to think. Was Sylvestri right?

After leaving Master Stellan's office, Vernestra had gone to find Imri and Reath. On the walk back to the Senate building, the two of them regaled her with anecdotes from Samara the Blue's writings and the likelihood Imri's abilities could be directly tied to his Genetian heritage. Then she and Imri had bid Reath farewell and headed over to the series of buildings that housed the Galactic Senate. Senator Starros had been expecting them, and Vernestra had found her to be warm and friendly in a way her daughter, Avon, was not. Avon distrusted most people, analyzing them like they were specimens. Senator Starros made jokes and thanked Vernestra and Imri for keeping Avon safe during their mishap on Wevo.

"I know that it is the pride of the Jedi to protect the peace of the galaxy, but I want to thank you again for saving my daughter, as well," Senator Starros had said, her expression open and grateful. "I have faith that someone as accomplished as you, Jedi Vern, will be a perfect fit for this very important task."

And then she had hustled Imri and Vernestra into a nearby sitting room to wait while she met with another set of guests. Vernestra had not even been certain what job she and Imri were being assigned, and the scene that happened after had been as distressing for her and Imri as it had been for the human girl, Sylvestri Yarrow. The parade of emotions had been confusing, and Vernestra was starting to understand why Avon was so naturally wary.

But now that she considered the event—the flattery, the needless compliments, the strange introduction to Xylan

Graf—Vernestra could see that she'd been a game piece in a much larger plot.

It was not something she liked.

They arrived at the platform and waited for the private speeder. Kyrie tried to point out a few of the sights on the nearby skyline, but only Imri seemed to be paying attention. Sylvestri shifted her weight from foot to foot impatiently but ignored everyone around her.

Vernestra studied the girl next to her. Her skin was dark, and her kinky hair was a cloud around her head. She wore simple blue mechanic's coveralls, and she seemed much larger than she was. Imri towered over her, and she was even a few centimeters shorter than Vernestra if not for her hair. And yet, Vernestra had the feeling she would be formidable in a fight.

"I think you're right," she said in a low voice. "I'm sorry I embarrassed your friend."

Sylvestri turned toward Vernestra with a frown. "He's not my friend. He's just someone who owes me money. I don't trust him, and neither should you. Actually, you shouldn't trust anyone on this miserable planet. My mother used to say politics was where truth went to die, and I'm starting to get what she meant."

Vernestra blinked in surprise but didn't have time to parse Sylvestri's logic. Their airspeeder arrived, and everyone piled in—Imri and Vernestra in the back, Sylvestri in the middle, and the aide up front with a droid that was piloting.

Sylvestri immediately stretched out on the row of seats and went to sleep, her soft snores echoing throughout the vehicle.

"Maybe she just needed a nap," Imri murmured to Vernestra, and the Jedi couldn't hold back her smile.

"How are you doing? Any more attacks?" Vernestra asked Imri, and the boy shook his head.

"No. Those exercises Samara the Blue wrote down really are helpful. I feel good. Mostly."

A pang of guilt twanged through Vernestra, but she squashed it so Imri wouldn't sense her disappointment in herself. She should've been the one to give Imri exercises to calm his senses when he got overwhelmed.

"Imri, I wanted to ask you a question. Earlier you mentioned hearing a woman whispering to you. What was that about?" Vernestra asked, pretending to a calm she did not feel.

"About a woman both alive and dead?" Imri said. He shook his head. "I don't know. I think I might have just been too connected to you. You've been very concerned lately, even though I know you try to hide it."

Vernestra bit her lip and nodded. That was entirely too close to the truth. "I didn't get any sleep on the way to Coruscant because I have been worrying about how to stop the Nihil, and wishing the Order could do more. The way we keep striking at the Nihil . . . battle after battle, and yet they still terrorize so many," Vernestra said. Imri didn't need to know about her strange hyperspace vision. She would keep that to herself as much and for as long as possible.

The speeder stopped with a jolt. Sylvestri was the first one on her feet, knuckling her eyes with a wide yawn as she exited. The platform was situated in the middle of the building just like in the Senate, and Kyrie gave them all a polite smile but did not exit the speeder.

"Professor Wolk's office is on the first floor. Just take the lift down there and you'll see it on the right. Good luck!" she said, the speeder zooming off before anyone could ask her any questions.

"Did she seem in a hurry to you?" Imri asked.

"She probably just has boots to lick," Sylvestri said, putting her hands on her hips.

"Hey, Padawan, new Knight. What are you doing?" came a voice from behind them. Vernestra turned to see Jordanna Sparkburn and Remy walking toward them, and she swallowed a sigh. Great, just what she needed. Someone else who was prickly for no good reason.

"Jordanna! Good to see you again. How has your sightseeing gone?" Vernestra asked, trying to radiate positivity toward the other woman.

Jordanna shrugged. She wore a nicer version of her homesteader clothing, a plain black tunic with gray fitted trousers underneath. "We've walked a good part of the district and it's all starting to look the same, so I was just heading toward the San Tekka corporate office."

Vernestra blinked. She'd expected hostility from Jordanna, but instead the woman seemed to be in a pretty good mood. Vernestra opened her mouth to answer when she realized that Jordanna wasn't paying attention to her at all. Instead her gaze was locked on Sylvestri, and the girl seemed to be similarly starstruck by the sight of Jordanna, her apparent bad mood forgotten.

"Syl," the San Tekka deputy said, voice little more than a whisper.

Sylvestri had gone ashen, and her eyes looked too wide for her face. "Jordanna? What are you doing here? I thought you couldn't leave Tiikae. Duty and all that."

Imri winced, and even Vernestra could feel the waves of sadness and longing radiating off of the pair. There was a story here, and it was one that did not belong to her or Imri.

"We're going to go on ahead," Vernestra said, shooting the two a bright smile and grabbing a deeply distracted Imri by the arm to drag him toward the lift. "Sylvestri, we'll meet you inside."

The two Jedi left the platform and headed toward the lift that would take them to the street level. Imri looked like he'd been hit by a speeder, partly upset and partly happy, and anyone who saw him would think he was unwell. The car came quickly, and once they were safely ensconced inside, Imri rounded on Vernestra.

"What was that? It felt like . . . they were a couple? And in love? But something bad happened, and Syl was sad and Jordanna was mad, but mostly at herself." Tears ran unchecked down his cheeks, as though it were his heart breaking.

Vernestra took a deep breath. Her reading hadn't been as good as Imri's, but it had been very close. "We've talked a lot about attachment and how dangerous it can be. But even for those who are free to pursue love, that chase can be fraught. I think that perhaps the love story between Jordanna and Sylvestri did not go as they had hoped. But they are together once again, because the Force works in mysterious ways. But those feelings between them might not work out. We can only hope that it doesn't end tragically."

"I know all this, Vern," Imri said, voice low. "I've watched holos. You're talking like you're afraid I'm going to fall in love."

Vernestra sighed. She felt like she was really bad at this. Why couldn't they just duel or meditate? This was a difficult conversation for her because she'd never once had any of those feelings, regardless of the people she met. She could tell when someone was attractive, and there were people she liked more than others, but she had never felt the push/pull of attraction so many other Padawans did when they came of age. She supposed that had made it easier for her, but that did not mean Imri's path would be as smooth.

"I just . . . I'm not telling you not to explore the feelings that you might have for another," Vernestra said, picking her way through the conversation. "Just . . . be mindful. Once there are other feelings involved, things get . . . complicated."

Imri scrubbed at his cheeks and flashed her a wide grin. "I get it, Vern. No worries. I truly was just wondering about Jordanna and Sylvestri. I've never felt someone who was so happy to see someone but also . . . scared. Like, fighting Drengir scared. I'm not about to run out and break any hearts. It's hard enough cutting myself off from the feelings of strangers. I can't even imagine a romantic partner."

Vernestra laughed, and luckily the lift chose that moment to arrive on their floor. They exited the car and Vernestra pulled the box out of her belt pouch, studying it once more.

"Do you think this professor will know what it is?" Imri asked. She'd filled him in on her conversation with Stellan on the way to the Senate so he would know everything she'd done. Not that it was much. Vernestra still wasn't sure what she was supposed to do on this assignment where no one seemed all that happy to have her around; the details had been lost in Xylan Graf's horror at being saddled with what he perceived to be children, but she believed things always worked out for the best, so she was only slightly annoyed. At least she still had the mystery of the puzzle box. Solving that could be the one thing she accomplished for the day.

"Maybe. I'm mostly curious what's inside."

"Do you really think the Nihil killed that family on Tiikae for it?" Imri asked, a troubled expression crossing his face as they began to walk down the path that led from the lift tower to the building proper. "It seems like such a waste of life."

"Yes," Vernestra said, jaw tight. "Which is why I want to know what's inside, if anything. It could be the box opens something else, a kind of puzzle key. I've heard that some cultures use such a thing as another level of security."

"Meaning that whatever is in the box is pretty valuable, huh?" Imri said, peering at it. "Maybe we should take it back to the Temple so the Council can keep it safe."

Vernestra didn't know why, but she felt a surge of wrongness at the suggestion. She had asked Imri about the mystery woman but hadn't told him that a vision had pointed Vernestra to the box in the first place. "No, I need to keep it. I think there's something I'm meant to do with it." The feeling was strange, and Vernestra couldn't have said where it came from, but the more she considered it, the more certain she was that the puzzle box needed to remain with her for the time being.

The main doors slid open, revealing a small foyer and then a long empty hallway with two others branching off to the left and right. There were a number of doors, all of them identical, and not a single one was labeled. Vernestra stopped and put her hands on her hips. "Just how are we supposed to figure out which one belongs to Professor Wolk?"

Vernestra turned to Imri, and that was when a door on the right at the end of the hallway exploded.

TWENTY

Syl was having a dream. Or a nightmare. She couldn't decide which.

"Hey," Jordanna said, giving her a small smile. Remy began to purr loudly, the vollka closing the distance to wind herself around Syl affectionately, nearly knocking the girl off her feet.

"Hey," Syl said back, scratching Remy between her horns, a move that would've cost just about anyone else an appendage. She was amazed she could even speak. She wanted to run after Vern and Imri, use their presence to defuse the awkwardness and pretend her heart wasn't alternately doing flips and dying. Remy butted her head against Syl, hitting her chest, and Syl gave in and smiled, moving her hand to scratch the blue-and-green hunting cat behind the ears. "You got pushier."

"She missed you," Jordanna said, her shoulders slumping. "I did, too."

The admission sent a sharp jolt of pain shooting through Syl's chest, and just like that she was back on Tiikae, waiting, hoping that she would see Jordanna and Remy come across the desolate landscape to the boarding ramp of the *Switchback*, hoping and waiting for them to appear as the red sun rose, and finally giving up and realizing they never would.

"I asked you to come with me," Syl said, giving Remy a kiss on top of her massive head before letting go of the cat. "You could have told your aunt that you didn't want to be the deputy and come with us."

"I know," Jordanna said, her voice heavy with . . . was that regret? Syl didn't let herself hope or wonder. She held herself tightly. As long as she didn't let it hurt, it wouldn't.

But, stars, it was good to see Jordanna again.

"I should probably go catch up with Vern and Imri," Syl said, gesturing toward the lift.

"Let me come with you," Jordanna said. Syl had never seen her like this: hesitant, questioning. She'd always been a woman of few words, but that was only because she thought actions spoke louder. She was only two years older than Syl, but at twenty Jordanna was so self-assured, so confident that Syl had felt silly arguing with her. Now it seemed as though some vital light within her had dimmed, and it made Syl want to know what had happened to her since they'd last spoken.

She also just wanted to spend time with Jordanna. Already Syl could feel that unnamable force pulling her toward the dark-haired girl, and she cursed herself for her weakness. She wanted to be aloof, to hurt Jordanna the way Jordanna had hurt her, but she didn't have the appetite for it. All she wanted to do was find a cafe and snuggle with Jordanna in a corner while Remy menaced anyone who came too close.

"Okay," Syl said when she realized the silence had drifted on a bit too long. Jordanna smiled a little, a mixture of relief and sadness in it, and Syl wondered what was happening inside her ex-girlfriend's head. Was Jordanna also sick-happy to see Syl?

They approached the lift and stepped in, the silence between them weighty and uncomfortable. Remy, who took up more than half the space in the car, pawed at Jordanna and let loose a low growl.

"Okay, okay," she muttered. Jordanna took a deep breath. "I have something to tell you."

Syl swallowed dryly, her heart somehow in her throat. "What?"

"I was wrong. I should've left with you when you asked."

Syl froze. Was this real? Was she hallucinating? This couldn't be real.

For so long she'd imagined this moment. Of course, in her daydreams they weren't in a lift on Coruscant; they were somewhere pretty and romantic, or even on their own ship. Jordanna would sweep in with her murderous cat and freckles and apologize beautifully, swearing never to leave Syl's side again. And then they would kiss like humans did in the holo adventures, passionately and to music.

This was not that. At all.

"Hey, I just," Jordanna said as the doors opened, "I just wanted to say I was sorry." And then she shrugged.

She *shrugged*.

Syl froze, and every last happy-sad feeling was incinerated by the flames of her rage. Did Jordanna really think it would be that easy? That she could say sorry and it would erase months of aching and crying and looking for a tall girl with dark curls and a lopsided grin around every single corner on every planet in the galaxy? All that hoping and waiting and wishing, did Jordanna really think it could be so easily erased?

Syl clenched her hands into fists. "How nice for you," she said before stomping out of the lift. She got the briefest impression of Jordanna's look of surprise before she strode to the door of the building that contained Professor Wolk's office. There was a strange rumble, and Syl found herself looking up toward the sky, expecting lightning. Did Coruscant even have weather? Or was that something else the planet found too provincial to indulge?

Syl turned back to the main doors only to have Jordanna shove her violently to the ground as two blaster bolts went singing overhead.

"What in the seven cursed valleys was that?" Syl yelled. "Who's shooting at me now?"

"Stay here," Jordanna said, running into the building, toward the danger, Remy right behind her. Syl sat on the ground and rested her head on her knees, her heart pounding and her eyes burning with unshed tears.

She had to stay angry. Her anger was the only thing that would keep Jordanna from breaking her heart all over again.

TWENTY-ONE

Vernestra threw up her hands, using the Force to block the majority of the debris that flew toward her and Imri. But she wasn't quite quick enough, and a few pieces of masonry got through. A piece of stone, sharp as a razor, sliced her cheek. Imri grunted as another piece sliced across the top of his left arm, splitting the sleeve of his tunic and painting the pale material scarlet.

Vernestra drew her lightsaber, and Imri did the same.

"They're still here," Imri said, and Vernestra nodded. She could sense someone with ill intent nearby, presumably the bomber, waiting around to take in their handiwork. But it was hard to see anything through the smoke that billowed down the hallway, filling the foyer.

A body came sprinting through the smoke, headed right for Vernestra and Imri. Vernestra put her hand out and pushed the person to the left with the Force, keeping herself from doing anything more when she realized the Gungan looking at her with wide eyes was terrified.

"They're trying to kill me," he said, and less than a heartbeat later a blaster bolt came through the smoke, hitting the Gungan right in the middle of the back. Two more followed, zipping past the Jedi and back toward the main doors.

"Imri!" Vernestra said, pointing to the injured man before sprinting through the smoke to find the shooter. She didn't wait to see if her meaning was clear; she didn't want to waste any time stopping the person responsible for the violence.

At first Vernestra's eyes burned and she coughed as she ran through the area nearest the explosion, but once she was clear of the smoke, she saw a Twi'lek man running along the corridor, a blaster in his hand. He turned once and fired at Vernestra, and she threw herself to the right to avoid the blaster bolt before powering up her lightsaber—the blade casting a brilliant violet glow in the corridor—and giving earnest chase, using the Force liberally so that each stride propelled her twice as far as normal. Using the Force in such a way wasn't advisable, as it was a great way to wear oneself out, but if the man escaped into the crowds of Coruscant, Vernestra would never be able to find him.

The Twi'lek fired wildly over his shoulder, and Vernestra blocked the bolts easily with her lightsaber. As she ran, she cast around for something to slow the Twi'lek down, but she needn't have bothered. Republic security forces came exploding down a corridor in the distance, and the Twi'lek skidded to a stop, firing at the guards at the end of the hallway.

They returned fire, and they were much better shots than the Twi'lek. Mostly because there were so many of them all firing at once. Vernestra skidded to a stop, bringing her lightsaber up and twisting the bezel so the blade fell into a whip. She spun the whip around in a quick circle to deflect the hail of blaster fire. The Twi'lek had no such defense, and he fell to the ground in a limp heap.

"Stop shooting! I'm a Jedi!" Vernestra called. For a moment she had the perverse notion that maybe the security forces didn't like Jedi any more than Syl did and they would keep shooting, but then the blaster fire stopped and Vernestra was able to power down her lightwhip and holster it.

"Jedi, well met," said a tall Balosar woman, her antenna-palps the only thing marking her as not human. "I'm Ashdree Marq."

"Vernestra Rwoh," Vernestra said, hands on her hips. Her chest heaved from running, and a keen sense of sadness bloomed in her at the sight of the dead Twi'lek. So much death, so much wasted life, and for what? Nothing, as far as Vernestra could see.

"Can you tell me what happened here?"

Vernestra explained to Ashdree what she had seen, including the injured Gungan, while the rest of the security team ran back toward the fire burning at the end of the hall. "I have to get back to my Padawan. He's by the entry with a Gungan who was injured in the attack," Vernestra said, and the woman nodded.

"I'll walk with you."

As they walked, Ashdree continued to ask questions, parsing every detail of what Vernestra had seen, which wasn't much. By the time they passed the destroyed office, the fire put out and the smoke quickly dissipating, they were both frustrated.

"Honestly, I couldn't tell you why that man destroyed the office or shot the Gungan," Vernestra said. "It all seems so senseless. Do you get a lot of these kinds of attacks?"

"Never," Ashdree said, two spots of color appearing high on her pale cheeks. "We monitor all of these hallways from a central location and are able to spot troublemakers long before anything happens."

"So then, you saw him when he came in?" Vernestra asked.

The woman pursed her lips and shook her head. "We never saw him. We saw a Jedi with her lightsaber out running down the hallway. We'll investigate, but most likely someone did something to our feed. It's been happening more and more lately."

Vernestra stepped back into the foyer with a frown on her face, and the expression only deepened into a scowl when she saw Jordanna with her arm around Imri, comforting him. Sylvestri Yarrow stood a little bit off to the side, looking put out, Remy leaning against her. The vollka had taken a shine to the girl, and Vernestra felt like that made sense. It was obvious Sylvestri and Jordanna knew each other from before, and the cat's behavior only reinforced that idea.

"Imri, are you okay?" Vernestra said. Jordanna gave her a sharp look, but it faded as she took in Vernestra.

"You're bleeding," she said, pulling a kerchief out of her back pocket and handing it to the Jedi.

"Thanks," she said, putting the cloth to her cheek. "We should get you to the clinic at the Temple, Imri, get that arm looked at."

"Oh, I'm good," Imri said, showing it to Vernestra. The tear in his tunic remained, but the skin underneath was pink and smooth. "Jordanna put a medpac on it for me. One with bacta, even!"

Jordanna gave an embarrassed smile. "One of the perks of being a San Tekka, even if only a dirt-grubbing cousin: deep pockets. I have a little bacta spray if you'd like some for your cheek."

"I'm fine, thank you. Did you see what happened?" Vernestra asked. The day hadn't gone how she'd expected, and her frustrations were beginning to pile up into true aggravation. She could only endure so much before she lost her temper. She was a Jedi, not a statue.

"No, Professor Wolk was dead when we arrived," Sylvestri said, sadness on her face.

Vernestra's anger melted away and confusion took its place. "Professor Wolk? The Gungan was Professor Wolk?"

"Yeah," Sylvestri said, her expression troubled. "Yesterday he said that someone was trying to kill him. It looks like they finally succeeded. This planet is supposed to be the jewel of the Republic, but judging from the number of people running around trying to kill folks, they've got some real problems right here in Galactic City." The sadness on the girl's face made Vernestra wonder what her relationship was to the Gungan.

"Who else has had an attempt on their life?" Vernestra asked.

"Well, me. But that's probably more Xylan Graf's fault than anything else."

Jordanna rounded on her. "Why didn't you tell me you were in danger?"

"Until about fifteen minutes ago I didn't even know you were alive, much less on Coruscant," Sylvestri shot back. "You didn't exactly respond to any of the messages I sent."

"Yes, I did! You didn't respond to any of mine!"

Vernestra looked from Jordanna to Sylvestri and realized she had fallen right into the middle of one of her least favorite holo adventures: the overwrought romance.

"I'm starting to get a headache," Imri said, going to stand next to Vernestra. "And I'm also starting to feel really hungry since we missed lunch."

Vernestra patted him once on his shoulder before turning back to Sylvestri. "Why do you think Xylan Graf was behind this?" she asked before anyone else could talk.

Sylvestri pursed her lips and shook her head. "Something about the guy really just puts me off."

"Me too," Imri said. When everyone looked to him, he gave a sheepish smile and shrugged. "And not just because he insulted us, either. He's hiding something, but I don't know what it is."

"Plots on plots on plots. Sod it all, but I could use something to drink," Sylvestri said with a sigh before turning back to Vernestra. "Besides, if you have a hyperspace question, you should probably go back and make nice with Xylan Graf, because with Professor Wolk gone, he is your next best bet on Coruscant. That is, unless someone tries to kill him, as well. Who knows, maybe the reason I was attacked is because they thought it was Xylan's room and he was the real target. Everyone on this planet is more than a little shady."

Vernestra sighed. It seemed like there was much more to this simple assignment than met the eye.

TWENTY-TWO

Reath fought a yawn as the senators asked Master Cohmac the same handful of questions over and over again, phrased slightly different each time. Only a couple of the members of the Jedi Council were present, Master Yarael Poof and Master Stellan, in whose meeting chambers they sat. There were four senators present, and Reath had already forgotten their names, much to his chagrin. But it had been a long day, and it was showing no signs of ending.

Reath desperately wished he could return to the library. It seemed silly that they had traveled all the way from Starlight

Beacon for this inquiry, especially since most of the questions the senators were asking had answers within the report they'd filed. Yes, the Republic should be concerned by the civil war on Genetia. No, there did not seem to be any outside influences. Yes, a peacekeeping force might be a good idea to minimize the loss of life.

The door to the chamber opened, and a dark-skinned human woman walked into the room. Master Stellan stood with an apologetic smile to the assemblage. "Friends, I'm afraid that is all the time we have. I will be sending along the copy of the report Master Cohmac filed in regards to his recent trip, and I hope this time has been enlightening for you."

The senators stood, grumbling, and as they filed out, with Master Yarael close behind, Reath stood to follow.

"Master Cohmac, Padawan Reath, please stay. My next meeting concerns you," Master Stellan said.

Reath looked to Master Cohmac, but his master gave him a short head shake, meaning that he didn't have any idea what Master Stellan could want with them, either.

Once everyone else was gone, except the dark-skinned woman who had interrupted the meeting, Master Stellan gestured for them to sit once more. Reath and Master Cohmac settled back into the chairs they'd just vacated while the woman, who Reath could now see carried a datapad bearing the seal of the Senate, and Master Stellan took nearby seats.

"Cohmac, Reath, this is Senator Ghirra Starros. She's been working very closely with the Council on our unified Nihil response the past few weeks."

"Jedi, it's good to meet you. I don't have a lot of time, but I do want to tell you I have a personal investment in ensuring the Nihil threat is put to rest sooner rather than later. Which is why I need your help in this matter." She gave Reath and Master Cohmac a tight smile, and rage rolled off of her in frustrated waves. The Nihil had done something very personal to this woman, and Reath wondered how many other senators were like her.

"Earlier today I met with Xylan Graf, the grandson of the head of the Graf family. For the past few weeks he's been agitating to assume the expired lease for the Berenge sector. The San Tekkas held it decades ago in order to conduct a handful of more dangerous hyperspace experiments, because the vast emptiness of the sector ensures that there is low interference from mass shadows. A few of us in the Senate had hoped to set aside the lease for academic study, not corporate experiments, especially since it became a popular shortcut after the San Tekkas stopped using the area. I'm afraid I cannot push off his request any longer since the Senate would make good use of the funds, especially since the offensive against the Nihil has exceeded early cost estimates. Earlier today I asked Vern Rwoh and Imri Cantaros to help Xylan survey the sector, and he took the offer of . . . someone so young as an insult."

"Vernestra is a Jedi Knight," Reath said, feeling the need to defend his friend.

"Yes, but I'm afraid I cannot get this through to Xylan, and with the planning for the unified assault ramping up, I don't have time to placate the Grafs and their hurt feelings. I need a stopgap solution."

Stellan smiled at Senator Starros indulgently. "How can we help you, Ghirra?"

The smile she gave Stellan was warm, perhaps a bit too familiar, and Master Cohmac frowned slightly. No one else would have noticed it, but as his Padawan, Reath was used to noticing his master's shifts in moods. There was something he didn't care for about Senator Starros, but Reath couldn't fathom what it might be. The woman seemed competent and friendly.

"What I'm asking is if you would be amenable to delaying your return to Starlight Beacon and assisting me in supporting this mission, as well," Senator Starros said, directing her request to Reath and Master Cohmac. "The thing is, there have been reports that the Nihil are working on a destructive weapon in the Berenge sector, and I am partly concerned that this is merely Xylan Graf playing at something far more dangerous. The Grafs have always been less than completely aboveboard in their business dealings, and I worry this is something more than they are saying. A handful of Jedi would be far more effective in squashing this than our own defensive forces, just in case there is something more nefarious afoot."

"Do you truly believe the Nihil are building some kind of weapon?" Master Cohmac asked.

"One of my experts thought so, and someone murdered him today," Senator Starros said, pursing her lips. "It seems laughable. The Nihil are not quite that sophisticated, but I'm loathe to take the chance. We already have so many other battles to fight. We have to strip away every advantage possible from the Nihil."

Master Cohmac nodded. "I agree. Reath and I will be happy to join the other Jedi already committed to this mission."

"Excellent," Senator Starros said, standing with a smile. "It will most likely just be a quick trip there and back with nothing exciting to report, but in case it isn't, know that you will have my immediate assistance should you need it. I will send a message to Xylan Graf and let him know to expect you tomorrow. May the Force be with you." She took her leave without another word.

Reath felt a curious anxiety burble up in his middle. "Master Cohmac, Master Stellan, I, uh, have a bad feeling about this."

"Oh, this is most definitely some kind of trap," Master Stellan said with a grin. "I've had my suspicions that someone very important was helping the Nihil, providing them with information, and Ghirra shares my suspicions. But that it could be the Graf family is far beyond what I imagined. Please don't tell anyone but Vernestra when you meet up with her. We want to catch the Grafs in the act." Master Stellan pulled on the hairs at his chin as he thought. "If we can cut the Nihil off from every single last one of their resources, we can end this conflict sooner rather than later. They've already killed millions. Our goal has to be to ensure that not one more life is lost."

Master Cohmac and Reath nodded and took their leave. As they walked, the anxious feeling refused to let go of Reath, and he knew better than to ignore his instincts.

"Master Cohmac, I feel like there is something much bigger happening here. I don't like this."

"I agree. Force help us, there are far too many people with their own agendas right now for me to rest easy. But one thing at a time. We must keep this information to ourselves for now as Master Stellan requested. I know you have a deep respect for Vernestra, and we will tell her as soon as we can. Stellan Gios always does what's best for the Order."

Reath wanted to ask, "What about what's best for the Force?" but he had a feeling he would not like the answer to that question.

TWENTY-THREE

Syl sat in a booth in a nearby diner with two Jedi, her ex-girlfriend, a disgruntled vollka, and a pounding headache, and tried not to feel like everything around her was crashing down.

When she had run into the Senate building after Jordanna, Beti ready for action, Syl had seen the boy Imri talking to Professor Wolk as the Gungan choked out his last breaths, and she had known that it didn't matter how she felt about Jordanna Sparkburn. Syl didn't have time for anger or remorse; she had to get through this deal she'd made with Xylan Graf and get back out to the frontier. There was something more civilized, in her mind, about fighting pirates and struggling for survival among the stars than lying to government officials and dying because of a blaster bolt to the back in a fancy building.

She didn't care about her mother's hidden life any longer. Syl would let the past stay dead. Since Professor Wolk was gone, so was the one person who had any real knowledge of the woman Chancey Yarrow had been. The only version that remained of her mother was the one from her memory, and that was a comforting realization.

That was enough to help Syl decide that she didn't want to know the truth. She wanted her Graf-funded ship and a line of credit. To the center of a red sun with everyone else. A quick call to Neeto in Port Haileap had verified that he'd already gotten the ten thousand credits Xylan had promised as a down payment. He might be a lot of things, but Xylan Graf seemed to be a man of his word, so Syl's only concern had to be keeping up her end of the bargain and putting the trip to Coruscant in her past like all her other bad decisions.

It was too bad one of her mistakes kept giving her meaningful glances across the table.

After the Republic security forces had shooed them from the building, they'd tried returning to Senator Starros's office, but it turned out that Senate security was suddenly a whole lot tighter, and they'd had to settle for sending a message to the senator detailing what had happened.

They had nothing to do but wait, and Syl had nowhere to go but back to Xylan Graf's tower, which meant she was forced to sit with the Jedi while they tried to puzzle out the significance of Wolk's murder. Syl had nothing worthwhile to add, so she nursed her moof juice and said nothing.

She couldn't help glancing across the table at Jordanna, her thoughts turning back to the first time they'd met. Syl's mother had decided that Syl needed some time spent studying hyperdrive and sublight engine repair, so she'd dropped her at a rooming house on Tiikae with a family of Ugnaughts who were known for their uncanny ability to rebuild just about anything.

"A month isn't all that long, and by the time Neeto and I have finished this run, I expect that you'll have learned how to break down and repair a hyperdrive. It's a vital skill for any hauler," Chancey Yarrow had said as Sylvestri stood in the middle of a dusty landing field, clutching her knapsack and trying not to feel like she was being abandoned. It wasn't the first time Chancey Yarrow had dropped her daughter in some out-of-the-way location in the galaxy to learn a skill, but it was the first time she'd done it so suddenly and with no warning. "Klanna and Roy will take good care of you. They're old friends. Give them all of the respect that you would give me."

And then Syl's mother had climbed aboard the *Switchback* and left.

For the next few days, Syl tried to learn everything she could from Roy, who was patient and plainspoken, but it turned out that hyperdrive repair was complicated and boring, so Syl found ways to keep herself out of Roy's difficult work as much as possible while still earning her keep. One day it was working on an ancient speeder bike—repulsorlift repair was much simpler than the finicky requirements of a hyperdrive—and Syl was halfway through resetting the reverse gravitational timer when Jordanna walked in to check on the bike.

Syl took one look at Jordanna's dark eyes and long dark curls and had the feeling of falling from a great height. When the other girl smiled, Syl swore her heart exploded.

The holos were always talking about love at first reckoning, usually romances that ended in tragedy, so Syl should've known better than to follow her heart when she got walloped by Jordanna's appearance in Roy's shop. But she couldn't help herself, and the next few weeks became days full of stolen kisses and nights of staying up late and watching the auroras paint Tiikae's sky in radiation-flecked rainbows.

Somehow Syl convinced herself that her mother might never return to Tiikae, that she could move in with Jordanna once her aunt, who was also her mentor, retired and Jordanna became the deputy in charge. But then one day the *Switchback* touched down in a landing field and Syl could feel the inevitable heartbreak looming large.

"Come with me," she'd said to Jordanna, the night before Syl was scheduled to leave. Chancey was always willing to take on a competent crew member, and her mother had agreed that Jordanna's skills in defense, which far surpassed

Syl's, would be an asset to the ship. "We could see the whole galaxy together! In another few months I'm going to buy my own ship, and just imagine how that could be. You, me, and Remy hauling and living a life that we choose."

But Jordanna had smiled sadly. "Syl, I'm training to be the deputy. I'm a San Tekka, and someone has to care for the vassals here. Surely you understand that? I have responsibilities, same as you. Plus, I can't leave Tiikae. It's my home."

Somehow Syl had expected Jordanna to change her mind; so when she didn't show the next morning, not even to say goodbye, Syl had tried to pack away her broken heart and forget about the falling/soaring feeling of being in love.

But now here she was, sitting across from the girl who had broken her heart, and it was entirely too hard to remember the pain of loving her and not just the thrill.

"Do you think the Twi'lek was a Nihil?" Imri asked, his voice bringing Syl out of the memory and back to the awkward reality of her afternoon. The Padawan emptied his cup and began to look around expectantly. He eyed the server droid each time it made a circle near their table, and Syl finally waved it down for him so the boy could order some food and another drink. "Thanks," he murmured.

Vernestra frowned. "I certainly hope not. With the Nihil's penchant for violence, that would bode ill for the Core Worlds."

Syl said nothing, just downed the rest of her juice and

stood. The Jedi paused in their discussion and turned toward her.

"I'm going for a walk."

"We agreed it would be safer to stick together," Jordanna said with a frown, looking to both Vernestra and Imri for support. "Especially since someone has already tried to kill you."

Syl grimaced. She didn't know why she'd let that bit of information slip out at the office building. Survivor's guilt, maybe? She'd been trying to lighten the mood at Coruscant's expense, but these Jedi had entirely too much seriousness to get a joke, even a bad one. Even Jordanna, whom she'd remembered as intense but with a sense of humor, had gone deadly serious.

Either way, now the Jedi saw her as a body to protect, and Jordanna agreed with them, even though her Beti was probably much more effective than those silly light swords they carried around.

"So how about we talk about our assignment instead of poor dead Professor Wolk?" Syl said. "Because it's obvious that whatever happened to him, we're never going to figure out why he died." Plus, every mention of Professor Wolk was like a flashing red light in her brain saying: *Hey, should you really have made that deal with Xylan Graf?* It was getting harder to ignore her misgivings, and it hadn't even been a day since she'd made the deal.

"Oh, no, he was most certainly killed to throw suspicion

on my family. So in a way, both our mission and his death are linked."

Everyone turned to watch as Basha and Xylan approached, the Gigoran gently moving aside an orange-skinned Dressellian when the man would have careened into Xylan on the way to the exit. Xylan did not seem to notice; he swept aside his cape and sat on the edge of the booth next to Imri, taking the space Syl had just vacated.

Jordanna grinned and slid over, patting the space next to her. Syl sank down onto the bench with a heavy sigh. She would ignore the happy jump her heart gave when Jordanna's thigh pressed against hers. She was focused on her deal with Xylan Graf, but her nervous system apparently did not get the message.

"Lord Graf—er, sorry, Xylan," Vernestra said. "I apologize, but perhaps you could enlighten us as to what exactly is happening? Especially since you say they are linked? I'm afraid Imri and I never truly got the full details of what it is that you seek."

Xylan nodded and very quickly brought the Jedi up to speed about his family's fight for the Berenge sector lease and Professor Wolk's conspiracy theories. "Professor Wolk was supposed to accompany us to the sector so I could disprove his theory and the lease application could proceed, but with him dead I am once more at a loss as to how to convince that thrice-cursed Ghirra Starros to see things my way."

Xylan blinked and turned to Jordanna. "I'm sorry, I don't think we've met."

"Jordanna Sparkburn. Perhaps I can be of assistance? I have to believe the more people who can confirm that the sector is free of the Nihil, the better for your application." Syl noticed that she kept her San Tekka affiliation to herself, most likely because the San Tekkas and the Grafs were always at odds. There had even been a handful of holo adventures about their family feud, although the names were always changed to avoid lawsuits.

"Absolutely not," Syl began, but Xylan held up his hand.

"Sylvestri, please. Our task has just become much more difficult than we thought. We are going to need all of the assistance we can get." Xylan leaned back with a smile. "Plus the testimony of a San Tekka would perhaps be even more exculpatory than that old Gungan's."

Jordanna let loose a husky laugh. "How did you know?"

Xylan smiled icily. "It's my job to know the comings and goings of my competition, especially when they are spotted in the vicinity of Senate office buildings. But I truly would be happy to have you along, if only to demonstrate the superior tactics of the Grafs."

"Sounds like fun," Jordanna said.

Syl swore under her breath. She was going to buy a hundred new blaster rifles against Xylan's line of credit as soon as this job was done.

"Syl said someone tried to kill her, as well," Imri said, pulling Syl's attention away from her future purchases. "Do you think they were trying to use her to cast some kind of suspicion on you?" The Jedi brightened as the server droid brought another moof juice and a plate of crunchy starch sticks. He picked up a handful and pointed to Syl with one of the snacks. "Does she know how to build such a weapon? Did you think she was working with the Nihil? Is that why you lied to her?" At a glare from Vernestra, Imri's eyes widened and he shoved the starch sticks in his mouth and chewed. "Sorry," he mumbled around the food. "I have a lot of questions."

The eyes of everyone at the table were now on Syl. She waited for Xylan to answer, but he inclined his head toward her. Syl sighed. There was no point in trying to keep the secret. The Jedi would find out sooner or later.

She just had to make sure that what they knew didn't tip them off to her lie.

"I don't know anything, but Professor Wolk thought my mother might be behind it. She was killed by the Nihil a few months ago. But Wolk thought she'd done something like, I don't know, faked her death. Like in one of the holo dramas." Syl swallowed the lump that formed in her throat every time she thought about her mother. Was her grief enough to keep the Jedi from sensing that she was hiding something? "That was why I wanted to talk to Professor Wolk. Just to see if maybe he had some kind of proof that she was still alive and that she was behind all of this."

"Oh," Imri said, his pale cheeks shading to crimson. "I'm sorry. I sensed a secret in you, but I didn't realize it was so, um, personal."

Syl raised an eyebrow at the boy. "Secrets usually are. Personal, that is. And stop trying to read my mind."

Imri opened his mouth to respond, but before he could, Vernestra spoke up. "The Force doesn't work like that. Besides," she said with a kind smile, "reading your mind would be next to impossible. Your will is much too strong."

"That's what I always told her," Jordanna said with a small smile.

"Fine. Stop it, anyway," Syl snapped. Jordanna's compliment both irked and warmed Syl, but she was a bit relieved to know the Jedi couldn't see right through her lie of omission. "So, what now? Wolk is dead, Jordanna and Remy are coming with us, and we still have work to do."

Xylan shrugged. "That seems to be about it, to be honest. I await confirmation from Senator Starros that she will still give this undertaking her full blessing, even without the benefit of Wolk's input." He seemed completely unbothered, not even a tiny bit nervous about what would come next. That was odd. A man was dead and his project was in jeopardy of being derailed, but there was not a lick of worry in his expression. What else was afoot? Xylan Graf was so good that Syl wasn't sure what was a lie and what was the truth.

And judging from the expressions on the faces of the Jedi, they weren't, either.

Syl sighed. Yep, just as she thought. Xylan Graf was probably working a con so long that she would be toothless before it finally came to fruition. Syl pushed aside her worry. None of this was her problem. She just needed to get to Berenge and back so she could get her ship and be on her merry way.

"Jedi Vern, why did you need to see Professor Wolk?" Xylan asked, changing the subject.

Everyone's attention turned toward the Mirialan, and Vernestra looked discomfited to be the center of Xylan's attention.

"Oh, I, ah, have a puzzle box. I thought maybe he could understand the glyphs." She reached into her belt pouch and pulled out a blue-and-black box engraved with strange squiggles.

Xylan frowned and held out his hand, taking the box and turning it over. "I've seen a box like this. My grandmother has a handful of them."

"So, can you open it?" Vernestra asked, leaning forward a bit. Syl snagged one of the starch sticks from the rapidly dwindling pile and crunched through it. Under the table Remy nudged up against her, and she handed a few to the vollka, as well.

Xylan shook his head and handed the box back to Vernestra. "No, I only know a couple of these symbols. This is old hyperspace prospector shorthand. But I think my grandmother would be able to read it. And you are in luck, because our next stop before we head out to the Berenge sector is my family compound out near Neral's moon."

Everyone at the table fell silent, and Syl was the first to recover. "I'm sorry, why are we going to Neral's moon and not straight to the Berenge sector? Am I the only one lost here?"

"Not at all," Vernestra said, frowning. "Why would we take such a detour?"

"Because that is where my ship is. An undertaking such as this requires something more than a pleasure craft," Xylan said with a smile that made Syl want to punch him.

"You don't have a ship here on Coruscant?" Syl asked, crossing her arms.

"Not one with highly experimental weapons," he answered smoothly, standing. "The family compound also doubles as a research center for the military defense branch of the Graf Corporation, so we're going to need to go there to retrieve some assets. Just in case." Xylan looked thoughtful for a moment before smiling wide. "You should all spend the night at my tower! We will make an occasion of it. I have plenty of space for all of you, and it would mean that we could get acquainted with one another before we leave. I love having guests, and it would be an honor to host Jedi. Think of it as an apology for my crass behavior earlier today," he said, directing the last bit to Imri and Vernestra.

"Sounds like a plan," Jordanna said with a toothy grin and a long look at both Syl and Vernestra. Syl met Vernestra's gaze across the table, and from the Jedi's expression she was as unhappy about their proposed sleepover as Syl was.

Jordanna, Jedi, and Xylan Graf. Syl was more than out of her depth.

She was drowning.

But there was nothing to do but see it through. The prize that waited for her on the other side would be worth it. She hoped.

So Syl squared her shoulders and pushed the maelstrom of her fears and concerns as deep into her core as it would go.

It wasn't like Syl had anywhere else to stay, anyhow. Might as well take advantage of every last bit of hospitality she could squeeze from the Graf scion.

Xylan clapped his hands and grinned. "Great, now that everything is decided, let us find a decent meal somewhere nearby. Because this is not it," he said, looking askance at the remaining starch sticks.

Syl grinned. She was not about to endure another meal of tiny plates and unsatisfying portions with Xylan Graf. Good thing she knew a place.

"How do you all feel about joppa stew?" she asked.

It was only after they were on their way to a nearby eatery that Syl realized no one had asked Xylan what he meant by retrieving family assets "just in case."

TWENTY-FOUR

Nan paced. She and Dr. Uttersond weren't allowed anywhere on the station but the room next to where they'd put the Oracle, Mari San Tekka, and Nan was starting to feel a tiny bit cabin crazy.

The hours and days and nights all blended into one another. This place wasn't like any other Nihil base that Nan had been to. Being a Nihil was usually thrilling, not mind-numbingly boring. She had nothing to do, nowhere to go. No gambling, no fighting, no drinking. Not a stim to be had. And even though chemical enhancers usually weren't Nan's style, it was more the principle of the thing. To be a Nihil was to live without rules, and yet the Gravity's Heart seemed to have missed the message.

There wasn't even a communal eating hall where Nan could watch the spontaneous fights that made being a Nihil so fun. Instead, Chancey Yarrow had all Nan's meals delivered to her, and her hourly bio breaks were carefully watched by a Quarren woman who looked like she was waiting for an excuse to kill Nan.

Two days into her captivity, Nan decided she hated the Gravity's Heart. All this because she'd killed one little stupid spiky-faced Weequay? It was absolutely bizarre.

The worst part was that no one was looking for her, because no one cared. The doctor was perfectly happy to be locked in a room with only occasional checks on his charge. He watched holo after holo, everything from overwrought romances to high-stakes adventures, and when Nan had asked him about it, he'd given her a puzzled look.

"This is the first vacation I have had in nearly a decade. My work will wait until I am ready for it," he'd said. "Besides, these are still Nihil. If you want a little carnage, your chance will come eventually."

Nan decided in that moment she would do anything to get off the Gravity's Heart and have a little fun.

Which is how she ended up flying the *Whisperkill* to an unknown location in the Hynestian sector a day later, Chancey Yarrow and a handful of her most loyal Nihil along for the ride.

She had no idea where she was going or why, but at least she wasn't stuck on the Gravity's Heart while the doctor watched another romance holo.

TWENTY-FIVE

Vernestra was halfway through Twenty-Seven Meditations for Clarity when Sylvestri Yarrow walked into the main sitting room on the floor they'd been given in Xylan Graf's tower. Vernestra felt the exact moment when the girl spotted her, because Syl's sleepy haze evaporated and a keen sense of dread emanated from the girl. No wonder Syl was worried about Jedi reading her mind. She projected her emotions like a holo. It didn't take the Force to see what she was thinking; just a glance at her dark face was more than enough.

Vernestra uncrossed her legs, letting go of the Force so she could place her feet on the plush carpet of the sitting area without forgetting how to stand. Bodies were sometimes awkward after such a deep connection with the Force. "Good morning. How was your sleep?" Vernestra asked, perhaps a tad too brightly. She wanted to get along with Syl as much as possible, but she was also keenly aware that pushing the girl would have the opposite effect.

"Fine," Syl said. The mechanic's coveralls from the previous day were gone, and the girl wore a pair of loose black pants that hung low on her hips, with a fitted red top and a black jacket, the straps of her backpack holster crisscrossing her chest. The butt of her blaster rifle was just visible over the girl's right shoulder, her holster strapped a little higher than it had been the day before. "You can go back to your, um, thinking. I was just looking for Xylan."

"Oh, I haven't seen him. The lift is locked, so we're trapped on this floor for the time being, but there is a droid around here somewhere if you're hungry or would like some tea."

"Okay. Thanks." The girl turned to leave, and Vernestra realized that she didn't want her to go.

"Can I ask you a question?"

Syl turned around, her expression wary. "Sure, why not?"

"Why don't you like Jedi? If you don't want to say, that's fine, but I thought maybe I should ask since we're going to be working together for the next few days."

Syl grimaced before flopping onto a nearby couch. "It's not that I don't like Jedi. That's kind of silly. It's that I always wonder why you're never around when people need you. The

Nihil have been out there for years, prowling the frontier, but it wasn't until they killed so many people on Valo that the Jedi took them seriously. You lot should have gone after them long ago," she said. Vernestra sat down on the couch opposite Syl.

"Oh, that's not—" Before Syl could finish her sentence, the couch shifted, and Vernestra had to jump to her feet as a massive creature nuzzled up to her, looking for pets.

"That's Xylan's Grand Theljian snow dog, Plinka. She likes to pretend she's somewhere to sit," Syl said with a laugh. "Don't worry, she got me, too."

"I didn't even notice. I should pay better attention," Vernestra said. With the Force she should've been able to sense Plinka's presence, but Vernestra was so worried about their upcoming mission she hadn't even detected the creature.

Syl stood with a frown and turned toward the nearby lift doors. "Did you say the lift was locked?"

"Oh, yeah, why?"

"I don't think Xylan is the type to lock us onto a floor, and this is the guest floor. Why is his dog here?" Syl said.

A sense of wrongness twanged through Vernestra, and she turned to Syl just as the girl pulled out her blaster rifle.

"I'll get Imri, you get Jordanna," Vernestra said, and Syl nodded and ran off without another word.

Vernestra had barely knocked on the door assigned to Imri when it slid open. "Something's wrong," he said. The boy was dressed already, and he followed Vernestra back to the sitting area where Jordanna and Remy were stretched out on a couch, Syl pacing and giving the lift doors meaningful looks.

"What makes you think there's something wrong?" Jordanna asked. She showed none of the alarm of the rest of the group.

"The lift is locked, and Xylan left Plinka here," Syl said, pointing to the large beast, who was trying, quite unsuccessfully, to get Remy to play. The vollka yawned and curled up on the edge of the couch.

"Did any of you try the intercoms?" Jordanna asked. "It's not uncommon to lock the lifts during the rest period. It makes it easier to stop any potential threats."

Everyone stared at Jordanna and she shrugged. "There are a lot of people who think kidnapping someone is a good way to make a few quick credits."

"He left his dog, though," Syl said, as though that fell somewhere near abandoning a ship full of children to Zygerrian slavers.

Jordanna gave Syl an affectionate smile. "Maybe there's a reason Xylan left his dog here. Perhaps this is her floor. I'm pretty sure my cousins have an entire set of rooms for their menagerie."

Vernestra looked to Syl, and she could tell the other girl felt as silly as she did. Had they both really panicked?

The lift dinged, and the doors opened to reveal Xylan Graf and his bodyguard, the silky-haired Gigoran with an incredibly white coat of fur. Behind them were Master Cohmac and Reath, and Vernestra's worry melted away.

"Master Cohmac. Reath. Are you accompanying us?" Vernestra asked.

Master Cohmac nodded, and Reath gave Vernestra a sheepish grin. "It seems like adventure keeps finding me, whether I want it to or not."

"Great," Sylvestri muttered, holstering her blaster rifle and crossing her arms. "Now there are four of them."

"Well, this is probably a waste of time, so you might be in for a very boring couple of weeks," Xylan Graf said, ignoring Sylvestri and speaking directly to Reath. He wore a much more sedate ensemble than the day before, and Vernestra was somewhat disappointed he hadn't included a cape. He had made quite the scene when he'd flipped his cape so dramatically back in Senator Starros's office. There would be little chance of such displays with the serviceable black pants and green tunic he wore now.

Xylan stepped farther into the room with Basha and frowned as he took in the group. "Is there something amiss?"

"The lift was locked and we thought something was wrong," Syl said, stepping forward. She thumped her chest in the manner of the frontier. "Sylvestri Yarrow," she said, introducing herself to Master Cohmac and Reath.

"Well met. Jedi Master Cohmac Vitus, and this is my Padawan, Reath Silas. We are all here on behalf of Master Stellan Gios just in case things are more fraught than they initially appear." His slight inclination in the direction of Vernestra and Imri made clear that they were included in his statement.

"Well, the more the merrier, I suppose. It's not like there is an imminent threat to the galaxy or anything," Sylvestri said. Her face looked like she'd bitten into a sour pastry as she stared down Xylan Graf. Vernestra realized that the girl didn't really want to be there. Vernestra hadn't bothered to wonder what was in this for Sylvestri, and now she did.

"About the lift?" Sylvestri said, turning back to Xylan.

"Ah, yes, there was a bit of an incident last night," Xylan said with a polite smile. "Whenever we have such a thing happen there are certain precautions in place, and locking down the lift is part of that. I hope none of you were alarmed."

"Another attack?" Vernestra asked.

Xylan nodded. "Yes. Although it was ill-advised. The ruffians got nothing but a few blaster burns. My tower was built with defense in mind—I am a Graf, after all—so there is no way anyone is going to get in unless I want them to."

"Told you," Jordanna said, winking at Sylvestri in a playful way from where she was still sprawled on the couch.

"Rich people are weird," Sylvestri muttered, shaking her head. Vernestra had to agree. The upper levels of Coruscant were supposed to be some of the safest places in the Republic. Was so much caution really necessary?

"Are we heading out?" Jordanna asked. She didn't make any move to rise, and Vernestra wondered keenly just why it was that the San Tekka deputy had decided to invite herself along. Was this because she was chasing after Sylvestri? Was she waiting for the right moment to make some sort of grand gesture like they did in the romance holos? Perhaps, since Jordanna seemed like she didn't really care about anything but her own momentary whims. That wasn't how a Jedi acted, and Vernestra found the behavior intriguing and a bit irksome. Jordanna seemed very irresponsible, and yet she'd defended Tiikae from all manner of threats. It was a curious conundrum.

"Yes," Xylan said, answering Jordanna's question and jolting Vernestra from her thoughts. "But first let us adjourn to the dining room and enjoy a light repast while I review our next steps to ensure we all understand the goal of this expedition."

Xylan led the way through the sitting room to an area set aside for dining. Like the rest of the floor, it was built with entertaining in mind, but also comfort, so the low table at the center of the wide-open room was surrounded by multihued cushions that looked like they should be reclined on. Everyone found their place, Xylan sitting at the head of the table and the Gigoran kneeling behind him to his left. Syl sank onto the cushion to Xylan's left and Jordanna sat down right next to her, Remy still in the sitting room from whence they'd come. Cohmac and Reath sat across from Syl and Jordanna, and Vernestra took a seat next to them, Imri sinking onto a set of cushions, as well. There was still space for at least a dozen more guests, and Vernestra imagined that when the room was full, the chatter of conversation was deafening.

A trio of droids appeared and began setting out various covered dishes. "The dishes with red lids contain meat," Xylan said with a smile at Syl. It was less friendly and more like he knew something special about her. Syl's resulting scowl was interesting, but Jordanna's quick look from one to the other was even more intriguing.

Once everyone had filled the plates before them, Master Cohmac began speaking. "Lord Graf—"

"Xylan, please," he interrupted, and Master Cohmac inclined his head.

"Xylan, now that we are all assembled, perhaps this is a good time to explain your interest in this specific sector of space. Because I get the sense that Senator Starros has a limited understanding of your request."

Xylan smiled, but Vernestra could feel the waves of frustration that emanated from him before he managed to regain control of his emotions. "Ah, Master Cohmac, you are correct. Now that we are about to be on our way, I must confess that the lease my family seeks is only part of the story, and in the interest of complete transparency I am happy to share as much as I can with you, keeping in mind that I may withhold some details in the interest of not showing my hand to the competition." This last part was said with a nod of acknowledgment to Jordanna, who was feeding a plate of sausages to the vollka who had appeared behind her chair.

"Fair enough, and I'm happy to fill in any details about the sector," Jordanna said, smiling sweetly at Xylan.

Next to Vernestra, Imri shifted uncomfortably. "They really hate each other," he murmured to Vernestra, and she nodded.

"Their family feud is legendary. From what I understand, them even being in the same room is a feat," she said before turning her attention back to what Xylan was saying.

"A few centuries ago, the Republic was in the habit of handing out leases for unoccupied sectors near member planets, most notably areas that could be used for hyperspace experiments. The Berenge sector was the best of these, and both my family and the San Tekkas found ourselves vying for the same bit of space. There were certain qualities within that area that we thought would make it optimal for riskier experiments."

"One of which is the lack of active planetary life," Jordanna said. "No risk of accidentally destroying a star system or having debris go hurtling toward a planet, like we saw with the Emergences last year."

Xylan's lips tightened at being interrupted, but he nodded. "After the San Tekka lease expired two decades ago, my family immediately applied for it. But we were summarily blocked by a group of academics led by Professor Wolk, who indicated that the unique properties of the sector make it ideal for academic inquiry. The sector is little more than an administrative grouping of planetless stars, devoid of settlements and, most importantly, rogue realspace objects to cast shadows into hyperspace, and for that reason there are a number of routes through the sector, a handful of them private Graf lanes. So we have a very, very strong interest in occupying the sector."

"But Professor Wolk also thought there was a Nihil weapon in the sector," Master Cohmac said, and Xylan nodded.

"Yes, but the old Gungan also thought the Nihil were responsible for the Great Disaster and the resulting Emergences," he said with a laugh, shaking his head. "The man was full of wild theories he couldn't prove."

"But you lost your ship in hyperspace, right?" Jordanna asked Syl, and the girl's eyes widened.

"Not quite. I, uh, lost it to the Nihil. When they killed my mother," Syl said while staring at her plate.

Xylan clucked his tongue. "Syl, there is no point in lying." Her head snapped up and she stared at the man as he turned back to the rest of the group. "Just like our dear Sylvestri, I loathe speaking ill of the dead, but Professor Wolk had a wild theory about the missing ships and how things were getting pulled out of hyperspace. He thought Sylvestri's mother, who was killed in a Nihil attack, had faked her death so that she could build a gravity-well projector in the sector. He tried to convince Syl that her sudden ejection from hyperspace was not caused by a malfunctioning hyperdrive, but rather a weapon created by her mother. Utterly nonsensical."

"You don't believe the Nihil built a highly experimental hyperspace weapon?" Master Cohmac said, his dark brows drawing together with worry.

"Absolutely not," Xylan said with a wave of dismissal. "The cost alone would be prohibitive. But Senator Starros seems to think the Nihil are more than the space trash they are, and if I want to secure the lease on the sector, I have to assuage her fears. The original plan was to prove to her and Wolk once and for all that his 'theories' were more about securing the sector for his own interests than an issue of security."

"What about the attempt on Syl's life?" Jordanna said. "Someone did try to kill her."

"Yes, and the Graf family has a lot of enemies," Xylan said with a tight smile. "Your own brood has tried to kill Grandmere no fewer than a dozen times. I tend to think that was just a case of mistaken identity."

Neither Jordanna nor Sylvestri seemed convinced by Xylan's smooth response, but they also did not offer any further arguments.

"Why hasn't the Republic sent a cruiser out that way to investigate? That should be simple enough," Reath said.

"They have, trust me," Xylan said with a long-suffering sigh. "And I have also sent scout droids. The energy readings are always normal. Wolk's theory was that the weapon was only detectable while in use."

"If this is a Nihil plot, then we will need to keep the Order and the Republic apprised of our movements," Master Cohmac said, and Xylan inclined his head. "So that it can be handled before any more lives are lost."

"Of course," he said. "But I am certain there will be nothing in the sector, and once we fly a simple grid through most of the space, it will be up to all of you to help me validate the findings that Senator Starros already has."

"Why Jedi?" Sylvestri asked suddenly. "I mean, four Jedi is a lot. I've heard a single Jedi can take out an entire Nihil Storm. Seems to me you'd be more useful to the galaxy and the Republic fighting those marauders than taking a spin through the Berenge sector." Her emotions were a jumble, and Vernestra wondered if all this talk of her mother was too much. Every time the woman was even mentioned Sylvestri turned ashen and her expression became morose, her grief obvious. This could not be an easy conversation for her.

Master Cohmac smiled at the dark-skinned girl. "There are already a number of Jedi engaged in assisting the Republic in flushing out the Nihil. But to your point, I had also wondered why we were being called in to settle . . . a business dispute. The Order is always willing to assist when asked, but I had similar thoughts."

Xylan shrugged languidly. "Senator Starros seems to think that the Jedi are above reproach and demanded that you lot be neutral observers. And I am willing to do anything to put this silliness to rest."

The droids came and cleared the serving dishes from the table, and as they did so, the center opened to reveal a holo display. A map of the galaxy glowed in the middle of the table, and Vernestra found herself more than a little impressed at the sight. She pushed aside her plate of half-eaten fruit and pastries to focus more fully on Xylan's words.

"We are here, on Coruscant. I have a transport that will take us here, to Neral's moon, which is a two-day trip by way of private Graf hyperspace routes."

"How can a hyperspace route be private?" Imri asked.

"Because no one has the beacon codes but my family, and they do not appear in any navicomputer but ours," Xylan said smoothly. "Without the beacons to navigate by, it's entirely possible for a ship to run into problems with hyperspace. Navigational beacons guarantee a safe passage by giving pilots an idea of their path and helping them steer clear of any possible obstacles. There are a number of beacons left behind from the Hyperspace Rush, and a number of those belong to the Graf family and are encrypted so that only we can read their positioning data. By using those private paths, we can get to the Hynestian sector and the main family satellite much faster than traveling the public routes."

On the holo map in the center of the table, a yellow line appeared, mapping out their route.

"And the Graf family compound is where your real ship is?" Syl asked.

"Oh, yes. The *Vengeful Goddess* is a very experimental ship. Cutting-edge laser cannons, four sublight engines, even a point-five-rated hyperdrive with tandem-processing navicomputer that operates twice as fast as most others. My family bought a shipyard on Corellia nearly a decade ago, and this ship is poised to be the blueprint for the Republic security forces once they see the beauty of the design. I daresay once you've flown her you will be hard-pressed to go back to more standard haulers," he said with a wink at Sylvestri, as though they were sharing a joke. The girl only scowled in return.

"I also have a number of smaller fighters that we can use. Other prototypes. Nothing as sophisticated as your Vectors, but effective all the same. We will want everyone who can fly piloting a ship to make the survey go faster."

Imri opened his mouth to say something, and Vernestra elbowed him in the side. "Not a word," she muttered while amusement danced across her Padawan's pale face.

"And after that?" Master Cohmac asked. Vernestra wondered how he'd gotten assigned to this mission. Had Stellan always considered sending along the Jedi Master? For some reason, that irked Vernestra a bit. Perhaps it was because just the day before, Xylan Graf had called her a child.

"After that we fly out and run a close grid search of the sector until we've mapped the space. Onerous, but that is what

Senator Starros wants, and so she shall have it," Xylan said.

"If you think there are Nihil, we should notify the Republic and the Order," Master Cohmac said. "It is illogical that we should walk into a trap."

"There is currently no proof the Nihil are operating in the Berenge sector," Xylan said smoothly. "Even poor Professor Wolk could find nothing conclusive to indicate any sort of presence in the region. All of his scout droids came back with completely normal readings, the same as mine. I am loathe to waste the Republic and the Order's time when there are very real threats to be handled. You have heard of the renewed fighting in the Hetzal system?"

"Yes," Master Cohmac said, watching Xylan as he took a drink of tea. "I see your conundrum." Vernestra realized that Master Cohmac did not trust Xylan Graf any more than Sylvestri Yarrow did. They would have to be on alert for anything suspicious, just in case there was something dangerous that Xylan wasn't telling them.

"But trust that at the first sign of trouble we will alert the Republic," Xylan said with a dismissive wave.

"What are we waiting for?" Sylvestri said, standing. "We should leave as soon as possible."

Xylan Graf gave a slow smile and nodded. "Yes, let us be on our way."

TWENTY-SIX

Syl was so glad to be quit of Coruscant that she nearly did backflips once Xylan's pleasure yacht, the *Resplendent Pearl*, cleared the last of the planet's hazy skyline. Sure, she was stuck working for a rich man who lied so much that the truth was near impossible to find, a man who had now wrapped her up in his web of lies, and everywhere she looked there were Jedi, but she was finally doing something. Syl was a woman of action, not politics. If she'd had her way, she would've jumped in a ship and flown to the Berenge sector straightaway, blast whatever waited for her there.

She had to finish out her obligation and get back to Port

Haileap as soon as possible. Syl hated all of this—the back-and-forth conversations, the lying, the possibility of intrigue. She was a hauler, not a politician. She just wanted her ship and her line of credit so she could get on with her life.

Perhaps sensing a bit of Syl's agitation, Xylan had announced to everyone as they got settled that Syl was their pilot, and Syl had never been so glad to have a cockpit all to herself. She had tried to keep her feelings about everything— the lies, Jordanna's sudden appearance—to herself, but from the anguished looks the Jedi—most especially Imri—kept shooting her, she had the distinct impression she had failed at every attempt.

And it wasn't that she didn't like the Jedi or even had a problem with them, they just made her nervous. Being around them was like walking a tightrope over a sarlacc pit. When she'd stumbled bleary-eyed into the sitting room that morning, Vernestra had looked dead, she was so still. That wasn't normal. There was no reason for Syl to pretend it was.

Still, she was a bit glad to have them along, in case things took a bad turn.

"Hey, there."

Syl turned around in the pilot's seat to find Jordanna and Remy standing in the doorway to the cockpit. Remy squeezed past Jordanna to bump her feline face against Syl's, the vollka's horns tangling in the girl's hair a bit, and she laughed and scratched the hunting cat before pushing her away. Her heart gave that same little jump it always did when she saw Jordanna, and she pushed her joy down as far as it would go, searching for her anger instead.

She had to protect her heart. No matter what.

"Hey, yourself. Didn't Xylan want to ask you a few questions about Remy and her species?" Syl said, a not-so-subtle hint that Jordanna should be somewhere else.

"Bah. He can find that in a databank," she said, sitting in the copilot's seat. "I wanted a chance to talk to you alone."

"I figured we've said everything we need to say to each other."

"Not true," Jordanna said, kicking her booted feet up on a metal box that held part of the navicomputer. "Where did your mother go when she left you on Tiikae for a month?"

Syl was disappointed that Jordanna wanted to talk about her mother. Not that Syl was actually itching to have a heartfelt conversation with Jordanna. But Chancey Yarrow was the last thing Syl wanted to think about as she flew Xylan's pleasure yacht out of Coruscant's gravitational field.

But now that Jordanna had mentioned it, Syl realized that she couldn't account for the four weeks her mother had left her on Tiikae. When her mother had picked her up, Syl had been so heartbroken over having to leave Jordanna that she'd retreated into herself for weeks, only coming out of her funk when her mother had been killed by the Nihil and she'd had no choice.

The timing was just too good.

"You think my mother dumped me on Tiikae so she

could what? Meet with the Nihil and broker a contract?" Syl asked, her knuckles white from gripping the yoke too hard. She was careful not to look over at the other woman. Thinking back to that time in her life was not something Syl liked to do, and she was afraid that Jordanna might get a glimpse of what she had gone through in those terrible months. But more than that, she had been very good at not thinking too long or hard about what Professor Wolk told her, because the truth was she didn't want to consider that he could be in any way correct. Better to take money from the Graf family than spend her days piecing together suspicions.

And here was Jordanna, shining a bright light into the shadows of it all.

"That's not what I said," Jordanna began, but Syl shook her head.

"But that's what you think. Otherwise, why bring it up now?"

"I don't know. But isn't it strange for her to just leave you behind like that?" Jordanna asked, and Syl huffed out a breath.

"No. That's the thing. She was always leaving me with this friend or that to learn some new skill. I always thought it was normal. But now you think it means my mother is some, what? Some Nihil lackey? If you'd spent a single moment with Chancey Yarrow, you would know that she is not a person who suffers needless cruelty."

"'People leave, it's what they do. It doesn't mean they

don't love you,'" Jordanna said, and Syl turned to look at her. "You told me that once, and I always thought it was such a strange thing to say. But now I guess I get it."

"I asked you to come with me," Syl said, even though she knew the issue was much bigger than that. "Me saying that had nothing to do with my mother."

"I know. And I won't let you out of my sight again," Jordanna said. "But I'm worried. What will you do if we get to the Berenge sector and she's there, sitting behind a giant cannon, shooting at passing haulers?"

The image was so ridiculous that Syl laughed, the sound more bitter than she'd intended. "Can we please talk about something that isn't my mother or the Nihil or Xylan Graf?" she said, exasperation lacing her every word.

"Sure. What do you think of the Jedi?"

Syl sighed. "I haven't known them long enough to make a decision."

"Of course you have. It's written all over your face every time you look at them."

Syl bit her lip. "They're weird, okay? There's something about them that feels . . . old. Even Vernestra, who is a year younger than me. I was expecting, I don't know, someone more heroic? They seem capable but a bit naive. I mean, Master Cohmac is basically like a skinny librarian or something, judging from how he talks. I was expecting someone more impressive."

"Yeah," Jordanna said, and when Syl glanced at her, her

dark eyes had gone distant, looking into another time. "I felt the same way about them when we were on Tiikae. Good people, but maybe a little . . . detached from the struggles of the frontier. I can tell you that the Jedi are very, very bad at change. At adapting to the world around them. Jedi are brave and determined and heroic, but none of that amounts to a week of rations without the ability to perceive the truth of the galaxy around you. Their Force might lead them to a larger truth, and I'm glad they're standing with the Republic against the Nihil, but they just aren't like us."

"What are you saying?" Syl asked.

"I think that maybe they cut themselves off from too much of life, so that the things they fight for are ideas, not people. It's not a bad thing. I guess that must just be how it is when you see all of the galaxy and its secrets laid out before you in distinct degrees of good and bad."

"Do you really think the Jedi are so, I don't know, simple?"

"I think the Force keeps them on a path that most of us only dream of. Just think how easy your life would be if you always knew the exact right thing to do."

Syl didn't think it was that easy for the Jedi, since both Vernestra and Imri had looked worried or concerned about things since she'd met them, but it did sound like a sort of idealized kind of existence. Perhaps that was why overall they seemed peaceful. Because they had the answer everyone was looking for.

Syl had once thought that answer for her was Jordanna,

but now she wasn't sure. That moment, piloting a nice ship with Jordanna and Remy in the cockpit to keep her company, had once been a dream. But now Syl wondered if she had wanted too little and if what Jordanna was offering was too late.

It wasn't something Syl ever thought she'd have to consider. Did she still love Jordanna? Or had their time together been fueled by the emotional flash burn of a crush?

"I don't know how you can say the Jedi don't care about people. Isn't the Force life itself?" Syl didn't know why she felt the need to defend the Jedi, but she did. Jordanna mocking them seemed a little like trying to tip a bantha for fun: it wasn't the herd beasts' fault they were so dull. Sometimes people were just who they were, and there was nothing to be done about it.

"People make up all life, that's true. But the Force doesn't always take into account people. It's so much bigger than the small problems of settlers or senators. And sometimes if you are looking at the forest you miss what is happening in the trees." Jordanna sounded sad as she spoke, and Syl wondered if there was more to her deciding to come along than a chance to stop whatever it was the Nihil might be up to or have another stolen moment with Syl.

What had happened on Tiikae since the last time Syl saw her ex-girlfriend?

A sedate chime echoed through the console in front of Syl, signaling they'd cleared enough of Coruscant's relevant gravity that they could make the jump to hyperspace. "Even this ship's alerts are fancy," she murmured.

There was a bump and a jolt as Syl made the jump to hyperspace. After a moment of silence, she sighed. "Okay, Jordanna, what is going on? This is a really different conversation than anything before. Remember all the nights you kept telling me how great the Force was? Now you sound like you don't much like the Jedi." Jordanna had been a bit of a Force enthusiast, her interests usually focused on the numerous ways cultures related to it, and she had even said she wanted to study the Force if she ever left Tiikae and went to a university. It might have just been the late-night musings of two girls with time to waste, but Jordanna believed the Force was real, unlike her aunt, the deputy who had only seen the Jedi as assets to keep order on Tiikae.

"The Order and the Force are two different things. It's just something I've been thinking about a lot, why people end up Jedi or even deputies. And it's not a matter of liking or disliking, it's about understanding the truth of a thing. Do you know why people join the Nihil?"

"Because they're monsters?"

Jordanna laughed. "No, because we all want a place to belong. The Nihil have given the castoffs and losers of the galaxy a home. They've given people with nothing something, and that is a very powerful thing. Are they bad? Of course. But they're bad because it's all a lie based around violence." Jordanna yawned. "Sorry, hyperspace always makes me sleepy. It's an old San Tekka trick. Want to put a baby to sleep? Drop into hyperspace. Now I can never stay awake during a jump."

"Why are you telling me all of this?" Syl asked, turning her chair toward Jordanna. It was strange; they'd been apart no more than six months, and in some ways it felt like the time had been but a heartbeat. She still felt comfortable around Jordanna like no one else she'd ever met, like she'd finally found the person she was meant to be with. But in other ways, Jordanna was like a completely different person. The way her face changed when she thought no one was looking, like she couldn't quite escape some terrible memory that always lurked on the edges of her mind.

"Because it's a fun fact about my family?" Jordanna asked.

"No, all this stuff about the Jedi."

The other girl laughed, even though Syl didn't find her obvious redirect funny. "Have you ever heard of the Church of the Force? My uncles are very into it, something that people have become enamored with on Naboo. They mentioned it to me in passing during my last situation report a month or so ago, and I've been thinking of it ever since. I want to know what it means to be good. Don't you wonder about that? I have spent the past six months trying to keep people alive and failing at it quite spectacularly." She laughed humorlessly. "But I don't know if that makes me good or not. How do I make a difference in a galaxy that seems to bend naturally toward destruction? That's why I left Tiikae. Because it didn't feel like I was doing a whole lot there, and I thought maybe I could make the galaxy better by, I don't know, being proactive instead of reactive. If that makes sense."

Syl's pulse thrummed in her chest. This was why she had fallen for Jordanna in the first place: she was always thinking about things in a way that made Syl want to think deeply, as well. Jordanna should have been a philosopher sitting in an atrium someplace like Naboo, where they valued such musings, not a deputy on a hardscrabble planet where every day was a struggle just to survive.

"Well, don't look at me," Syl said with a shrug. "I am strictly here for the money."

Jordanna laughed. "Right. And you traveled all the way to Coruscant for the sightseeing. You are such a terrible liar."

"Why are you here, Jordanna?" Syl said suddenly, her mixed feelings finally settling on a single issue. Jordanna was too good at seeing the truth of Syl, and if her ex-girlfriend asked her directly about her dealings with Xylan, all her doubts would come pouring out. "And I don't mean philosophically. I mean, why are you right here, right now? With me?"

"Because I've spent too much time fighting, and I realized that when I had a chance, I didn't fight for the one thing I cared about." She stared at Syl, her gaze full of heat, and it was in that moment Syl realized she was blinkered.

She couldn't protect her heart from Jordanna breaking

it because the other girl already held it in her hands. Syl was still hopelessly in love with her.

Jordanna grinned. "I love it when you have absolutely no comeback. Anyway, I plan on spending the rest of this mission convincing you that you should give me another chance, so just know that's coming. Prepare to be wooed!"

Syl's face heated when she considered all the ways Jordanna could try to charm her. "Are you sure you aren't just having a bad week? You do like to change your mind a lot," Syl muttered.

"Not this time, and you should really, really never play sabacc, the way your very pretty face reveals your emotions." Jordanna stretched. "Things will work out for the best and as they must. That is what I know, because even though I'm not a Jedi, I do believe in the Force. Now, I am going to take a nap. Wake me up when it's time to eat."

Like Remy, Jordanna closed her eyes and was soon quietly snoring. Syl pulled her attention away from Jordanna and pulled up the navicomputer's screen. She looked at the coordinates and frowned.

They seemed wrong. Syl recognized one of the beacons, which was in the Dalnan sector, not the Hynestian. She only knew it by heart because she had once transposed the numbers in the flight calculations and flown them toward the frost planet Hynestia instead of Haileap, much to her mother's anger. It had been a costly mistake that taught Syl to always, *always* double- and triple-check her routes.

So why were they flying toward Haileap now?

Syl went to a nearby cabinet and pulled out the navicron that contained the time-phased star chart. Navigating via star charts was old-fashioned, but most ships carried one just in case the navicomputer went belly-up. Syl's mother had made her learn how to navigate this way before she'd ever let her fly the *Switchback*. As Syl compared the locations in the navicomputer with the flight path that had been registered with the Republic, a sensation of dread began to overwhelm her.

They weren't going anywhere near Neral's moon. They were headed to a spot of empty space not terribly far from Port Haileap.

Just what was Xylan Graf playing at?

And, more important, did the Jedi on board know?

TWENTY-SEVEN

Vernestra was sitting on the floor in the cargo area with Master Cohmac, Reath, and Imri when the ship gave the characteristic bump that meant they'd entered hyperspace. For the past few hours, ever since they'd boarded the ship, Master Cohmac had been walking them through a guided meditation that was meant to help them better work together in case they became engaged in battle, something he felt was inevitable despite Xylan Graf's platitudes.

"I think we should take a break," Master Cohmac said, standing from where he sat cross-legged on the floor. "Imri, Reath, why don't you go see if there's anything you can do to help Basha with the food preparation?"

The Padawans nodded and departed down the corridor that led back toward the center of the ship. Vernestra had barely climbed to her feet when Master Cohmac looked over at her.

"Here is your chance to ask me your questions," he said, and Vernestra felt her face heat.

"My apologies, Master Cohmac, I did not realize I was being so obvious."

"You're young, Jedi. You may be skilled, but I have been doing this for a long time. I could tell from your surprise when Reath and I exited the lift this morning that you wanted to ask me whether or not Stellan had sent me along to keep an eye on you."

"Did he?" Vernestra asked, and Master Cohmac smiled.

"Yes. But not for the reasons you suspect. I stopped by to speak with him after he received your message. Good idea, sending him one that was encrypted."

Before they'd gone to the diner in the aftermath of Professor Wolk's death, Vernestra had decided to send Master Stellan a message alerting him not only to the academic's passing but to the strange nature of her meeting with Senator Starros and Xylan Graf. But she'd received no response, so she had figured maybe she was just being a bit silly.

"So Master Stellan didn't send you along because, well, because he thought Imri and I couldn't handle this by ourselves?"

Master Cohmac shook his head. "Not at all. He was worried that perhaps Senator Starros had not been completely honest about her request for your assistance, and your message confirmed those suspicions. There are some politics at play here, and even I'm not entirely sure what Xylan Graf's or Senator Starros's motivations might be."

Vernestra's shoulders slumped. "I feel like I keep mucking things up." She'd felt the dishonesty coming from Xylan, but she'd second-guessed herself and thought it was because of something else.

"No, you did what you thought was right," Master Cohmac said. "I'm going to be quite blunt with you, Vernestra, but your master did you no favors pushing you to become a Knight so early. And I think it was a mistake to allow you to take a Padawan so soon."

Vernestra jerked as though she'd been slapped, but before she could say anything, Cohmac continued.

"Not because you aren't capable or don't have good control of the Force. And not because you aren't good at mentoring the boy. But because I worry that your current trajectory is unsustainable."

"I'm fine," Vernestra said, her words clipped.

"I am certain you are. But take this lesson with you from an old Jedi who has seen far too much pain in his time. Being a Knight is about more than just connecting to the Force. It's about having an understanding of the galaxy around us. You are responsible and have done an excellent job helping Imri understand and use his abilities. But you are young, and you don't have a huge amount of experience. People will take advantage of that, Vernestra. Senator Starros wanted to embarrass Xylan Graf and his family, and I have little doubt she tried to use you to do that. The Grafs, however, have influence beyond that of Starros, and Stellan asked me to come along to eliminate any appearance of bias by the Order. I cannot tell which one, Xylan Graf or Senator Starros, is being honest with us. But my feeling is the answer is neither of them. And that is what a Jedi must always remember: the galaxy is full of those who would use the Order and the Force for their own purposes, but our allegiance must always be to maintaining the balance of the Force. So we go where we are called."

Vernestra felt small and embarrassed. She'd been so happy about Stellan's confidence in her, she hadn't even thought to question the larger ramifications. But Sylvestri had understood. She had known that Vernestra was being used as a game piece, and not a very important one at that.

"The Jedi have a responsibility to stop the Nihil," Vernestra finally said. "As does the Republic. They are murderers and thieves, and as long as we allow them to prey on the frontier, the galaxy will be the worse for their presence. They've already killed millions of people! Helping the Republic stop the Nihil is what we should be doing. Master Cohmac, I keep thinking about what Sylvestri Yarrow said this morning, and I agree. We shouldn't be here. We should be out helping save lives, not settling business disputes."

A look of chagrin flickered across Master Cohmac's face. "The Republic exists to keep order, but sometimes there are also members of the Republic who use the pretense of providing assistance to see to their own affairs, and I'm afraid you may have run into one of those situations with this assignment. I have a feeling Senator Starros is playing a deeper game than any of us realize at the moment. And the same can be said of the Grafs, who have a long history with the Order, from the research I have done. But I agree, we have a larger task ahead of us as stewards of the light."

"We have to stop the Nihil, Master Cohmac, even if it puts us in the orbit of questionable allies. You've seen what they're capable of. It's the Jedi who must lead that charge. And that is where we should be right now."

"Perhaps," said Master Cohmac. "This does feel quite a bit like a distraction, and I have no love for the Grafs, as they have shown themselves to be capable of terrible things and are suspected of worse." A look of disgust briefly flashed across Master Cohmac's face before he schooled his expression back to one of polite interest. "There is a great deal of space between the will of the Force and the will of either the Republic or the Jedi Order. But that is a discussion for another time. Just know that my presence here has nothing to do with your abilities and everything to do with politics."

He rested his hand on Vernestra's shoulder for a moment

before departing the cargo bay, leaving her to herself and her maelstrom of emotions. She was feeling more and more off balance these days, and it was not an experience she liked.

She sank down on the metal floor. She didn't want to feel the anger and frustration that sat heavy in her middle, but it was important to recognize this moment for what it was: a chance to grow. She had learned an important lesson. The Jedi may recognize her worth, but there would always be outsiders who would doubt her, who would see her as a tool for their own ends. And she could not let that turn her bitter. Rather, she had to understand it was part of life in the galaxy and accept it as she did everything else.

That did not mean she didn't feel angry.

Vernestra closed her eyes. She had to find her center, to let go of the anger she felt at Senator Starros and Xylan Graf, at being manipulated. Vernestra took a deep breath and felt everything shift, as though the world had tilted ever so slightly to the left. She opened her eyes and found herself somewhere completely different.

Jedi. I have been calling for you, came a whispery voice. It sounded neither male nor female, and the Basic spoken carried an unfamiliar lilt. *You draw near.*

Vernestra blinked. Like last time, the vision felt incredibly real. She stood in a ship, a different one than Xylan's, the corridors built from a hodgepodge of material that made it look like a giant scrap heap. This time the entire vision was washed in hyperspace blue, everything in gradients of the hue, so Vernestra knew her old affliction had not fully gone away as she'd thought.

But was this a real place or just a Force-created musing?

You already have the answer, the voice said, even though Vernestra was certain she had not spoken aloud. *The way is clear.*

She was half tempted to try to return to her body, but she knew that was not how this worked. She would have to fully embrace the vision before it would release her, and she could only hope that would be before anyone found her body.

"You called for me," Vernestra said into the empty corridor. "Show yourself."

You must come to me, the voice said, and Vernestra followed the sound of it down a curving hallway. Until it branched. After a moment of hesitation, she took the path to the left, the walls painted with strange symbols. Not the ones on the puzzle box she still carried, but symbols that seemed to be taken from several different languages. She finally realized they were mathematical calculations, the numbers strange in a few of the theorems. But what purpose did they serve?

So close, my child, the voice said. *So close.*

Vernestra began to run, giving it her all as she had back in the office building when she chased the Twi'lek who had killed Professor Wolk. But here in the vision she couldn't reach the Force, so her footfalls were all her, running flat out, her boots echoing hollowly in the eerie space. She was so close, only meters away from a room that glowed with the perfect blue of hyperspace. But the more she ran, the more she realized she wasn't going anywhere.

She began to push herself, straining to get to the voice. Her heart pounded and her breathing became labored. Just a little farther, just a little more and the mystery would be ended.

"Vern! Wake up!"

Vernestra startled. Her heart pounded as the vision faded and she slammed back to reality inside her body. She was lying flat on her back, Imri looking down at her, his eyes wide and his pale cheeks flushed.

"Vern. Are you okay?"

Vernestra sat up and looked around. She was in the small cargo bay of the *Resplendent Pearl* once more. Imri watched her with a concerned expression, but he was fortunately the only one in the cargo area with her.

"Yeah, I'm fine. Are we still in hyperspace?" Her head throbbed, and she took a deep breath and let it out.

Imri frowned. "Yep. Is that why you were, uh—actually, where were you?"

Vernestra rested her head in her hands. "I think I was having a vision."

Imri shook his head. "Vern, you weren't here. I mean, your body was, and if Syl or Xylan found you they may have thought you were just sleeping, but anyone else . . ." His voice trailed off, and Vernestra didn't have to wonder what he meant by "anyone else." Any Jedi would've wondered why she was meditating so deeply, deeper than most Jedi regularly went into the Force. So in a way Vernestra was glad that Imri had been the one to find her; it would mean fewer questions to answer.

But she was more concerned that it was happening at all.

"Imri, I have to tell you something. Something that few Jedi know about me."

Imri frowned. "Is this about your lightwhip?"

"No. I actually haven't told anyone in the main temple about that yet. When I was a Padawan I used to have . . . episodes. It didn't happen all of the time, only sometimes when we traveled a long way and were in hyperspace for a very long time. I have visions, only they're less like visions and more like leaving my body to go visit other places. I'm still not quite sure what they are."

Imri blinked, his eyes going wide and his mouth forming a circle of surprise. "Deep meditation can be very dangerous, Vern."

"I know, which is why it's important to understand that this thing I do, it isn't on purpose. I can't control it, Imri. And I thought I was finished with it after I passed my trials. Master Stellan was always convinced that it was something I could train, hone to an actual skill. But I've tried, and . . . well, I can't. I've told Master Stellan that I've put it aside, but the reality is that I've never been able to do it on purpose. I'm sure Master Stellan made note of it with the Temple when I was a Padawan, and I'm hopeful that no one asks me to use it.

Because I can't." It felt like something Vernestra should confess to Master Stellan or Master Cohmac, not her Padawan. But she had always kept an open and honest line of communication with Imri, and it was too late to change that now.

"So why is it happening now?" Imri asked, his expression thoughtful. "It hasn't happened as long as you've been my master, has it?"

Vernestra shook her head. "No, and I don't know why now. I'm not sure whether something has triggered it or if it's like your sensitivity to emotions, a skill that's slowly getting stronger."

"You've noticed that, huh?" Imri asked, shifting from foot to foot. "I didn't want to think that was what was happening, but it's getting harder and harder to block everyone else out. Even with the exercises from Samara the Blue. I think it might be something to do with being half Genetian, but I'm . . . concerned."

Vernestra's head pounded, an aftereffect she remembered from previous bouts of hyperspace tripping, and she swallowed a sigh. "I think concerned is a good way to feel. For me, I think I'm going through this again because there's something happening, something big, and I need to be there to help someone. But what it is? I don't know. And as for your abilities, hopefully once we get through this mission we can return to the Temple on Coruscant and see if there isn't some help to be had from the Council. There are other humans from Genetia in the Order. Perhaps some of their experiences can help shed some light on your abilities and how best to control them."

Imri nodded and gave Vernestra a sheepish grin. "Well, as your Padawan, I have your back. I promise, I won't let anyone sneak up on you."

Vernestra smiled. "And I have your back, as it should be."

"There you are."

Both Imri and Vernestra turned to see Sylvestri standing in the doorway to the main hall.

Imri helped Vernestra to her feet, and the Jedi smiled at the pilot. "Is it time to eat?" he asked.

"Soon, but I wanted to talk to you about something else."

"Oh, did you have questions about the Force?" Vernestra said. She could sense the questions swirling around Sylvestri, and teaching others about the Force was one of Vernestra's favorite things to do.

"What? No. I don't care about the Force. Well, I mean, not at the moment. Look," Sylvestri said, glancing left and right as she closed the short distance to Vernestra and Imri. "I was double-checking the coordinates in the navicomputer and checking them against a time-phased star chart—"

"Isn't that a little old-fashioned?" Vernestra asked with a frown.

"Yes, but my ship's navicomputer has been blinkered for a while, so it's old habit. Anyway, these coordinates that

Xylan set aren't taking us anywhere near Neral's moon. We're headed right toward the Dalnan sector."

"Did you ask him about them?" Imri said, and Sylvestri snorted.

"Absolutely not. I came down here to see if you knew about it," Sylvestri said, her gaze boring into Vernestra.

Vernestra shook her head. "This is the first I have heard. And I share your concern. Our first step should be asking Xylan about it."

Sylvestri shook her head. "If there is one thing I know about Xylan Graf, it's that he always has an explanation that sounds completely plausible, even if the logic is fuzzier than a bemeer fruit. Look, I told you that Xylan Graf isn't my friend, and I meant that. My only interest in coming along on this trip was to make a few credits and maybe figure out my next steps as a hauler. But he's up to something. I just don't know what. I'm telling you this so you can tell the rest of your friends and we can be ready for whatever it is that's waiting for us on the other end of this haul."

Before Vernestra could say anything else, Sylvestri spun on her heel and walked away, the sound of her boots echoing back toward the cockpit.

"Do you think Xylan Graf is working with the Nihil?" Imri asked, his pale brows pulled together into a contemplative frown.

"Perhaps. Master Cohmac definitely does not trust him, or the Graf family. Sylvestri's warning is right: we need to be on our guard. But we should also have Master Cohmac speak to him about this."

"Do you think he'll deny it?"

"Yes. But we should be able to detect if he is lying outright. Either way, we should remember that danger could lurk anywhere. It's anyone's guess what will be waiting for us, and I don't want to be caught unaware."

As they walked toward the crew mess, Vernestra's thoughts turned back toward the vision she'd had. Well, the place she'd been pulled to, really. The last time, she'd seen the boarding house on Tiikae and the vision had implored her to find the box. Now the cube was a perplexing weight in her belt pouch.

Could Xylan Graf be taking them to the place she'd just been? The strange, eerily empty ship with the unusual calculations on the walls? Was that the Graf family compound? Vernestra didn't know, but Sylvestri's warning would not go unheeded.

Vernestra would relay the message to Cohmac and Reath at the earliest possible junction and do what she always did: hope the Force was with them.

TWENTY-EIGHT

Nan knew money when she saw it. The old woman talking with Chancey Yarrow was the kind of rich where her face looked young even though her body betrayed the fact that she was ancient. The entire station smelled of flowers and freshness, and plants bloomed everywhere, a feat of engineering that screamed, *I have entirely too many credits.* It wasn't like the Amaxine station where Nan had run afoul of the Jedi the year before; this was a place that was well maintained and full of people moving about their business. There was a dome, for the love of stars. Nan tried to imagine the cost of the fuel just to keep everything humming along, the air breathable and humid, and realized that it was a mind-numbingly high number.

These people weren't just rich; they had the kind of money that made the impossible possible, and Nan's fingers itched to do a little smash and grab. How much was that old woman's jewelry worth, after all?

"Don't even think about it," said the Nautolan woman standing next to Nan, her well-muscled arms crossed. Her name was Jara, and Nan only knew this because Chancey had said it a couple of times in conversation. No one had bothered to give Nan their names. She occupied a strange space within this hierarchy, not quite a prisoner but not free to be left to her own devices, either.

Nan still didn't know why Chancey Yarrow had even invited her to come along. The whole trip had the feeling of a test. The Nihil were constantly testing one another, pushing boundaries and waiting for someone to break, so that didn't bother her. She was good at navigating such intricacies. What did bother her was that, of all places, they'd gone to a station that reeked of money.

They should be taking from this old woman, not sharing recipes with her or whatever it was that was happening.

Nan had landed the *Whisperkill* in a small docking bay with an overabundance of pleasure yachts and other too-shiny ships, the walls of the space looking like something straight from Naboo, too fancy and with a multitude of swirls and silver plating. It looked like an even more ostentatious and filigreed version of the Republic's bloated eyesore Starlight Beacon. Not that Nan had been to the legendary station, but she had seen the holo docs about the marvel that it was, most of which had been funded by the Graf family, namely Catriona Graf.

The same woman who now glared at Chancey Yarrow, who seemed utterly nonplussed by the luxury that surrounded them.

"What are we doing here?" Nan asked, only half expecting the purple woman standing next to her to answer.

"Negotiating," she said.

She'd thought maybe they would bring along the Oracle, but it became clear halfway through their travels that what they wanted was a ship that could easily be discarded. They thought that was Nan's ship.

They had another think coming.

The old woman suddenly gave Chancey a curt nod and walked back toward the entrance to the grand compound, the Gigoran and Twi'lek guards that flanked her covering her retreat. Chancey walked back, her dark face wearing a wide smile.

"We have a number of hours before they arrive. The Matriarch has agreed to let us set up our ambush here and has agreed to our new terms, understanding that they will be beneficial to both of us. Prepare yourselves."

Besides Nan, there were maybe five Nihil, and they

laughed and whooped as they ran back to the ship. Nan turned to go with them, and Chancey Yarrow stopped her.

"Nan, you stay with me," Chancey said. She still wore a knee-length dress in a swirling Hosnian pattern, and her braids had been twisted to lie flat against her head, the better to wear the mask that dangled from her neck.

Nan felt a thread of unease uncurl in her middle. The woman did not look like she was going to kill Nan, but wasn't that how the best professionals worked? You never saw the blade coming.

"I have spoken to Lourna Dee about you, and she told me that you are unwaveringly faithful to Marchion Ro. Is this true?"

Nan felt a small flip-flop in her middle. Did Chancey know that Nan had sent a message to a San Tekka conglomerate office about Mari San Tekka being held captive on the Gravity's Heart?

Nan's goal had been simple: she would set it up so the San Tekkas would attack the Gravity's Heart, providing a distraction for her escape. She'd figured that even if they thought Mari was dead, they'd want the honor of punishing her kidnappers. It's what Nan would want. Vengeance was a simple, satisfying thing, and surely the San Tekkas would agree. There was, of course, no guarantee they would take the bait. But if they did, well, it was too delicious to consider.

Nan had already talked with Uttersond about what to do in an attack, and the doctor had told her that the Oracle's pod would easily levitate due to an internal repulsorlift frame. It was a good plan, assuming the pieces fell into place. And if they didn't? Well, Nan would be no worse off than she had been.

As long as no one suspected that she'd sent the coordinates to the San Tekkas.

"I am the most loyal to Marchion Ro," Nan said, crossing her arms and staring down Chancey "It's why he trusted me to protect his Oracle. The fact that you have me here will not go unnoticed."

"Mari San Tekka is as safe as a more-than-a-hundred-year-old human woman can be. I asked because what we are about to do is by direct request of Marchion Ro, and I want to make sure that I can trust you to follow my instructions. If we pull this off, your Ro will hold you in the highest esteem."

Nan perked up. "I'm listening."

"Good," Chancey Yarrow said, explaining the rest of her plan. "Oh, and nicely done with your little message to the San Tekkas. It never went out, of course. I'm not so gullible as to not track all incoming and outgoing communications. But I appreciate your resourcefulness in light of what looked to be an unwinnable situation."

Nan blinked. "You aren't mad?" She had a knife in her boot, but it was her only weapon, and if she killed Chancey there would be little hope of escape.

The woman smiled, and for a moment Nan thought she was dead. But Chancey made no move to attack. "You are wasted on Marchion Ro. He does not realize the asset he has in his arsenal, and you have no idea of the wealth you could make working for yourself. Clean you up a bit so that you aren't so obviously Nihil, and you could be a worthwhile spy. But that is a conversation for another day. Now, let us go over this again."

Nan couldn't help grinning as the woman continued to talk, and she realized she had vastly underestimated the deviousness of the scientist.

Maybe Nan would get to have a little fun after all.

TWENTY-NINE

Syl walked into the crew mess for the second meal and found Xylan holding court, laughing over something with Basha while Master Cohmac stood stone-faced nearby. Jordanna still napped in the cockpit, Remy taking up all the available floor space, and Vernestra and Imri sat with Reath on a bench seat in the back corner, whispering among themselves, frowns all around. It was a contradiction in vibes, and Syl wanted to turn back around and hide out in the cockpit.

Syl knew she was no diplomat. She let her temper get the better of her more often than not, which was one more reason being around so many Jedi was irksome. Their perpetual calm only served to remind Syl of her many failings, her temper being the one her mother had chastised her for the most. When Syl had found that the navicomputer coordinates had been changed, her instinct was to strap on Beti and demand a few direct answers from Xylan Graf. But instead she'd decided to go to the Jedi, who had been less than helpful. And now they were a good distance to their goal with no clue as to what was waiting for them at the end of the trip.

Syl might not mind lying to a senator, but it turned out that she didn't have the stomach to go up against Jedi.

So Syl was already near a breaking point when she walked into the crew mess and saw Xylan looking as carefree as ever. Especially when he turned toward her and gave her his usual infuriatingly handsome grin.

"Syl! How do you like flying the *Resplendent Pearl*? She's quite a beauty, is she not?"

"Why are we going to the Dalnan sector and not the Hynestian?" Syl blurted out. As soon as the words were out of her mouth, she regretted her impulsiveness. She'd planned on letting the Jedi take the lead on the issue, use their creepy mind-reading abilities to question Xylan. But she was such an anxious blend of emotions in that moment that she'd been unable to hold her tongue.

Xylan's smile didn't budge; in fact, he laughed. He *laughed*.

Syl crossed her arms as he stood and walked toward her. He clapped his right hand onto her shoulder like they were old friends, and Syl's fingers twitched with the urge to punch him right in his face just to see if that would rattle him.

"The more time I spend with you, Sylvestri Yarrow, the more I like you." He was being genuine as far as Syl could tell, and before she could respond, he whirled toward the rest of the group. "Syl is correct. I did change the coordinates in the navicomputer right before we left Coruscant. But I would rather wait until Jordanna joins us before I explain everything to all of you."

"Well then, good thing I'm done with my nap," Jordanna said, stretching as she walked into the crew mess. She winked at Syl and affectionately bumped the other girl's shoulder with hers, subtly enough that the rest of the room didn't notice.

Syl ignored her.

"Oh, excellent," Xylan said, clapping his hands together. "Well, since you are all looking at me like I stole the last gnostra-berry cake, let me be blunt: there are too many who would wish this expedition to be a failure, so to make certain our endeavor was a success, I filed a false flight plan."

"So why didn't you tell us the truth?" Master Cohmac asked, his expression inscrutable.

"Well, we have a San Tekka with us," he said, gesturing to Jordanna, who yawned widely in response. "I figured if anyone was going to try to interfere in our task it would be her. And yet, per my new agreement with Senator Starros, I need her to help verify my claims of the Berenge sector's vacancy."

Jordanna laughed. "That's ridiculous. If the San Tekkas wanted you dead, you'd be dead. And it wouldn't be me doing the killing. You know that as well as I do."

"Perhaps," Xylan said. "But with this many Jedi around, I knew you wouldn't dare make a move once we'd left Coruscant, so I just had to make sure we weren't followed. At this rate we'll be to Everbloom, my grandmother's estate, before you can summon any reinforcements."

Jordanna shook her head but said nothing in response.

"My plan also keeps us safe from the Nihil, who have some of their number working for the Republic, I'm certain of it. It's the only way to account for their uncanny ability to continually hit large, expensive cargos."

"I think assuming that the Republic is in league with the Nihil is very, very foolhardy," Master Cohmac said. The older Jedi did not look quite as relaxed as he had before, tension radiating through his body. Syl didn't think the Jedi Master would attack Xylan, but even Basha turned to pay closer attention to the conversation.

"No, you are correct, Master Cohmac. My family has been tracking the Nihil attacks since before the destruction of the *Legacy Run*. It's a matter of good business, you see. The Republic cannot be everywhere, and knowing the patterns of the pirates in any given area is a large part of assuring our shipments get where they need to go. But there have been some things about the Nihil that just do not add up. The first is their use of hyperspace, which Professor Wolk was trying to understand, but the second was how much they seem to know about the Republic's response. In the past month the Jedi have undertaken several large-scale operations against the Nihil, and it hasn't seemed to affect them as much as it should have. That leads one to think that there are, indeed, a few operators within the government who are savvy enough to play both sides. And I, for one, did not want to take a chance with any distractions from our goal. But I do apologize for withholding the information."

The Jedi leaned back, a contemplative look on his face, and Xylan turned to the rest of the group.

"With that being said, we will be at the Graf family compound late tomorrow. Rest up until then, because I have arranged for us to only stay a short time before heading out to the Berenge sector. And Syl," he said as he walked toward the door that led to the crew quarters in the back of the ship, "next time, just ask. I feel like you should trust me a bit more after all we've been through." He patted her on the head like she was Plinka, and Syl ground her teeth to keep herself from violence.

He left, Basha climbing to her feet and lumbering after him, and Syl shook her head.

"A logical-sounding explanation for everything," she said. "I really hate that guy." She mostly hated that his logic had been pretty sound, much more so than that of his past tales.

"In this case, he is telling the truth," Master Cohmac said. "I didn't detect any subterfuge from him as he spoke. So whatever the truth might be, he *believes* that someone within the Republic is working with the Nihil."

"Should we send a message to Master Stellan?" Vernestra asked. Syl recognized the name. Footage of him, ragged and dusty, cradling the injured Chancellor Soh, had been all over the holonet for weeks after the attack.

"Not yet," Master Cohmac said. "Whoever is in charge of the Nihil cells is smart enough to make it look like they're losing, and yet for the most part they are carrying on with business as usual. I fear that sending a message to Stellan might tip our hand, because whether we like it or not, Xylan has bought us an element of surprise just in case there is something else afoot. We'll wait until we have something a little more certain than suspicions. But for now, let's eat. It's not going to get any better cold, I'm afraid."

"Hey, we followed the recipe," Reath said. "It's just, rations are what they are."

"They should at least be edible," Vern said, teasing the boy, who blushed in response. Syl wondered if every single Jedi knew the others. Sure seemed like.

As everyone turned to the covered dishes the Padawans had prepared, Syl found herself annoyed once more. Jordanna tried to catch her eye across the table, but Syl ignored her, turning her focus inward. There were too many questions and not enough answers. All she had wanted was to warn the Republic about the Nihil so they could do something, and now here she was neck-deep in lies.

She just hoped none of them would come back to hurt her.

THIRTY

Vernestra hadn't thought she would ever see anything more impressive than Starlight Beacon, that gleaming city in the midst of space, but the Graf family compound—which Xylan had told everyone was called Everbloom, for the gardens that were always in season—came very, very close. She had been expecting the family compound to be located on a minor moon or some such, but when the *Resplendent Pearl* approached a gleaming space station on the far edge of the Dalnan sector, Vernestra realized that she had grossly underestimated the power of credits. There was even a dome. Who had engineered the thing?

"It's gaudy," Xylan Graf said, coming up next to her

where she stood near the observational portal in the crew mess. Vernestra turned and gave him a polite smile. Sylvestri didn't trust the man; her suspicious dislike radiated off of her in waves every time he entered the room, and Vernestra got the impression that the girl's instincts were correct. There was something too friendly, too smooth about him. He reminded Vernestra a bit of the blaster salesman she'd known back in Port Haileap. The man had been cited for defrauding people several times, and Vernestra sensed that Xylan also had a very loose understanding of the concept of truth.

"It reminds me of Starlight Beacon," Vernestra said.

"Oh, it should. Much of the design for that station came from the work done here on Everbloom over the last one hundred years. Some of the best aeronautic and structural engineers have worked on this place. The Matriarch, my grandmother, had once toyed with the idea of adding life-supportive apparatus to an asteroid, but it was far cheaper to just build it from the ground up. This also allows her to move about the galaxy at will."

"It moves?" Vernestra said, trying to imagine the massive station making its way through space.

"Of course. It even jumps through hyperspace. But I didn't tell you that. Come on, we'll be landing soon and there are protocols to be followed."

Vernestra nodded and trailed behind Xylan as he made his way down to the cargo hold. The side of the wall there would open up to reveal the boarding ramp once they landed, and Xylan had declared that the Jedi should be presented to his grandmother, the head of the Graf clan, in a formal introduction at her request. Only Syl was excused from the shenanigans, mostly because she'd crossed her arms and scowled when Xylan had first presented the idea to everyone.

If Xylan was expecting a parade-quality entrance, he was going to be disappointed. All the Jedi wore their mission attire. Xylan, who seemed to have forgotten the purpose of their trip, had dressed himself in a bodysuit made of what looked to be some kind of purple leather, the front open to his navel in a deep V that revealed a good bit of his brown chest and made Master Cohmac raise an appreciative eyebrow when he thought no one was watching. Xylan also wore a silver cape over his right shoulder, and Vernestra felt that this was his true self. These flamboyant fashions were as much a part of his identity as a lightsaber was part of a Jedi's.

"You ready for the show?" Jordanna said, standing with her arms crossed. She'd insisted that she have a good view for "the nonsense pomp and circumstance Grafs are known for." There had been no heat to the statement, just a cool truth. Remy sat at her feet, the vollka shooting Imri half-lidded glares every time he looked at her, his desire to pet her clear in his grin.

"This seems like a bit much for a ship," Vernestra said.

A niggling apprehension chilled the skin along Vernestra's arms, but she couldn't have said whether the feeling was tied to Imri scooting closer to Remy or something else entirely. "I'm guessing Everbloom does not receive Jedi too often."

"I believe this falls under the category of diplomacy," Reath said with a sheepish grin. The Padawan had been preoccupied ever since they'd left Coruscant, and Vernestra wondered if he already missed the planet.

Imri sidled closer to the vollka, and she casually yawned, showing him rows of very sharp teeth. He rethought his campaign to pet her and went to stand next to Vernestra, his expression pained.

"Don't worry, at some point she'll come around," she said.

"No, that's not it," he said.

"Are you okay?" Vernestra asked.

"I'm fine. Syl is very, very suspicious about all of this, and I'm trying not to let her fear seep into me," Imri said. "But I keep getting the feeling that there's something not right. Someone is definitely hiding something bad."

"Who are you sensing it from?" Vernestra asked, because she'd had the same feeling all morning, as well. The closer they'd gotten to the Graf family compound, the more uneasy she'd grown. But she couldn't identify just what it was making her feel that way: her own instincts or Syl's misgivings.

"I'm not sure," Imri murmured.

There was a soft bump and then another as the ship

touched down. Over the intercom Sylvestri announced that they'd landed. Xylan turned to the assembled Jedi and gave them a polite smile.

"Xylan," Basha said, stepping forward. "You should take a step back. Let the Jedi lead."

Xylan laughed. "Why ever would I do that? A Graf leads from the front."

"Basha," Imri said, eyes wide. Vernestra spun toward the giant and sensed what Imri had. That was who had been withholding the truth from them.

The Gigoran grabbed Xylan Graf by the waist and yanked him backward off his feet as the boarding ramp lowered, revealing the treachery that lay beyond. A group of people wearing masks stood at the base, led by a woman in a swirling blue dress and a blue mask that sparkled like the heart of hyperspace.

It was a trap.

Xylan's eyes widened as he struggled ineffectively in Basha's arms. "What are you doing? You aren't supposed to be here!"

"You're out of time, Xylan," came the muffled voice of the woman. "We've renegotiated terms."

Vernestra had no time to wonder who she was. There was a popping noise as canisters of gas were deployed. Vernestra drew her lightsaber. Remy yowled and ran back toward the living areas of the ship, escaping the fight. The vollka was smart. Purple gas rapidly filled the interior of the cargo hold, billowing thick and terrible.

"Rebreathers!" Master Cohmac shouted.

The Jedi had taken to carrying the devices after the assault on Valo, and it was a good thing. They were bulky and unwieldy, but it was better than choking on the fog of war. As soon as Vernestra had taken a couple of clear, deep breaths, she coolly assessed the chaos.

Jordanna pulled a blaster and fired at the Nihil but was hit square in the chest by a bolt, crumpling to the ground. Reath ran over to assist Xylan Graf, but the Gigoran, Basha, whose vocalizer seemed to also be functioning as some sort of gas mask, picked Reath up while holding Xylan with only one arm and flung him across the cargo bay, where he landed in a heap. Xylan Graf began to cough, and Basha turned and lumbered toward the interior of the ship, the cargo bay door sliding shut behind her and trapping the Jedi.

Imri ducked to avoid the blaster bolts. The cargo hold was on the smaller side, and there was no space for him to safely draw his lightsaber, so he took a step backward to give the older Jedi space to work. Master Cohmac stepped backward, trying to use the Force to push the gas away. But it was no use. Especially once the Nihil started shooting.

Reath went down first, a blaster bolt catching him in the chest. Master Cohmac powered up his lightsaber and immediately fell forward as a blaster bolt hit him from out of nowhere, the bright blue of his lightsaber extinguishing before the hilt rolled under a stack of crates. Vernestra tried to hold her lightsaber aloft, tried to fight her way forward. She had to stop the Nihil.

The gas hung in the air in a thick cloud, and Vernestra found herself fighting through the miasma. The first swing of her lightsaber took out a human man, severing his hand so that his blaster fell to the ground. While he was screaming Vernestra elbowed him in the face, sending his mask into his nose with a sickening crunch. She could have cleaved him in half, but she wouldn't kill anyone if she didn't have to.

That was a mistake.

He fell at her feet, but as he went down, he leveled a kick at her knee that she managed to avoid.

But not the punch from the left that knocked loose her rebreather.

Vernestra fell to her knees, and a flurry of blaster fire rained upon her. She tried to repel the bolts but was too slow, the energy from one causing her to drop her lightsaber. As she tried to climb back to her feet, a hand came out of the gloom and ripped the rebreather off of her face.

"Imri, run. Warn Sylvestri," Vernestra said, her last thought for her Padawan, who had stepped forward with his powered-up lightsaber, the last Jedi standing. But a stray blaster bolt caught him, and he crumpled before her eyes.

Vernestra began coughing as she inhaled the gas filling the cargo hold. It made her head spin, and the blaster bolt that singed her cheek knocked her off balance as she tried to avoid it. Then she was on the ground, her chest heaving as her body was racked with coughs.

And then there was nothing to do but succumb to the darkness.

THIRTY-ONE

Syl finished the landing procedures and stretched. It had been a relief when Xylan Graf told her that she could remain on the ship while the Jedi went to glad-hand with the Graf matriarch. After the disastrous trip to meet Senator Starros, Syl wasn't certain that she could smile pretty and tell one of the richest women in the galaxy what she wanted to hear, and apparently Xylan Graf had shared her concerns. So here she was in the cockpit until that mess was finished, and then she would make her way into the compound with Basha like she was the hired help.

It should've bothered her, but it didn't. Syl knew who she

was, and servant was closer to the truth than woman of consequence. Let the Jedi politick; she was going to enjoy the
peace and quiet. It gave her a chance to cool her heels in the
cockpit and catch up on her holos. She was woefully behind
on *Love on the Rift* due to everything. A moment to just be the
girl she had been before she'd gone to Coruscant on a mis-
guided mission seemed like the perfect way to pass the time.

Syl had just powered up the holo screen—of course Xylan
had a set in his cockpit; Syl should've checked earlier—when
Remy came skidding into the small space. The vollka hissed,
and every single hair stood on end.

Syl did not have to be a Jedi to know that something
was wrong.

The comm unit had a number of different channels pre-
programmed, so Syl clicked through them until she found the
ship's internal comms. She keyed the button, but instead of
hearing Jedi making polite introductions, she heard coughing followed by blaster fire and the unmistakable thumping
of bodies hitting the floor.

"Imri, run. Warn Sylvestri," came across the speaker, and
Syl's heart skipped a beat and then resumed in triple time.
Her fears were coming true, and she couldn't even count on
the Jedi for help.

Syl ran through her options. She could try launching the
ship again, but it had no weapons that she'd been able to find
besides the most basic of laser cannons. She could run down
to the cargo hold and try to figure out what had happened,

but if something had taken out four Jedi, Syl would be an afterthought.

Syl tried to change lanes in her mind. She had Beti and Remy, who paced in the small area, turning back toward the hallway every few seconds and hissing, her horns crackling with energy. Between the two of them they should be able to do some damage, as long as they took someone by surprise.

"Remy, stay here unless I call you," Syl said to the vollka, who most likely had zero idea what she'd said. This was it; this would be known as the moment she lost her mind. Since she wasn't likely to be alive much longer, it was the least of her worries.

Curse that Xylan Graf. She never should've agreed to help him. In a few short days, she'd been shot at, bored to tears with hyperspace theory, and forced to play politics, and now she was trying to save Jedi from something bad enough that even the vollka was bristling with terror. All because Syl had wanted his money and a fancy meal. All this stress because Xylan Graf had deep pockets and she was greedy.

If she made it out of this mess alive, she would never lie again. She was telling the truth and minding her own business forevermore.

Syl took a deep breath and left the cockpit, walking back toward the crew mess, stepping lightly so her boots wouldn't echo on the metal floor. She'd only gone a few steps when Basha appeared before her, an unconscious Xylan Graf cradled in her arms.

"You should return to the cockpit until we are summoned by the Matriarch," the Gigoran said in her mechanical voice.

"I think I'd like to stretch my legs, if you don't mind. Looks like your boy maybe got into that Toniray after all." Syl laughed. "By the way, I keep meaning to ask, what kind of soap do you use on your fur? It is just the shiniest." She was babbling, which was not unlike her. But this was the worst time for it.

"Sylvestri Yarrow, please return to the cockpit until I come for you," Basha said, refusing to move. She was large enough that she blocked the entirety of the hallway, and the only way to get to the cargo hold was by way of the stairs on the other side of the crew mess.

"Yeah, I'm not going to do that," Syl said, giving Basha a grin.

The Gigoran was not amused.

Basha swung a heavy hand toward Syl, and the girl ducked before dropping into a crouch. She usually hated her small size, but in the narrow space of the ship's corridor, it was an asset.

Syl went to all fours, thinking that she could fight back by taking out Basha's knees, and as she did so, the vollka roared. Syl got only the briefest impression of a blue-green blur launching over her head, Remy going for Basha's throat while the Gigoran dropped Xylan to defend herself. Oof, he was going to feel that when he awoke.

Syl hadn't wanted to hurt Basha, but Remy had no such

reservations. Syl wondered what exactly the vollka had seen down in the cargo bay.

The Gigoran backpedaled down the hallway, Remy stalking her as she fled toward the crew mess. Basha's white fur was stained red from the wound Remy had inflicted. Lightning seemed to arc throughout the corridor, the vollka's horns charging up for an attack, and Syl felt the tingle of the energy along her scalp, her mouth agape as she watched the vollka unleash electricity. A bolt hit the Gigoran, and she grunted, the vocalizer translating the sound into a burst of static.

Syl took a deep breath, picked herself up from the ground, drew Beti, and charged after Basha, hurdling Xylan Graf as she did.

There was no going back now. She was all in.

Basha fell backward over a chair in the crew mess, dazed from the electrical attack, and Syl ran past her even as Remy circled Basha, looking for another opening.

"Not now, cat! Let's get Jordanna." Syl realized that the worry burbling in her middle, acidic and hot, wasn't for the Jedi but for her ex-girlfriend. So much for trying to keep her emotions in check.

The scrabble of paws running next to her made Syl feel a little better. The vollka was a fierce weapon when she chose to be, and Syl's odds were infinitely better with such an ally.

Syl reached the cargo bay doors, but no amount of mashing the buttons would open the mechanism. She pointed Beti at the lock system and fired once, twice, three times, the rifle kicking terribly but her aim true. On the fourth shot, the lock gave way, and Syl was able to slide the door along the track half a meter and peer through the opening.

As the door opened Syl tried to prepare herself for anything, but the purple gas that lay in a heavy carpet on the floor was not one of the things she'd counted on. There were several people in masks clapping each other on the back, and the sounds of wreckpunk blared through a music player in the cargo hold, the Nihil apparently celebrating their victory. But the loud music had allowed Syl to take the marauders by surprise. Reath was slung over one of their shoulders as a man exited down the cargo ramp, and she could see the unmistakable outlines of the rest of the Jedi lying on the floor.

Somehow, some way, the Nihil had ambushed them.

Syl didn't need to see anything else. She leveled her blaster and fired at the nearest Nihil, a human, hitting him dead center in the chest. Without waiting for him to fall, she fired at a masked figure running down the ramp, missing them but hitting another Nihil instead. She'd shot a Nautolan woman in the back. Not very sporting but effective nonetheless.

The Nihil started firing back.

Syl ducked back around the cargo bay door, using the heavy metal as a shield. The music suddenly stopped; Syl had ruined the party, and she couldn't help smiling even though they were shooting at her. Blaster fire riddled the other side, and people began shouting, the words muffled and indistinct. Syl counted to six—much better than three, which everyone would expect—and darted back into the opening, hitting a Kage man who looked nearly human except for his too-pale gray skin.

The shooting on the other side stopped, and a whirring noise started up, like a giant fan. Remy paced behind Syl, keeping to the cover but also clearly eager to get to where Jordanna lay on the floor of the cargo hold, a singe mark in the center of her chest.

"Syl, you don't owe these Jedi anything," came a voice. It was a familiar one, and in the heat of the moment Syl couldn't quite place it.

"Get blinkered, Nihil scum!"

"Sylvestri Yarrow, you will put away Beti and walk out here with your hands up before you get hurt."

Syl's heart skipped a beat, and then another, and she had to close her eyes and take a deep breath as her heart picked up a triple beat. It couldn't be. She was imagining things.

Syl swallowed dryly. She knew the voice. Of course she did. There was no imagining it.

"I don't know you," Syl yelled, refusing to believe the awful truth. Her eyes burned with hot tears, and the past few months came slamming back. All the tears she'd cried, all her moments of doubt—all of it sat heavy on her heart in that moment.

"Yes, you do. Xylan Graf was supposed to tell you the truth, make things easier, but I see he seems to have fouled that up even worse than everything else."

Syl peeked around the edge of the cargo bay door, her rifle held muzzle down at her side. There, standing in the cargo hold, was Chancey Yarrow. Her mother looked just like she had the last time Syl had seen her: hair braided in even rows, the ends tied up at the base of her skull in a complicated widow's knot. But the mask hanging from her neck, the same blue as hyperspace, was new and its meaning unmistakable: Chancey Yarrow was most definitely working with the Nihil.

"You're supposed to be dead," Syl said, her voice flat. It wasn't what she wanted to say. Not even close. But her brain was in survival mode, and it was only by sheer will that she hadn't shot at the specter standing before her. Just to make sure she wasn't imagining it. "If you're working with the Nihil, you'd be better off dead."

"I know, and we have a lot to discuss. But I need to take care of this first, and then I promise I will tell you everything," she said, smiling at her daughter.

And then Chancey Yarrow, the woman Syl had mourned for the past six months, shot her daughter in the middle of the chest.

THIRTY-TWO

Vernestra woke in pain. Debilitating pain that ran from the top of her head all the way to her toes and then back again. She couldn't think, could barely breathe, and it took her a long minute to realize that she was screaming.

Her throat was raw with the force of it, and as she registered the pain and the dryness in her throat, the agony throughout her body began to fade, leaving behind pins and needles of sensation.

"In another few seconds the pain should fade completely. Please just relax until then. I have a glass of juice for you when you're ready."

Vernestra blinked at the calm voice, but she found it hard to focus on anything but the discomfort of her existence. She'd never experienced such intense pain.

"The gas the Nihil used was manufactured by the Zygerrians to subdue revolts among the enslaved. It is a very, very brutal thing. On behalf of the Matriarch, I apologize for this terrible incident happening on Everbloom. We had no anticipation of any such attack, and if we had, we would have taken stronger measures."

Vernestra blinked again, but this time the simple act didn't feel like a week of intense Force running practice. She sat up and took in her surroundings. She lay on a soft floor in a room without any decoration, the walls a dingy beige, and a Twi'lek woman with lavender skin watched her. She held a tray with a glass of blue juice on it, and with a kind smile she offered the glass to Vernestra.

"My name is Saffa, and I'm to take you to see the Matriarch when you are feeling up to it."

"Where's everyone else?" Vernestra reached a shaky hand out toward the juice and felt a surge of pride when she managed to pick up the glass and take a long drink without dropping it. In her mind the sight of Imri taking a blaster bolt to the chest replayed over and over again. He had to be alive somewhere, since she'd been hit, as well, and here she was, still alive. Why would the Nihil use stun blasters instead of the more lethal option? It didn't make much sense.

"They are, like you, recovering. And they will join us shortly."

Vernestra tried to climb to her feet and immediately fell back to the floor, the cup falling from her hand and rolling away.

"I will fetch you more juice," Saffa said, bending at the waist before deftly picking up the cup and leaving the room. The door was left open as she departed, showing that Vernestra wasn't a prisoner even if it seemed like she should be.

What in the seven fiery moons was going on?

Vernestra closed her eyes and tried reaching for the Force, but there was nothing. The rush of awareness she usually got when she reached for the Force, like the sound of far-off water, was completely absent. It was alarming. No, it was more than that. Vernestra was terrified. She had spent most of her life—all her life that she could remember, at least—reaching for the Force and finding it there, like the sound of rain on a window or a nearby creek burbling along merrily. And now here she was, completely and utterly cut off from it. She knew it was because the gas still clouded her mind and she could not focus properly to reach the Force. But it was still jarring.

Vernestra hiccupped and blinked back tears. She was alive. She would get through this.

And when she did she was going to make sure Stellan and the rest of the Jedi Council got an earful about the Graf family.

There was a reason they were all still alive, and Vernestra

doubted it was because this had been an unplanned attack. The Nihil had been waiting for them.

The sound of running footsteps came down the hallway, and someone shot past Vernestra's door before doubling back. She struggled into a sitting position before sighing as she saw Jordanna Sparkburn standing in the doorway, a massive blaster in her hands.

"Isn't that Syl's?" Vernestra asked.

"Yeah, Beti," Jordanna said. She looked angry enough to spit fire. "They took Syl and the Padawans. You've got to get up and get moving so we can go after them."

"What? How do you know?" Vernestra said.

"Because they aren't here. The more you move around, the quicker the effects will fade. Here."

Jordanna walked into the room and helped Vernestra to her feet, the older girl the perfect height for Vernestra to lean on since she was nearly a head taller.

"Where are we going?" Vernestra asked.

"To find Cohmac and then steal a ship. I've been running around the compound since I woke up. There was some Aleena yammering on about how happy she was to have me at Everbloom, but the last thing I remember was Basha snatching up Xylan before I was shot, thankfully with a stun bolt. Remy found me and led me to you. And you are the first person I was able to find. Most of these rooms are empty."

"Just what exactly is going on here?" Vernestra murmured as she and Jordanna began to make their slow way down the corridor. As they walked Vernestra took her time to study her surroundings. She'd been half afraid the walls would end up being the same as those she had seen in her vision, but this was definitely not the same place. These walls looked expensive and nice, not run-down. Vernestra got the feeling that the walls were blank because they were waiting for something, not because they were supposed to be.

"Lady Vernestra! Lady Jordanna! Please return to your rooms until the Matriarch can speak with you." The patter of pursuing feet came toward them, and Jordanna kept walking, the only sign that she'd heard the servants an increase in speed.

Vernestra turned around to look over her shoulder and saw the Twi'lek from her room, as well as an Aleena woman, small and reptilian with a black-and-yellow mottled appearance and a rapidly swelling eye. "Did you hit the servant tending to you?"

"Yes, Jedi, sometimes punching your way out of a situation is the best idea." Jordanna glanced at Vernestra out of the corner of her eye. "She wouldn't tell me anything and she wouldn't let me leave, so I got a little violent. Sorry, I'm short on trust right about now. Curse these Grafs. They keep living down to their name."

Vernestra hiccuped and then started to laugh, the sound hollow and weak. The corner of Jordanna's mouth quirked. "I suppose there was probably a better way to handle that. But I've had a pretty awful week."

"Well, we just got dosed with Zygerrian crowd-control gas, so I can imagine. How are you walking around already?"

Jordanna's mirth faded. "The more times you're exposed to the gas, the less effect it has. Don't forget I've been fighting the Nihil on Tiikae for a while. I've had my share of that stuff, among others."

Vernestra sobered. She was starting to understand why Jordanna was so hardened. No one should have to endure so much fighting.

Jordanna's expression brightened. "Look! Isn't that Master Cohmac?"

Up ahead was a Belugan woman standing in the hallway a meter away from Master Cohmac, who leaned against the doorjamb. Her fleshy sideburns quivered with alarm while the Jedi Master scowled at her. He had his hand raised, reaching for the Force, but nothing was happening.

"Master Cohmac!" Jordanna called.

He lowered his hand as the Belugan woman ran off, croaking in agitation. "Where are we, and what happened?" Master Cohmac said through gritted teeth.

Before anyone could answer him, a cool hand grabbed Vernestra's arm, and the Twi'lek woman pulled Vernestra back a little, halting Jordanna's forward progress. "Please, you should really come back to the room until—"

She didn't get to finish her sentence, because Remy exploded into existence right between Jordanna and the Twi'lek, driving the servant backward. Vernestra hadn't noticed the vollka stalking alongside them, and her horns crackled as she growled deep in her throat. Remy's fur was matted with blood and dirt, and she looked a little worse for wear, but she seemed mostly all right.

"I wouldn't mess with her right now," Jordanna said with a chuckle. "She is not in a good mood." Jordanna moved to stand next to Master Cohmac, who gave her an incredulous glance.

"How are you upright already?" he asked. "I feel completely flattened."

"I've tangled with the Nihil a few times." Jordanna rested her hand on Remy's head as the vollka moved away from the servant and pressed against Jordanna's hip. "More important, Sylvestri Yarrow and your Padawans are gone," she said, voice low.

"Do we know where?" Master Cohmac asked.

Jordanna shook her head. "I'm guessing the Nihil grabbed them, and that they fled when the compound security came out to protect the ship. They must have wanted us alive, which is why we're still breathing. We were set up."

"Yes, you were. But not how you might think. It seems that my grandson was not the only one played for a fool," came a creaky voice from the end of the hallway down which the servants had fled.

A Gigoran—but not Basha, judging by the light gray fur—walked beside a tall woman with ashen hair pulled into a complicated updo on the top of her head. Her pale face was bereft of age lines, and one side of it had been tattooed with blue swirls that could have been some ancient language or just a pretty design. Her face was curiously smooth even though her body radiated age. There was no malice emanating from her; in fact, she seemed to be truly annoyed and upset at how the Jedi had been treated.

Vernestra realized that she was sensing the woman, and she reached for the Force in earnest. The feel of it came flooding back to her, like a river undammed and rushing forth, and she gasped at how quickly she felt better once she could connect to the energy of the Force. The effects of the gas that had left her mind disorganized and unfocused were now gone, and feeling normal mentally went a long way to making Vernestra feel a bit steadier physically.

Vernestra stood on her own, leaving behind Jordanna's assistance just as Master Cohmac began to straighten, and the old woman gave them a tight smile. "Ah, I see the sassaberry juice is doing its job. It is designed to help the body flush out impurities. It is an excellent restorative to counteract the effects of poisonous gas. I will make sure I send some along with you when you return to the Temple. As an apology for the unfortunate incident that occurred."

Master Cohmac straightened up to his full height. "Lady Graf, thank you for the, ah, hospitality. But I am afraid I must demand the immediate return of our missing Padawans and our lightsabers."

"Of course," she said. "And please, call me the Matriarch.

I would like to formally welcome you to Everbloom, although my greeting is an unfortunate afterthought since your initial welcome was so terrible. Kantuck, please return the lightsabers to the Jedi."

The Gigoran lumbered forward. In his massive hands he held four lightsabers. Vernestra took hers and Imri's, and Master Cohmac reached out and took the remaining two. When he glanced at Jordanna, she shook her head.

"Don't worry, I have Syl's Beti," she said, hefting the blaster rifle. She leveled it at the old woman. "Which brings me to the most pressing issue: where's my girlfriend?"

Vernestra blinked and immediately looked to Master Cohmac. She'd felt the emotions swirling between the two of them, but she hadn't been aware they had committed to each other. Master Cohmac seemed amused at the declaration.

"Does Sylvestri Yarrow know she's your girlfriend?" he asked.

"Not yet! Which is why I'd better find out where she is in the next five seconds," Jordanna said with a cold grin at the Matriarch.

"And our Padawans, Reath and Imri. You were obviously working with the Nihil, so where are they?" Vernestra asked, and the Matriarch gave her a polite smile.

"I'm sorry, there were no others," the old woman said. "And since when do Jedi shoot people for fun?"

"I'm no Jedi. I'm a San Tekka," Jordanna said, and the old woman took half a step back.

"You'd better start talking," Master Cohmac said, his voice hard.

"Fine," the old woman sighed, as though they were the ones being unreasonable. "Xylan thought he might have a lead on some experimental technology, and he reached out to a contact he had made through the Nihil. He has been compensating certain members of that faction in order to protect our shipments for the past year or so, ever since the *Legacy Run* was destroyed. His contact was amenable to sharing their discoveries on the condition he could bring them a girl: Sylvestri Yarrow. Apparently they thought she would be useful in helping their scientist remain focused."

"So the Graf family has been working with the Nihil?" Master Cohmac said, and the Matriarch shrugged, the gesture strange coming from a woman so polished.

"Absolutely not. When I discovered the truth, I insisted that Xylan cease his machinations immediately. But you know how children can be," she said with a languid wave. "So impulsive."

"So where is my Padawan?" Vernestra said, voice even. Catriona Graf was lying, but they had more pressing issues. Imri, Reath, and Sylvestri were in danger. A keen edge of panic had begun to burble up in Vernestra's heart, and she pulled on the Force to ground herself in action and not emotion.

"Threaten me as you will, but I cannot give you answers I do not have. The Nihil came here to demand their payment, threatening my life in the process, and I agreed to let them take what my stupid grandson had promised them here. I feel I must reiterate that I did not know he had Jedi with him. Since when does the Republic send Jedi on 'scientific inquiries,' which is what this trip was supposed to be? I expected the whole thing to be quick and painless and this whole unsavory business to be put behind me by now."

"Quick and painless for who?" Jordanna asked, and the yawning silence was all the answer necessary.

"Tranquility, Jordanna," Cohmac said, using his hand to lower the blaster rifle. To the Matriarch he said, "You do understand that there will be consequences for this? Your grandson lied to a senator and is party to the kidnapping of two Padawans and a civilian. This is no small matter."

"I am fully prepared to answer for my grandson's actions, but I think perhaps you might want to find your friends with all haste. Or I would be happy to let you use my comm unit to call the proper authorities. It shouldn't be more than a day or two before someone can reach this part of the sector."

Vernestra took a deep breath and let it out. Catriona Graf was lying about her involvement. She knew far more than she was sharing. But she was right. It would be some time before any peacekeepers could arrive to detain the old woman, and they needed to find Reath, Imri, and Sylvestri as soon as possible. Could they really just let the woman go in order to find the others?

Jordanna clearly had no trouble deciding what was more important. "You will give us your fastest ship and directions to find them."

Master Cohmac gave a curt nod of agreement. "Whatever else awaits you will be for the Republic to decide."

"The ship is yours, but I have no idea how you'll find the Nihil. They took their cobbled-together ship and left to wherever it is that the Nihil go," the woman said with a dismissive wave. "It isn't like I have a map of possible Nihil locations. Well, I do, but I've already given that to the Republic and I would assume they've taken care of those hideouts."

You already have the answer.

Vernestra startled at the memory of the voice in her mind, and she thought with unnaturally sharp clarity of the puzzle box in the pouch hanging from her belt. The Force or something, someone else prodding her along? She decided in that moment she didn't care.

"Do you recognize this?" Vernestra fished the box out and thrust it at Catriona Graf, relieved it was still in her belt pouch. The woman looked down her nose at Vernestra. At first she seemed like she was going to ignore the question, but then the Matriarch took the puzzle box and turned it over in her hands.

"I do. These sigils are old prospector markings. A notation of sorts in case their life was lost while forging new paths between beacons. This means *increase, decrease, home,* and so on." The old woman turned the puzzle box around and around in her hands, a slow smile coming over her face. "I haven't seen one of these since I was very small."

"Can you open it?" Jordanna asked, and the Matriarch raised a single brow.

"Why, of course." She pressed three of the sides in quick order, and the cube opened like a flower, lying flat. "The answer is 'Always return home.' It's an old prospector saying."

"If you can't go forward, go back from whence you came," Jordanna murmured. At Vernestra's puzzled gaze, she shrugged. "It's an old San Tekka saying."

"An old hyperspace prospector saying." The Matriarch sniffed. "The San Tekkas are not the only family who spent lives during the rush."

Jordanna looked like she was considering saying something else, but she swallowed the retort. Most likely she knew this was not something they had time for. They needed to find the Nihil who had taken their people as soon as possible.

The Matriarch handed the box back to Vernestra and dusted her hands off like she was brushing away the commoner. "I can see that you are all in distress, so please know that anything you need is at your disposal."

"A ship, like Master Cohmac said," Jordanna said. "With extra big guns. Xylan said you had one of his."

"Ah, yes. The *Vengeful Goddess.* A frivolous thing, to be sure. It's simply ridiculous to think so many guns would be necessary to haul cargo. But, it is yours," she said with a smile. "As an apology."

Jordanna crossed her arms. "What about Xylan?"

"My grandson? Oh, I will deal with him."

"The Republic will deal with him," Master Cohmac said.

The Matriarch waved the statement away. "Yes, I suppose that is true. Now, I suggest you lot be on your way before I change my mind. I daresay it wouldn't look good for the Order to be accused of harassing citizens in their homes. Unless the Jedi are now ruffians for the Republic?"

There was silence as they all watched the Matriarch and her bodyguard walk away.

"I don't like her," Jordanna said. "And not just because she's a Graf."

"Agreed," Master Cohmac said. "And I don't buy a word of what she says. She can try to blame Xylan for this, but he had help. But she is correct that it's not our place to decide, so we will leave it for the Republic to deal with in the proper manner."

"There is definitely more she isn't telling us, and I wish I knew what it was," Vernestra said, her frustration for a moment pushing aside her worry over Imri.

"We can only work with the truth before us. What's in the cube, Vern?" Jordanna said.

Vernestra held it out so everyone could see the projection of a little girl laughing and running through the tall grass on some far-off planet. The scene skipped so it was in a modest house, the little girl playing with a set of blocks. She pointed at the numbers and clapped her hands. "Look, Daddy! I did it. That's where it should start. Right there."

"Who is that?" Jordanna wondered aloud. "She looks familiar for some reason. Why were the Nihil willing to kill for this on Tiikae?"

"I don't know who that is, but what is that?" Vernestra said, pointing to the numbers on the ground.

"On her blocks?" Master Cohmac said, coming closer.

"Yes. She said that's where it should start," Vernestra said. "What does that mean?"

"If this was taken during the Hyperspace Rush it might be a start point," Jordanna said with a frown. "For navigation. Come on, I have an idea. Let's get to that ship."

"I will be happy to lead you to the *Goddess*," said the Twi'lek servant, who had remained behind.

"Run," Vernestra said, and as they set out for the ship, Vernestra prayed she wouldn't be too late.

THIRTY-THREE

Syl was angrier than she'd been in a very, very long time as she lay on the deck of some unknown ship, her hands bound in front of her. Reath and Imri lay to her right, both unconscious, their occasional groans of pain reminders that they still lived.

But for how long?

Syl's chest stretched and ached as she moved, and she considered that seeing her mother again had not gone the way she'd thought it would. Her mother was alive. Her mother had *shot* her. But she had shot her because she was Nihil.

Her mother was alive and working for the Nihil.

And that made Syl a complex combination of angry and

sad. She could feel the heat of it in her heart, and it wasn't just lingering heat from the stun blast her mother had shot her with. It was rage, pure and unfiltered, and Syl hadn't felt it toward her mother since she'd been twelve and her mother had refused to let her go with a friend to Zeltros for a festival.

Her mother was alive.

Her mother was a liar.

Her mother was working with the Nihil, which was the thought that threatened to unravel Syl every time it crossed her mind. How could she, knowing the havoc and pain the marauders had rained down on the galaxy? They'd had friends on the *Legacy Run*, other Byne Guild members who had died trying to hold their ship together. They knew at least a dozen haulers who had gone missing in the months since the pirates had expanded their operation beyond the fringes of the frontier.

There were millions of reasons not to cooperate with the Nihil, but apparently Chancey Yarrow had found at least one reason to cooperate that justified faking her death and leaving her daughter behind to fend for herself. How long had Chancey even been dealing with the Nihil? Had Syl unwittingly been working for the Nihil her entire life, Chancey's random abandonments meaning more than just an opportunity to be free from her daughter in the name of education? The strange pieces of her childhood rearranged themselves into a new, unsettling pattern. It made too much sense not to be true.

And that made Syl angry, because it hurt to know that she could be tossed aside so easily.

A far-off door slid open and Syl closed her eyes, letting her body go limp as footsteps echoed toward her across the ship. She forced her breathing to slow, and as the steps stopped a short distance away, she began to bide her time.

"Blast it, Reath. Why do you keep crossing my path?" someone said—someone not much older than Syl from what she could tell.

This was her chance.

Syl ignored the screaming from her muscles as she opened her eyes and swung her legs around, knocking the girl off her feet. As she fell backward Syl scrambled onto her chest, using her legs to pin the pale human girl's arms at her sides. She smiled up at Syl, completely unalarmed.

"Kinky," she said, and Syl swung her bound hands at the side of the girl's head.

"You aren't my type," Syl muttered. With the girl unconscious, Syl searched her for any kind of weapon but found nothing.

"Don't break her. From what I understand, she's the Eye's favorite. I'm also trying to see if she can be useful, since she seems to be very resourceful."

Syl turned to see her mother sitting in the corner of the room, legs crossed, completely relaxed. She'd been watching the entire time, and somehow Syl had missed her presence.

"Always take in the entirety of your surroundings. I

cannot believe you're still forgetting that part of the lesson."
Chancey Yarrow looked just the same as she had the last time
Syl had seen her, and the familiar sight made Syl's heart give
a painful leap before settling back into despair.

"Where was the part of your lessons that included sign-
ing up with murderers for my own goals? I think I missed
that," Syl said, climbing to her feet. She should've known this
was one of her mother's games when her hands were bound
in front of her instead of behind her like the Jedi.

"Stop being so dramatic. You're lucky I only stunned you.
I could have killed you."

"And I could have stayed home. So many lost opportu-
nities."

For the first time Syl looked back on her childhood from
a different perspective, as the daughter of a woman who had
spent a number of years in a military college. Of course it
was true. Hadn't Chancey Yarrow run her daughter through
exercise after exercise with the precision of a drill instructor?
Syl had always taken it for granted; after all, hauling was
dangerous, and crews had to always be prepared for pirates,
cheats, and swindlers. It wasn't unusual for haulers to focus
so much on security and self-defense. But that was the problem with being knee-deep in a sarlacc pit. You never saw the
danger until it was too late.

"Can you take these off or at least tell me what you think
is going to happen next? You're not going to be able to keep
the Jedi incapacitated forever."

"These are just Padawan learners. I was smart enough to leave the rest behind. As well as Jordanna. I'm not sure how you linked back up with her after all of this time, but you are a fool for even talking to the girl. How many times are you going to let a San Tekka break your heart?"

Syl swallowed dryly, her heart thrumming with hope. Jordanna would come for her, and the Jedi would come for their Padawans. Syl had watched the way they worked together; there was affection there even if the Jedi were not known for it. Master Cohmac and Vernestra would come for their Padawans.

"How long?" Syl asked, changing the subject. "How long have you been working for the Nihil?"

"Not long, not as long as it should have been. I was stubborn, but they finally made me an offer that I could not resist."

Doubt flashed through Syl's mind, her mother's words striking too close to her newest fear—that her mother had always been a monster and she had mistaken cruelty for love; so she gestured around the ship, which looked the worse for wear. "Just what is this place, exactly?"

"The culmination of years of work. You remember your auntie Lourna, don't you?"

The image of a slender Twi'lek woman with a penchant for black jumpsuits came to mind. She'd spent a year with Lourna learning how to defend herself in close quarters. The first time they'd practiced, she'd knocked Syl unconscious.

When Syl had awoken Lourna had told her she was lucky to be alive and that no one would be pulling their punches. By the time Chancey came back for Syl, her arm had been broken twice, and she was pretty sure her jaw was fractured a couple of times, as well.

Syl had been thirteen.

"Yeah, I remember her."

"We've stayed in touch over the years as she has built her reputation. About a year ago she told me of an oracle who navigated hyperspace like no other. She offered me the chance to finally prove my theory correct, to be able to finally build my machine while aided by the greatest navigational mind that had ever existed. Lourna believed in me and thought that it was wholly possible to create a device that replicated the gravity of a heavenly body in realspace, thus weaponizing hyperspace." Syl had never heard her mother talk like this. Well, that wasn't entirely true. She sounded exactly like the recording Professor Wolk had played. Seemed like the holos hadn't been altered after all.

"Well, bully for you," Syl said. Exhaustion, emotional and physical, swept through her, and she sat down hard next to an empty crate. She felt like she'd just woken up from a nightmare only to find out it was all true. "Why did you kidnap me and the Jedi?"

"Oh, those Padawans are tribute for the Eye."

Syl blinked. "Who in the twin suns is the Eye?"

"He is the soul of the Nihil, the center of the Storms and

a visionary who also understands that the Republic doesn't deserve the respect it demands. He's working on something, and he needs Jedi to test it on." She said it so casually, like it was no big deal to kidnap people and give them to a man who thought destroying a planet was a clever pastime. And while the rhetoric about the Republic sounded familiar, Syl doubted that a man who killed civilians at a festival was anything so noble as a political dissident. No, the Nihil were nothing but murderers and thieves, no matter how Chancey Yarrow tried to rewrite their backstory.

That was when Syl realized she had never truly known her mother. How could she have not seen this part of her for all these years? "You can't give people away to be experimented on. What is wrong with you?"

Syl's mother had always been odd, different from other mothers, but something else had happened and she was now working within a reality removed from the one where Syl dwelled. Was it the influence of the Nihil, or Lourna? Was she making up a story to push Syl away, to protect her? But if that was the case, why had she brought Syl along with the Jedi?

Syl didn't know, and she didn't care. She wanted off of the ship and away from this woman, her fear overriding any sense of familial obligation. Better she had died in the first Nihil attack, which Syl now realized had probably been orchestrated by Lourna as a way for Chancey Yarrow to "die" so no one would suspect anything was amiss.

Poor Professor Wolk. He had been right all along. That made Syl wonder if Xylan had been working with the Nihil from the beginning, the attempt on her life at the hotel Xylan's way of getting Syl to trust him.

And she'd been stupid enough not only to take his money but to lie for him. If she'd just told Senator Starros the truth, she would've been so much better off.

Syl pushed the thought aside. She had more pressing matters at the moment than her regrets or Xylan Graf's motivations.

"Okay, got it, Jedi go to the Nihil as test subjects. And what about me? I'm alive for a reason." She knew her mother too well. Chancey Yarrow was always thinking several steps ahead of anyone else, and if she'd had her blaster set to stun it was because she'd needed Syl alive. She worried that this incarnation of her mother would kill her if it became necessary.

"Darling, you are the only one who can help me with my work," Chancey said, her smile so full of love and affection that Syl wanted to cry. How was she supposed to reconcile the monster her mother had become with the woman she'd grown up worshipping? Even if they had been the same person all along?

"The Gravity's Heart is a massive undertaking, and while I have managed to convince a few top scientists to help me"— Syl was certain by "convince" Chancey meant something far less benign—"they are a lazy lot and need constant oversight.

Who else would I want at my side but my daughter? How else can I keep you safe?" There was something in her mother's voice that proved her words for a lie, and Syl could so clearly, finally see the truth: her mother was trying to protect her. Maybe she hadn't faked her death, not like Syl thought.

Lourna had kidnapped her, and somehow Chancey had maneuvered herself into being in control of the situation. And now she had brought Syl to her prison all in the name of familial love, but Syl was really on the Gravity's Heart because her mother was trying to keep her safe.

By bringing her into the belly of the beast. It was such a stupid, risky thing to do, and it was exactly what Syl would expect from her mother.

So Professor Wolk had been right, but not exactly. Because he apparently had forgotten just how resourceful Chancey Yarrow could be when her back was to the wall.

"We can get out of here," Syl whispered, scooting closer to her mother. "You don't have to stay here."

Chancey's face twisted into sadness before her usual serene expression returned. "The Nihil have spies everywhere. Lourna told me they have sympathizers within the Senate itself. Where in the galaxy do you think we could run to?"

Syl couldn't help the hysterical laughter that burbled up, and when it burst forth she was powerless to stop it. She could only shake her head as her eyes watered.

"If you think," Syl gasped out, once she could finally get a measure of control, "that I am ever going to help you, that

I would pay for my life with the lives of others, then you are sorely mistaken. I would rather die than help you. My mother raised me to believe that the galaxy was uncaring and vast but that didn't mean we should be selfish and irresponsible." Saying the words out loud filled Syl with shame. She should've been smarter than to get mixed up with Xylan Graf. She should've remembered her morals and not been so tempted by credits. She wouldn't make the same mistake again.

Chancey's calm smile faded and her eyes narrowed. "You always were a sulky child," she muttered, climbing to her feet from her throne of packing crates. "You'll come around. I'll leave Nan here. When she wakes she's probably going to want a word with you. Perhaps some time spent with her will convince you that survival in this galaxy sometimes means indulging in unsavory activities."

Without another word she left, the storage room's only door sliding shut and the sound of a lock engaging strangely loud in the small space. Syl tried very hard not to cry as she found herself buried in despair.

She was only mostly successful.

The one thought that warmed her was that at least Jordanna and Remy were safe.

THIRTY-FOUR

The *Vengeful Goddess* was a beautiful ship, and as Jordanna sat in the copilot's seat, Vernestra hanging back by tacit agreement, she'd gone so far as to caress the control panel.

"Oh, Syl would love you," Jordanna said to the ship. And even though Vernestra had only spent a few days with Sylvestri Yarrow, she found herself agreeing.

She hoped Sylvestri would get the chance to admire the ship herself.

Once they'd left Everbloom and hit the inky blackness of space outside of the Graf compound, Master Cohmac turned on the comms station to call back to the Temple and tell them everything, including the Grafs' treachery. While he did that, Jordanna turned to Vernestra. "Would you like to do the honors?"

"You really think the code in the blocks is a location?" Vernestra asked.

Jordanna nodded, and Vernestra entered the code into the navicomputer with surprisingly steady fingers.

"Got it," Jordanna said. "It's a beacon in the Berenge sector, unsurprisingly."

"Unsurprising, why?" asked Vernestra.

"It was our first home. At least that's the lore. My aunt told me that the entire family had once lived in their ships in the sector, basically nomads. But that all changed when Mari San Tekka went missing. She was a genius, and helped take my family from haulers with too little sense to real prospectors. When she was lost as a little girl, the San Tekkas abandoned the Berenge sector and let the lease expire. That place, well"—Jordanna frowned, her expression pensive—"it's a little bit cursed."

"Let us go investigate and hope for the best," Master Cohmac said somberly.

As soon as the ship jumped to hyperspace, Vernestra found a spot to sit in the empty cargo hold. So far meditating in hyperspace had been useful, and Vernestra wanted to hope that the Force would deliver them to Sylvestri, Imri, and

Reath before anything else happened to them. She ignored her too-rapid heartbeat and the way her palms were slicked with sweat.

She would hope that the Force saw fit to grant her one more vision.

Vernestra began to breathe, deep and even, her body sinking into the familiar rhythms of meditation. She felt herself deep within the Force, a wave in a vast ocean, pulled from her body, like slipping into a warm bath after a long day. Only she wasn't settling into heated water; she was being drawn out into the cosmic Force.

She tried to stop it from happening. She reached for her physical form, trying to sink back into her body like they taught Jedi when they first learned to meditate, so they would not become too lost in the vastness of the Force, but she couldn't stop her headlong plunge into the magnificence of the galaxy.

This was the first time Vernestra had ever been aware of the beginning of one of her visions, and she could sense that she was being both pushed toward a certain place in the galaxy and pulled. Was this what a Wayseeker did? If so, Vernestra could understand why certain Jedi felt compelled to follow that path. There was a purposefulness to it that was reassuring even as it was unsettling.

She looked around, or rather saw with her displaced consciousness that she was back in the massive ship she had journeyed to last time. She didn't hesitate, running down the corridors she'd already traversed, heading to where the voice had beckoned in her previous vision.

Hurry, hurry. I have so little time left.

Vernestra rounded the corner of the empty ship and slid to a stop before a door. It opened easily as she approached, and in the room were rows of navicomputers and a medical pod that had seen better days. Machines beeped and whirred, and as Vernestra looked down at the pod, she saw a frail old human woman, her pale skin lined and folded in on itself.

Yes. We must hurry. I have a gift for you. One last Path before I pass on. It was always meant for you.

The old woman opened her eyes and didn't, and Vernestra had a sensation of seeing two versions of the woman: the one she wished for people to see and the one that truly existed. Was it a trick of the Force or created by the nature of the old woman's affliction? She didn't know, and she had the sensation that something was very wrong with the old woman and had been for a long time.

"Gone traveling," the woman said. "But I have a Path for you."

"Vern! Wake up!"

Vernestra stiffened. Jordanna and Master Cohmac both stood over her, and Vernestra's heart pounded as her face flushed in embarrassment.

"Are you okay?" Master Cohmac asked.

"Yes. I was having a vision," Vernestra said, feeling unsteady.

Master Cohmac quirked an eyebrow. "And was it useful?"

"More and more it seems," Vernestra murmured. Jordanna returned to the cockpit, and Remy licked Vernestra's hand as though she was worried.

"You'd better be nice to Imri when we find him," Vernestra said to the vollka, voice clogged with worry, and the cat responded by grooming herself in a very inelegant way.

Master Cohmac cleared his throat. "We have a couple of hours before we get to the end of our jump. You should get some rest so you're at a hundred percent when we arrive." He offered Vernestra a hand up, and she took it, climbing to her feet and following the other Jedi back toward the cockpit.

Master Cohmac settled back into the pilot's seat. "I don't suppose your vision gave you any insight into where Reath and Imri are?"

Vernestra shook her head. "No, but I feel like we're going the right way, that this trip will lead us to them."

Master Cohmac's expression did not change, even though Vernestra figured he had to be as concerned about Reath as she was about Imri. "If this is the way they came, they most likely took just as long as we will to traverse hyperspace, so we should refresh ourselves. They could only be at most a couple hours ahead of us. And I sense that we will have a battle on our hands. I've sent notice to a nearby temple to request assistance."

"Will they come, though?" asked Jordanna, her arms crossed.

"They'll come if they can," Vernestra said.

Jordanna shook her head. "I wish I could be so sure." There were shadows in her expression that made Vernestra think there had been calls for help before that went unanswered, and Vernestra thought once more of all the planets like Tiikae that had spent too long at the mercy of the Nihil.

Master Cohmac raised a hand to forestall any further discussion. "We must focus on what we can, and for now that must be resting and saving our strength for the battle ahead."

Vernestra nodded and left the cockpit to return to the cargo hold and meditate a bit more, hoping this time for a vision of Imri and Reath, safe and sound.

She hoped that the Force was leading them where they needed to be.

Imri and Reath's lives depended on it.

THIRTY-FIVE

As soon as the *Vengeful Goddess* exited hyperspace, all Vernestra's senses stood on alert. She'd had no more visions, but the meditation had left her calm and centered and ready to take on whatever came next.

A tingle ran over her skin, and she jumped up from where she and Jordanna lounged in the crew mess to sprint through the ship to the cockpit. Jordanna followed.

"Master Cohmac! I sensed—" Vernestra's voice cut off as she looked out the viewport to the space beyond. "What is that?"

"I think," Jordanna said, her voice low, "that is the Nihil's not-so-secret weapon."

What looked to be a giant wheel cobbled together from hundreds of ships spun slowly in the emptiness of space. Flashes of light emanated from it, like someone was still busy working to add new ships to the wheel, the engines randomly firing to keep the thing spinning. This was undoubtedly the dilapidated ship from Vernestra's vision, but she wasn't ready to share that bit of information with anyone just yet.

But it was a good sign that they had made the right choice in jumping to the beacon from the puzzle box.

"Look," Jordanna said, pointing to a ship that appeared before them. "There's the welcoming party."

"I think I can handle whatever they send our way until reinforcements arrive," Master Cohmac said, powering up the ship's guns.

"We can't wait for help. We have to find a way on board that station," Jordanna said.

"Use the escape pod. I'll distract them as you fly toward the station," Master Cohmac said, standing from the pilot's chair. He flipped a few switches on the comms unit. "I'm also going to send an updated request, and this time I am sending to the main temple on Coruscant as well as the local Republic coalition frequency. Stellan will want to know what we've found out here, but we need reinforcements, fast."

"Here's hoping someone is listening," Jordanna muttered. Master Cohmac merely raised an eyebrow in her direction.

"You should hurry," Cohmac said, and Vernestra and Jordanna nodded before taking off.

"There are comm headsets in the weapons cabinet located in the armory," Jordanna called as she followed Vernestra down the corridor toward the escape pod. Her heart pounded, and she couldn't help trying to reach out to Imri as she fitted a comms unit to her head, adjusting her hair so the gathered mass wouldn't interfere with the headset.

But no matter how much Vernestra reached for Imri within the Force, she couldn't sense him. There was not a hint of his presence, which she had to believe meant he was still unconscious, under the power of the gas the Nihil had used on them.

"Here," Jordanna said, pulling out a set of masks and throwing one to Vernestra.

"Good idea," Vernestra said, fitting the mask over her head. The last thing she wanted was to get hit with the purple gas again. There would be no taking her by surprise this time.

When they reached the escape pod, Jordanna held back. "I'm a terrible pilot," she said. "So you fly."

Vernestra grinned and jumped in the pilot's seat. Despite her worry about Reath and Imri, it felt good to have the chance to fly again. Remy squeezed into the space before the doors closed, the vollka pacing around the shuttle in agitation. Within a handful of seconds, the escape pod was powered up and Vernestra was launching the capsule, turning it so they headed straight for the spinning station.

Laser fire skidded across the escape pod's shields, and Jordanna sighed.

"So much for the element of surprise. Oh, what do we have here?" She began to flip switches and laughed as she powered up the weapons. "Two gun arrays on an escape pod? I like the way these Grafs think."

"That seems like overkill," Vernestra said, unable to keep the concern from her voice.

"Oh, it is. But it's also brilliant. Ready?"

"Yes," said Vernestra, swinging the pod hard to the right to avoid a skiff barrel-rolling right at them. It was one of a dozen ships launching from the spinning station, and Vernestra did not think reinforcements were going to arrive in time. They were on their own.

"Master Cohmac?"

"Clear what you need to get to the docking area. I'll try to distract the rest until our reinforcements arrive. May the Force be with you." His comlink cut out as he concentrated on the ships bearing down on him, and Vernestra took a deep breath.

There was nothing to do but focus on surviving.

The skiff came around for another pass, and Jordanna let loose a barrage of laser fire that caught the Path drive, detonating the ship in a display of sparks and blue flames.

"I like that they give us a nice spot to aim for," she said, cackling as the pod flew past the wreckage. "Stupid Nihil."

Some of the debris from the other ship hit the escape pod, the metal screaming as it took a direct hit along the side.

"Um, maybe try to avoid the wreckage next time,"

Jordanna said, already targeting another Nihil ship that bore down on them, this one looking like a pleasure yacht hacked together with pieces from a cargo hauler in an oddly shaped mess.

"How is that thing even flying?" Vernestra wondered aloud.

"Nihil ingenuity, I guess." Jordanna shot at the ship, but it flashed out of existence before returning behind them.

"Did they just jump behind us?" Vernestra asked, and Jordanna swore.

"Reckless bastards," she muttered as they were fired on from the rear. "There's only a few kilometers to the station. Can you make a run for it? These smaller guns are beginning to overheat, and the longer we're out here, the worse our chances get."

Jordanna was right. Already a dozen different alarms beeped or flashed at Vernestra, and their shields were at a measly fifteen percent availability. Any more of this and they would be history.

"I have an idea," Vernestra said, flipping switches. "Hold on."

Behind them, Remy yowled her displeasure and crouched down, pressing her belly to the floor.

"Yeah, I got a bad feeling, as well," Jordanna said.

Vernestra might be just okay at flying, but she was excellent at crashing.

THIRTY-SIX

Reath woke to a feeling of panic pressing on him from all sides. Which made sense, because something was definitely on fire.

He sat up, his head pounding as he blinked at the sight before him. Syl was slamming her hands against a closed door, swearing liberally as she demanded to be let out. A thin trickle of smoke filtered in under the door, and the sounds of running feet and shouting came from the other side, but no one answered Syl's pleas.

"Hey," Imri said as Reath looked over at him. "Everything hurts. How are we even alive?"

Reath grimaced at the younger Padawan. "No idea," he

said, gesturing at the singed material of his tabard. "I guess it was a stun blast. Do you know where we are?"

"No," Imri said, wincing.

"We're on the Gravity's Heart, the Nihil hyperspace weapon," Syl said, coming to stand near the Jedi. "We're locked in here, but it sort of sounds like someone's attacking, so we need to come up with a plan quickly. Any ideas?"

Reath struggled to his feet, the movement awkward since his hands were bound behind his back. "I have no lightsaber. Do we have any weapons?"

"No. She didn't even have any," Syl said, pointing to the girl huddled next to some crates in the far corner. A brilliant bruise colored the side of her face, and she gave Syl a sullen glance.

"You're lucky I don't have a weapon, otherwise you'd be dead."

Syl snorted. "Good luck with that."

"Nan?" Reath said, unable to fully believe what he was seeing. He reached for the Force before giving up on it. He was still entirely too weak for anything impressive.

"Hey, Reath. Glad to see you aren't dead. Think you can get us out of here?" she said with a crooked smile.

"How does she know you?" Imri asked, his pale face twisted into a scowl. "She's Nihil."

"We were on a station together a while back. I saved her life and she grudgingly returned the favor," Reath said, his voice flat.

Nan shrugged. "It wasn't personal."

"If you want I can hit her again," Syl offered, and Reath shook his head.

"I don't supposed these crates have anything useful?" he asked, changing the subject.

"You mean like a key for these?" Syl said, holding up her manacled hands in front of her. "Not that I saw. I was hoping you guys could use your magic to open them up."

Both Imri and Reath shook their heads, and Syl sighed. "Well, I guess I'm back to my previous plan." She began kicking the door again, yelling as she did so. Reath realized she was kicking an access panel, and he walked over to stand next to her.

"If you can get that access panel open, we may be able to override the locking mechanism on the door," he said.

Syl began to kick the panel in earnest, and the metal plate fell to the side. Reath bent down to look at the wires inside and grinned.

"Excellent. If you can yank that red and that yellow wire, that should release the door."

Syl bent down and pulled the wires Reath had indicated, jumping back as the mechanism sparked. The door slid open a scant few centimeters, but it was enough for Syl to wedge her fingers in and pry it open the rest of the way.

The door had no sooner opened than Nan jumped to her feet, knocking Syl out of the way and running off down the corridor.

"Should we chase her?" Imri said, coming to stand next to Reath and Syl.

"Nah, we need to find a ride off of this heap," Syl said. "Any ideas? You know, since we have no weapons and this ship is full of Nihil."

"One thing at a time," Reath said. "And, agreed. I don't think I can use the Force right now. My head is still woozy."

"Same," Imri said.

"Okay, good to know," Syl said. "Then I suggest we run, hopefully away from the fighting."

They took off down the hallway, and as they began to pick up the pace, there was a far-off explosion and the very clear sound of rending metal.

"What was that?" Syl shouted as they continued to sprint down the hallway.

"I don't know," Imri shouted back. "But I will say that I hope it's your girlfriend and she is really, really angry."

"Jordanna is not my girlfriend," Syl growled.

Reath didn't quite understand the back and forth; he was certain he had missed something, but then they were sliding into a room with a medical pod and his focus was on the thing that dominated the center of the room. The door slid shut behind them, locking into place.

"What is that?" Syl asked, her eyes wide and a look of disgust twisting her features as she stared at the pod.

"She needs help," Imri said, gaze far away.

Reath's bad feeling bloomed into full-blown worry.

"One move and you are all dead," said a Chadra-Fan with a prosthetic leg. He held a blaster in one hand and a canister of gas in the other, and as a unit Reath, Imri, and Syl backed up toward the medical pod.

"I guess we should have run the other way," Syl said, and Reath had the terrible realization she was right.

THIRTY-SEVEN

Vernestra twisted the yoke hard, sending the escape pod careening into a spiral, like it had been hit. She pointed the nose right at an approaching Nihil ship, daring it to challenge her.

The craft blinked out of existence, leaving the path to the space station's docking area clear.

"Hold on!" Vernestra yelled. She pushed the escape pod at full throttle, the docking bay approaching entirely too fast. Jordanna yelped in alarm, and Remy yowled.

Vernestra didn't so much land the escape pod as slam it into the landing deck of the massive station, metal screaming as the craft slammed into another ship in the docking bay before flipping end over end. Vernestra's world turned upside down before the craft stopped right side up. Jordanna said nothing as they came to a halt next to several other ships, most of which looked like they were either salvage or scrap.

"You really *are* good at crashing ships," Jordanna said, seeming a bit ill.

"Okay, that wasn't that bad, considering."

Jordanna said nothing, just unfastened her seat restraint before undoing the strange belt she wore. Then she began to piece together a ring from the random pieces on her belt. Remy reappeared behind them and growled low in her throat, and Vernestra couldn't help feeling uneasy.

"What's that?" Vernestra asked.

"This is what I use in hopeless situations," she said, still twisting the pieces together. There was also a pair of gloves that she pulled onto her hands, strange things that looked to be made of some sort of flexible metal alloy. "Which, if you haven't noticed, this is. You aren't going to like it." Outside the escape pod viewport, a half dozen Nihil approached, blasters drawn.

"How do you know that?" Vernestra asked.

"Because the one time I used the Merry Maker, Master Oprand gave me a lecture to end all. This is a Nihil weapon I took off of one of them when they brought the Drengir to Tiikae."

Vernestra did not like the idea of using anything the Nihil had created. The weapon Jordanna was piecing together looked a bit like discarded components of several lightsabers, but before Jordanna could finish, blaster fire rained down on them, shattering the escape pod's front window, and Vernestra was diving for the rear of the craft while pulling free her lightsaber.

"Jordanna!"

"I'm okay, Vern. Do me a favor. Stay where you are for the next few moments while I handle this."

Before Vernestra could object, Jordanna stood and raised her hand toward the side door of the escape pod.

"Can you get that out of the way for me?" she asked, and Vernestra nodded.

The metal bent and flew outward, taking out an approaching human woman, carrying her across the hangar bay, and pinning her against a ship. In the same moment, Jordanna threw the circlet she'd built. It glowed pink like a strange sort of vibro-blade, but Jordanna sent it spinning with no care or elegance, the thing arcing through the air and cutting through everything it touched.

It sliced through the nearest masked Nihil like a hot knife through soft cheese and then arced again before hitting the next one. Vernestra's stomach dropped at the carnage left behind, the men cleaved in half like overripe fruits. This was not the way of the Jedi; this was unbridled massacre.

And it was only beginning.

The remaining Nihil tried to shoot at the spinning hoop or run away from it, but they were unsuccessful. The pink circle returned to Jordanna, who caught it with her strange gloves, the effort making her grunt before she flung it at a new opponent. Once, twice. The third time the pink circle returned to Jordanna, almost everyone in the hangar was dead.

Vernestra strode toward the other woman, a sick feeling in her middle. "Jordanna, that's enough."

"There are still Nihil for me to take care of." Jordanna's voice was flat, far away, and the look in her eyes was vacant, like she saw not the piecemeal station before them but someplace else entirely.

"You have to stop," Vernestra said, pointing to the pink circle with her lightsaber. But the circle did not stop. Jordanna held her hand out, making small adjustments so that it sliced through a masked Nihil woman running back down the hallway, hitting her arm but leaving her otherwise unharmed. The hangar bay was littered with no fewer than a dozen Nihil, all of them killed in a matter of heartbeats. Jordanna ignored them as she began to run after the fleeing Nihil.

"No, enough!" Vernestra said, putting her hand out and using the Force to push Jordanna off her feet. The woman fell, her foot slipping in a puddle of green blood from one of the Nihil she had killed, and as she leapt back to her feet, the pink circlet returned to her, hovering over her head like a menacing crown before falling into her gloved hand.

"Fine," Jordanna said, powering down the weapon so

it was just a pitiful-looking metallic hoop without any of the murderous energy that had made it so lethal. "But next time I stand before the Nihil, I will not leave a single one of them alive. No one will survive." Her expression was hard, and Vernestra had no doubt that if she had not been there Jordanna would have lost her focus and chased down every single Nihil on the station.

"No more. All this indiscriminate killing isn't good," Vernestra said, feeling a bit silly for stating the obvious. But it was more than that. For the first time Vernestra could sense the sadness that Imri had told her seeped from Jordanna. It surrounded the older girl like a miasma, and Vernestra found her own worry growing even stronger as she considered the burden Jordanna carried with her.

Once more Vernestra found herself pondering how fighting the Nihil, and the relentless bloodshed they left in their wake, was changing the galaxy. What kind of person had Jordanna been before her life became a struggle for survival. The girl she was with Sylvestri Yarrow was nothing like the emotionless killer that stood before Vernestra.

Jordanna had killed the Nihil in self-defense, but there was something about it that didn't sit right with Vernestra.

"Perhaps," Jordanna said, shrugging, her face a blank mask. "But I also think perhaps the Force could want me to help out a bit. After all, someone has to stop the Nihil. We are all the Republic, right?"

"I don't know," Vernestra said, not wanting to get into

a philosophical argument about the Force. Could the Force really be connected to such a brutal weapon? It was better in Jordanna's hands than a Nihil's, but as bad as a blaster was, this seemed so much worse.

Before Vernestra could say anything else, Remy scented the air and yowled, running off in the same direction the Nihil had fled.

"Wait, do you hear that?" Jordanna said, very neatly changing the subject. She ran after the vollka, her circlet still clutched in her hand, and Vernestra had to sprint to catch up.

When she rounded the corner, Jordanna and Remy were nowhere to be seen, and Vernestra slid to a stop. Her heart began to thrum and her head began to pound, and it was difficult to breathe. At first she thought it might be the effect of some kind of gas, and she wrestled with the mask that hung from her belt. But halfway through the movement, she stopped, realizing that it was something else entirely.

The hallway was the one from her vision.

Vernestra clutched her lightsaber and walked without thinking. She broke into a run. A mixture of dread and excitement drove her forward, because whatever was waiting for her at the end of the long hallway would be equal parts good and bad.

Luckily Vernestra knew the way. Her visions had been true.

Vernestra didn't hesitate. She made her way through the creaking emptiness of the station. There was something about the space that felt ominous and cold, as though the walls had borne witness to untold miseries, the negative energy seeping into them. It made her want to leave the station, to escape its dim confines. But she couldn't leave without finding Imri and Reath or identifying the voice from her visions.

Force willing they were all located in the same place.

Vernestra rounded one last corner and then ran flat out to a brightly lit doorway. She had thrown away any last vestiges of caution and entered the room ready to fight, but when she crossed the threshold, she found Jordanna bent over an unconscious Reath. A canister of gas was leaking pitifully in the corner, Syl putting an empty trash can over it as she coughed. Imri stood nearby, his face scrunched in pain.

"Where were you?" Jordanna demanded. Her circlet was still powered down, and it hung around her neck like a very ugly necklace. "I've been trying to call you through the comlink."

"Oh, I didn't hear you," Vernestra said. She felt disoriented, as though her trip had been made to seem much faster than it was. She'd been right behind Jordanna. Hadn't she?

"Imri, are you okay?" Vernestra asked, not understanding how she had lost a bit of time.

"Yes, but she isn't," he said, nodding toward the old woman lying in a medical pod. The light within the pod burned the same blue as hyperspace, and to anyone but a Force user it would look as though the old woman inside was sleeping peacefully. But Vernestra could sense that the woman's brain had stopped functioning, though her heart beat on and her chest rose and fell as though she were breathing.

"What is that?" Imri asked, voice choked with a combination of pity and disgust.

"I think the pod is keeping her alive even though her spirit has passed on."

"Is that?" Jordanna walked closer to the pod, and her breath hitched as she looked down at the woman inside. "Is that Mari San Tekka?" she whispered.

"Who is Mari San Tekka?" Vernestra asked, coming to stand next to Jordanna.

"She was a girl who went missing. They say she helped turn my family's tide of loss and pain into profit toward the end of the rush, but that her parents paid for our good fortune in heartbreak," Jordanna said. "She would have been a distant cousin."

Gone traveling, the whispery voice from Vernestra's vision had said. It was curious. Vernestra could see the old woman in the pod speaking to her, but she sensed that this body had no occupant, as though the woman's spirit had departed in death but somehow refused to fully abandon her flesh.

"I had a vision of her. She said she had something for me."

Yes. We must hurry. I have a gift for you. One last Path before I pass on. It was always meant for you. The memory was fresh and gave Vernestra the odd sensation that she was talking to the dead woman.

"Vernestra, can you hear her?" Jordanna asked.

"No, it's just a memory of my vision," Vernestra said.

"So, at least you know your visions are of true things sometimes," Imri said. "This place makes me uneasy. We need to get out of here."

"Especially before that gas-slinging Chadra-Fan wakes up," Syl said, pointing to the man slumped in the corner. "He seems to be responsible for this woman, and there is nothing good that can come of that."

"I agree," Reath said, sitting up with a groan. "Why is my head pounding?"

"Side effect of the gas canister the Chadra-Fan threw at you," Jordanna said, offering Reath a hand up.

He groaned as he stood and leaned heavily on her. "How is it I'm the only one who got hit with the gas? Just my lucky day, I guess."

"The effects should quickly fade," Jordanna said with a grin. She looked over Reath's head, her gaze on Syl. "Hey, you."

"Hey, yourself. Is that my Beti?" Syl said, pointing at the modified blaster rifle strapped across Jordanna's back.

"I figured you'd want a friend," Jordanna said with a smile, offering Syl the blaster. Syl smiled back and held up her bound hands.

"A little help, first?"

Vernestra sliced through the manacles, freeing first Syl and then Reath and Imri. She then approached the medical pod. "Since she's your kin, what should we do with her?"

Jordanna looked at the old woman and sighed. "Since

she's gone we should give her peace by powering down the pod. I can tell the family what I found when we return to Coruscant. If we get back to Coruscant."

"The puzzle box must have been hers once upon a time. You should take that, as well," Vernestra said, her own voice sounding far away. There was still something here, some task to be done, and she did not want to leave the old woman just yet. At the edges of Vernestra's senses she could feel the station vibrating under her feet in a distressing way. "I will send your ancestor on her way. You lead the others to safety."

"I think the station is starting to break apart. We need to get out of here," Sylvestri Yarrow said, pointing to the door.

"You're probably right. Cohmac said we should hurry," Jordanna said, pointing at the comlink she wore.

Jordanna half carried, half dragged Reath out of the room, Imri and Syl right behind them. As they left, the station began to list to one side, and there were explosions far off that echoed through the small space.

For half a heartbeat Vernestra hesitated, but then she closed her eyes and reached out to the half-dead woman. The woman reached back, the connection like and unlike a Force bond. For a moment nothing happened, but then Vernestra began to see flashes of the old woman's life: a childhood spent on an idyllic planet, her first trip through hyperspace, and then something different—the blue of hyperspace, seeming less random and more deliberate, diverting and flowing in the same way Vernestra perceived the Force, a rushing, branching fluid thing that could be charted and mapped and explored.

And then Vernestra saw it—the Path, a proper thing to be named and followed and remembered. Vernestra felt the memory of it being carved on her mind. No matter what happened, she would know how to get there, the place beyond the edge of the galaxy, a place where no living thing should go and no one had gone for a very, very long time.

And then Vernestra was alone, all by herself, and the presence of the old woman was fading, retreating across a distance where Vernestra could not follow. But the Path to that far-off place was within Vernestra, and she finally understood why Master Stellan had been so enraptured with the idea of Vernestra's hyperspace visions. Traversing hyperspace the same way a Jedi traveled through the Force was a difficult thing to do, and this frail old woman had spent a lifetime making her way across the hidden paths of the galaxy.

A talent exploited by the Nihil in all the worst ways.

"Thank you," Vernestra said, placing her hand against the glass of the medical pod as the old woman inside collapsed in on herself. There was no longer the dual perception of the woman—of her body and her spirit. There was only her corpse, long dead, the physical form that had kept her prisoner until she could offer up one last Path to Vernestra.

"Vern! We've got to get moving!" cried Syl from the hallway.

Vernestra used her lightsaber to slice through the hoses connected to Mari San Tekka's pod. Alarms flashed and the light within the medical pod went dark, hiding the corpse inside from view.

And then Vernestra dashed out of the room and ran for her life.

THIRTY-EIGHT

They met no resistance as they sprinted through the hallways, Remy leading the way back to the hangar bay. Syl got a glimpse of a battle raging outside of the station as they passed a viewport, and she grinned.

"Looks like you guys brought some friends," she yelled as they ran down the corridor.

Jordanna nodded and tapped the comlink in her ear. "Master Cohmac said our reinforcements arrived. They aren't firing directly on the station, but it's taking a lot of damage in the battle."

"Let's hope we can find a ride," Vernestra said, running up behind them.

The Nihil weren't the kind of people who stuck around once things went belly-up, and that was for the best. It meant they could escape that much quicker.

The hallway opened up onto the hangar bay just as the entire world tilted. From behind them came the sound of creaking metal and then a hollow boom as part of the station collapsed. Beyond the hangar a number of ships flew past, shooting at one another, including a spindly, fragile-looking craft that Syl had never seen before.

"What is that?" Syl said, yelling to be heard over the din of the station creaking and groaning as it came apart.

"Vectors," Reath said, groaning as he stood on his own, letting go of Jordanna. "A lot of them."

"And a Longbeam," Vernestra said.

"Master Stellan summoned Master Elzar from the temple on Dubrovia, which is not far. He brought along a few coalition peacekeepers who were in the area. Master Cohmac says they are making short work of the Nihil," Vernestra said with a smile to the group, relaying the conversation happening over her comlink.

"Who did this?" Reath asked, voice almost too quiet to be heard.

And that was when Syl saw the carnage that littered the edge of the hangar bay. Bodies, seemingly hacked to pieces, all of them Nihil.

Reath glanced at Vernestra, who shook her head a bit, her eyes wide with concern. But her gaze flicked to Jordanna, just barely, and Syl turned to look at the girl she loved.

Jordanna's face was expressionless, nearly slack, and a tendril of panic unfurled in Syl's chest. Was it happening again? Had Syl placed her love and trust in someone she didn't truly know?

"Jor?" she asked.

"Later," Jordanna said, the word seeming to cause her physical pain.

For a moment no one moved, the Jedi dismayed, Syl wondering how Jordanna could wreak such havoc. But then there was another explosion, and the moment passed.

"Well, let's get out of here before we end up space trash. Where's your ship?" Syl asked, her voice mostly fine.

Jordanna cleared her throat, her gaze going toward a piece of wreckage still smoking off to the side. "Vern sort of crashed the pod."

"In my defense, it got us here," she said.

Syl sighed. "Well, let's hope one of these scrap heaps can fly."

Remy suddenly stiffened, letting out a yowl before taking off across the hangar bay.

"She must smell something familiar," Jordanna said. "We should follow her."

They took off across the hangar bay, too, Vernestra bringing up the rear. They had only gone a few steps when blaster fire rained down on them. Syl dove behind a nearby crate while everyone else took cover, as well.

She peeked over the top of the crate, and there, sitting maybe twenty meters away, was the *Switchback*.

And standing on the boarding ramp was Chancey Yarrow.

"Mom, stop shooting! It's finished."

"Don't be ridiculous. This is merely a hiccup for people like Lourna."

No one else would notice the fear in Chancey's voice, but it was all that Syl could hear. "Give up and come with us. It doesn't have to be like this."

"I did not raise you to be soft, Sylvestri Yarrow," she yelled back. "I am taking my ship and getting out of here before this place is completely destroyed. I taught you to be a survivor. This is your last chance to make the right decision."

Syl wasn't a little kid anymore. She understood that her mother was a desperate woman, pushed into doing a terrible thing to survive. That didn't make it right. But the pain in her chest was real. This was the last time she would see her mother, and it wasn't as the woman who had taught her to be strong, to defend herself and do what was right, even in tough circumstances. Syl refused to let it make her sad.

The blaster suddenly flew out of Chancey Yarrow's hand, Vernestra standing nearby with her own hand outstretched toward Syl's mother. The Jedi pulled the blaster to her, and Chancey Yarrow didn't bother waiting to see what would happen next. She stepped backward into the *Switchback* and raised the ramp, her gaze remaining on Syl all the while. *I'm leaving you here to die,* her eyes seemed to say, and Syl realized that her mother truly was dead, after all. Whether it was fear or something else that had killed her bright spirit didn't matter. Chancey had chosen her path.

And Syl would choose her own.

The ship began to power up, and Jordanna, Reath, and Imri all peeked out from where they'd taken cover.

"There goes our ride," Imri yelled, face twisted with worry.

Remy seemed to pop into existence next to Syl, yowling at her.

"Maybe not!" Syl gestured for them to follow her but slid to a stop. "Where's Vern?"

"Here! I found a ship. Well, Remy found it."

Vernestra stood next to a skiff, not much bigger than an emergency escape shuttle. It would be a tight fit, but they could make it work. They didn't really have any other choice.

"There's no guns," Syl said.

Vernestra shrugged. "What do you need guns for? You have Jedi."

"I'd rather have the guns," Syl muttered, gesturing to the battle that still raged outside of the hangar.

But there was no being picky, so she piled into the shuttle with everyone else.

It was a tight fit, with everyone trying to find space. Imri plopped onto the floor next to the door, and Remy laid down next to him with a sigh, resting her massive head in his lap, her horns catching in the singed material of his tabard. His eyes went wide, and Jordanna smiled.

There was a brief moment of confusion as Vernestra and Sylvestri jockeyed for the pilot's seat, but the Jedi relinquished it with a smile. "I did just crash, and you are a professional."

Syl laughed, the moment of brightness almost making her forget that her mother had just left her to die on the slowly collapsing weapon she'd built.

"Hey, are you all right?" Jordanna said. She'd ended up in the copilot's chair, although Syl wasn't quite sure how. She reckoned it had something to do with the whispering coming from the back of the ship.

"Yes, I'm going to be fine. We're going to be fine," Syl said. And then she leaned over, grabbing the front of Jordanna's shirt and pulling her forward until their lips touched. She didn't know what had happened in the hangar bay, but she knew she loved Jordanna.

Surely they could figure it out.

"Hey! Can we save the kissing for after we're safe?" Reath called. "We aren't rescued yet."

Syl let go of Jordanna with a smile that was reflected on her girlfriend's face, and finished powering up the shuttle with no issues.

"All right, next stop, anywhere but here," Syl said, swallowing as she looked at the chaos she would have to negotiate outside of the hangar bay. "May the Force be with us."

THIRTY-NINE

Vernestra had never been the subject of a Council meeting, and she decided that she didn't much care for it.

Imri stood next to her, his temple attire brand new like hers, and fidgeted. The day before, she'd managed to get him to sit with another Jedi Master who also was quite adept at discerning the feelings of others. The Mirialan man had been very impressed with Imri's abilities and had gone through a number of meditation exercises designed to give Imri more control over his sensitivity, which was common in human Jedi who could trace their bloodlines to Genetia. Vernestra was hopeful that it was working, since now Imri seemed to be more worried about getting lunch than the emotions of those around them.

"Jedi Vernestra Rwoh, do you think your young age led Xylan Graf to believe he could more easily use you as a bargaining chip in his dealings with the Nihil?" asked Master Rosason.

It had been going on like this for the past hour, and Vernestra smiled serenely as she answered yet another version of the same question. "Master, I am a Jedi, as is Master Cohmac and Padawans Reath and Imri. Xylan Graf will have to be the one to explain his actions to you. I cannot surmise what his plan was. As far as we knew, Xylan had convinced the Republic to fund a scientific mission to the Berenge sector. Master Cohmac's abundance of caution was responsible for making certain that the coalition forces from the Hetzal system could respond in a timely manner."

Nothing remained of the Gravity's Heart. After Vernestra and the rest had escaped from the station, they'd been able to land their small craft on one of the three Longbeams that had arrived to subdue the Nihil. The battle had been short and effective, and a number of the pirates had been taken into custody. And then the Longbeams had fired on the severely damaged station until nothing but dust was left.

"You have seen the documents provided by Senator Starros, Master Rosason. And Catriona Graf has already confirmed that the leader of the Nihil, their Eye, is Lourna Dee. Catriona and Xylan Graf have also provided us with information about Lourna Dee's ship, including a tracking beacon, since the craft was built by the Grafs. This is less a Nihil plot and more one funded and conceived by a member of the Graf clan," Master Stellan said. "We should take this as a moment to realize that the Nihil are more resourceful than we'd previously thought. They are collaborating with affluent citizens, and we cannot let this stand. And that should begin with a public trial holding the Grafs accountable, but it should end with the Jedi devoting themselves to this conflict above all else. We managed to stop them this time. Who is to say we will discover their next plot before it costs the Republic lives? What we need is a fully coordinated response with the Republic, not the piecemeal actions we've taken over the past couple months."

"The Jedi are not soldiers, and what you are describing sounds perilously close to war," said Master Rosason. "And that should never be the inclination of the Order. It should always be a means of last resort."

Vernestra let her mind wander as the Council began to discuss the matter, and she was startled by Master Stellan suddenly standing.

"If there is nothing else for Vernestra and her Padawan learner, I suggest we dismiss them and have this conversation amongst ourselves." When no one said anything, he nodded to Vernestra. "You are both dismissed."

Vernestra and Imri bowed and left the Council chambers,

only to find Master Cohmac and Reath standing outside, waiting for their turn to go in.

"How did it go?" Master Cohmac asked.

"Well, I was apparently taken in by Xylan Graf because I was too young to be made a Knight, despite my many accomplishments," Vernestra said, unable to hide her frustration. None of it was true, but that didn't seem to be clear to Master Rosason.

Master Cohmac sighed. "Don't worry, they'll tell me that perhaps I have spent too long in academic pursuits to fully recognize the danger before me. We did the best we could with the information we had, Vern, and that's all there is to it."

She took a deep breath and steadied herself. "I suppose you're right. Do you know if you'll be returning to Starlight Beacon after this?"

Master Cohmac frowned. "I'm not certain. Do you need a ride?"

Vernestra shook her head and smiled. "No, we have one. Be well, Master Cohmac, Reath."

"It was great working with you!" Reath called as Vernestra and Imri turned to leave. Vernestra caught the Padawan's blush as he ducked his head, and wondered what that was about. But she didn't have long to consider it as she noticed Imri's frown.

"What?"

"You didn't tell them about your connection with Mari San Tekka, or the Path she gave you." After Syl had flown them to the nearest Longbeam, a task made easier by the battle winding down as they'd left the Gravity's Heart, Vernestra had told Imri about her conversation with the half-dead woman.

"No. I spoke with Master Stellan and told him we had found her and that I had given the puzzle box to Jordanna to return to her family. But I don't think he is quite ready to know about the Path. I think it's something we'll need in the future, but for now I feel like we should keep it to ourselves." Vernestra had meditated for a long time on whether or not to show her former master the modifications she'd made to her lightsaber and tell him how her hyperspace visions had led her to find the woman responsible for giving the Nihil their unnatural mastery of hyperspace. She had, in the end, decided to keep the information to herself. Why, she couldn't quite say, but she could feel it wasn't a thing to share just yet, the way she only felt when the Force was leading her toward a decision. She was certain that the Path would be necessary but that there were other, more pressing matters at hand.

Plus, she didn't have to tell Master Stellan everything. She was no longer his Padawan, and it was time to start making her own way in the galaxy.

And that meant she would keep her own counsel on some things. Or at least only share them with her Padawan.

"Come on," Vernestra said, resting a hand on Imri's shoulder. "We have a ride to catch."

FORTY

Syl stopped in front of the gleaming ship and frowned. "This isn't mine," she said to the Republic official standing in front of the boarding ramp.

The Devaronian rubbed his horns, sighed, and looked down at his tablet. He had the look of someone who'd run out of patience. "Are you not Sylvestri Yarrow?"

"I am, but I don't know how this is my ship."

He held the tablet out so Syl could see it. "It says right here that this ship was signed over to you yesterday on behalf of Graf Holdings, Unlimited. Good thing, too. Most of their assets have been frozen since then. Or so I hear."

Syl looked at the ship and swallowed dryly. When the

message had been sent to her hotel—not a flop but also not
the sumptuous lodgings where she'd nearly been killed by an
assassin she now knew had been hired by none other than
Xylan himself—she'd expected to find the *Switchback*, confiscated by the Jedi after they'd begun to round up the Nihil in
the aftermath of the battle of the Berenge sector.

But this ship was something else entirely, and Syl found
herself hard-pressed to believe it was hers.

"What's it called?" she asked, and the Republic official
sighed.

"You don't know the name of your own ship?"

"I was attacked by Nihil and have a head injury. You
know how fragile we humans are," she said.

The Devaronian rolled his eyes. "The *Vengeful Goddess*.
But I can change it if you don't like the name."

Oh, she liked it. Very much.

Once Syl signed for the ship, the Devaronian took his
leave, muttering about dirt grubbers from the frontier, but
Syl ignored him. She had a ship to explore.

Syl made her way to the cockpit without hesitation. She
powered up the systems, weapons, hyperdrive, and sublight
engines. There really were four, and Syl almost wept with joy.
The *Switchback* only had two. This ship was truly in a class
by itself.

There were weapons she had never heard of, and more of
them than any ship of that size really needed, but she didn't
care. It was all hers.

"Did you see this?" called a voice behind Syl. She turned around to see Jordanna walking down the hallway toward her, dressed in a bodysuit of black Wellsian leather. Syl blinked, and it took a moment for her brain to start thinking again after seeing Jordanna in something besides frontier homespun.

"See what?" Syl asked finally, figuring Jordanna wasn't asking about her new look.

She smiled knowingly and handed Syl an envelope. Inside was a peculiar token and a handwritten note from Xylan Graf. Paper? The man wasted no opportunity to flaunt his wealth.

Syl read the note:

Apologies for my subterfuge, but I always keep my word. Mostly. Here is your ship, and while my funds have been frozen by the Republic and the rest of my assets seized, I have a friend on Takodana who is always looking for enterprising new partners. You should look her up, and give her this when you get there.

"Takodana?" Syl said, gazing down at the token as she handed the note to Jordanna to read. "There's nothing but pirates there."

"I don't know, maybe we should check it out," Jordanna said.

"We," Syl said, and Jordanna grinned.

"You, me, and Remy."

"What about your family?" Syl asked, heart pounding painfully.

Jordanna shrugged. "There are enough San Tekka cousins that someone else can step in as deputy if the vassals ever return to Tiikae. I've got my heart set on other things."

Syl crossed her arms, the token heavy in her hand. "Is it really that easy?"

After they'd given their statements to the Republic officials, they'd found themselves with nothing but time to kill. So they'd managed to sneak away and talk. A lot.

And Syl's heart remained the same. But still, she worried that somehow, some way she was making a mistake.

Maybe she just wasn't used to being happy.

"Usually, no. Escaping my family is not always possible. But the revelation that the Nihil were working with the Grafs and had Mari San Tekka has put the family on high alert, throwing all of their resources in with the rest of the coalition forces. They're too busy to care what I'm about right now."

Syl bit her lip. "I heard there were new attacks."

"Well, then, let's head to Takodana," Jordanna said with a mischievous grin. "It'll be a new start. For both of us."

"I have to stop by Port Haileap and get the rest of my crew first," Syl said. She'd sent Neeto a message, and the Sullustan was anxious to get back out among the stars. He would lose his mind when he saw what their new ship looked like.

Plus, she had so much to tell him. How would she break it to Neeto that, in the end, her mother had been loyal to the Nihil? It was hard enough for Syl to believe it herself.

"Helloooo! Syl? Are you here?" came a call from outside

the ship. Voices drifted up to Jordanna and Syl in the cockpit. "Imri, if you keep trying to pet that vollka, you're going to end up missing a hand."

Jordanna's eyes widened in horror, and Syl laughed. She stood and pulled Jordanna into her arms, kissing her like she'd dreamed of doing for months. As Jordanna's lips met hers, everything bad in the world melted away, leaving just the pounding of her heart and the warmth of Jordanna in her arms.

Syl leaned back a little and smiled up at Jordanna. "We have to give some friends a ride to Starlight first. I didn't think you'd mind."

"Vern! Look! She finally likes me. See how she rolled over?"

"Imri, that belly is a trap. Haven't you ever met a cat?"

Jordanna looked at Syl, and she couldn't help laughing. It was going to be an interesting trip to Starlight Beacon—that was for sure.

"It's a good thing I love you," Jordanna said with a sigh.

And Syl couldn't agree more.

FORTY-ONE

Nan sat in the copilot's seat and said nothing as Chancey Yarrow steered the ship toward the now familiar landmark of Everbloom. When Nan had run from the still-bound Jedi for her own ship, she hadn't expected to find it gone, or Chancey Yarrow striding purposefully toward another ship in the hangar bay.

She certainly hadn't expected the woman to offer her a ride.

"All right, little spy. You need to follow my lead if you want to live," Chancey Yarrow said, landing her decrepit ship in the wide-open yard of the Graf compound as a number of heavily armed Gigorans ran to meet them. "Unless you want to try your luck with Marchion Ro."

Nan bit her lip. Chancey's threat was not without merit. Nan had lost the Oracle and Ro's devious Chadra-Fan, and returning to the *Gaze Electric* empty-handed would be folly. Nan was a survivor long before she was Nihil, and maybe it was time for a short hiatus from Lord Ro's tasks.

Nan's heart ached though. All she wanted was to return to the Eye, to have him appreciate how hard she had fought to survive. And maybe one day she could. But she would need something good, some piece of information that he wouldn't be able to resist, to get back into his good graces. The Oracle was gone, which meant so were the Paths. The Nihil would need something else to give them an edge over the Republic and the Jedi.

Nan was willing to bide her time until the moment was right. So much of life was being patient, and Nan could wait to return to the Eye.

The *Switchback* was overrun by the Graf family forces. Chancey raised her hands above her head, and Nan did the same. The security forces leveled blasters at them and escorted them off the ship, and as they walked Nan cast frequent glances at Chancey. The older woman's expression was serene, as though she were on a nature walk instead of being marched across the vast plain that led up to the ridiculous expanse of the Graf family manor.

The Matriarch was out front, just like last time they'd come, but now a young man with a well-groomed beard and an outlandish outfit stood next to the stately old woman. He looked as nonplussed as Chancey, like this whole thing was another regular afternoon.

"No weapons," said the Gigoran nearest to Nan, the vocalizer making her voice strange. The Gigoran was missing large swathes of hair near her throat, and a still-healing scar puckered the skin.

"Thank you, Basha," the old woman said. "Chancey, you have kept your word."

"As I said I would. You'll find the routes and my preliminary data in the datacrons located in the cargo hold. But more to the point: I've proven my hypothesis. Hyperspace can be vulnerable to attack, and not the heavy-handed sort Marchion Ro favors. A more sophisticated kind of upheaval, one that takes planning and study and must be refined."

"Yes, I was interested in the early research your Gravity's Heart provided," the Matriarch said with a frosty smile. "And we have decided to accept your offer."

"I've signed the *Vengeful Goddess* over to your daughter," Xylan Graf said. "My representative said she and a tall, dark-haired woman already claimed the ship. And Maz assured me that they sent along a message and have agreed to speak with her."

"Good. Maz will look after Syl as much as she can," Chancey Yarrow said. She sagged, as though finally releasing a heavy burden. "And you are sure you can keep me safe?"

The Matriarch sniffed. "The Nihil are still pirates. Nothing can penetrate Everbloom's defenses short of a full-scale Republic attack."

Chancey nodded. "And my laboratory?"

"Waiting for you whenever you're ready," Xylan said with a smooth smile. "An unlisted station built into an asteroid in the Hynestian sector. It will become the premier facility for hyperspace research and development under your guidance. There are worse ways to spend one's retirement."

"Indeed," the older Graf said with a smile that never reached her eyes. "Who is this, by the by?"

"This is the potential informant I promised you."

Being referred to as an informant was not good, and Nan assessed her options for escape.

There weren't any.

"A pity we lost all of the Jedi," the Matriarch said, pursing her lips. "They would have provided a nice distraction for Ro when he realizes we've double-crossed him."

"Wait, what do you mean?" Nan asked, her earlier fear surging once more.

Chancey Yarrow sighed heavily. "Lourna Dee and the Grafs cooked this plan up long ago. They offered me a chance to test out my theories and the resources to build the weapon."

Nan blinked as the pieces slid into place. "You always knew that you would get caught."

Xylan Graf laughed. "Of course. A weapon that can kick

ships out of hyperspace? That was always going to be discovered, sooner or later."

"The key was making Ro believe it so we could have access to Mari San Tekka," the Graf matriarch said. "We know someone within the Senate has been working with Ro from the beginning. Eventually he would be convinced that what we had was the real deal."

"The weapon truly only worked three or four times," Chancey Yarrow said. "But with the Graf family screaming about lost ships, it was convincing enough that Ro agreed to Lourna's request to have his oracle spend some time on the Gravity's Heart. She was the final piece of the mapping data that we needed to one day create a more successful version of the gravity-well projector, one that can predict timing as well as direction."

"Why are you telling me this?" Nan asked, a sick feeling beginning to bloom in her middle.

"Because I want you to know that you can do better than licking Ro's boots," said Chancey. "Families like the Grafs are always looking for someone to provide information."

"And we pay handsomely," the Matriarch said, her gaze hard. "Now, you have a choice. You can either work with us, or we can return you to Ro's ship. And we haven't much time. Lourna will be captured quickly by the Jedi, and once that happens the Republic will no doubt seek to bring us to what they consider justice. We have no intention of giving them the satisfaction."

"You'll have some time to decide what story you tell him," Chancey said, crossing her arms and looking bored. "He's still off on his most recent sojourn. And even if you tell him the truth of the Gravity's Heart, he won't have time to do anything about it. The Jedi and the Republic have the Tempests on the run, and it is just a matter of time before every single Nihil in the galaxy is dead or imprisoned."

Nan blinked and took a deep breath. She'd been a lot of things in her life, always whatever was required to survive. But she had never, ever been her own woman.

Information brokers did well enough for themselves, and being on the payroll of a family like the Grafs? Well, that was something else, indeed.

So Nan did what she did best: she took care of herself.

"What do you want to know?"